The Ritual
Copyright © 2021 by Shantel Tessier
All rights reserved.

For more information about the author and her books, visit her website— https://shanteltessier.com/
You can join her reader group. It's the only place to get exclusive teasers, first to know about current projects and release dates. And also have chances to win some amazing giveaways- https://www.facebook.com/groups/TheSinfulSide

Editor: Jenny Sims and Amanda Rash
Formatter: CP Smith
Cover model: Cooper A.
Photographer: Wander Aguiar
Cover designer: Melissa Cunningham

PLAYLIST

"Make Hate to Me" by Citizen Soldier
"Needles" Seether
"Like Lovers Do" Hey Violet
"Numb" 8 Graves
"Killing Me Slowly" Bad Wolves
"Guest Room" Echos
"I Don't Give a Fuck" MISSIO, Zeale
"Everybody Gets High" MISSIO
"Taste of You" Rezz, Dove Cameron
"Sick Like Me" In This Moment
"Bad Intentions" Niykee Heaton
"Mirrors" Natalia Kills, Migos, OG Parker
"If You Want Love" NF
"Broken" Lifehouse
"Honesty" Halsey
"Oh Lord" In This Moment
"All The Time" Jeremih, Lil Wayne, Natasha Mosley

WARNING

For those of you who wish to go in blind, please remember this dark romance is a work of fiction, and I do NOT condone any situations or actions that take place between these characters. Continue to the ***prologue***, but just remember that I warned you. If you do NOT want to go in blind, please read the **trigger warnings** listed below.

AUTHOR'S NOTE:

Nothing about this is to be taken seriously. It is strictly a work of fiction and for your smut pleasure.

The Ritual may contain triggers for some.

Trigger Warnings include but are not limited to:

Graphic violence, non/dub con, branding, forced sex fantasy, drug/alcohol use, masks, breath play, bondage, kidnapping, anal.

If you have any questions, feel free to email me, and one of my assistants or I will get back to you. shanteltessierassistant@gmail.com

Some things to know about ***The Ritual***
It is not an RH
It is told in dual POVs
OTT (over the top) H
J/P (jealous and possessive) H
A Dark College Romance

THE RITUAL

USA TODAY & WALL STREET JOURNAL BESTSELLING AUTHOR

SHANTEL TESSIER

PROLOGUE
L.O.R.D.

A LORD TAKES *his oath seriously. Only blood will solidify their commitment to serve those who demand their complete devotion.*

*He is a **Leader**, believes in **Order**, knows when to **Rule**, and is a **Deity**.*

A Lord must be initiated in order to become a member but can be removed at any time for any reason. If he makes it past the three trials of initiation, he will forever know power and wealth. But not all Lords are built the same. Some are stronger, smarter, hungrier than others.

*They are challenged just to see how far their **loyalty** will go.*

*They are pushed to their limits in order to prove their **devotion**.*

*They are willing to show their **commitment**.*

Nothing except their life will suffice.

Limits will be tested, and morals forgotten.

A Lord can be a judge, jury, and executioner. He holds power that is unmatched by anyone, other than his brother.

If they manage to complete all trials of initiation, he will be granted a reward—a chosen one. She is his gift for his servitude.

ONE

INITIATION

RYAT

LOYALTY
FRESHMAN YEAR AT BARRINGTON UNIVERSITY

I KNEEL IN the middle of the darkly lit room along with twenty other men. My hands are secured tightly behind my back with a pair of handcuffs. My shirt is torn, and blood drips from my busted lips. I'm panting, still trying to catch my breath while my heart beats like a drum in my chest. It's hard to hear over the blood rushing in my ears, and I'm sweating profusely.

We were dragged out of our beds in the middle of the night to serve. Our freshman classes at Barrington University start in two weeks, but we already have to show our loyalty to the Lords.

"You will always have to prove yourself," my father once told me.

"You were each given a task," the man calls out as he paces in front of us. His black combat boots slap against the concrete floor with each step, the sound echoing off the walls. "Kill or be killed. Now how many of you can fulfill it?"

"I can," I state, lifting my head to stick my chin out in the warm and sticky air. Sweat covers my brow after the fight. It's rigged. You are supposed to lose. The point is to wear you down. See just how much you have to give. How far you can go. I made sure to win mine.

No matter what it took.

He smirks down at me like I'm fucking joking. "Ryat. You seem so confident in yourself."

"I know what I'm capable of handling," I say through gritted teeth. I don't like being second-guessed. We were each raised for this—to be a Lord.

Wealth got us here.

Yet our determination will separate us by the time it's over.

The man looks at the guy on my left and nods. The guy walks behind me and yanks me to stand by the back of my shirt. He undoes the cuffs, and I rip the shredded material up and over my head before dropping my hands to my sides when what I really want to do is rub my sore wrists.

Never show weakness. A Lord does not feel. He's a machine.

The man steps up to me with a knife in hand. He holds it out handle first to me, his black eyes almost glowing with excitement. "Show us what you can do."

Taking it from him, I walk over to the chair bolted to the floor. I yank the bloody sheet off the chair to reveal a man tied to it. His hands are cuffed behind his back, and his feet are spread wide and secured to the chair legs.

I'm not surprised I know him—he's a Lord. Or was. The fact that he's restrained tells me he's not anymore. But that doesn't change my orders.

Kill without questions.

You want to be powerful? Then you realize you are a threat to those who want your position. In order to succeed, you don't have to be stronger, just deadlier.

The man shakes his head, his brown eyes pleading with me to spare his life. Multiple layers of duct tape are placed over his mouth—those who spill secrets will be silenced. He thrashes in his chair.

Walking behind him, I look down at his cuffed wrists. He wears a ring on his right hand; it's a circle with three horizontal lines across the middle. It stands for power.

Not just anyone would know what it means, but I do. Because I wear the same one. Everyone in this room does. But just because you get one doesn't mean you'll keep it.

I reach down and grab his hand. He begins to shout behind the tape as he tries to fight me, but I remove the ring easily and walk back around to stand in front of him.

"You don't deserve this," I say to him, placing it in my pocket. "You betrayed us, your brothers, yourself. The payment for that is death."

When he throws his head back and screams into the tape, I press the knife to his neck, right below his jawline. His breathing fills the room, and his body strains, waiting for the first cut.

A Lord does not show mercy. Blood and tears are what we demand from those who betray us.

I press the tip of the knife into his neck, puncturing his skin enough for a thin line of blood to drip from the wound.

He begins to cry, tears running down his already bloody face.

"I uphold my duty. For I am a Lord. I know no boundaries when it comes to my servitude. I will obey, serve, and dominate," I recite our oath. "For my brother, I am a friend. I shall lay my life down for thee or take it." I stab the knife into his right thigh, forcing a muffled scream from his taped lips before yanking it out, letting the blood soak into his jeans while it drips off the end of the knife onto the concrete floor. "For we are what others wish to be." Circling him, I run the tip down his forearm, splitting the skin like I did his neck. "We will be held accountable for our actions." I stab him in the left thigh and tug it out as his sobbing continues. "For they represent who we truly are."

Jerking on the collar of his shirt, I rip it down the middle to expose his chest and stomach. The same crest that's on our rings is burned into his chest. It's what we are given once we pass our trials. Gripping the skin, I pull on it as far as I can with my right hand, then slide the blade through it with my left, cutting it from his body.

He sobs, snot flying out of his nose as the blood pours from the gaping hole in his skin. His body begins to shake while he fists his hands and thrashes in his chair. I throw the skin to the floor to rest at his feet. A souvenir for later.

I walk behind him. The only sound in the room is his cries muffled by the duct tape. I grab his hair, yanking his head back, and force his hips off the chair. His Adam's apple bobs when he swallows. I look down into his tear-filled eyes. "And you, my brother ... are a traitor." Then I slice the blade across his neck, splitting it wide open. His body goes slack in the chair as the blood pours from the open wound like a waterfall, drenching his clothes instantly.

"Impressive." The man who handed me the knife begins to clap while silence now fills the room. Walking over to me, I throw the bloody knife up in the air, catching it by the tip of the blade and holding it out to him.

He comes to a stop and gives me a devious smile. "I knew you'd be one to watch." With that, he takes the knife, then turns and walks away.

I stand, still breathing heavily, now covered in not only my blood but a fellow brother's. Lifting my head, I look up at the two-way mirror on the second-floor balcony, knowing I'm being watched and knowing that I just passed my first test with flying colors.

TWO

INITIATION

RYAT

DEVOTION
SOPHOMORE YEAR AT BARRINGTON UNIVERSITY

THE RAIN FALLS from the sky, soaking my clothes and making them stick to my skin. I kneel in the middle of the ring. Water mixed with my blood swirls on the ground around me.

I take a second to catch my breath and regain a little bit of strength because the rain makes it harder to connect. My opponent stands opposite me with his fisted hands up, covering his face while he bounces from foot to foot like he's a fighter getting paid millions to show off to the world for a pay-per-view fight.

I guess, in a way, it is a show. Just not televised. And there is no payout. Your reward is you get to keep breathing.

"Get up," he yells at me. "Get the fuck up, Ryat!"

Smiling, I make my way to my feet and drop my hands to my sides, letting him think he has me. As if I'm that fucking weak not to fight back.

He charges me, and I step to my left at the last second as he drops his shoulder. I kick my leg out, tripping him. He lands on his face, sliding in the puddle of water, and the crowd hollers.

"Tell me, Jacob. Just how bad do you want to die?" I ask and hear the others laugh at my question.

An audience is always needed. Your fellow brothers must witness your devotion. Otherwise, it doesn't exist.

He gets to his feet and spins around to face me. Growling, he shows me his teeth before charging me again. This time, I don't move out of the way. Instead, I meet him head-on with my fist. The blow knocks him back, and blood flies from his mouth. My knuckles split from the force.

Lifting my hand to my mouth, I lick the blood and rain off them. "Tastes like victory," I mock.

Wiping the blood from his busted face, he stumbles, eyes blinking rapidly. I clocked him pretty good. "You ..." he chokes out. "You ..."

"Ryat," I remind him of my name since he seems to have forgotten.

He charges me once again, this time much slower than the last. Sidestepping him, I lift my arm and let him run into it. My forearm hits his Adam's apple, knocking him off his feet and flat on his back.

He rolls over onto his side, coughing and grabbing at his throat. I take the chance and kick him in the face and blood gushes from his now broken nose.

I fall to my knees, straddling him. My hands wrap around his throat, cutting off his air.

His hands slap my arms, feet kick, and hips buck underneath me, but he doesn't have a chance.

As my grip tightens, his eyes bulge. "You will not beat me," I growl.

When a Lord fights, he fights to the end. There can only be one winner. Only one left standing. And I refuse to be anything but.

THREE

INITIATION

RYAT

COMMITMENT
JUNIOR YEAR AT BARRINGTON UNIVERSITY

I ENTER THE house as quietly as a church mouse. The order was simple. I was given a location in Chicago, a name—Nathaniel Myers—and a picture.

Take him out.

I make my way down the hallway and up the winding staircase to the second floor. Taking a right, I stop at a closed door. Reaching up, I place my finger to my lips to tell Matt to be quiet. He's like a fucking bull in a china shop. We were given a partner for this assignment to see how we work with others, but I prefer to be on my own. Not only do I have to watch my back but now I've also got to watch his as well.

Matt nods once, running his hand down over his face before gripping the gun, holding it down to his side. Matt and I have been friends for three years now. Ever since we moved into the house of Lords and started Barrington University in Pennsylvania. But that doesn't mean I want to work beside him. I just do better on my own.

Opening the door, I enter the room, seeing a man and woman lying on a bed with the sheets pushed down to their waist. She's topless, her big paid-for tits on full display. A tattoo of a rose underneath her right one. The guy lies on his stomach, hands shoved under his pillow. I'm sure there's a gun under there at all times. He probably sleeps with his finger on the trigger.

Walking over to the side of the bed, I place the barrel of my suppressor to his head and pull the trigger, getting it over with. I could draw it out, but why take that chance? Too many things can go wrong. And it's not like you get points for creativity.

The woman stirs, and Matt goes over to her side of the bed, ripping the covers off her even more. She's completely naked.

"Matt," I hiss. "Let's go."

He pulls the knife from his back pocket, flipping it open. "She ..."

"Is not on the list," I whisper-shout. We don't deviate from our orders.

He reaches out and grabs one of her breasts, making her shift and let out a moan.

I round the foot of the bed, coming up behind him, and point the end of my suppressor at his head. "Get the fuck out of here. Right now," I demand.

He chuckles, lifting his hands in surrender. "Just having a little fun, Ryat." Turning around, he faces me, but I keep my gun pointed between his blue eyes. "Aren't you tired of doing what the Lords say? Don't you want some pussy?"

My teeth grind. "There are rules for a reason." I'm not saying they make sense, but I've come too far to break them now.

"Fuck the rules," he snaps, loudly making her shift onto her side. Reaching down, he undoes the buttons on his jeans, followed by his zipper. "I'm going to fuck her. You can do whatever you want with your cock." He rips his belt from his jeans and turns to face her.

A shrill scream makes both of us jump. She crawls across her dead husband and runs out of the room.

"Son of a bitch," Matt yells, chasing after her.

I roll my eyes. This is why I prefer to work alone. I follow them into the hallway to find Matt standing at the banister. I come up beside him, placing my gun down at my side with one hand while the other grips the railing. Looking down over it, I see the woman facedown on the first floor with blood slowly pooling around her onto the white marble floor.

I turn to look at him, and demand, "Did she fall over, or did you throw her?"

"She fucking fell," he snaps, immediately defensive.

I shake my head, teeth grinding. "Come on. Let's get the fuck out of here and call it in to be cleaned up."

FOUR

INITIATION

RYAT

THE BACKS OF my knees are hit, knocking me down onto them. I grind my teeth to keep from making a sound when they impact the concrete. Blood rushes in my ears, and my heart beats wildly in my chest.

This is what I live for!

The adrenaline rush is unlike anything I've ever known—an addiction. Something that can't be bought off the streets or drank from a bottle.

The hood is ripped off my head, and I blink, looking around to adjust my eyesight. I'm in the center of a room. Seats filled with men dressed in thousand-dollar suits circle the large space. You wouldn't know they're all killers if you saw them on the street. The room is filled with power. Some are senators, while others are CEOs of multibillion dollar companies. A Lord is made to feed off another. It's like anything else—someone has to be at the top, and another has to hold up the bottom. But still, powerful nonetheless. After graduation, we're each strategically placed where we fit best in the world.

My eyes fall to what looks to be a birdbath sitting in the middle with a small fire going, and my breathing picks up.

"Restrain him," someone calls out.

I'm shoved face-first to the floor. My arms are yanked behind my back and handcuffed. I growl as I'm jerked back to a kneeling position. A belt is wrapped around my neck and is pulled from behind while a boot presses into my back right between my shoulder blades.

I bare my teeth, trying to breathe with what little air I have.

"Ryat Alexander Archer, you have completed all trials of initiation. Do you wish to proceed?"

"Yes, sir," I manage to growl out.

He nods, placing his hands behind his back. "Remove his shirt."

Another man comes up to me and cuts the collar of my shirt, then rips it down the center. He leaves it hanging off my shoulders and walks away.

Instinct has me fighting the restraints, and the man behind me pulls tighter on the belt, shoving his boot farther into my back, cutting off my air in the process. I fist my cuffed hands and watch the man place a hot iron into the fire.

"A Lord must be willing to go above and beyond for his title. He must show strength and have what it takes." He pulls the hot iron from the flames and turns to face me, the end burning red. "If you shall fail your position as a Lord, we will take what was earned." He looks over to his right and adds, "Silence him."

A hand fists my hair, yanking my head back to stare up at the black ceiling. If I was able to breathe, I'd growl at the motherfucker who is touching me. A small cloth is shoved into my mouth, and I bite down on it, knowing what's coming.

"Ryat Alexander Archer, welcome to the Lords. For you shall reap the benefits of your sacrifice." Then the hot iron is pressed to my chest, searing the crest to my body.

FIVE

RYAT

I WALK INTO the empty office, looking out through the floor-to-ceiling windows behind a set of couches. The city lights illuminate the night. It's one in the morning and my first time here.

Making my way down the hallway, I knock on the last door.

"Come in," a man calls out.

Entering, I close it behind me. A man sits behind a desk in front of the floor-to-ceiling windows. A single lamp glows from the corner of his desk, and I wonder if this is so people won't know he's in his office at this time of night. "You wanted to see me, sir?"

"Have a seat, Ryat." He gestures to the chair across from him.

Doing as I'm told, I cross my arms over my chest. My senior Lord ceremony was three weeks ago. Classes at Barrington University start in two. For three long years, I've proven myself to the Lords. And now I'm one of them. But this morning, I got a call to be seen by a fellow Lord. It's not uncommon but definitely had me curious as to what the fuck he wants.

He pulls a picture out of the pocket of his Armani suit jacket and slides it across the black surface. "Here is your first assignment."

Picking it up, I look it over but quickly lift my eyes to him once again. "What about her?" I ask confused.

"She is to be yours."

My gift—a chosen one.

Freshman year, we all took an oath, knowing that we all might not make it. During our senior year, we are rewarded for our servitude with sex. We're allowed to take more than one chosen one. We can share her with the other Lords if we'd like. It happens a lot. I don't know how many damn orgies I've watched over the past three years. There are no rules for us once we take on a chosen. Only for the women. If they accept—they have to willingly take the oath to belong to us—then they are ours. If a friend wants her for a night, we have the power to say yes or no. But if they are caught stepping out, they are punished. Humiliation is key.

I snort at his answer and throw the picture down. "No, seriously."

His light brown eyes just stare at me, jaw set in a hard line. The man looks too young to be in the position that he has. Not many wrinkles and in good shape, a full head of dark hair that he keeps slicked back. But that's a Lord for you. We put all the hard work in during our first three years of college. Once we graduate from Barrington, we rule.

I look away, running my hand through my hair, and choose my words differently. "She doesn't belong to me."

"She does ... for now." The man nods once.

She's a junior this year at Barrington. I know her but have never spoken to her. No reason to. Like I said, she doesn't belong to me. Releasing a sigh at his silence, I pick it back up. She stands in the middle of a parking lot next to her white Audi R8. Staring down at her cell, she's oblivious that someone is watching her, taking pictures of her. She wears a pair of low-cut jeans and a white T-shirt. Her dark hair is down, the wind blowing it in her face.

"This has to be wrong," I urge, shaking my head. "She is ..."

"Are you denying a direct order?" he asks, tilting his head to the side.

I grind my teeth. "No. It's just ..."

"Good." He stands, ripping the picture from my hands. "Do what must be done and make it happen."

Nodding my head, I stand as well. "Yes, sir." Then I turn and exit his office, knowing that I'll do whatever must be done.

Blakely Anderson will be mine.

BLAKELY

I'M PRACTICALLY RUNNING down the hallway trying to find my first class. Books in one hand, my schedule in the other. My bag has fallen off my shoulder and sits in the crook of my arm. Coming to where I think I'm supposed to be, I stop at the door, and my shoulders fall.

Room 125

I'm supposed to go to room 152. "Ugh." I throw my head back. "Son of a bitch."

This is my junior year at Barrington University, so you would think I'd know the college by now, but I don't. This place is the size of a large city, spanning over three thousand acres. Over twenty buildings hold the classes, plus apartments and houses because they don't have dorms here. That's not acceptable for the rich.

I spin around to head in a different direction but hit a brick wall. The impact throws me back onto my ass. The books go flying along with my paper and bag.

"Watch where you're fucking going!"

I look up from the floor to see a man standing in front of me. Emerald eyes so dark they're almost frighteningly glare down at me. His dark brown hair is trimmed shorter on the sides, and the longer pieces on top are unkempt, giving it that messy, "I just rolled out of bed" look. He's got a straight nose, and there's a tic in his chiseled, smooth jaw. He's dressed in dark denim jeans that hug his thighs, a black T-shirt shows off his broad shoulders and muscular arms, and tennis shoes. Ryat Archer stands there looking every bit pissed off as he does every second of every day.

"Sorry," I mutter, pushing my glasses back on my nose. I was running too late this morning to take the time to screw with my contacts. They hate me.

Reaching out my hand, I wait for him to grab it and help me up.

He uncrosses his arms and shoves his hands into the front pockets of his jeans, letting me know I'm on my own. His eyes drop to my chest, and he tilts his head to the side as they continue down over my stomach and bare legs. Slowly, he takes in my T-shirt and jean shorts. My breathing picks up, and fear creeps along my spine like a spider crawling on my skin. He looks at me like I'm a problem he needs to take care of. Something in his way to conquering the world.

The hairs on the back of my neck rise while my nipples harden when his gaze lands between my legs. Everything in me tells me to run—any other woman would—but I stay sprawled out on the floor like an idiot. The air gets thicker, making it hard to breathe, which just makes my tits bounce when I manage to suck in a deep breath.

He takes a step forward, the tip of his shoe knocking into the bottom of mine. "There are animals that roam these halls. If you're not careful, one will catch you." Those threatening eyes reach mine once again, and he smiles down at me. It's not any friendlier than his glare. Instead, I get this feeling he wants to rip my throat open with his perfectly white teeth—a million-dollar smile comes to mind.

I swallow nervously, my mouth all of a sudden dry. "I ..."

"Blakely? God, Blakely?" I hear a familiar voice. "Why are you on the floor?" Matt comes up behind me. Bending down, he places his arms underneath mine and lifts me to my feet. "What happened?"

I don't answer. Matt is picking up my books, bag, and schedule while I just stand here staring at Ryat like a deer in headlights. His eyes haven't left mine since he delivered the threat. I fully understood it. This is what you expect from anyone attending Barrington.

Cruel.

Evil.

God complex.

This is what happens when children grow up getting anything and everything they want. And I'm not talking about a teddy bear from the store. No, I'm talking about that one-of-a-kind two-million-dollar car before they even have a license.

"Everything okay here?" Matt asks.

I look down to see he's left my books stacked on the floor by our feet. My eyes go to Matt, and he's got all his attention on Ryat. They're not friends. Not anymore, anyway. They were once, but something happened last year, and let's just say they hate each other now.

"Blakely?" Matt snaps, making me jump.

Instead of answering him, my eyes shoot to Ryat once again.

Ryat arches a dark brow at me, his green eyes still boring into mine. They're less threatening now and more playful. This is a game to him. *Is everything okay here?* "Yeah," I answer Matt.

I don't know Ryat very well, but I'm aware of his reputation. You don't want to be on his shit list.

Ryat blinks, breaking contact, and looks over at Matt. Wiping the smile off his face, Ryat steps into him. I hold my breath as Matt cowers. "Keep your bitch on a leash." He then looks over at me, his eyes quickly running over my body once again, making my breath quicken. "Otherwise, one may assume she's a stray." He puts his attention back on Matt. "And well, let's just say you of all people should know that someone may choose to take her from you."

With that, he reaches up and shoves Matt into the wall, then walks past us to carry on with his day.

"What the fuck?" Matt hisses, pushing off the wall and watching

Ryat walk away without even bothering to give us a second glance. "Blakely?" He places his hands on my shoulders. "Did he push you down?" His hands run down over my arms.

"No ... not exactly." I continue to watch Ryat. The hallway isn't crowded by any means, but even if it was, you'd still be able to spot him. He's about six-three and two hundred and fifty pounds of muscle. He walks with an ease—as if he has all day to get where he's going.

"Did he touch you?" Matt growls.

Ryat pulls his cell out of his pocket and starts texting before he takes a right down another hall. Disappearing out of sight.

"Blakely?"

"What?" I snap, turning to look at Matt now that Ryat's completely gone.

"What the fuck happened?" he demands. "Were you talking to Ryat?" His eyes narrow on me in suspicion.

Of course. Now Matt is mad at me. Another man threatens his relationship with me, and it's my fault. *Always is.*

"Nothing." I push him off. "What happened between you two?" I demand, crossing my arms over my chest. They live in the same house—house of Lords. They're both members of the L.O.R.D.—Leader, Order, Ruler, and Deity—a secret society made up centuries ago by men to feed their misogynistic and egotistical attitudes. I only know what very little Matt has told me over the past three years, which is practically nothing. Their oath keeps them from talking about it.

"How the hell should I know?" He shrugs.

I eye him skeptically. "You're saying you have no clue why he hates you?" I find that hard to believe.

"Ryat is an asshole," he adds as if I didn't already know that.

Yes, but he completely avoided my question. "Whatever. I'm late to class."

I leave him standing there to go on with my day and manage to find the right room. Making my way up the stairs to the top row of the auditorium classroom, I sit down on the end next to my best friend since kindergarten and rub my elbow. It hurts after I fell on it.

"Where were you?" she asks.

I nod. "Got caught up."

She rolls her eyes. "Let me guess, Matt?"

"Something like that."

"Hey, look what I found." She reaches into her bag and pulls out a piece of paper. Unfolding it, she sets it down on my desk.

"What is it?"

"Our first official college party of junior year," she squeals.

I pick it up and read over it. It's a black piece of paper with **The Ritual** written across the top in white letters. From what I know, the *Lords* do this every year. I've heard girls talking about it here and there, but whenever I ask Matt about it, he shuts me down and says they've been sworn to secrecy.

"It wouldn't be a secret society, Blakely, if we told everyone what goes on, on the inside," he once said to me, and I rolled my eyes.

I begin to read over it.

I vow.

You vow.

We vow.

The ritual is what one must do in order to become a chosen.

A chosen must be willing to surrender in all that they do.

I look over at her and raise a brow. "Is this shit for real?" Does she even know what this means? I've never actually seen a flyer about it before with rules listed. I just thought it was a stupid rumor that some girls started to feel wanted. Some will do anything to get some dick.

She nods. "I hope so."

Rolling my eyes, I look back at it.

A chosen is protected under the ritual. Any and all must treat them as such.

"No." I wad it up and throw it back at her. "That's stupid. Or fucked up. Either way, you know I can't go." Matt would kill me if I showed up at the house of Lords.

"Matt can't tell you what you can and can't do, Blakely," she argues.

I ignore that and focus my attention on the professor down at the front of the room. I start thinking about what Ryat said in the hallway. He called me a stray. Said that someone may *choose* to take me away. Which is stupid because he knows I'm with Matt.

"Wait?" I say a little too loud and sink down into my seat when the kid to the left shushes me. "Give me that back," I whisper.

Running my hand over it, I try to flatten out the wrinkles the best I can on my desk. "Who chooses?" I ask her, my eyes scanning over it.

"I'm not sure." She shrugs, leaning over and looking at it too.

The girl in front of us turns around and glares.

"Sorry," I whisper.

Her eyes drop to the paper, and then she spins around, throwing her blond hair over her shoulder. I pull out my cell and send Matt a quick text. I know he doesn't have a class this hour. He was going to hang out at the library for a little bit this morning.

Me: What does it mean for a Lord to choose someone?

WE EXIT CLASS, and I pull out my cell once again to see if Matt has responded. He read it immediately but has yet to reply. I sigh, placing it in my back pocket.

Sarah starts hanging on my arm. "Come on. Let's go," she whines. "We're running out of time to actually have fun. It's junior year. We spent all summer back home. We swore this year would be different. That we would actually go and do things. It's just one party. What could it hurt? Not like we already have plans."

"I ..."

"Are you guys talking about the ritual?" the girl who sat in front of me asks.

"Yes," Sarah answers.

"Well, I wouldn't go if I were you." She clutches her books to her chest. "It's evil. Vile. Demented. Just some guys on a high horse who like to fuck around with women."

"How so?" I ask, interested. Something about how Ryat worded it to Matt has my curiosity piqued. You can't take something that doesn't belong to you.

"Tyson Crawford." She states the name like we should know who that is.

We don't. "Who is that?"

"He was a senior at Barrington a few years ago. He chose Whitney Minson as his. Well, once she performed the vow ceremony ..." She trails off, her eyes going from side to side to see if anyone is listening to her. When satisfied no one is paying attention, she steps in closer to us. "He tied her facedown on his bed, naked, gagged, and blindfolded. Left her there all day while he went to his classes. He had cameras all over his room with a live feed of it on his phone. Then once he went home, he fucked her, which he also recorded and sent to her boyfriend—the boyfriend she was cheating on after she took the vow to be Tyson's."

"Damn. Savage. I like it." Sarah laughs.

The girl's eyes narrow on her. "It was disgusting," she spits out.

"Then what?" I ask. I feel like there's more to that story there.

"Well, she belonged to him. She was his chosen one," she says, all but rolling her eyes.

"Meaning?" I urge, still not understanding this chosen shit. "Someone can't just decide to have you," I state the obvious. "Women aren't fucking property."

Dropping her voice to a whisper, she says, "The Lords can do whatever the fuck they want. Their oath promises them that."

"How do you know about all of this? Were you a chosen?" I wonder.

"Fuck no." She scoffs as if offended that I could even think that. Then she turns around and practically runs off like it's a sin to be seen with us.

"Oh, we're going," Sarah says matter-of-factly.

"Ritual? Vow ceremony? Sounds like some fucked-up shit." I shake my head.

"Matt's a member. How bad can it be?" She laughs. "He's a pussy."

I don't argue with that. When I look up, Ryat walks by with two other guys who I know as Gunner and Prickett. Fellow Lord members. A Lord member is always easy to spot because they wear a ring—a crest. No one who isn't a Lord knows what it actually means, though. Right now, the three are oblivious to everyone around them, deep in their own conversation. I imagine this is what they're always like. Thinking they're untouchable.

My hands fist, wrinkling the paper once again. The words he said to Matt ... what the girl just said to us. I've known they took an oath—a stupid one at that, but I don't know what all this chosen shit is about. I guess I've just never paid that much attention to what goes on behind the doors at the house of Lords. The members are required to all live together, and it's not near campus.

Making up my mind, I take off down the hall. I pass by, then turn around and stop in front of them, making all three come to a halt.

"Well, hello sexy." Gunner, the one on the right, smiles at me, his baby-blue eyes dropping to my bare legs.

"Bitch, remember?" I ask Ryat, who stands in the middle, crossing my arms over my chest. He had referred to me as Matt's bitch, but he knows my fucking name.

The corners of his lips turn up, giving me a smirk, looking more playful than before. "I see the pathetic boy toy still hasn't put that leash on you." His stunning green eyes drop to my neck, and he shakes his head while making a tsking sound. "Can't say I didn't warn him."

Heat rushes up my body, and my face goes red with embarrassment. Why did that feel like another threat? And why does my heart begin to race at the thought of being his prey?

"Free game?" Prickett, the one on the far left, asks.

My eyes snap to his. "Excuse me?" I bark. Pretty sure it's the first time I've ever heard him speak. I don't talk or hang out with any fellow Lords. Matt is the only one I know on a personal level. He's always kept me as far away from them as possible, and I never minded that.

"They always are," Ryat answers him.

"Well, who do we have here?" Sarah asks, sliding up next to me.

"Sarah." Gunner lifts his hand to rub his chin while his eyes devour her. "Nice to see you again."

"Seems so." Her eyes drop to his crotch, and I roll mine.

"What did you mean by someone else may choose me?" I ask Ryat, sticking my hip out.

All three men stiffen, and their eyes narrow on me. He steps forward, his body entering my space. I suck in a shaky breath when he reaches out, taking a strand of hair and tucking it behind my ear. His fingers gently brush my skin, and I shiver at the contact. He bends down, his green eyes devouring mine when he whispers, "Why don't you ask Matt why he's not allowed to choose you."

I pull away, taking a step back, and frown. "He's my boyfriend." What does he mean Matt wouldn't be able to choose me? And what the hell is he choosing me for?

"Keep saying that like it means something," Ryat remarks, making the others laugh.

I yank Sarah away from them, not really sure what I planned to accomplish by that. But I'll definitely be talking to Matt about this.

As we're walking down the hallway, she looks over her shoulder to glance back. "Ryat is staring at your ass like he wants to eat it." She chuckles.

"Yeah ... well, that won't be happening."

SIX

RYAT

I WATCH THE brunette stomp her way down the hall, getting as far away from me as possible. Blakely is exactly what I expected her to be. Long dark hair and big baby-blue eyes hidden behind her black-rimmed glasses. She looks so innocent with a Barbie doll face and sun-kissed skin. Great fucking body. Big tits, considering how small she is everywhere else, with a bubble ass. Can't be taller than five-four without hooker heels on.

I know who she is. I also know that it doesn't matter that she's promised to Matt. He's pissed off the Lords and lost his chance at her being his chosen.

Prickett thinks she's free game, but that's the furthest from the truth.

She's mine.

It wasn't a coincidence that she ran into me this morning. I put myself in her way and waited for her to look up and notice me. I've been following her ever since I was told to choose her two weeks ago. Learning her schedule and the places she goes. She lives a very boring life, that's for sure.

I was, however, surprised that I liked the way she looked, staring up at me from on her ass. Vulnerable. Easy prey.

"That's Matt's girl? They're still together?" Gunner asks, pulling his cell out of his pocket.

"He seems to think so." *She won't be for long.*

"She had the flyer in her hand," Prickett states.

"I saw." By the way it was wadded up, I think it's safe to assume she's not coming. My comment about strays and chose to be taken must have piqued her interest. Good. I want her asking around and finding out just who I am. I'm definitely more of a man than Matt. All she has to do is ask him.

"Dude, she's got to be a virgin." Gunner laughs. "Sure you want to fuck with that? Take someone without some experience."

"Doubtful," I mutter.

I know she and Matt have never had sex, but that doesn't mean she hasn't fucked someone else. But that would be the icing on the cake, wouldn't it? If I took his woman and fucked her before he ever had the chance. Plus, it just makes her ten times more interesting. And my cock even more desperate for her.

"She's on the list," Gunner adds, scrolling through names on his cell.

I already knew she was on there. Blakely Rae Anderson is to be chosen. Just not by the guy she expects, but definitely the better choice.

BLAKELY

"Matt?" I call out when I spot him in the library sitting at a table. And what do you know? He's texting away on his phone. "You better be responding to me."

"Shh." He shushes me, standing up while pocketing his cell. "Keep it down." He grabs my arm and yanks me down an aisle where we're alone. "What are you doing? Don't you have class right now?"

"Why are you ignoring me?" I demand.

"I'm busy, Blakely," he growls, stepping away from me.

"Not too busy to talk to someone else apparently," I hiss.

"I'm not doing this right now." He runs his hands through his dark hair. "I don't have the time ..."

I grab his arm, but he just shoves me off. "Why can't you choose me?"

He glares down at me, his jaw hardening, and steps into me, pressing my back into the bookshelves. "What did you just ask me?"

I swallow and place my hands on his chest, trying to push him back a step. Matt is a big guy. He lives to work out. His physical appearance is very important to him. He played football all through high school.

I'm too weak and small to even make him budge. "Why can't you choose me?" I ask, softening my voice. "What does that even mean?"

"I'm only going to say this once," he growls, stepping even closer. Placing both hands out on the bookshelf behind me, he cages me in. "Drop this. Right now. It does not concern you."

Why is he avoiding this? How bad can it be? "But Ryat ..."

"I don't give a fuck what that piece of shit says, Blakely. Stay the fuck away from him. Stay away from the house of Lords." He pushes off the bookshelf, stepping back. "And go to fucking class."

SEVEN

RYAT

I SIT IN the chair with Matt to my right. We haven't spoken one word to each other since last night in Chicago. We were given one hit and ended up killing his wife as well.

The door opens, and I sit up straighter.

"What the fuck happened?" Lincoln demands.

"The job was completed," Matt snaps, immediately going into defensive mode just like he did with me at the house last night.

The moment we made the call that we finished the job, we were on a private jet and brought back to Pennsylvania to the house of Lords and escorted to this room where they've made us wait. Which is never good. I've seen men come in here and never walk out.

"You killed his wife," Lincoln argues. "She was to stay alive. I don't know how you see that as a job completed."

Matt growls. "She got in the way."

"Is that true, Ryat?" He looks at me. "She was a problem, standing in your way of completing your assignment, and you had to terminate her as well?" Arching a brow, he waits for my answer.

I just stare at him, crossing my arms over my chest. I'm not a fucking rat, but I'm also not going to lie for Matt. He stepped out of line. We have rules that we have to abide by. Otherwise, what in the fuck are we doing here? I'm not killing for sport. I do what needs to be done. Period.

Lincoln sighs, running his hand down his face. He's clearly stressed. "You're on probation, Matt."

"What?" He jumps to his feet. "What the fuck, Linc? You know that's bullshit!"

"I know that you killed a very important bitch," Lincoln snaps, getting in his face. "And now I have to clean up your mess!"

"Who the fuck was she?" Matt demands.

"That's none of your business," Lincoln shouts in his face.

"You just said she was important," he argues.

"Get the fuck out of my office, Matt, before I strip you of your Lord title," he screams, pointing at the door.

Matt spins around and shoves the chair over before he storms out, slamming the door behind him.

I push up off the armrests and turn to exit as well.

"Wait, Ryat," Lincoln growls.

I turn to face him, and he plops down behind his desk. "I need to know what happened." He links his fingers together on the surface.

I say nothing.

"Goddammit," he hisses, leaning back in his seat. "You have to give me something."

"I did what was required of me. He's dead," I say simply.

He nods once. "So, Matt killed the woman."

I look away from him and grind my teeth. They already suspected it was Matt, but I just confirmed it. This is why I don't fucking talk.

"I'm not sure what to do, Ryat," he states.

I look back at him, and he tilts his head from side to side, contemplating his next move. "I could put you on probation as well."

I fist my hands, not really all that surprised. I figured they'd punish me in order to get me to talk. Then he reaches over and pushes a button on his office phone. "Send him in."

The door opens behind me, and I see a man walk in. I don't know him personally, but I've heard of him. His list of bodies is a mile long. A sadistic son of a bitch. He killed three of his brothers his senior year. Everyone in the house of Lords feared him. He's a legend, really.

"Ryat Archer?" He reaches out his right hand to me.

"Yes, sir." I do the same and shake it.

He gestures for me to sit back down in my seat, so I do. "What is this about?" I ask, looking back and forth between the two men.

"Well, son …" He sits on the leather couch, unbuttoning his black suit jacket. "I'd like a favor from you."

I lean forward, placing my elbows on my thighs. This is how they'll get

me to talk? Threaten to put me on probation and then ask me for a favor? In
return, I ask to no longer be on probation. "And what will I get in return?"

He throws his head back, laughing, making his body shake. Then he
looks over at Lincoln. "I like this kid."

"Told you," Lincoln says cryptically.

"The Lords are all about accommodating their brothers who are willing
to go above and beyond." He leans back, getting comfortable. "So, Ryat ...
the real question is, what is it that you want?"

I sit in my black W Motors Lykan Hypersport, tucked back in the
parking lot of Blake's apartment complex. It sits right off campus.

The first thing you are taught when becoming a Lord is that
you do your intel. You think of every scenario that gives you an
advantage to win.

The light flips on in her bedroom, and I sit up straighter when
she walks past her window, finally arriving home. Stopping in the
corner, she reaches down and lifts her shirt up and over her head.
My cock grows hard instantly as I watch the motion cause her hair
to fall over her back.

It doesn't matter that I can only see her shadow. It's good
enough. For now.

Walking out of sight, I see another light come on in an adjoining
room, her bathroom. I've been watching her enough to know the
layout of her apartment. It's even harder to see through the stained
glass, but still enough to make out the side view of her large breasts.
The curve of them and her flat stomach followed by her great ass.

"Fuck." I unzip my jeans and pull out my dick. Spitting on my
hand, I slowly start to stroke it, imagining I have one hand in her
hair that's shoving her mouth on my cock.

She steps in what I know is her shower, and I see water spraying
onto her body. Closing my eyes, I pick up the pace with my hand
and see her on her knees inside the shower. Her pretty blue eyes
look up at me while her parted lips just beg to be fucked.

"Whatever my girl wants," I pant, my hips bucking in the driver's
seat.

I wrap my hands into her wet, dark hair and slide my cock inside
her hot, wet mouth and begin to fuck it. "Blake." I moan, my hand
picking up the pace as I imagine her pretty blue eyes crying while I
fuck that pretty face.

My balls tighten, and my breath quickens seconds before I come
in my hand. "Fuck," I hiss, reaching up, I remove my shirt and use

it to clean up my mess.

Looking up at her window, I see the light to her bathroom turn off, then the one to her bedroom.

Taking a deep breath, I lean my head against the headrest, trying to calm my racing heart.

"Soon, Blake. Soon." I won't have to use my hand or imagination. I'll have her mouth, pussy, and ass to use.

I will fucking own her.

JUNIOR YEAR

I exit the room and start walking down the hallway to my bedroom. Shoving the door open, I slam it shut to find Matt sitting on the side of my bed. "Get the fuck out." I walk past him toward my adjoining bathroom.

He jumps to his feet. "What in the fuck did you tell Lincoln?"

Spinning around, I shove his chest. "I didn't say shit!"

He stumbles back and then shakes his head, giving a rough laugh. "You should have my back."

"And you should have known not to fucking touch her," I shout back.

"If you would have let me fuck her ..."

"You mean rape her?" I correct him. "Fuck, Matt! What in the hell were you thinking?" Abstinence is part of our oath, until our senior year when we are granted a chosen. If I had told Lincoln that he was going to rape the woman, he'd for sure be stripped of his Lord title.

Matt runs his hands through his hair, letting out a frustrated breath. "I don't know, man. Blakely and I have been fighting—"

I snort, interrupting him. "You've been fighting with your girlfriend, so you decide to disobey an order with the Lords? They'll kick you out."

"I'm fine." He waves me off. "What did Lincoln have to say to you after I left?"

He only mentions Lincoln, which means he doesn't know another man was brought in to speak to me. "I didn't rat you out." I avoid his question.

"Well, what did you fucking say?" Matt snaps.

"That's none of your damn business." I turn my back on him, ending this conversation.

He grabs my shirt and yanks me from the bathroom back into my bedroom. I swing, my body twisting, and my fist connects with his jaw. "Don't fucking push me, Matt," I growl, clenching and unclenching my hand, feeling it already starting to swell from the hit.

Rubbing his jaw, he steps up to me, chest to chest, and I bow mine, ready to knock his ass out when he speaks. "If I find out you fucked me over, I'll end you, Ryat."

I smile at that. "I'd like to see you try."

With that, he spins and exits my room, slamming the bedroom door on his way out.

BLAKELY

IT'S A FRIDAY night, and I'm lying in my bed watching a horror movie on Netflix while scrolling through my social media page. Not seeing anything interesting, I close out the app and turn up the TV, thinking over my time here at Barrington University since classes started two weeks ago.

I haven't run into dipshit anymore. But Matt's been acting weird ever since I stormed into the library demanding answers. That he didn't give me. He's always bringing up Ryat. Every day, he asks me if I've seen or spoken to him. When I say no, he says okay, but I can see it in his eyes that he doesn't believe me. And it's starting to bother me. I've never cheated on him before, never even flirted with another guy, so the fact that it's got him questioning my loyalty is pissing me off.

I've been the one begging him for sex, and he's the one who turns me down. Always telling me that he promised my parents we'd wait for our wedding night. *That's bullshit.* Who the hell waits these days? We've fooled around, but he always stops it before it goes too far, leaving my body begging for more.

"We're going," Sarah states, entering my bedroom and plopping down on the end of my bed.

"But ..."

"No buts." She shakes her head. "We've done nothing but stay in, and I didn't leave Texas just to stay home all the fucking time. Plus, Matt is out of town." She winks at me.

He went home for the weekend. I wanted to ask why he didn't invite me, but I also didn't want to see my parents, so I kept my mouth shut. "What does that have to do with anything?"

"You can let loose and have fun without him accusing you of wanting to fuck Ryat." She's overheard several of our arguments in the past couple of weeks. The walls in our apartment are too thin. Or maybe we just fight too loud.

"Please." She resorts to begging when I remain in bed just staring at her. "Just this time ... It's just one party."

It's been a while since I've had a girls' night with her. Matt's never been a big fan of Sarah's. He says that she's too flirtatious with everyone. He's been very vocal about his hatred for her over the years. When we're all back home in Texas, he'd always show up or make plans for us with his parents, so I'd have to cancel mine with her. She never seemed to get mad at me for that. Funny how I'm just now noticing that he would do that. "Fine," I growl, throwing the covers off. I do want to get out and have some fun. "We'll find out what this chosen shit means," I add.

"Yes!" She jumps to her feet. "I'll go get dressed." Storming out of my room, she yells over her shoulder, "Wear something slutty."

I laugh, entering my closet.

An hour later, we're pulling up to an open gate outside the house of Lords. It's about fifteen minutes from Barrington's campus off a two-lane road. It was a hotel back in the day that was given to them. All members must live in the house during their duration of college. Matt moved in his freshman year. You're not welcome to be here unless they are throwing a party. Otherwise, the gate is closed, and the property is off-limits to outsiders.

Two men stand on either side of the gate dressed in black cloaks and white masks, resembling skeletons.

A building comes into view at the end of a long and curvy drive. The renovated hotel stands five stories tall with large windows. Its white brick with black shutters makes it look designed for the rich. Six columns are decorated with black garland wrapped around them from top to bottom. Spotlights are placed strategically on the ground to illuminate the site of the party.

It has a large roundabout with a pond in the middle with a fountain on either side and a white arched walkway across the center. Men and women stand on it with their drinks, some smoking cigarettes.

After pulling into a parking spot to the left, we get out of the car. "Are you sure we're invited?" I ask.

"Of course." She waves me off. "Everyone is."

"But Matt has never let me come here." Not even during the parties. He said even though I was *off-limits*, he didn't even want me around the members. I never knew what he meant, and when I asked, he would get mad, blow up at me, then avoid me for a few days.

You can hear "Make Hate to Me" by Citizen Soldier blaring from the inside of the house.

Both glass doors are wide open, and we step inside. The marble floors, expensive décor, and artifacts make my mouth fall open. Now, I've grown up around money. My father owns a multibillion dollar business. My mother isn't nearly as wealthy as my father, but she's known around the world for her swimsuit spreads. That's how they met. He saw her picture once and flew halfway across the world just to buy her coffee. Three months later, they were married. I was born six months later. Pretty sure my mom got knocked up that first night on purpose—trap the wealthy man type of situation. Then after they had me, they were done. I always begged for a sibling. Not like it would have taken time out of their days. I was raised by nannies and tutors. But this is on another level.

Everything is white as snow and polished to perfection. The walls are painted white with black and white pictures. The one on the wall to my left is a large picture of the Eiffel Tower. I've been there several times, and I've never seen it prettier than in this photo. Straight ahead is a grand staircase covered in black carpet with a matching banister. On the second floor, the platform opens up, giving the option to go left or right. The upper level is also open in the middle, allowing you to look up at the high, black-painted ceiling where chandeliers hang down to the first floor. I see multiple doors that lead to some of the rooms. An elevator in the left-hand corner must take you to the third and fourth floors.

"This place is amazing," she whispers in awe.

"Phones, keys, and ID."

We both turn to the right to see a man standing behind a concierge desk. He wears a black mask with Xs over his eyes and stitches for lips along with a black cloak.

"Phones, keys, and ID," he repeats loudly over the music, holding out two baggies for us.

Walking over to him, I take them. "Why?" Sarah asks.

"Because those are the rules. Either drop your shit in the bag or get the fuck out," he barks, handing the kid next to us a bag. He doesn't think twice about digging his belongings out of his pockets and placing them in the bag. He zips it up before giving it back.

The guy in the mask writes on it and then places it in a cubby behind him on the wall.

"Come on." She bats her eyes at me. "What could it hurt? It'll be fun." Then she starts placing her things inside hers.

"Right?" *What could it hurt?* This is what I wanted to do. Get out and get some answers.

Handing him back the bag, he gives us two pieces of paper. "Write your name on the tag and place it on your shirt." Then he clicks the pen and hands it to me.

Bending over, I write my name and then give it to her to do the same with her name tag.

"This is wild. I've never been to a party like this." She grabs my arm and starts bouncing up and down excitedly. "Is this for a prize?" she asks him.

He throws his head back, laughing. We can't see his face, but the angle gives us a clear view of his Adam's apple moving from his laughter. "This is the start of the ritual," he states once he's calmed himself.

"What is that exactly?" I ask because I still haven't gotten a direct answer.

"Don't get too concerned. I doubt you two have anything to worry about," he answers cryptically and then dismisses us, moving on to the next set of girls who just walked in.

"Let's go find some alcohol." She drags me through a hallway and into a kitchen. The room is large with industrial-size stainless-steel appliances. To the right is a bar area where people currently occupy.

It looks like any other college party. The only difference is some are dressed as the guy up front—masks and cloaks. "Who are these people?" I whisper-shout in her ear over "Needles" by Seether.

She shrugs. "If I had my phone, I'd google it."

Something tells me Google isn't going to know shit about the situation we've found ourselves in. *Ritual?* Sounds churchy to me that involves blood and a sacrifice. I wonder if it's the Lords that are dressed differently. It's no secret at Barrington who the members are as far as I know. You don't hear much talk about them, but all I know is what Matt has told me, which isn't much. I've just always assumed they were like a fraternity.

Going over to the island, I see small glass bowls lined up side by side. Each one contains pills of various colors and shapes. I recognize some as Xanax, Percocet, and Adderall. Things my mother will pop every now and then when she's either stressed or has a headache.

"What do you want?" Sarah asks me, looking over the drinks lined up.

"I'll have a rum and Coke, please."

She nods her head and starts to pour me a drink. Once done, she makes herself one. We tap them together in cheers. Taking a drink, I cough. "Dear Lord." I hiss in a breath. "Trying to kill me?"

She laughs. "No. But a good liquor coma sounds good."

She was in rehab twice while in high school. Her mother came home during our freshman year to find her passed out on the floor in her own vomit. She took some Oxy. She's not suicidal, but she wanted them to see her. When that didn't work, she went to a party, got drunk off her ass, and wrapped her father's one-of-a-kind car around a tree. She didn't even have her license yet.

Obviously, rehab wasn't any help. I think her parents were just glad she left for college after her senior year. *She was someone else's problem* kind of attitude.

"Come on. Let's go see what this place is all about." She grabs my arm and pulls me out of the kitchen and through a hallway. We step into an open room. I'm guessing it was once a ballroom with high cathedral ceilings. The walls vary in shade from white and gray. The black granite floor has white vines running through it. It's gorgeous, just like everything else I've seen so far.

The music is louder here. A DJ is set up in a corner at the front of the room, and he too wears a black mask and matching cloak. A long table seats every bit of twenty-four, but only one side is occupied. Twelve people sit side by side, all wearing the same black masks and cloaks overlooking the room.

"What the fuck?" I whisper in her ear over "Like Lovers Do" by Hey Violet.

"I like it." She nods quickly, taking a drink. "Mysterious."

It can't be that bad, right? Not if Matt is involved. He's a Polo and loafers while playing golf kind of guy. Not a mysterious, I'll chase you down in an alley and kill you type of vibe. "It's like a cult," I mumble to her. "If they try to brand our asses, we run for it." Fuck the keys, cell phone, and ID. I can get new ones.

She laughs like I'm joking.

EIGHT

BLAKELY

Two HOURS AND three drinks later, I'm pretty fucking drunk. Sarah's damn near gone. We're laughing and dancing to "Mad Hatter" by Melanie Martinez.

I get this spine-chilling feeling and stop dancing. I quickly look around, but I can't focus on anything. My hair slaps me in the face, and I shove it back behind my ear the best I can. Only for it to fall back in my way.

"What?" She notices and stops dancing. "You going to get sick?"

"No. I ..." My eyes stop on the table at the front of the ballroom. It sits high up on a platform, giving the ones seated there a clear view of the crowd. Two of them are now standing behind it, facing one another. Their hand movements let me know they're deep in conversation. The one on the very end is typing away on a phone, making me wonder why we had to give ours up. The one in the middle. It's a man. I can tell by the way he's sitting. He's laid back in his seat with his right hand up, resting on the side of his mask. It causes the sleeve of his cloak to slide down, and I can see the black and silver watch on his wrist. The flashing lights hit it, almost blinding me.

The one sitting next to him leans in and must say something because the guy's mask moves up and down as if he's agreeing.

Those feelings return, making my breathing pick up while I stare at him. Bringing the drink to my lips, I go to take a sip, but I'm hit from behind, knocked forward, making me spill it down my face and shirt. "What the fuck?" I spin around.

"Sorry ... Blakely?"

I blink up at another guy dressed in a black cloak and mask. "How do you know ...?"

He rips his mask off, and I stare up at a set of wide blue eyes. They instantly narrow on me as I blink. "Blakely?" he growls. "What are you ... What are you doing here?"

I can't speak. Instead, my eyes go to the bleach blonde he's still holding. She clings to him like the typical drunk girl who can't stand on her own.

"What in the fuck is this?" Sarah demands, stepping forward. "Who the fuck is this bitch?" She's always been an angry drunk. Senior year of high school, she got trashed and punched her ex-boyfriend in the face for not having any gum. The cops were called, parents showed up. It was a nightmare.

"Hey," the girl whines and then laughs. "I'm his girlfriend."

"No," Sarah snaps, yanking my arm, and pulls me forward. More alcohol rolls over the rim of my cup and onto my clothes. "This is his fucking girlfriend."

She frowns and looks up at him. "Huh? Baby, what's she ..." *Hiccup.* "Talking about?"

"Nothing," Matt tells her.

Sarah laughs, but it holds no humor.

His words snap me out of my trance. We started dating my freshman year when I moved here to Pennsylvania from Texas for college. We knew each other in high school, grew up in the same city, but I wasn't allowed to date then. *Not until you're in college, Blakely. That's when you're old enough to understand a relationship,* my mother had said.

I've remained a virgin for him. I've begged him to fuck me, and every damn time, he's turned me down. Here I am, twenty years old, and the only thing I've fucked is a dildo that I'm not even sure how to use and a vibrator that I keep plugged into the wall when I feel like screaming for a release. He fucked Gabby Simmons his sophomore year in high school. His number kept climbing after that. And it looks like it hasn't stopped.

He steps forward. "Blakely ..."

I grab Sarah's drink out of her hand and toss it into his face. Thankfully, it had more than mine. He gasps, and his girlfriend cups her mouth, softening her laugh.

"Fuck," he growls, running his hand down it, wiping off the excess alcohol before shoving his damn mask over it like I have more to throw at him.

"This is over," I tell him.

"Blakely—"

"Enjoy," I tell her, interrupting him with a big fuck-you smile and walking off.

Making my way to the kitchen, I stop at the island. Placing both of my hands on the edge, I bow my head. My sweaty, tangled hair falls to cover my face, and I sniff, trying to calm my breathing. I will not cry here. This will not be the last time I see him. I'm stuck here until he graduates at the end of this year.

"Here." Sarah pushes my hair back with her free hand, and I see she has a new drink for me in the other. Smells like vodka this time. I take it and throw it back, not caring how much gets on my already wet shirt. "He's shit anyway, girl. Fuck him. Well, not literally. But you know ..."

What will my parents say when I come home for the holidays, and they ask why he's not with me? How will I explain this? It's practically an arranged marriage without the ring and signed contract. Maybe that's why he's cheating. Because he knows no matter what, I have to end up with him. Two families forming one. "Do you think this is why he never let me come here?" I ask her. "Because he's been with her the whole time?"

She looks away and sighs, thinking the same thing I am.

Is this why he has been questioning me about Ryat? They say the one accusing you of cheating is usually the bastard stepping out. How long has he been with her? Weeks, months, years? It could be any of those answers.

She didn't look familiar. But Barrington is massive. She might not even go there. He's made her his girlfriend? He didn't even acknowledge me when Sarah corrected her that I was his girlfriend. Have I never even been?

"Fuck him," I hiss.

"Yeah!" She gives me a drunken smile. "Let's go back out there and dance some more. Okay? Show that piece of shit what he'll miss."

"Okay." I throw back some more of my drink and then set it down, not wanting to wear anymore of it.

RYAT

I sit back, watching Blakely through the two holes in my mask as she makes her way back to the dance floor. The chair vibrates my ass from the speakers being right behind us while "Numb" by 8 Graves plays. My right knee bounces with anticipation.

I choose you!

I'm guessing that since she threw a drink in her piece-of-shit boyfriend's face while another girl was hanging all over him means he's no longer in my way.

Makes things a little easier for me. Not like I'd let that motherfucker stop what I plan on doing. His fuckup is my gain. She'll willingly allow me to take her as mine. Never underestimate a woman hell-bent on revenge. She'll do anything to make an ex regret what he didn't appreciate.

I didn't think she'd show, but it couldn't have gone better if I'd planned it. She's here while Matt's with Ashley. He never would let Blakely come to our house. Didn't want her seeing what goes on. How the Lords operate. Kept her as far away from the members as possible. He knew that she wasn't his guarantee. Not until after graduation anyway. He'll marry her because that's what his father told him to do, and she'll hate him because he's shit.

A solid foundation for a marriage, if you ask me.

Blakely throws her hands up and sways her hips to the music, causing her wet shirt to rise. My eyes drop to her pierced belly button and run down her exposed skin to where her jeans sit low on her hips. I run my tongue along my teeth, wishing they were her body.

"Three hundred and twenty-five so far," Lance speaks into my ear.

I nod but say nothing. It's amazing what boring rich kids will do for a little excitement. As the seniors at Barrington this year, we're upholding a century-old tradition by throwing this party to kick off the school year.

The ritual is a game the Lords made up to pass the fucking time.

Imagine having more money than you could ever spend. More than your grandkids could ever spend. More than your great-grandkids ... well, you get the point.

Somewhere, something has to give. After graduation, you begin your new role in the world as a Lord and settle down with some bitch who'll fuck the pool boy any chance she gets. She'll have the nannies raise your ungrateful children while you're flying around the world working, fucking a one-night stand in your penthouse suite that you met in a bar and won't bother to remember her name.

Yeah, I'm cynical. Love doesn't exist. Convenience does. Most of us are already set to marry that certain person who will make our lives a living hell. There's a reason the rich stay rich—arrangements are set in place before we even come along. Empires are combined to remain indestructible. Contracts signed, promises spoken, and alliances made to ensure our futures remain on top.

My eyes find her again just as she turns around and walks out of the ballroom. "Watch the floor," I say, getting to my feet.

"Got it." Chance waves me off.

I step down off the platform and make my way through the crowd. Finding her in the hallway, I watch her push open a door and stumble inside. She exits immediately. My girl is drunk off her ass. I've been watching her ever since I saw her step onto the dance floor. At one point, I knew she felt my stare. I wonder what she would think if she knew what I plan on doing to her.

She opens another door and quickly looks away, mumbling, "*Sorry,*" to whoever she just witnessed fucking inside by the way her cheeks redden.

I smile.

Stumbling, she places her hand on the wall to keep herself from falling into it. Looking into the next room, she steps inside, and I do the same. What are the odds? It's my room.

Closing the door behind me, I flip on the light.

NINE
BLAKELY

"SARAH ..." I SPIN around, expecting her to have followed me, but I freeze when I see one of those mask-covered men standing in the room with me. "Oh, uh ..." My eyes go to the door as I take a step back, stumbling into the footboard.

He steps into me, and I suck in a breath when he lifts his hands to push my hair back. I watch wide-eyed and half-paralyzed as he lowers his hand down over my shirt, pressing the material softly to my chest. He gets to my breasts and tilts his head to the side. The pressure of my bra rubbing on my nipple makes it harden.

I gasp when he rips off my name tag. He wads it up in his hand and tosses it to the floor, landing at our feet.

"Matt ...?" I swallow, my tongue heavy.

The figure shakes his head, and I whimper. Why do I believe it's not him? And why don't I care? "I'm sorry ..." I lick my numb lips. "I shouldn't have ... I'll leave." I stumble over my words as I go to walk around him.

But his hand comes out, wrapping around my waist and pulling my back to the front of his body. My breath rushes out of my lungs. "I'd rather you not," he whispers roughly into my ear.

I try to think if I've heard his voice before, but the song "Killing Me Slowly" by Bad Wolves is too loud, and my mind is foggy.

A chill runs up my back, making me shiver. Without permission, his free hand yanks my shirt up, and then his warm hand lands on my stomach. My heart races when his hand starts making its way up my rib cage and to my bra.

I swallow nervously, and my thighs tighten when he slides his hand under the material and up over my sensitive breasts. I should be embarrassed for two reasons. One, he's a stranger, and two, my chest is wet from the alcohol spilled on it. But that's not the case. As I lean my head back on his chest, a moan escapes my numb lips. I lick them just in case I'm drooling. I've imagined what it would feel like to be touched. To know what it's like to be sexually wanted for so long. I wish I wasn't so drunk, so I could really take it in.

"I was watching you earlier," he admits shamelessly into my ear. "He's over you. Let me help you get over him."

His words once again tell me it's not Matt. But he saw us? Was that why I felt like I was being watched before I found Matt with that girl? It was him? "I ..."

"Shh." His hand around my waist lowers to my jeans. His fingers softly run back and forth along the top of the material, making my body break out in goose bumps. "Will you let me help you?"

My head is swimming, the room tilting. My heart is racing, my body on fire. All of a sudden, everything is hot. Getting undressed sounds like an amazing idea. I nod and breathe, "Yeah." Why not? I'm single now. Matt has someone. Why can't I? It's not like I loved him. It's the fact that he was fucking cheating on me when he wouldn't even fuck me.

"Stay right where you are," he orders. "Understand?"

Swallowing the lingering taste of vodka from that last drink, I answer, "Yes."

He lets go, and I watch him walk out from behind me and over to the door. He locks it, then turns to face me.

I look up at him. He's got an all-white mask on. It's got black lines through it in various places to make it look like it's cracked. The eyes have black circles around them, and the lips are filled in the same color. For some reason, it's not as frightening as it should be. Maybe that's the alcohol talking. I've never done something so bold before. So reckless. Something that is a hundred percent my decision.

My mother would throw a fit if she knew I was drunk at this party, let alone locked in a room with a stranger who hasn't shown me his face.

Stepping into me, he lifts his right hand and once again runs it down my face and neck, pausing on my pulse. It's racing. My breathing ragged. I feel like I might pass out soon. Dropping his hand, he walks behind me again, and I hear a drawer open and close. Then darkness covers my eyes.

I lift my hands to remove it. "What ...?"

The material falls to my feet, and my arms are grabbed and yanked behind my back. Then I'm bent over the side of the bed. I'd scream, but my breath gets caught in my throat. He holds my wrists crossed with one hand while I hear the sound of metal before something cold is tightened around each wrist.

"Stay," he growls before I feel the loss of his body.

I'm panting, my body shaking while I wait here like an obedient dog, pulling on what I can only think to be handcuffs. Seconds later, that material is placed back over my eyes, taking away my sight. It's tied in a knot, securing it in its place.

He grabs me by my hair, yanking me to stand, and I cry out, surprised it didn't rip the blindfold off. "You can take it off when I'm done with you." His voice is rougher than it was a second ago. Almost angry.

It makes my legs tighten and pussy throb. I moan in acceptance for whatever the stranger wants to do with me. My body has been screaming in silence for years for someone to touch it. To have their way with it. I can't satisfy it. Not like I crave. Imagine having to scratch an itch that you can't reach no matter how hard you try. Or trying to scream underwater for help, knowing that no one can hear you.

Matt turned me down countless times. I once tried to seduce him on the golf course, and he yelled at me when we got back to his parents', telling me it was embarrassing how I rubbed my ass against him while his friends were only a few feet away. No one was paying any attention to us, and it's not like I was naked. I was wearing a skirt. All he had to do was lift it up and touch me.

The man slaps my ass, making me jump and cry out. "Answer me," he demands in my ear.

Did he ask me a question? I try to rack my drunk brain but come up with nothing, so I just say, "Yes."

His hands come around the front of my jeans, and he unzips them.

"Yes," I repeat again just in case he didn't hear me the first time as the song changes to "Guest Room" by Echos. I know I'm going to agree to whatever the fuck this stranger wants from me. Hoping he can show me what my body was meant to do because I feel like I've been missing something.

RYAT

I TOSS HER onto the bed, lying on her back. She cries out when she lands on her restrained wrists. I yank my mask off and drop it to the floor, then I remove her heels before pulling her jeans down her legs.

"Yes." She moans, arching her back.

I remove her underwear as well and place them in my pocket. She won't be getting those back. Crawling onto the bed, I spread her legs while running my hands up her thighs. They shake, and she's panting. I imagine her like this with Matt, and my fingers dig into her skin. I hope the bastard saw me following her off the dance floor.

Whimpering, she gets my attention, and I let up on her. Spreading her legs wider, I lean down and look over her pussy. It's clean-shaven and glistening already, making my mouth start to water instantly. Running my thumb over it, I spread her open and lower my face, licking her pretty cunt.

Her hips jump, and I hold them down in place.

"Oh, God ..." She trails off.

She's wet, so I slip a finger into her easily. It's warm and so fucking tight. I pause as Gunner's words come back to me from the other day. "Blakely," I say, pushing a second one into her, making her hiss in a breath.

She arches her neck, lips parted, and whimpers. "Yeah?" She's too drunk to even realize I called her by her name.

"Have you ever been fucked?" I ask her, removing my fingers and pushing them into her again while twisting them to where they turn inside her and reach upward slowly. I'm taking my time because I don't want to hurt the poor girl. Not yet. But once she's my chosen, all bets are off.

This is what the oath is for—restraint. It's about thinking things through and outliving our opponent. Wear them down. Show no mercy. We are stronger than them.

"No." She bucks her hips.

"Fuck," I growl before sinking my teeth into her thigh and making her flinch on a soft cry. My cock is so fucking hard, it's pressing painfully against the inside of my jeans. For three years, I've done what was asked of me. I can't break that oath now. I just have to wait a little longer.

Removing my fingers, I replace them with my tongue and lick her wet pussy, making her moan. I do it again and throw her legs over my shoulders to get a better hold on her writhing body while I show her why I'm the better choice for her.

Matt is going to hate me because I'm going to fuck his future wife.

She will be my chosen, and I will use her in more ways than she ever knew possible. I'll leave scars he'll have to look at every day, knowing I once fucking owned her.

TEN

BLAKELY

"You really don't remember?" Sarah asks me while walking down the hallway of Barrington Monday morning.

"Nope," I answer.

She frowns, tilting her head to the side in thought. After a long pause, she speaks. "Well, that sucks."

"Right? What about you?"

She shakes her head. "We must have had a great time."

I laugh as she smiles. I allowed a stranger to blindfold and cuff my wrists behind my back, and I'm not even sure we had sex. I do, however, remember him throwing me onto the bed and going down on me. I fucking screamed, or at least I did in my head as I came all over his face. Then I think I blacked out.

I woke up the next morning in my bed, Sarah in hers, and my car in the parking lot of our apartment complex. Our cell phones, IDs, and my car keys were sitting on the kitchen counter with no explanation of how they got there. However, my underwear was missing, but otherwise, I was dressed in the clothes I went wearing.

We did nothing but lay on the couch, wrapped in blankets, eating greasy cheeseburgers trying to get rid of our hangovers. She was sick most of the day, and I felt like I was dying. Thankfully, we feel much better today.

"Have you heard from Matt?" she asks.

"Another no," I growl. I do, however, remember that motherfucker and his *girlfriend*. He's the main reason I even let the stranger touch me. I'm more pissed at Matt than I am at the fact I may have lost my virginity and can't remember it. When I woke up in my bed Saturday morning, I was pretty sore between my legs with bite marks on my inner thigh.

"He hasn't even called to try to explain himself? Ask for forgiveness?"

I shake my head.

"What a piece of shit," she snaps and softens her voice. "I'm sorry."

"It's fine." You know what they say—better to find out now rather than five years down the road and three kids later.

My cell phone rings in my back pocket, and I pull it out to see it's my mother. "I'll meet you in class." Walking off, I answer, "Hello?"

"Good morning, dear. How are things going?"

I wonder if she's calling because Matt's mother has informed her of our breakup. They are best friends. "Fine," I answer, testing the waters.

"Nothing new to tell me?" she asks in that voice that tells me she already knows something.

"No," I lie.

She sighs heavily. "Well, I just spoke to Kimberly, and she said that she heard you and Matt got into a fight this past weekend."

"A fight?" I snort; the pussy lied to his mother. "He was cheating on me, Mom. We broke up." Why should I have to hide who he really is? Plus, telling her now is better than doing it in person. She can chase me from room to room, and our house is big. Now I can tell her how I feel, then hang up and go about my day.

"You know that no relationship is perfect, right?" she responds.

My mouth falls open. I know she's not implying what I think she is. "You can't be serious?"

"Of course, I am. I think your father and I have given you a false representation of what marriage is like."

"So, you think I should put up with someone being unfaithful?" I snap.

"I think that sacrifices are made in a marriage—"

"Well, thankfully, I haven't married him," I interrupt her, my blood boiling. I don't know why I'm mad because I knew she'd be this way. That's why I was afraid to tell her what happened.

"The wedding is still on, Blakely," she states.

She wants it to be next summer after I graduate. She and Kimberly have been planning it for years. "Mom ..."

"You have plenty of time to work through things. This is an opportunity for you."

I blink. *An opportunity?* "For what?" I wonder.

"You'll see." She hangs up.

I pull the phone from my ear and just stare at it. What the hell is she referring to? An opportunity for what? To see how far he'll go to make it up to me? The fucker hasn't even reached out to me. Silence speaks louder than any gift a man can give you. If he wanted to, he would and all that shit. If a woman would just pay attention, a man will tell her everything she needs to know without him even saying a damn word.

My mother once went two weeks without even looking my father's way. He bought her a vacation home—an oceanfront estate in South Hampton—after that. She forgave him quicker than a stack of cards falling over from a breeze. Now I understand it.

An opportunity to see what I can get out of him. Too bad there's nothing that fucker could give me that would make me forgive his cheating ass.

I silence my phone before placing it back in my pocket and have that feeling creeping up my spine again. Like someone is watching me.

Looking up, I find a set of emerald eyes. Ryat is leaning up against the far wall. A girl with short, bleach blonde hair stands in front of him, and she's speaking to him, but he's looking at me. He doesn't seem to care that I caught him staring.

Then like he never even saw me standing here, he looks down at the girl who continues their conversation. He nods a few times, and then his lips start moving, but I can't hear what they're talking about.

A guy bumps my shoulder, pushing me to the side, not even bothering to say he's sorry. I spin around, looking at all the faces that fill the hall. My breathing picks up, thinking about the weekend at the house of Lords. It could literally be anybody. I didn't think about it that night, but now that I'm sober, it's got me wondering. What if it *was* Matt? I asked him, and he said no, but that doesn't mean he was telling the truth. Fuck, he's already been lying to me. What's one more? I try to remember what his voice sounded like, but I can't. I do remember him saying that Matt was over me. He had been watching me. But maybe that was his way of telling me he was done with me. He didn't like that I caught him and left him. He wanted that power.

Or I'm overthinking it, and it's someone else. It could have been someone who doesn't even go to Barrington. It's a college town tucked back in the mountains of Pennsylvania, but that doesn't mean people don't vacation here. Some cabins sit in these mountains that cost millions, and we're only an hour from a large city. People come out here all the time to get away for the weekend. But why the cloaks and masks? That part doesn't make sense. Were the Lords dressed that way, or was it something else?

The reasonable answer has to be Matt. He knew I was there. He knew I was mad at him, and that was his way to get even. He fucks someone and then makes me think I fucked someone else. No hard feelings. It's a trick he played on me.

"Hey?"

I turn around to see Matt standing in front of me as if I had summoned him. "Hey?" I laugh maniacally. I'm pretty sure I'm having a fucking mental breakdown, and the first thing he decides to say to me after I find him cheating is *hey*?

"We need to talk." His eyes narrow on me with accusation.

Talk? What is there to say? I think about what my mother said to me, and I decide to use this chance as an opportunity. Just not the kind she meant. "I think we said enough at the party." I cross my arms over my chest.

He runs a hand through his hair. "I wanted to talk to you ..." He pauses and looks over my shoulder, squaring his. His eyes come back to mine. "Ashley got sick, and we had to leave before I could find you again."

"Wait?" I hold up my hand. "So, we didn't see each other again?" I'm not even surprised he left with her.

He frowns. "No."

So, it wasn't him I spread my legs for. For some reason, that makes me feel better. I'd rather it be a complete stranger, anyone but him.

"Why?" he asks.

"No reason." I blow him off, going to step away, but he grabs my upper arm and yanks me to a stop.

"What the fuck did that mean, Blakely?" he growls, getting in my face.

I lick my lips and give him a sweet smile. *Fuck you, Matt.* "I just realized you weren't the guy I fucked that night." Okay, so I'm not a hundred percent sure I had sex, but I want him to think I did. He not only cheated, but he also lied to me because he told me he was going back to Texas for the weekend. He thought he'd be safe at the house of Lords, knowing I wouldn't be there. Fuck, what if I hadn't gone? How long would he have kept this from me? Would we still be pretending we're a couple?

"What?" he shouts, tightening his hand on my upper arm. "You what?"

"You're hurting me." I try to pull away, but he yanks me closer to him.

Lowering his face to mine, he snaps, "You better be joking, Blakely. I swear to God ..."

"Problem?"

I look over to see Ryat has joined the conversation, now standing next to us.

Matt growls at him. "Go away."

"I wasn't speaking to you." His green eyes meet mine, crossing his arms over his chest. "Is this man bothering you?" The tone of his voice doesn't sound concerned in the least. A total contradiction to his question.

Matt snorts. "I'm her boyfriend. You know that. Now fuck off, Ryat."

"No, you're not. And yes, he is," I answer him. Finally able to yank my arm free of Matt's grip, rubbing the sensitive skin.

"You just admitted to cheating on me, and you're saying I'm the problem?" Matt shouts, getting everyone's attention.

"You were cheating on me." I shove my finger into his hard chest. "And that's why I dumped your lying ass."

He runs his hands through his hair, releasing a deep breath. His body is tense, and he looks like he's about to punch something. "I knew you'd be just another fucking whore. You've been throwing yourself at me for years."

I want to be embarrassed that he just said I beg him for sex, but I can't. I'm in too much shock that he's mad I cheated on him when he was the one who was actually cheating. I broke up with him, then messed around with a stranger. Not the other way around.

Ryat looks back at Matt and tilts his head to the side. "Looks like someone chose your bitch." He shrugs carelessly. "Told you that would happen."

"You son of ..."

"Matt?"

What the actual fuck? His girlfriend also joins our conversation. Does she go to Barrington? If so, what year is she? "What's going on?" she asks, coming up to us, her eyes searching all of ours.

Matt thins his lips. I wait for him to push her away, to explain all of this to me. He said we needed to talk, so now is his best chance if I've ever seen one. He can fill her in on us, and I can find out just how long he's been screwing her.

Instead, he takes her hand and yanks her down the hall. She throws a look of concern over her shoulder at me, and I have a second of pity for her. I bet she didn't even know about me.

"Unbelievable," I mutter to myself, a laugh escaping my lips. What did I really expect from Matt, though? He has already proven to me what kind of man he is. I just never paid much attention. Now my eyes are wide open.

I see Ryat lower his lips to my ear out of the corner of my eye. My laughter stops, and I hold my breath as he whispers, "Told you he was over you."

I inhale sharply as he pulls away. Reaching up, he slowly runs his hand through my hair while his eyes search mine. Blood is rushing in my ears, heart hammering in my chest. I'm speechless. No! It can't be. Can it?

It was Ryat? If so, did he plan that? Was it because of his hatred for Matt?

Tilting his head to the side, he drops his eyes to my lips. "You've been asking about a chosen." His eyes come back to mine. "All you need to know is this ..." Stepping into me, he gently pulls my head back by my hair, forcing me to look up at him. I swallow nervously. "It means that what I did to you was just the beginning." Lowering his lips to my ear, he adds, "I'll own you, Blake." He shortens my name, his free hand comes up, and he trails a finger down my neck over my racing pulse, making my body break out in goose bumps. "And I think that's exactly what you want." With that, he takes a step back, leaving me to watch him walk away, my pussy now wet and shocked that it was him.

RYAT

It's BEEN A week since the party at the house of Lords, and she's been on my mind every second of every day. I see her here and there, but I don't approach her. I don't have to. The way she avoids me tells me exactly what I need to know—she thinks of me. I doubt she remembers much from that night. She was wasted, and in a sense, I took advantage of her in more ways than one. I'm not even sorry.

Making my way up the stairs to the third floor, I enter the library at Barrington. It's after ten o'clock on a Friday night, and she's here studying like the good little girl she is.

Looking around, I scan the rows of tables and empty chairs. The students are getting drunk and fucking. No one here has to study. Parents pay for their kids to attend this college, knowing it guarantees them perfect grades. But Blakely—I know she's here—I know where she's at all the time. If I'm not following her, I'm watching her.

Shoving my hands into the front pockets of my jeans, I start to walk past the rows of bookshelves, looking down either side for her.

Passing the second to last one, I pause and take a step back. She stands at the end, an open book in her hands, staring down at it, lost in her own little world. Such a stupid move. Anyone could drag her out of here kicking and screaming, and no one would ever know. She'd just disappear. *Poof.* Like magic. Thankfully for her, I'm not going to do that. Instead, I pull out my cell phone and take a pic of her. Then I send it to her.

I overheard her conversation with Matt in the hallway on Monday. She thought he was the guy she allowed to go down on her at the party. I wanted her to know it was me. I did that to her. It was just the beginning of what I can do. I gave her what little information she needed in order to want more. She's already curious, but now I want her needy. Begging for what Matt hasn't been able to give her.

I don't hear it go off, but she readjusts the book in one hand to hold it while grabbing her cell with the other. She opens it up, and her body stiffens when she sees the incoming picture message. I watch the way her tits start to bounce at her intake of breath, and I lick my lips.

Her head snaps up, and her wide blue eyes meet mine. "Ryat?" she asks nervously, her eyes shooting behind me. I stand at the end of the aisle, trapping her between the bookcases and the wall behind her. She's got no way out. "What are you doing here?"

I have to refrain from smirking. She doesn't care that I took her number that night. Instead, her concern is why I'm here. Stalking her. I don't answer but start walking over to her. She turns to fully face me, and she takes a few steps back. Big mistake. It just places her back against the wall, giving me an even better advantage of keeping her here.

Ripping the book from her hands, I drop it to the floor by our feet. She looks up at me, her pretty blue eyes searching mine. She's got her glasses on tonight, and I find them sexy as fuck. Stepping into her, I reach up and cup her face, my free hand sliding behind her back to pull her into me. Leaning down, I trail my lips along her ear, and she melts into me. Her soft yet firm body presses into me, and I whisper, "I can still taste you."

She inhales sharply at my words, her hands gripping my shirt.

"You tasted like goddamn honey," I growl, my hand moving into her long, thick hair. "So fucking sweet." She whimpers. "So fucking addicting." My cock is hard, straining against my jeans. I want to fuck her pretty face right here. I don't know how Matt was ever able to deny her.

"Wait," she breathes. Her hands start to push me away, and I take a step back. I need her to accept me for now. After the vow ceremony, I can force her to do whatever I want.

I drop my hands to my sides but don't speak. Instead, I just stare at her. Taking in the way her cheeks blush and her lips part while her breathing picks up. I imagine her doing that while I pin her down, her legs wrapped around my hips. My cock fucking that tight pussy and her screaming my name while I pull out and come all over her pretty face.

She bows her head and pushes her hair behind her ear. *She's nervous.* It's cute to see her like this around me. Especially since I've already had my tongue shoved up her cunt.

"I want to know what you meant." Lifting her eyes, she looks up at me through her dark lashes, adjusting her glasses up on her nose.

I act stupid. "About?"

"The chosen one." Licking her lips, she crosses her arms over her chest. "What does it mean? I don't understand—"

"You don't have to," I interrupt her.

Her lips thin, and she looks away from me, huffing. "Why would someone willingly give themselves to something that they know nothing about?"

Is that why she's here? She's trying to find a book about a Lord? Although I can understand her concern, it doesn't mean I sympathize enough to give her what she wants. As a Lord, we don't know everything going in. Another Lord cannot share secrets with someone who isn't a member. So, even my father couldn't tell me much about it. It was just something I had to do. Just like her—she's a direct order that I have to follow. I won't lose my Lord title for her. I've worked too hard and sacrificed too much to let her get away. So, I give her a little something to think about.

Choosing my question carefully, I ask, "Haven't you ever wanted to do something for yourself?"

She rolls her eyes. "Of course."

I know when I'm done with her, she will be Matt's wife. It won't matter if she hates him or not. She will spend the rest of her life serving him. But before then, she'll serve me.

"I've tried to look it up online ..."

I laugh, and her eyes shoot daggers at me. "You won't find anything about a Lord or chosen one on the internet."

Growling, she stomps her foot. "Then where?"

Stepping back into her, I place my hands flat against the wall on either side of her head. She stiffens, sucking in a breath. "You won't find anything about us anywhere. Because the Lords don't discuss their lives with outsiders," I say simply.

The tip of her tongue peeks out before she sucks her bottom lip in and nibbles on it. "If I ..." She pauses. "Choose to be your chosen one." Lowering her voice, she whispers, "Will you hurt me?"

Giving her a smirk, I answer truthfully. "Yes."

She whimpers, her eyes falling closed.

"But ... I'll also make you like it."

Her eyes open, and she stares up at me. I can see it. She's so fucking curious. Blakely Anderson is starving for something that not just any man can give her. But I can. I'll show her just what Matt refused to. "Matt didn't want you, Blake," I say. Dropping my hand from the wall, I run it down her neck, feeling her pulse race. "But I do." Not a total lie. I might have never looked at her twice if not for the order to make her my chosen. But I see her now. And she's exactly what I fucking need. A toy to use. A body to fuck. And sweet fucking revenge.

"You only want me because of Matt," she states, sticking out her chin as if she can read my mind.

I smile but don't correct her. Blakely's a smart woman. Instead, I say, "And that's the exact reason you'll choose to be mine." With that, I push off the wall, giving her my back, and leave her standing there to think about our conversation.

ELEVEN

BLAKELY

MONDAY AFTERNOON, I enter the apartment and walk into my bedroom. It's been a long day. I'm exhausted and want nothing more than to lie down in bed and go to sleep. I didn't sleep all weekend. Instead, I lay in bed thinking over what Ryat said to me in the library Friday night.

He's right about several things. But he was wrong about me only wanting to be his because of Matt. I've let him dictate my life for too long. For what? A pretend relationship? The thought of being Ryat's chosen is only that—being his.

Removing the hoodie, I go to toss it onto the bed but pause when I spot a small black box already sitting on it.

"Sarah?" I call out. As far as I know, she's still in class.

That wasn't there when I left this morning. Walking over to it, I open it up to see a note that says **drink me** sitting next to a small vial of clear liquid. I've never seen anything like it before. I've popped pills back in high school with Sarah but never done anything liquid other than alcohol. Something tells me this isn't vodka.

There's also a small picture underneath it. I pick it up and flip it over. It's of me in the library—the same one that Ryat sent me before I found him standing in the library. My head snaps up, doing a quick look around my room. My heart accelerates, and I stare back down at it in my hand. "Hello?" I call out again. "Is someone here?"

No answer.

"Ryat?" I ask, swallowing nervously. He took that picture, so he had to have left this box. How did he get in? Did he ask Sarah to help him?

I jump when my cell rings. Dropping the vial and picture back onto the bed, I grab my phone and hit answer. "Hello?" I say, trying to calm my racing heart.

"You embarrassed him?" my mother snaps in my ear.

"What?" I ask, doing another quick look around my room. I walk to my closet and look inside it, but it's all clear.

"Matt," she growls. "Kimberly said you embarrassed him in front of his peers on Friday."

"I'm not talking about this, Mom," I say, going into my bathroom. Still alone.

"I don't know what the hell is happening there, but know this, Blakely Rae. You will not mess this up for the family. You will get married to Matt. Keep this up, and it'll be much sooner than expected." She hangs up.

I come back to my room and plop down on the side of my bed.

The vial sits next to me, and tears fill my eyes. I can't stop it. I can't control it. My life has never been mine. Why did I think it would be now? I will be Mrs. Blakely Winston no matter what I do. The thought is crippling, knowing I'll live a lie in a loveless marriage. I did have feelings for Matt. It took me a while, but I was okay with spending forever with him.

Now? I despise him. I'll never respect him, and I'll never willingly marry him. My mother will have to drag me down the aisle if that's the case.

Ryat? Do I think his sudden interest in me has to do with Matt? Absolutely. Do I care? No. As far as I'm concerned, Matt can kiss my ass. If he can do whatever he wants, so can I. And that includes letting Ryat have his way with me.

Making up my mind, I pop the top off the vial and toss back the odorless and soapy tasting liquid, drinking it like the note said.

Fuck it!

RYAT

I ENTER HER apartment, knowing that she's home alone. I made sure of it. Pushing her bedroom door open, I find her lying on the bed. She's on her back, her hands up by her head. Eyes closed and breathing deeply. Passed out.

She took the GHB.

I figured she would. People in our world are always looking for a way to escape reality. I needed another taste of her, and there are rules for a reason.

Walking over to the side of the bed, I pull the covers off her to find she had changed into an oversized T-shirt before it kicked in. I fist the material in my hands, thinking it belongs to her cheating ex. Yanking it up, I see she's got on a pair of black lace underwear. Letting go of the shirt, I place my hand on her flat stomach and slide the tips of my fingers into the fabric. Teasing myself.

My cock is hard, straining against my zipper. I want to fuck her so bad. Ever since I saw her sprawled out on the floor, I wanted to take her dark hair in my hands and shove my dick down her throat and make her pretty blue eyes cry.

The rules of the ritual are simple.

The chosen must offer herself. She has shown me interest by showing up at the party. If there was any doubt what she was doing there—my bedroom proved she wanted something. Even if it was just revenge on Matt. I'll take that. That's something I can use.

Typically, the chosen one and the Lord know each other. They've been friends, or they've dated. Few instances are like Blakely and me—when the Lord is forced to pick a certain chosen one. There are women at Barrington who would kill to be a chosen. Serving a Lord is an honor for them. Matt has kept her in the dark for a reason. He didn't want her to know what was going on. He thought it didn't matter, and she was a sure thing for him. Now that's no longer a possibility. So, his reasons for keeping her in the dark have changed.

I wouldn't say she would have been my first choice because I never thought of her like that. Is she hot? Yeah. But I knew she was off-limits. Even after I was given the order, I had reservations. That was until I started planting myself in her life. I've been following her for several weeks now. Then after the little taste she gave me—I've been salivating, wanting more. If I had revealed myself to her in my bedroom that night, she wouldn't have allowed me to touch her.

If the chosen one accepts, she is yours until you no longer have use for her. She won't remember that motherfucker's name after I have my way with her.

Slowly, I hook my fingers into her underwear and pull them down her tan legs, letting my knuckles graze her smooth skin. Gripping her thighs, I push them apart and crawl onto the bed to kneel between them. I look over her shaved pussy, bringing the fabric to my face. I inhale, my cock jerking in my pants. Fuck, I need to be inside her, but that can't happen tonight. Not yet.

The rules are clear, but they don't say anything about playing with her. They allow us just enough to hang ourselves. The Lords are always testing us.

I throw the underwear to the floor and slide my hands up the inside of her thighs to her cunt. I bite my lip, spreading her lips open for me. "Goddamn," I whisper, slipping a finger inside her.

She's not wet, but I didn't expect her to be. Bringing my finger to my mouth, I suck on it up to my knuckle and then slide it back in, gently testing the waters while my eyes go to her face.

Her head is tilted to the left, her dark hair covering her pillow, and her breathing remains unfazed. I reach up with my free hand and shove her shirt up farther to expose her chest to me. I smile at the fact she's not wearing a bra. Her breasts are fucking amazing. Round and firm, they fit in my hand perfectly with pretty pink nipples and small areolas.

Looking back down at her pussy, it's getting wetter. I remove my finger and add another one. She still doesn't move.

My girl has proven that I own her, and I can't wait to show her just what that means.

I start to get more and more aggressive. Her head moves to the other side, and a whimper escapes her lips. I didn't give her very much GHB because of her small size. I didn't want her to experience too many side effects. I just needed her to be drowsy and impaired to the point I could play with her. Plus, it can increase an urge for sex.

She arches her back for me, her lips parting, and I watch the way her nipples harden as her pussy tightens around my fingers.

I readjust myself on the bed, placing my left hand by her head. I lean all my weight on it while forcing a third finger into her tight cunt. My cock twitches with anticipation to be inside her. To be the first there. To own her.

Her breath catches, and I gently kiss the corner of her lips. "Beautiful."

"Ryat." She moans.

"Yeah, Blake. It's me," I tell her, and she whimpers. Even drugged and only half-conscious, she knows I'm the one touching her.

I begin to finger-fuck her roughly while my thumb plays with her clit. Her body rocks back and forth, making her tits bounce and the bed squeak. She lets out a cry when her pussy clamps down, and she comes all over my fingers.

Something about having her like this—having total control over her body—is very powerful. Knowing she willingly took something I gave her without any knowledge of what it was. She's craving to be owned, to be dominated, to be mine.

I stop, and her eyes remain closed. Bringing my fingers to her mouth, I rub them over her parted lips, smearing her cum across them like icing. "Soon, little one," I tell her before I stick them in my own mouth, licking them clean. Tasting that fucking honey that I've been craving after she gave herself to me in my bedroom.

Pushing off the bed, I move to a sitting position between her shaking legs. I reach down and grab the collar of the oversized shirt and rip it down the middle. "I'll burn this," I say to myself, pulling her arms out of it, knowing that I'm one step closer to owning her and erasing any trace of Matt.

Reaching into my back pocket, I pull out the card and lay it on her nightstand. Now I wait.

TWELVE

BLAKELY

CHOSEN ONE

I READ OVER the white card in my hand that was left on my nightstand Monday night after *he* visited me.

Lifting my eyes to the cathedral, I sink my teeth into my bottom lip to nibble on it nervously. It's what one would think of—large and medieval-looking with the high walls and spiers on the top. It sits in the middle of nowhere off the two-lane road. It reminds me of something you'd see in a scary movie where some kids come to a haunted building to explore. Only they all end up dead in various rooms due to blunt force trauma, and the villain smears their blood along the walls.

Okay, maybe I've watched too many scary movies lately.

An old white cross sits above the main entrance. You can see where it once was upright due to the discoloration, but at some point, it has fallen. The wind rocks it slightly back and forth, making a creaking sound just adding to the ick factor. It could not be scarier if it was made for a movie set.

It's cold out tonight. My body shakes, and my teeth chatter while I stand in a low-cut black mini dress that barely covers my ass and red Gucci heels. I have all my weight on the balls of my feet. Otherwise, they'd sink into the soft ground.

I did my makeup heavy with smokey eyes, thick eyeliner, and red lipstick. I probably look like a cheap hooker walking the streets to find a John. But I won't be getting paid for what I'm about to do. No. I'm going to freely give it away. Hand it over to a man who I know will use it. Abuse it.

Looking back down at the card, I flip it over to see **The Ritual Vow Ceremony** typed out along with the address that I had to google. It was exactly thirty minutes from campus, tucked back in the middle of nowhere. Below that, it reads—*once the chosen accepts her duty, she is bound to serve him.*

I'm getting to be part of a "ritual" of the Lords. I know it seems as creepy as it sounds, but I need something new in my life. It's been missing something for as long as I can remember. And Ryat made me realize what that is.

"Haven't you ever wanted to do something for yourself?"

His question in the library made me think. From a young age, I've had dreams of what I wanted for a future, but my parents have shot them down one by one. I wanted to go to Stanford, but that wasn't an option.

"Barrington is where you'll go." My mother told me that when I was twelve. No argument.

I like Barrington, don't get me wrong, but it just wasn't my first choice. I wanted to be normal for once. I went to a private school all my life, so Barrington feels no different. It's secluded in the middle of Pennsylvania. It's for rich kids—the elite. The ones with criminal records a mile long that *daddies* have paid off and judges have brushed under the rug. What could possibly go wrong when you put them all in one place? They are the men and women born and bred to take over their family's business one day. The degrees are formalities. You need the accolades on paper even though they're just handed that billion-dollar empire once they graduate.

I guess that's another factor that led me here to the middle of nowhere at this cathedral—bored out of my fucking mind. Every day of my entire life has been planned out for me. The sports I was allowed to play, the grades I had to make. The man I'll marry.

It's been painfully exhausting. Do you ever just want to shut it all off? Not have to think about the next second of your life? Go on an unplanned road trip? Have a one-night stand with the cute guy you scrolled past on your timeline? Social media makes you think you have all this freedom, but you don't. Not really. You're stuck behind a device watching others live out their dreams. You post selfies of fake smiles and expensive clothes, hoping that someone will envy you.

Reassure you just how good you have it. All the while hating your life. "Smile, dear, you never know who is watching you," my mother always tells me.

Desperation is never pretty.

Ryat is my way out. Being a chosen one is my escape. Well, at least for now. Who knows how long it'll last? Maybe it's all for pretend, but it's something I want to do.

Taking in a deep breath, I begin to climb the stairs into the building. Pushing open the heavy doors, they squeak, informing whoever is here of my arrival.

My heart hammers in my chest while I walk down the central aisle. Figures fill the large pews on either side. They're all dressed in black cloaks and white masks. I wasn't raised religious, so I've never been to church before. I always expected places like this to be the color of gold—shiny and expensive—to give you an overwhelming feeling of calmness. That couldn't be further from the truth.

It's old. The high ceilings are the same color as a dark night. You can see there were once paintings on them, but over time have faded to unrecognizable. The floor is covered in leaves and branches. It's just as cold as it was outside and the old stained-glass whistles from the heavy winds.

Ahead of me looks to be a large stage and altar. On both sides are long staircases that take you up to a loft overlooking the congregation. In the middle of the loft sits a tub for baptism sunk into the floor up against the ledge. The side facing us is all glass to allow the people of the church to witness. Three steps on either side step down into the water, and it has to be about four feet deep.

I make my way on shaky legs to the front, leaves and branches that cover parts of the rotting floor crunching under my heels. Old, outdated, and very abandoned-looking, this place is nothing like the hotel where they live. Makes me wonder why they would use it for anything.

Coming to a stop at the front, I notice in the first two rows, sitting next to the ones dressed in cloaks and masks, are women. None of which are covered. They're like me. Each wearing dresses and heels. The girl on the far end catches my attention.

It's Sarah.

I go to walk over to her but stop when I see the woman next to her. It's the blonde from the party at the house of Lords. Matt's *girlfriend*.

Is he here? If so, he's wearing a cloak and mask. The hairs on the back of my neck rise, thinking he's watching me, but I notice you can't see any of the women's hands or arms. Looking closer, I realize they must be behind their backs. My heart hammers, blood rushing in my ears at the eerie silence in such a large building. It's deafening.

I jump when a hand lands on my shoulder from behind. I try to turn around, but it prevents me from doing so. Instead, he runs his hands down my arms slowly, and I know he can feel me shaking. When he gets to my wrists, he gently brings them behind my back.

I close my eyes, knowing I'm going to accept what's coming. No matter what happens here tonight, it'll be because I took a chance. I chose to be here. I choose to be his for however long he decides he wants me.

He grips both of my wrists in one of his hands, then I hear the sound of metal. My chest rises and falls with each erratic intake of breath. I look out at Sarah, and she has her head down, staring at the floor. A quick glance down the first row shows them all doing it.

The cold metal wraps around my wrist, and he secures the handcuffs one at a time to the point they pinch my skin, making me whimper.

"Are they too tight?" I recognize Ryat's voice, pulling my hair off my shoulder.

"Yes," I answer softly.

"Good." Then he tightens them each one more click, and I hiss in a breath.

"Will you hurt me?"

"Yes."

I expect there to be pain involved, and a part of me is excited about that. Grabbing my upper arm, he yanks me back.

RYAT

I LEAD HER up the stairs with my hand on her upper arm, my fingers digging into her soft skin. I've been waiting for this day for too long. Seems like forever since I was told to take her as my chosen. But it's finally here. Making our way to the platform, I bring her over to the small pool-like structure that was added for us to perform the ritual.

The Lords were given this building a long time ago. The first thing they did was gut the inside. It's not your average cathedral. Things have been added to accommodate our traditions.

She fumbles to a stop at the edge, and I hear her breathing pick up. I'm about to tell her to get into the water, but she takes the first step herself. I bite back a smile. My girl wants to give herself to me, and I can't wait to make her mine.

Usually, this is done with the chosen naked, but she will be leaving her clothes on. I don't want anyone seeing her body. The point of the ritual is to cleanse them from their past sexual partners, but I'm extremely territorial over what's mine. I've watched women at Barrington for the last three years throw themselves around waiting for the day to be a chosen one. It just so happens that she's never had sex. But the vow ceremony must be performed, nonetheless, in order to solidify the ritual. He still kissed her, held her, and messed around with her, I'm sure. I want to wipe any piece of him remaining clean from her body.

As part of the ritual, we have to show ownership. You either fuck their mouth, pussy, or ass. It's not to please them. It's for us to claim them. So, since I'm selfish and refuse to show what I have, her mouth will do. Once we're done here, I'll take her out back and fuck that tight cunt in the woods, on the ground or up against a tree. It doesn't matter. Everyone will see she's mine from the bite marks on her legs and hickeys on her neck.

Blakely will be owned by a Lord. I will make sure everyone is well aware of that.

She takes the last step, the warm water coming up to her chest as I stand next to her. Letting go of her upper arm, I reach out and push the dark hair from her face, getting it wet with my fingers. She looks so pretty right now with her makeup done and hair fixed. I'm getting ready to ruin it. "Recite your vow," I order.

Her eyes widen for a brief second, and she licks her lips nervously. Then she takes in a deep breath. "I vow."

Good girl. She was paying attention to the flyer that she had wadded up in her hand. "You vow," I acknowledge and nod my head at her to say the last part with me.

"We vow," we say in unison.

Then I reach up, gripping her hair while I kick her feet out from underneath her and shove her under the water. Holding her there. She starts to fight immediately. So hard, that the water splashes over the top of the glass, falling to the first floor.

Yanking her up, she begins choking the moment her face breaks the surface. I drag her over to the stairs to my right and sit on the top one, letting go of her for a quick second to undo my belt followed by my jeans.

She's gasping for breath while coughing up water at the same time. It's the only sound in the church. Everyone below sits silent, patiently waiting for me to claim my chosen one. Matt included. I hope the fucker sees how much she wants this. Me.

She's hunched over the best she can without her face being in the water, most of her now wet hair covers it. She can't do anything about it since her hands are still cuffed behind her back.

I pull my hard cock out and stroke it a few times, allowing her an extra second to catch her breath, knowing I'm about to make it worse. Then I reach out, gently moving her hair from her face with my fingertips to get a look at her. Black puddles under her eyes before running down her cheeks. Her wet lashes are stuck together, and her parted lips are trembling while water runs off her chin. Her pretty blue eyes are red and full of apprehension.

It's too late now, little one. You belong to me.

I slide my hand through the water, gathering up all her long, wet hair to the back of her neck. Once I have it all, I grip it and yank her to me. "Kneel," I order, and her knees fall to the third step, below me, making her whimper. "Open your mouth."

Her wide eyes look over my dick, and I smile at the look of terror she has. She takes in one last deep breath and licks her lips before opening her pretty painted mouth for me. Gripping the base of my cock, I slide it into her mouth.

I'm not gentle.

Her gagging fills the space of the church, and the water once again rolls over the sides while I control her head. Up and down, it bounces on my dick. She's trying to fight me and pull away, but I don't let go. Instead, I grip her hair harder, forcing more of my cock down her throat. She closes her eyes tightly, and her face scrunches as I hit the back, making her gag again.

"Look at me," I demand.

Her eyes open, and I can see the tears run down her cheeks through the water already covering her face. "Relax and open up for me," I whisper to her, slowing my rhythm, giving her a second to catch her breath. She blinks, and new tears run down her face. I scoot forward, my ass hanging off the end of the step, getting in a better position.

I pull out, and she sucks in a gasp. "Open wide for me," I say softly, wiping the tears from her face with my free hand, smearing the black eyeliner and mascara. "Stick your tongue out and breathe through your nose."

Swallowing, she opens her mouth as wide as it'll go and sticks her tongue out.

I bring her head down, her mouth taking me in once again. I lean my head back and close my eyes, not caring to watch, just wanting to come. I hit the back of her throat, and her body fights me while the gagging returns. This time, I don't let up.

My balls tighten, and my breathing picks up. I shove her head down one last time and hold it there as I come, forcing her to swallow.

THIRTEEN

BLAKELY

I'M GASPING FOR a breath as his cum, water, and drool runs down my chin. My body shakes uncontrollably, my knees rubbed raw from the steps. Everything hurts from tensing, and my hands have gone numb from the handcuffs.

I remain kneeling as he lets go of me and stands. I look up at him through the tears that still fall and watch him stick his semi-hard dick into his wet jeans before zipping them up. He's big—in both length and girth. My jaw hurts from keeping it open, and my throat is sore from how rough he was.

Leaning down, he grabs my upper arm and pulls me to my feet. I'm not even sure I can walk; my legs are shaking so hard. He pulls me out of the water and over to the stairs. I drop my head to stare at my wet heels while water runs off our soaked clothes.

He releases my arm and grips my hair, yanking my head up, and I whimper. "Don't be ashamed, Blake," he whispers in my ear. "You're my chosen one. Be proud. I know I am."

Leading me down the stairs, we go left at the bottom, and I keep quiet as he takes me down a hallway and to a door.

We step outside. Looking around, I can't see much. It's dark outside, and there's only a single light on the building above us to illuminate this area.

The cathedral is surrounded by woods, and I squint, trying to see out into the trees. The wind picks up, and I shiver. My soaking wet dress clings to my body, and water still runs down my legs.

"What are we ...?"

He turns to me, grabs my shoulders, and spins me around, shoving my back into the building. I cry out as he crushes my restrained arms between the church and me. He steps into me and cuts it off, slapping a hand over my mouth.

Leaning his lips to my ear, he takes my lobe into his mouth and sucks on it, making a shiver run up my spine. Pulling away, he whispers roughly. "I'm going to fuck you right here, right now. That mouth is mine. That ass is mine. That cunt is mine. You're fucking mine."

I whimper as my pussy starts pulsing at his words. I can't imagine how rough he'll be on my body after what he just did to my mouth. I'm still not sure if we've already had sex since I passed out the first time and drugged myself the second time.

His emerald eyes are on fire. It makes my stomach turn at how much he wants from me. And at how much I want to give him. "You belong to me now, Blake. And I'm going to take what's mine."

He moves his hand from my mouth, and I suck in a breath. Taking a step back from me, I slump against the building. I'm not sure my legs can hold me up anymore. Gripping the hem of my dress, he yanks it up to bunch high on my waist. My breathing hitches when he digs his fingers into the top of my thong and pulls it down my trembling legs, and he has to help me step out of them.

"Please ..." I beg, pushing off the church just a bit to relieve my arms. My wrists hurt so bad, and my knees start to buckle, making me shuffle in my heels. "Undo the cuffs ..."

He shoves my underwear into my mouth and slaps his hand back over it, pinning my head to the building. Water fills my mouth, and I choke on it, making my body convulse against his before I can swallow it down. I blink, and he watches fresh tears fall from my eyes at the act.

He lowers his lips back to my ear while his free hand slides between our bodies and finds my pussy. "You don't know what belonging to me means yet. But I'm about to teach you, little one." He trails his lips down the side of my neck, and I tilt my head to the side to allow him access. "No one will hear me fuck you, and no one will ever watch me fuck you."

I breathe heavily through my nose while swallowing more water that soaked my underwear. "But everyone will know you belong to me." His fingers gently massage my clit, and I moan. "I will show off my trophy covered in bruises from my hands." He spreads my pussy and slides a finger inside me, forcing me to lift on my tiptoes. "Marks from my teeth." He bites down on my neck, and my body breaks out in goose bumps while I cry out into my gag. "You live for me now." He licks up the side of my neck to my ear. "And I for you." He thrusts in a second finger, and I suck in a deep breath from my nose, closing my watery eyes. "You serve and obey me. I protect and own you."

My legs shake, my feet ache, and my arms hurt from being pinned, but my pussy is dripping wet. And it's not because I was just in water minutes ago. I've never been treated like this. So dominated. My body is trembling in anticipation for what he's going to do to it. This is what it craves. What I've imagined it would be like. I might have never slept with Matt, but I've played with myself enough—my fingers and toys—that I'm so fucking ready for him.

"Now ... spread your legs and let me fuck my cunt."

RYAT

HER SMALL BODY trembles against mine, but she does as she's told. She spreads her feet the best she can, and I smile against her wet skin.

Mine!

She's going to make the perfect chosen one. So eager to learn. So willing to submit. I remove my fingers from her pussy, and she lets out a whimper. "Do not spit this out," I order, pulling my hand from her mouth.

She nods once. If I had tape, I'd add it, but I don't. Plus, this will be a test of just how well she will take her chosen one responsibility.

Reaching down, I undo my jeans and remove my cock. It's been hard this entire time. Her arms and wrists hurt? She should be a man. Sometimes you get so hard it's excruciating. It can bring you to your knees if you're not careful.

I step back into her, grip her right thigh, and lift her heel off the ground. Holding it against my hip, I look down and watch the head of my cock push its way into her sweet fucking cunt.

Mine!

I'm the first one to be there.

Her mumbled cry makes me smile as I force my way into her. She's so fucking tight. Well, the best I can in this position. I would prefer her ass up in the air so I can really get deep, but I'll do that when I get her back to my place.

I wasn't joking when I told her that everyone will know she belongs to me. I have all night to have her any way I want. To mark my territory. And I can't wait to see the look on Matt's face when I take her back to the house of Lords. He should have taken my warning as the threat it was. I won't make the same mistake he did. I'll put a leash on her so fucking short, she won't be able to breathe without my permission.

Dropping my face to her neck, I kiss her wet skin, pieces of her hair stick to my lips as I pull my hips back and shove them forward, forcing more incoherent noises from her gagged mouth.

"Fuck, Blake." Her already tight pussy clamps down on my dick, and my breathing picks up. My free hand drops to her other thigh, and I lift it as well, using my body to press her back into the building. I start fucking her hard with fast thrusts without protection. I will never use a condom with her. No reason to. I'm clean, and I know she is too.

I haven't had sex in over three years—since I took the oath the summer before my freshman year. This is why the tradition was started. It shows us what it's like to taste power. Owning her is just a small fraction of what I will do once I graduate from Barrington. The Lords don't want us spending our college years letting pussy get in our way. We have to prove that our loyalty to the Lords is more important than our dicks.

I forgot how good pussy feels. How warm, soft, and pliable as it stretches to accommodate my size. And she's so wet, yet there's still just enough resistance that I have to force it. It's taking my breath away. My hand just wasn't cutting it anymore.

My balls tighten on their own, and I grind my teeth, not wanting it to be over. But bringing her out here wasn't the best idea. There's always a chance someone could walk back here and see her, but the Lords are still inside going through the ritual. I wanted to be first tonight because I wasn't going to fucking wait any longer.

Knowing I can't hold it off, I drop her legs and pull out because I'm going to come any second.

Stepping back from her, I grab her dress and yank her forward, forcing her to her knees. Reaching into her mouth, I pull out her underwear and grip her hair at the crown with that hand, yanking her head back. "Open your mouth," I rush out through gritted teeth.

She parts her lips and stares up at me, tears running down her makeup-smeared face.

Fucking beautiful. Just like I knew she'd be.

I grip my wet cock with my free hand just in time to stroke it once before I come all over her face with a groan. The force behind it almost knocks me to my knees. Leaning forward, I have to let go of her hair to place my hand on the building behind her to keep myself upright.

Fuck me!

It was worth it. For it to be with her. Knowing that I can do that as much as I want whenever I want. It's an ego-stroking moment, for sure. The power of that alone is almost a high, like being inside her.

Pushing off the wall, I try to calm my breathing as I look down at my dick. There's not any blood that I can see. But I've fucked enough women before college to know that not all of them bleed. I figured the odds of her doing so were small. When I dropped her off at her apartment after the party, I went through her drawers and found all the toys that I'm guessing she uses on herself. Anything like that could have stretched her hymen over the years. Plus, she didn't bleed when I finger-fucked her. Shoving my dick into my jeans, I zip them up.

Crouching down to her level, I reach out and run my finger through the cum that's smeared across her cheek. "Tongue out," I order.

She swallows before parting her lips and doing so. "Good girl," I praise her, and she whimpers, her body shaking. Running my finger across her tongue, I clean it off. Then I run three fingers along her chin, picking up more, and stick them into her mouth, pressing them to the back of her throat and forcing her head back. She gags, eyes blinking with fresh tears, but she doesn't try to pull her head away. "Close."

Her lips close around my fingers the best she can, and her tongue wraps around them, making me groan when she sucks, wanting it to be my cock inside of her mouth again. When done right, a mouth can feel better than a pussy. Slowly, I pull them out, letting her lick them clean once again.

Satisfied with her obedience, especially with her lack of experience, I stand and reach into my back pocket, pulling out the handcuff key.

She drops her head and lets out a soft sob knowing she's being freed from the unforgiving metal binding her wrists. I walk behind her and grip her upper arm, pulling her to stand. She cries out and stumbles forward in her heels, but I hold her. I inspect her wrists and hands before I undo them. There's a little bit of blood running down her hands from them cutting into her skin, and they're blue from lack of circulation.

This is her doing.

I had asked her if they were too tight in front of the Lords. It was for show. When she said yes, I couldn't show any weakness, so I tightened them. But in all honesty, it was setting her up to fail. If she had said no, I would have tightened them too.

The ritual is crystal clear on how we treat our chosen during the vow ceremony. Whatever I do with her behind closed doors is a different story. But I won't go soft on her. That's not who I am.

I was trained by a fellow Lord, and Ty taught me what was expected. We are training these women for a higher power. Even I can't save her from her future. All I can do is prepare her.

She will know hell, but for now, I shall be her devil.

I undo the cuffs, and she lets out a soft cry before pulling her hands around to the front. I yank her dress back down into place and bend down, picking up her underwear before sticking it into my pocket. "Let's go," I say and grab her arm, leading her around the building and to her car parked out front.

FOURTEEN

BLAKELY

HE PUTS ME in my passenger seat and gets in the driver's seat. I had left my keys in the car, along with my purse and phone; he starts it up and drives us away from the building. I was in the middle of nowhere, so I wasn't worried about anyone taking anything.

I stay silent, rubbing my hands together. They tingle as the feeling finally returns to my fingers. My wrists are raw and bloody. I still have cum on my face, my hair, and on my chest. I'm not sure if I'm allowed to wipe it off. I'm freezing cold, sitting in my wet dress, and my underwear are in his pocket. My thighs burn, and my pussy is sore. It wasn't nearly as painful as I thought it was going to be, and it makes me wonder even more if I've already had sex with him. After everything that has happened since classes started, I don't regret my decision to live my life how I want.

Yeah, some would argue that my agreeing to be his chosen one strips away any say I have over my body, but I see it differently. I see freedom in knowing that I belong to him. Someone who physically wants me. A person can only handle so much rejection before they start to question why? What is wrong with me?

"Where are we going?" I whisper, biting my bottom lip nervously, wondering what now.

He looks over at me for a quick second before placing his eyes back on the road. "House of Lords," he answers before "I Don't Give A ..." by MISSIO and Zeala begins to fill the car.

WE PULL INTO the gate of the hotel, and he parks my car before opening my door for me.

Entering the place, it's odd being here without it crowded with people. No flashing lights or blaring music. Just silence. "Everyone is still at the vow ceremony," he states, knowing what I'm thinking.

He takes my hand and guides me to the bedroom where I once found my stranger in a mask. He steps into another door, and it's his private bathroom. A long mirror and counter with double sinks are in front of us. A door to the right is where the toilet must be. To the left is a shower that runs the full length of the bathroom. It's nothing but glass to see inside with three showerheads. One at each end and the third in the middle. The floor is white with dark gray walls. The countertop black. It's weird to see nothing is cluttering it like all the stuff I leave out on mine.

He lets go of my hand, turning around, and his emerald eyes meet mine. My breath catches at the look in them.

He's hungry.

They tell me everything that I was wondering. I know what we did in the woods was just a sample of what he wants from me.

"Take a shower." His eyes look over my cum-covered, makeup-smeared face and then down over my body. "Get cleaned up." Then he walks out, shutting me inside.

He didn't tell me to hurry, so I take my time. The water hurts my wrists, but it's not unbearable. I stand under the center sprayer and just enjoy the warm water before washing my hair with his shampoo. Then I use his bodywash, and it makes me wonder if this is why he brought me here. One more way to claim me. It's hard to deny a man if you bathe in his scent.

Turning off the water, I exit the shower and dry off with a white towel I found hanging on a hook, being careful with my wrists. Looking around, I realize I don't have anything to put on, but I have a feeling that's on purpose.

I open the cabinet under one of the sinks and find mouthwash. Unscrewing the lid, I throw some back. I swish it around before spitting it in the sink. I've swallowed water that had no telling what was in it and cum. Multiple times. I'd like to brush my teeth, but mouthwash will do for now.

Taking in a deep breath, I open the door and step out into his bedroom. It's what I would imagine a guy like Ryat to have—the dark walls are bare, and the bed is covered in black sheets, a black comforter, and two pillows with matching pillowcases. One tall dresser and one long dresser are dark gray. There's no TV or mirror hanging. I never paid attention last time I was in here. Too drunk and also blindfolded.

He's over by the long dresser with his back to me. He's still wearing his wet clothes, and I see the way his shirt sticks to his back and arms. You can see every outline of muscle. They tense as he moves, digging around for something.

I clear my throat, and he shoves the drawer shut. Turning around, his tongue comes out, and he licks his lips while his green eyes look me over. "Drop the towel," he orders, and my heart accelerates.

I reach up and untuck it from my underarms and let it fall to my feet. I already know he's seen all of me. I swallowed that liquid, changed my clothes, crawled into bed, and woke up naked hours later. He had undressed me.

He walks over, his eyes on my breasts. Coming to a stop, he reaches out and cups my right one, and I moan as he squeezes it. He's in no way gentle, but I love it. Whenever Matt and I would mess around, he'd be soft. I always felt like I wanted more.

Ryat lets go and slaps the side of it. Making the skin sting and the sound bounce off the walls in the room.

I jump back, gasping as a shock like electricity runs straight to my pussy, making it pulse and raise my hands to cover them. A cruel smile spreads across his face, knowing exactly what it did to me. Reaching behind, he pulls the handcuffs out of his back pocket, and I whimper at the sight of them. The cuts they left on my wrists start to throb once again.

"Put your hands down to your sides, or they'll go behind your back."

A choice. Willingly or forcefully. Why do I want him to force me? He arches a brow at my hesitation and steps closer to me, but at the last second, I decide to lower them to my sides.

"You're such a good girl," he whispers lovingly as he tosses the cuffs to the bed.

A weird sense of disappointment washes over me that I chickened out. He said he would hurt me, and I want that. If there's no pain, then how do you know you're alive?

"Aren't you?" he asks. Lifting his hand to run his knuckles over the tops of my breast, he forces my thoughts elsewhere. My nipples harden as they travel lower over them.

I want to be his good girl, but in a bad way. "Yes," I breathe. My body has never felt so alive. So needy for something that it's already had. I didn't get off when he fucked me. But I have a feeling that was the point. It was a show of ownership, even if no one was watching.

His eyes go to my neck. "Whose good girl are you?"

"Yours," I answer softly.

"Mine," he agrees.

He slaps the side of my breast again, and I yelp. It wasn't as hard as the first time, but it catches me off guard. My hands go to shoot up, but I shove them back down to my sides.

The corners of his lips slowly turn up before showing me his gorgeous smile. That alone has more wetness pooling between my legs. The man knows exactly what he's doing.

He does it again, harder this time, and I throw my head back, closing my eyes and letting out a cry. But it's not because it hurts. It feels so good.

He does the other one, and I moan this time, my body just slightly jerking, starting to adjust to the sting.

"You like that, don't you, Blake?" His voice is full of amusement. "So much potential for my chosen one."

I'm not sure what that means, and I'm not about to ask.

"Look at me," he orders, all sense of humor gone.

I open my eyes and lower my head to stare up at him. His gaze drops to my breasts. Reaching out, he takes both my hard nipples between his fingers, and he pinches them. Hard. I rise up on my tiptoes, screaming out, and he yanks me closer to him by them. I'm panting as he holds me in place. I fist my hands down by my sides, sucking in a deep breath.

Letting go of them, I cry again at the sensation it gives. It felt good. So good. "Get your heels." He nods to the bathroom door behind me and then turns, going back to the dresser.

I walk into the bathroom to find them lying on the floor where I had taken them off for my shower. They're still wet, and I pour what little bit of water remains inside into the sink and go back to the bedroom.

"Put them on," he orders, not even bothering to look at me.

Using the wall as support, I slide my feet into the six-inch Guccis. They're cold from the water, and my feet are already so sore from wearing them earlier. But I'm not telling him that. I kinda like the pain.

He turns around, and I notice he has something in his hand. He tosses it onto the bed. My eyes go to see what it is, but he reaches out and grabs me, pulling me toward him.

I trip in my heels, falling into him, and he catches me. Bringing me over to the foot of the bed, he spins me around to where I face it and lightly smacks my ass. "Spread your legs. As far as you can."

I see that he had thrown my underwear from earlier in the middle. He smacks my ass again, getting my attention. And I place my hands on the black footboard for support to spread them as far as they'll go. He bends down next to my left ankle, and I watch him reach under and pull out a chain. It's short, attached to a black leather cuff, and the other end is attached to the post. He wraps it around my ankle, securing the buckle. I pull on it just to see how much slack it has. There's none. Then he walks around to the other ankle, pulls it even farther to the other corner post, and does the same.

Standing behind me, he places his hand on my back and pushes me to lean over the footboard. It's a little higher than where my hips are, so I have to get up on my tiptoes to where it doesn't dig into my stomach.

The moment my face hits the bed, I feel the muscles in my legs pull tight from the position. I suck in a breath, trying to readjust myself, but it's not going to matter. I don't think it's supposed to be comfortable.

He walks over to the left side and bends down, grabbing another chain from underneath the bed. "Right arm."

I slide my left to him, and he just stares at me. "Right arm ...?" I trail off, repeating what he said, but he's on the left side of the bed.

Leaning over, he grips my right hand and yanks it across the bed toward him. He wraps the leather cuff around it, securing it, and I almost smile at the feel of them. They're not nearly as bad as the handcuffs. Then he walks back around behind me and to the right. This time, he doesn't even say anything. He just grabs my left hand, crossing it over my right one, and secures that wrist too.

My whole body is pulled tight, my upper body twisted like a pretzel. My neck and chin sit on my upper arms, which makes it hard to breathe.

He opens up the top drawer to the nightstand and pulls out a small roll of duct tape. My breathing picks up. He disappears behind me, and I try to look over my shoulders, but I can't. My arms crossed restrict the movement of my head.

His wet jeans rub against my thighs before he leans over my back, pressing my hips further into the footboard. The edge of the wood, digging into my skin, makes me whimper.

Reaching out, he grabs the underwear. With his free hand, he grips my chin and pulls it up off my arms, forcing my neck to arch back at a painful angle. Without saying a word, he shoves the underwear into my mouth, and then I hear the tape being ripped off. He slaps it over my lips, securing the underwear in my mouth like earlier. At least they're not drenched in water this time, but they're still damp.

He gathers all my hair and holds it at the base of my neck, still yanking my head back. "A chosen one must understand patience."

I try to adjust my already aching body, but nothing even budges an inch.

"She must understand obedience." His free hand comes around and grabs my neck, his fingers digging into the skin while taking my air away.

My body jerks, trying to fight it on its own, making the chains rattle and the bed shake.

"And she must understand that her body is no longer hers." He kisses my cheek and releases my throat. My face falls to rest on my arms again, and I take in a deep breath through my nose.

His hands touch my inner thighs, and I jump. "Every touch, every kiss, every ounce of pleasure your body receives will come from me." He softly runs them upward, and his thumb pushes into my still sore pussy.

I moan, pushing against it, my body humming. Heart hammering, I can feel my pulse racing.

"You will not even touch yourself." Pulling his thumb out, he then replaces it with two fingers, pushing them all the way in to his knuckles, and it hurts so good. I whimper and tears begin stinging my eyes. "If you disobey, you will be punished, little one."

I try to twist my hips as his fingers move in and out slowly. I know he's taunting me, making me wet and needy. Removing them, I hear him drop to his knees. And then his warm, wet tongue runs along my throbbing pussy.

I moan when he licks it. His hands come up to my ass, and he grips my cheeks, pulling them apart. I tense as his tongue continues to slowly move higher. I start trying to tell him to stop, but it's just mumbled nonsense while I yank on my restraints as hard as I can to no avail.

His fingers dig further into my cheeks when his tongue slides over my puckered ass. Then just as quickly, it's gone. He lightly kisses it with his lips before letting go of my ass cheeks. But I don't relax. I'm more tense than before.

No, no, no, I shake my head. Matt and I never did anything back there. He never tried, but I wouldn't have let him anyway.

Ryat chuckles at my unease. "There is no need to fight it, Blake." Slapping my cheek playfully, he adds, "I'm going to own that too."

RYAT

I ENTER THE cathedral, checking my watch. They maybe have an hour left.

Taking a back pew, I slide in and sit down, fanning my arms along the back of it. A rule of the Lords is that you watch your brothers accept their chosen ones. Otherwise, there wouldn't be a need to be present. You can't show ownership to an empty room. Plus, it makes all the younger members hungry. Reminds them why they have to abstain from getting their dick wet for three years.

I look up at the loft and see one of my brothers in the water. He's got a black hood over his chosen one's head while he fucks her from behind. She's completely naked, her fake tits pressed against the glass side of the square tub, and her hands are also cuffed behind her back.

Makes me think of Blakely. I left her tied and gagged to my bed to return here.

He comes and yanks her out of the pool. With them out, I can see just how low the water level is now. It's not even waist-deep. Fucking in a bowl will do that. The water has to go somewhere.

"Where's your girl?" Gunner asks, coming to sit in the pew in front of me. He turns in his seat to look at me.

"Not here," I state. It's none of his goddamn business where she's at. I made sure to lock my bedroom door so no one can get to her. And I gagged her for that exact reason. I don't want someone hearing her in there. The Lords may be here, but there is still staff there. Now that the seniors can actually use their dicks, it'll be nothing but fucking orgies. They'll pass their chosen ones from room to room while having other women join them. "Where's yours?" I counter. He picked her best friend, Sarah.

"She's passed out in my trunk." He smiles.

"How many more are there?" I ask, looking around the room. All the freshman, sophomores, and juniors are still seated in their masks and cloaks.

"Two," he answers, looking down at his watch.

Just then, I hear a woman say, "I vow." As she stands in the water.

"You vow," Prickett announces. "We vow," they say in unison, and then he shoves her underwater, where he places his foot on her back, holding her face down to the bottom.

I look back at Gunner, and he's checking his watch again. "Have somewhere to be?"

"Sarah will be up in about thirty," he answers.

Ahh, I nod. He's drugged her, and it'll be wearing off soon.

I hear the girl gasping as Prickett brings her up from the water, and immediately, he pulls her out and goes to town on her ass. I've seen enough Lords take their chosen ones over the last three years that I could go without seeing them anymore. I couldn't care less who and how they fuck.

Now that I've picked mine, I could do without everything else. I want to live in my bedroom with her. Fuck that, I want to move out of the house of Lords and go somewhere remote with her. Just us, no one around for miles. Then I wouldn't have to gag her, and I could listen to her scream my name for hours.

Prickett and his girl finish up, and he pulls her out of the water while she sobs. We make these women think they have a choice to be chosen. But not all are. We are given a list of names that must be chosen before senior year even starts. Manipulation isn't hard. If you have someone repeatedly tell you how great something is, you eventually want a taste.

One more.

Pulling out my cell, I pull up the live feed on my app. Blake is still in the same spot I left her. Just like I thought she'd be, but it still doesn't hurt to look. I have ten cameras set up in my room, so I can see her from any angle. Plus, two in my bathroom. The house is littered with them. Every Lord has the same app and chance to watch his chosen one. She's not struggling. I wouldn't be surprised if she passed out. It's been a long day, and I'm about to make it a very long night for her.

"I vow."

Closing out the app, I drop the phone to my lap and look up at the loft. Matt stands in the water with Ashley. "You vow," he growls.

I smile. Sorry fucking bastard.

"We vow," they say, and he grips the back of her neck, shoving her into the water facedown. She struggles, the water splashing around.

He's got her hands zip-tied behind her back, and her ankles are also tied together. There is no rule on how you restrain your chosen one. As long as it's done. Being held underwater will have anyone fighting, so the restraints help keep them from clawing our faces off. Plus, it's just another way for us to dominate them. She's naked, and he's already put a collar on her.

I sit up straighter when he continues to hold her underwater. He's baring his teeth like he's mad at her. As if it's her fault he fucked up and lost his toy.

She slows down, her body going slack altogether. *What the fuck ...?* I jump to my feet. "Matt," I shout in warning.

Everyone in the cathedral turns to look at me. I can't see their faces because of their masks, but I'm sure their eyes are wide. A Lord never tells another member how to treat his chosen one. Matt gives me a go to hell look and then yanks her up from the water by her hair. Her head hangs back, and she's completely still for a second before she spits water from her mouth. Sucking in a breath, she proceeds to cough.

Being a Lord isn't about harming our chosen ones. They are a reward. If you break it or kill it, you don't get to replace it with another one. He knows this.

Not going to say it's never happened because it has. More than once since I've joined. These women go down as missing persons and are never looked for. When the public isn't even aware your organization exists, no one suspects you committed the crime.

I turn and walk out of the cathedral, going back to play with Blakely. My cell rings when I fall into my car. "Hello?" I answer, letting the Bluetooth pick it up while I take off down the gravel road.

"Who did you end up with?" my father asks in greeting. He is a Lord. Most members got here because of their bloodline. My son or sons will one day be a Lord and so on. It is something that was not a choice but required of me. But I was more than ready and willing to accept.

"Blakely," I answer, pulling out onto the road.

"Good job, son," he says with a heavy breath.

"Did you ever doubt me?" I ask jokingly.

He chuckles. "No. Just make sure you do what needs to be done."

"Always."

"I'll see you this weekend." He hangs up, satisfied with our chat, and "Everybody Gets High" by MISSIO immediately fills my car.

Matt will not get anywhere near her. Not until I physically hand her over after graduation. And there won't be anything left of her for him to take.

———————

Unlocking my bedroom door, I walk inside and find her still naked, bent over my footboard tied, gagged, and eyes closed.

Deciding to let her have a few more minutes of sleep, I walk into the bathroom and undress out of my still wet clothes. I need a shower. Stepping inside, I close the door behind me and stare down at my hard cock. I squeeze some soap onto my hand and reach down. Wrapping my hand around the base, I stroke it, my hand tightening so painfully on it that it takes my breath away.

"What ...?" I stop and let go, placing both hands on the wall and stepping under the sprayer. I've had to do it myself for so long that it's like a habit now. The amount of porn I've watched over the past few years is enough to make a hooker blush. That's not to mention what I've seen happen here at the house of Lords. We knew going into our freshman year what our requirements were going to be. I lost my virginity when I was fifteen to our neighbor's daughter. She was the same age as me. It wasn't like we dated. We both wanted to fuck, and there was an easy decision. After that, I fucked my way through high school. The summer before I came to Barrington, I fucked as many as I could, knowing it'd be the last chance I got for a while. It didn't do any good. The moment I arrived and knew I'd have to do it myself was when I started craving it.

Tell someone they can't have something and watch them do anything in their power to get it done. Especially if they've already experienced it before and know how good it feels. We keep each other accountable. Men have been kicked out, stripped of their titles, and shunned for it. The Lords do not joke around. It is a zero-tolerance organization. There are no three strikes and you're out. They can decide at any moment to tell you to pack your shit and get the fuck out throughout your duration of college. If you accept and become a Lord and then fuck up. Well, let's just say, they chase you down and kill you.

Finishing up in the shower, I dry off and walk out into the bedroom, deciding it's time to wake her up. I open my nightstand and get the lube out first. Then walk to the end of the bed. Dropping my towel at my feet, I kick it away and run my fingers over her pussy. She's not that wet, but I didn't expect her to be. I squeeze some lube on my fingers and softly rub it over her pussy and up over her ass. She freaked out when I touched her there before I left to finish watching the vow ceremony, but she will learn that I own that as well, and I will have it. Even if that means she leaves me no choice but to take it.

I plunge a finger into her pussy, watching to see if she reacts. When she doesn't, I add a second one, and her head moves a little. "Wake up, Blake."

Removing my fingers, I grab my dick and slide into her, not waiting. She jerks, pulling on her restraints, coming around. Slapping her ass, I hear her mumbled moan. Looking down, I watch my cock move in and out of her. I can get deeper now than before, and I can go harder. Grabbing the footboard on either side of her hips, I do just that. Not wasting any time. I know she's sore, but going slow won't do her any good. Plus, that's just not me. I'm not going to give her any false hope that this is anything else than what this is.

I own her.

Her pussy clenches down on me, and I push into her, the headboard slapping the wall with each thrust. Leaning over her body, I grip her hair and yank her head off her arms. I wrap my free arm around her neck and hold her head in place. Her arms crossed in front of her pulled tight, hands fisted. "Feel that?" I ask her, making her whimper. "How fucking wet you are?" I pull out and shove my hips forward. "I love that," I say, and she clamps down on me. Growling in her ear, I slam my hips into her, and her breathing picks up, her body tensing. A mumbled cry fills my room as she comes.

I slow my rhythm and let go of her hair and neck. Her face drops to her arms when I pull out completely, and she sags against the bed. I push my thumb into her wet cunt a few times before replacing it with my cock once again.

When I slide my thumb up to her ass, she starts fighting me, but she's got no chance. I push my thumb over her lube-covered ass, just applying some pressure. "Relax," I say, slapping the side of her leg with my free hand. "It'll hurt less." Whimpering, she stops struggling. I pull my cock out of her pussy and slowly enter her while my thumb starts circling her ass, gently applying more pressure "Good girl," I say, repeating both. "Just breathe."

She's panting, her body trembling. I watch her back muscles tense while fighting the restraints. When I push my thumb into her ass, a muffled cry comes from her taped lips. "Such a tight ass," I say through gritted teeth. It's going to feel amazing when I take it. "I'm going to take it, Blake," I inform her. "My cum will fill this tight ass just like it will your pussy."

I leave my thumb inside her while my hips pick up their pace again—my cock fucking her cunt. I'm close.

My breathing picks up, filling the room while the headboard pounds into the wall. I try to hold it in, but it's just been too long. I remind myself that I have tomorrow and the next day and the next day. She belongs to me until graduation. I can do this as much as I want.

Feeling my balls tighten, I shove all the way into her one last time. My muscles tensing and my cock pulsing inside her fucking sweet cunt as I come.

I pull my thumb out first, and her body sags against the bed while I remove my cock. Leaving her like that for a minute, I bend down and grab the towel that I kicked away and run it over her, cleaning her up. Once done, I drop it and lean over her back. I rip the tape off her mouth and pull her underwear out. Then I get to work on releasing her arms and legs before entering my bathroom, grabbing some pills for her. Walking out, I see her sitting on the side of the bed, head down and hands in her lap. She's rubbing her wrists. "Here. Take these." I hold out my fist.

She looks up at me, and her tired eyes go wide with excitement. *Interesting.* "It's Advil to help with the soreness."

"Oh," she says, shoulders slumping in disappointment when I open my hand to show them to her.

"You thought I was going to drug you again," I comment.

Her cheeks redden, but she takes them from me. Her eyes fall to the floor, unable to meet mine.

Walking over to her, I gently cup her chin and lift it to where she has to look up at me. "Tell me." She's got something on her mind. And Blake needs to understand there is nothing she can't talk to me about. I'm not the kind of guy who runs to his friends and tells them what we did. If there's one thing about me, it's that I can keep a secret. In fact, I will be buried with many. What I do with her will be added to the others.

"Did we have sex that night?" she whispers. "That night you gave me the stuff to drink."

I tilt my head to the side at her question. Did she not think tonight was her first time?

She sighs at my silence. "I, uh ... it's just that I was really sore the next day ..."

"No," I answer. Of course, she was sore. I was rough with her. I hate to tell her, but she'll always be sore from now on.

"Oh." Once again, she looks disappointed by that answer.

"You told me you were a virgin in here the night of the party." I'm not going to tell her that's not why I didn't fuck her. Because honestly, it wouldn't have stopped me. It's the path I chose. The Lords can kick you out, strip you of your title and power. And as much as I wanted to, making her mine for the duration of my senior year is fucking better than just one time.

Her eyes widen, and her cheeks go red at the thought of her telling me that information. "Matt never would sleep with me," she whispers.

I hate her even mentioning his name, but I understand that he was a big part of her life. I'm going to erase any thought of him from her memory. She won't even know who he is when I return her to him. "You don't have to be embarrassed," I tell her. "I like that I was the first to fuck you." I let go of her chin and run my thumb over her lips.

Her breathing picks up as she asks, "What did you do ... that night at my apartment?"

"I can show you." I'd love to watch her watch me play with her while she was drugged. See if it turns her on. I have a feeling she'd get off on that.

"Really?" Her eyes widen and her nipples harden at that thought.

"Yeah, but not tonight." I pull the covers back, and she crawls under them naked. I slide in next to her, and she snuggles into my side. I go to shove her away but don't. Instead, I pull her closer, knowing that this house is full of almost a hundred men, and any one of them would gladly take her from me.

FIFTEEN

BLAKELY

THE FOLLOWING MORNING, we're walking down the hallway of my apartment complex and come up to my door. Two boxes are sitting outside of it. Ryat bends down to pick them up, and then takes the keys from my hand and unlocks the door, shoving it open for me.

"What's in those boxes?" I ask, entering.

"Curtains," he answers, locking it after he closes it.

"Curtains?" I wonder. "Why are you having things shipped to my apartment?"

"Because they are for your windows."

I follow him into the kitchen, and he opens the top drawer, pulling out the scissors and cuts the top, popping it open. "How did you know where those scissors were?" I ask, but he ignores me, repeating the process with the second box. "Why do I need those?" I go on.

"You've got an hour," he dismisses me.

Standing here, I look down at them, wondering what the hell he's doing when he spins me around and slaps my ass playfully, ordering, "Go get ready."

"It won't take me that long," I say, trying to figure out what the hell he's doing.

"You should pack a bag."

I didn't have anything at his place, so we had to stop by here this morning before my ten o'clock class. I start to walk toward my room but stop and turn to look at him. "Can we stay here?"

He stops fucking with the damn curtains and looks up at me. Brows scrunching. "Here?" he repeats.

I nod. "Yeah, the house is crowded." *And Matt is there.* "Can we stay here? At least sometimes? Or is that against a rule?" I have no clue what they are and aren't allowed to do. Matt would never tell me shit. I thought it was because he was trying to protect me, but now I think it's because he was hiding stuff from me.

"No. It's not against any rules," he answers, and I smile at his honesty but notice he doesn't answer my first question. "Go get ready." He returns his attention to my new curtains, making me roll my eyes.

I throw on some makeup—foundation, mascara, and blush. Then I brush my hair before running a straightener over the ends to try to calm it down quickly since I fell asleep with it wet last night, and then slip on a black tank top and a skirt. It resembles a tennis skirt with a wide waistband and pleats. The fabric is light and soft. I lean over the countertop and apply red lipstick and call it good.

I walk into my bedroom to find him standing in front of my window, admiring the black curtains that now hang from my window. He must have hung them while I was in the bathroom. "I'm ready."

He looks over his shoulder at me and then turns his entire body around, placing his hands on his hips. His eyes start at my chest and slowly run down to my heels, hardening to a darker green. "Change," he orders.

I laugh at that and walk into the kitchen. "I'm going to grab a drink really quick, then we can go." Bending over into the fridge, I pick up a bottle of water. Straightening, I turn and shut it. "Okay ..." I call out, but he's standing right there, making me jump. "Jesus, Ryat ..."

He grips my hair and yanks me forward. I cry out, dropping my water. Shoving me down, he bends me at the waist and drags me back to the bedroom, tossing me onto the bed facedown.

I go to get up, but he grabs my hands and yanks them behind my back. "Ryat ..." I gasp his name when he sits on my thighs, pinning me down, knowing exactly where this is going. He brings my arms parallel against my back, holding them with one hand, his fingers digging into my skin. Then I hear him removing his belt with his free hand. It wraps around my forearms a few times, then he fastens it, securing them in place.

My face is pushed into the comforter, smearing what little makeup I just applied. He gets up off my thighs and slaps them. "Put *my* ass in the air," he commands.

I close my eyes, my heart hammering still from him dragging me in here. Wiggling the best I can, I get up onto my knees and spread them as wide as I can, knowing what he wants. My entire body hurts from last night. My calves burn from the position I was in when he left me there. My shoulders hurt from being pulled across my body. My back is sore from how it was stretched over his footboard. I have bruises on my hips. And my feet from my heels. But my pussy? It's pulsing, begging to be touched. Fucked. It hurts in the best way and I hope it stays like this. A reminder of what he does to me.

I flinch when his hands touch my thighs. He runs them up to my ass, under my skirt, before he flips the soft material up and onto my back. Hooking his fingers into my underwear, he takes his time, slowly running them up and down the inside of the material, his knuckles barely grazing my pussy.

I suck in a shaky breath when he pulls them to the side, exposing myself to him.

"She's so wet," he praises, and I dig my face into the comforter so he can't hear my pathetic whimper. I always knew I'd get turned on by being dominated. "See how easy this was?" he goes on. "For someone to see what I have and take it?" Then I hear his zipper.

He doesn't give me any chance to prepare for his cock. No fingers. No tongue. He thrusts his hard dick into me, stretching me with his large size and making me scream. It hurts. Just like it did last night. I'm sore and sensitive, but I want to get off. I want to hear him moan my name. I love that he can't help himself. That he has this primal need to make me his. Over and over.

He shoves my legs farther apart with his, and the new angle has my ass dropping a little. He leans over my back, grips my hair, and yanks my face back, fucking me roughly until we're both coming and tears are running down my face.

RYAT

ONCE DONE, I pull out, and she sags to the bed. I rip the skirt off her and undo my belt. She stretches out and sniffs. Helping her to a sitting position, I then go over to her dresser and open the third drawer, pulling out a pair of jeans. "Wear these." I toss them onto the bed. "Keep your underwear on." I want her dressed in her cum-covered underwear all day. I'll make sure to stuff them into her mouth later. Give her a reminder of what I did to her when she disobeyed. I go to walk out of her room, but she stops me.

"How did you know where those were?"

I turn back around and stare at her. I fucked up her makeup, and her hair's now a tangled mess from my hands. Pretty much messed up everything she just did to herself in a matter of our twenty-minute fuck. Leaning up against the doorframe, I cross my arms over my chest.

Her eyes drop to her skirt in my hand. "Ryat?" She barks my name. "You knew where the scissors were. And now my jeans." Her voice rises.

I smile. She's cute when angry. I'll remember that.

"Did you ... did you go through my room when I wasn't here?"

I lay her unconscious body on her bed. Standing next to it, I watch her sleep. She passed out the moment she came on my face in my bed back at the house of Lord's party. I got her dressed, placed her in her car, and drove her back to her apartment while Gunner followed me in his car with a drunk, passed-out Sarah as well.

Blakely won't remember much come tomorrow. Too much alcohol will do that to you.

"Ready?" Gunner steps into her room to see if I'm ready for what we came here to do.

"Give me a minute," I answer. Going into her bathroom, I open her drawers, searching for something that will be very important once I choose her as mine.

Crouching down, I open the bottom cabinets under her sink and see hair products along with curling irons. Standing, I open the drawer next to her sink. "A-ha." I pull out the light pink container. Popping it open, I see the birth control and make sure she's on the correct day. Just because she has it doesn't mean she uses it. And she is. Just what I wanted to know. Now that I know she's a virgin, I want to make sure I don't have to use a condom. The last thing I need is to get her pregnant.

Putting it back where I found it, I exit her room and walk into the living room. I pull her cell, keys, and ID out of my back pocket and dump the stuff onto the countertop in the kitchen.

"I'm ready." I hold out my hand to Gunner while he removes Sarah's things from his.

"No," I tell her truthfully. "I went through it when I brought you home from the party at the Lords." I did more than just go through her stuff.

Her eyes drop to the floor, and her brows scrunch. "Last night ... last night you said you'd show me what you did to me when I drank that stuff." Her eyes snap back up to mine. "Did you place cameras in here that night too?"

"Yes." She'll never find them. Gunner and I were prepared to do our homework that night. We were here for well over two hours.

"How many?" she demands, getting to her feet, but she wobbles on shaky legs from my cock in her pussy. So she kicks her heels off for better stability.

"Enough."

"Ryat." She storms toward me. "You had no right!"

I reach out, grab her neck, and slam her into the wall next to the door. I put my face in hers, and our noses practically touch. She lets out a shaky breath. "As much as I'm loving this little attitude of yours." Her pretty blue eyes narrow to slits on mine. "We have somewhere to be. Get dressed, fix yourself, and let's go."

With that, I let go of her and walk into the kitchen, leaving her to get ready. I open the drawer next to the sink, grab a lighter, and hold it to the skirt, lighting it up and then dropping it into the sink. It was too short with easy access. She thought I was fucking joking when I told her to change. I wasn't. She's going to learn really quick that I don't joke about shit, and I have no problem proving that to her.

Just like the curtains. I got them because I once sat in my car and jacked off to her walking around naked in her room and taking a shower. I'm not going to allow another man to do the same. So, I had to add some protection for her.

She's fanning the smoke when she enters the open living room/ kitchen area. Now dressed in the jeans I picked out. Her makeup is fixed, but she has thrown her hair up into a messy bun instead of taking the time to do anything with it. "What are you burning?" she asks.

When I don't answer, she looks around, and her eyes go to the sink. "Is that my skirt?" she growls.

"*Was* your skirt," I correct her, and she fists her hands down by her side. "I have to leave town this weekend," I tell her, changing the subject. This probably won't be the last piece of clothing of hers that I get rid of.

She tilts her head to the side, letting out an exasperated breath. "Why?" Her tone tells me she doesn't really care. Just that she felt obligated to ask.

"Do not go to the house of Lords." So, I ignore her question.

Her lips turn down just the slightest at her confusion. "What? Why would I—?"

"Do not go there," I interrupt her.

"Sure, yeah." She nods her head as if I believe that shit lie she just told.

"That's not good enough, Blake," I snap.

She huffs. "Well, Sarah is there. Why can't I go there and see her? You'll be out of town. What else do I have to do?"

That's what I was afraid of. The house of Lords parties every fucking weekend after the vow ceremony. No cloaks, no masks. Just fucking orgies. Anyone and everyone will show up. I don't trust Matt around her. And I don't trust her not to get wasted with Sarah. Hell, the last time she did that, she let a guy tie her up and go down on her—me. So, I'm very well aware of what she's willing to do. She's been starving for physical attention longer than I have. I knew I couldn't have it; she was just rejected. I don't blame her for wanting it now, but I'm afraid she'll get too friendly with someone. Or someone may just see a passed-out drunk woman as an opportunity. I could have Prickett and Gunner watch out for her, but she is not their responsibility. She's mine.

I walk over to her, and she stiffens, expecting me to throw her to the floor or tie her up and fuck her. Instead, I say, "There will be plenty of parties for us to attend there. Just promise me that you won't go to the house of Lords without me. Ever." Unless she walks into the front doors with me hand in hand she does not need to be there. Period.

Her blue eyes search mine before she licks her lips and nods, softening her voice. "I promise." Sounding much more believable.

Cupping her cheek, I lean in and kiss her forehead while whispering, "Good girl," making her whimper.

I was taught to punish and humiliate when needed. But I was also shown the importance of praise. Blakely will learn to crave that from me as much as the other.

SIXTEEN

BLAKELY

I SIT SILENTLY in the passenger seat while he drives us to Barrington. My apartment isn't on campus, but it's definitely close enough that I could walk if need be.

"Are you going to show me what we did that night in my apartment?" I ask, breaking the awkward silence.

He remains quiet, driving through one of the many parking lots, looking for a space. I cross my arms over my chest and let out a huff. Finding a spot, he backs in. I'm reaching for the door when he holds out his phone to me. I let go of the door handle and look at him. He nods for me to take it.

Pulling it from his hand, I see it's paused on a video. I push play.

It's of me in my bedroom. I'm lying on my back, hands up by my head, and I'm passed out. Ryat walks into the room and over to the side of the bed. Ripping my shirt up, he places his hand on my stomach and slides it down and into my underwear. My nipples harden while I watch him push them down my legs before pushing my legs open. He then climbs on to the bed and sits between them. He starts fingering me, and my breathing accelerates while my body reacts to the video.

I watch as his fingers make me squirm in the bed, my body coming alive for him on its own. He gets rough, my body rocking back and forth, forcing me to come. He removes them and rubs them along my lips before sucking his own fingers clean.

I'm fucking panting as I watch this. It's the only sound you can hear inside the car while I clench my thighs shut. Thankfully, there's no audio on the video.

He then rips the shirt off me and walks out of the frame. The video stops. Without a word, I throw his phone into his lap, open the door and get out. I practically run across the parking lot to the building, needing to get away from him.

That should not have turned me on as much as it did. But the fact that I wasn't aware he was there makes my body break out in a sweat. The way he knew what it needed, what it liked.

I make my way to my first class for the day and sit down next to Sarah. She's got a big smile on her face. "How was your night?"

I blush and look down at my desk. Of course, she knows that I never slept with Matt but had tried. "Good. Yours?"

She places her elbow on her desk and her chin in her hand. "Amazing."

The girl in front of me turns around, glaring. "Please tell me you two didn't ..."

"Mind your own business," Sarah tells her.

"Maybe don't talk so loud," she snaps, then turns back around, throwing her hair over her shoulder just like last time.

We're walking out of class when I see Ryat across the hall. Just like before, he's standing with Gunner and that blonde. "Lunch?" I ask Sarah before she walks away.

"Sure," she throws over her shoulder.

I try to get closer to them without looking like I'm eavesdropping. I rush to the side hall and peek around the corner.

She stands in front of them, both of her hands on her hips. Her short bleach-blond hair is up in a high pony, and she's dressed in a pair of short shorts and a T-shirt with a set of black heels. Her back is to me so I can't see her face. Gunner is smirking, and Ryat looks bored as he stares down at her.

"Cindy Williams." I hear a familiar voice.

I jump and look over to see Matt is watching me eavesdrop. *Fuck.* Busted. By him of all people? "Who?" I ask, crossing my arms over my chest, not expecting an answer.

He smiles a cold and collected smile. Like this was his plan to get me to talk to him. "Her eldest brother ... he's five years older than me. He'll be president of the United States one day."

"Yeah, right." I laugh at that and this weird conversation we're having. It's the first time he's spoken to me since we got into our fight here in the hall.

"And Ryat ..." I stiffen when he says his name. "Ryat Archer will be the most ruthless and renowned judge in New York. Well, possibly in the US."

I frown, looking at him. "Why are you telling me this?" Why is he even talking to me at all? Wasn't he at the vow ceremony with that girl he was at the house of Lords with? Doesn't he know I belong to Ryat?

He snorts. "Cindy Williams will be Mrs. Cindy Archer."

My pulse accelerates at his words. Now I understand why he's talking to me. He thinks he can hurt me. He thinks I'm such a needy, lonely bitch that I've already gone and fallen for Ryat after one fucking night. Seriously? So, because a guy finally fucked me, I'm supposed to love him?

He steps into me, and it presses my back into the wall. "Matt ..." I warn.

Leaning into my ear, he whispers, "She will be his wife. She will have his kids. And she will be the one tied to his bed that he fucks."

A coldness runs up my spine. Not at his words but how he says them. The dark tone in his voice sends warning shivers down my spine.

He pulls back and smiles down at me. "Just like you will be all three of those things for me." Reaching out, he plays with a piece of hair that's fallen out of my messy bun. "Have fun while you can, Blakely. He may be fucking you for now, but I will be the one who will have you for the rest of your miserable fucking life. And I will never let you see the light of day." Leaning forward, he licks up the side of my face, making me taste vomit. "And you will pay for what you've done to me. Remember that he's playing with you now, but I will own you. Till death do us part. And that won't come fast enough for you." His eyes drop to the hickeys that Ryat left on my neck, then the bruises on my arms and wrists. "You may be his slut, but you will be my worthless whore." Then he walks off.

RYAT

"Why didn't you choose me?" Cindy asks, her hands on her hips. "I know my name was on that list," she snaps at me.

I say nothing. Not every girl gets chosen. We have fifteen seniors this year and hundreds of women's names on the list. That's why some Lords choose to have more than one. The list of women willing to be a chosen is a mile long.

Gunner laughs at her words. "Why the fuck would he pick you as his chosen? He's stuck fucking you every day after his graduation until he dies. Why would he add a year to that prison sentence?"

Baring her teeth, she lets out a growl and spins around, stomping off down the hall.

"Man, you are going to hate being her husband. She's going to be a miserable bitch." He slaps my shoulder, watching her sway her ass down the hall. "I'd keep her gagged twenty-four seven, strapped to a board down in the basement."

"That's the only plan I got." My parents arranged my marriage to Cindy Williams years ago. I was a senior in high school, and she was a junior. We lived in New York; her family lived in California. We took a family vacation to the Alps with them. Both of our fathers are Lords. And her two older brothers as well. Her father wanted her with a fellow Lord, and when my father told him I was going to have my freshman initiation the following school year, wedding bells started ringing.

We spent two weeks in the Alps. The first night there, she found her way to my room and woke me up with my dick in her mouth. I spent more time in bed fucking her than I did out skiing. She's okay when her mouth is full, but when it's not, all she does is run it. Nonstop.

"So, what are you going to do?" Gunner asks, getting my attention. I look over at him. "About what?"

"The ice queen. She's probably already on the phone with daddy, ratting you out that you chose Blakely instead of her."

I wave him off. "Let her. Nothing they can do about it." My father knew I was told to choose Blakely. He understands I had no choice, and he also knows that what he and my mother have arranged with the Williamses isn't going anywhere. Right now, my focus is to fuck up Matt and his pathetic life. "I got the right girl."

Gunner slaps my chest. "Speaking of your girl." He points down at the end of the hall.

I see Blakely walking in the opposite direction with her head down, gripping a stack of books in her hands to her chest. "See you back at the house of Lords," I tell him and take off down the hall. "Blake?" I holler at her, but she keeps going. "Blakely!" I call out her full name when she chooses to ignore me.

Catching up with her, I grab her shoulder and spin her around. She looks up at me, and she's got tears in her eyes. I frown. I just dropped her off an hour ago, and she totally avoided me. I knew her watching me get her off would get her worked up. "What's wrong?"

She looks back over where I was just standing and then back at me. Without answering, she begins to walk off again.

"Blake?" I snap, grabbing her arm. She tries to pull away from me, so I tighten my grip and drag her into a nearby room that just happens to be empty.

"Don't touch me," she screams, dropping all of her books to the floor as I shut the door behind us.

"What in the fuck is going on with you?" I demand, getting in her face.

Her eyes narrow up at me right before she slaps me. "Fuck you," she shouts. She goes to do it again, and I grab her wrists, spinning her around, and wrap my free hand around the front of her. I pin both of her arms to her chest, her back pressed to my front. "Fuck all of you." She sniffs, then her body softens against mine, and she starts crying.

"Hey." I let go of her and spin her around to face me, knowing something is seriously wrong. She drops her head, and I grip her chin, forcing her to look up at me. "You better tell me right fucking now what's going on with you."

Her bloodshot eyes search mine, and then she shakes her head, her nostrils flaring. "I took an oath to let you fuck me, Ryat. I don't have to give you anything else."

My teeth grind. "It doesn't work that way ..."

"Says who?" She snorts, yanking away from me. "You?" Her eyes drop to my shoes and run up over my jeans and T-shirt. When they reach mine, they're full of disdain. Then she quickly picks up her books before walking past me toward the door.

I step in front of her and slap my hand against it, blocking her exit. "Blake ..."

She looks at me, her blue eyes now blazing with fire. Something has happened that has pissed her the fuck off, and I don't like that she won't tell me what it is. "Unless you plan on ripping my clothes off and bending me over a desk, we're done here," she states, arching a brow.

This bitch is challenging me.

My cock is already hard at her little attitude, but I'm also speechless. Who knew Blakely was such a firecracker? I didn't. Matt always made her sound like a little flower that he had to protect from the softest breeze.

I let go of the door, raising my hands in surrender and stepping away. I'll let her leave right now because I have a better idea of how to remind her where she stands with me. I'm not Matt. I won't put up with this shit.

She yanks the door open and storms out, her heels clanking on the floor as the door falls shut, closing me in the classroom.

SEVENTEEN

BLAKELY

I SIT AT the kitchen bar in our apartment drinking a rum and Coke. It's my third. I skipped the rest of my classes today. Didn't give a shit to be there.

Matt got to me. He was right. It doesn't matter who I fuck today, tomorrow, or next week. The end will be the same. I'll be his. And now I've pissed him off. He pretty much told me he'd keep me caged in the dark as his sex slave.

What the fuck did I do to him? He was cheating on me. He never even told me about the ritual. How was I going to vow to be his if I didn't know about it? Ryat chose me, but Matt showed no interest in me whatsoever. Just our future as husband and wife. Let's not forget the girl he's been with for God knows how long.

I take another drink, the straw making a slurping sound as I realize I've reached the bottom. Then there's Ryat and his high horse. I'm not telling him shit about Matt and me. He's already possessive and controlling. If he knew what Matt said to me, he'd probably take it out on my ass, and I'm not going to allow that. I didn't do anything wrong.

Getting to my feet, I walk into the kitchen to pour myself another drink but realize the bottle is empty. "Great." I throw it into the sink, and it shatters, some of the pieces falling onto the floor. I step back, not wanting to get cut, and go over to the bar, picking up my cell to call Sarah.

"Hey, girl." She answers on the second ring.

"Wanna go out?" I ask her in greeting. Either she wants to or not. I don't have time to beat around the bush.

"Yeah," she answers excitedly. "Gunner and I—"

"Just me and you," I interrupt her. "I need a girls' night. And please don't tell Gunner where we're going. I'm avoiding Ryat right now."

"Of course," she says without hesitation. "You at the apartment?"

"Yep." I nod to myself.

"I'll be there in twenty." She hangs up. I set my cell down on the counter and make my way to my room and to my closet, leaving the mess of broken glass in the kitchen. I start digging through my clothes, looking for the most revealing thing I own. The motherfucker burned my skirt. Fuck him!

Smiling, I pull the dress off the rack. "Perfect."

I get undressed and step into the skirt, pulling it up to my waist. Then I raise the two pieces of fabric up and around my neck. Turning, I look at myself in the mirror and the crisscross halter cut-out dress. It shows off my stomach, chest, and all of my back. The crisscross material barely covers my tits. Looking down, I pull on the string on my right thigh, making the skirt bunch up even more.

Twenty minutes later, we're walking into Blackout. It's a four-story club on the outskirts of town. "Have you been here before?" I ask her while we check our stuff in at the front. No way am I carrying it all around with me while I dance and drink. Plus, me drunk with a phone isn't smart right now. I don't want to drunk text Ryat when I'm horny at two o'clock in the morning. Or do something worse like send him pics of my pussy while in the bathroom.

"No. Janice was telling me about it the other day."

I nod. Of course, our neighbor did. Last year, Sarah and I were woken up at three in the morning because the cops were banging on her door. They found drugs inside her place, and she spent three weeks in jail. We had to feed her cat and water the plants for her.

We shoulder our way past the crowd, and I grab the bar for stability. I should have worn flats. I've already had so much to drink; I'm going to be crawling out of here after closing.

A bartender walks over to us. "What will it be?" he yells out to us.

I go to hand him my bank card to start a tab when a guy beside me slides a hundred across the bar. "I got their drinks, Benny."

Looking up, I see a pair of dark eyes staring at me. A smirk covers his unshaven face, and his eyes drop to my tits.

"No thanks." I dismiss him, slapping my card on top of the bar.

He snorts. "Come on, let us buy your drinks for the night."

"Us?" Sarah asks.

"Name's Nathan," a guy to her right introduces himself, placing his forearm on the bar. "And this here is my friend Mitch." He gestures to the one next to me.

"Well, thanks for the offer, Nathan and Mitch, but we're good." I look at the bartender. "Rum and Coke. Two, please."

"Oh, come on." The one next to me picks up my card, and his free hand grabs my forearm. "You should be grateful we're offering to take care of you for the night." That smirk returns to his face. "You can pay us back later."

His words anger me. He expects us to get on our hands and knees and kiss his fucking shoes because he's offering to pay what? Maybe a couple of hundred dollars on drinks for us tonight? "No, thanks," I repeat and yank my arm away from him as I take my card from the other.

"Hey—"

"It wasn't a fucking hint, asshole." Sarah snaps, cutting him off. "The answer is no. Pick two different girls." She grabs my hand, yanking me from the bar. "Come on," she growls. "There are other bars here to get drinks at inside this club."

Looking back at them over my shoulder, I see another guy join them, but his back is toward me, so I can't get a look at his face. But I see a tattoo on the back of his neck that looks like a spider crawling out from underneath the collar of his shirt. My eyes go to the one who introduced himself as Mitch, and he's already glaring at me. Giving him my back, I throw my hair over my shoulder.

Fuck him!

RYAT

I HATE CLUBS. I'm not much of a partier. Even throughout high school, I didn't go to many. I hate people in general. Then you mix alcohol and drugs with it, and I just can't deal with them.

The house of Lords throws parties all the time, and although I tolerate them, I don't drink at them. Too many opportunities for shit to go wrong. I prefer to be levelheaded and in control. That way, if something goes down, I can handle it.

So, the fact that Gunner and I are at Blackout isn't helping my already sour mood. I've left Blakely alone since she threw her little fit earlier today at Barrington, but then Gunner called me and said we had a situation. I'm not happy about it.

The fact that I'm standing on one of the second-story balconies looking down onto the first floor and watching another man touch what's mine makes me see fucking red.

Pushing away from the railing, I rush down the hallway and see two men standing at the railing. Both have holsters on their belts with guns loaded. "Ryat." One nods at me.

Walking over to the edge, I point out Blakely and Sarah on the first floor. They're throwing back shots at the bar in the back. "See those two girls. One dressed in a white dress, the other in a black one?"

"Yeah. What about them?"

"No one touches them. Got it?"

He nods. "Yes, sir."

Satisfied that they will do what needs to be done if something happens, I finish walking down the hallway to the end and come to a door. I punch in the key to enter and push it open.

Ty is in the middle of fucking a server.

Her brown eyes widen when she sees Gunner and me enter the room. Shrieking, she presses her palms on the desk he has her bent over and tries to push herself up. Grabbing the back of her neck, he slams her face down onto the desk and continues to fuck her from behind. "Just let them watch," he tells her.

"Ty ..."

Leaning over her back, he reaches in front of her and pries her mouth open, sticking his fingers inside—two on each side—opening her mouth up so she can no longer argue with him. "Shut the fuck up," he growls.

Her face is scrunched, and she closes her eyes in embarrassment. That's Ty for you. He was always good at humiliation. The man taught me everything I know.

He pumps into her, their hips hitting the desk, making it rattle.

She moans, unable to help herself, and her fingers curl around the edge of the desk, holding on to it. She's fighting the inevitable. Drool starts to run down her dark-painted lips and onto the desk. Her hair covers parts of her face, and the room fills with her unintelligible sounds that he's forcing from her. Then her eyes roll back into her head just as he thrusts one last time—both of them cumming.

Pulling out of her, he removes the condom and tosses it into the trash can by his desk and sits down. "Now get the fuck out," he orders, and she gladly obliges, running as fast as she can past us, but stumbling out the door. "What can I do for you guys?"

"The basement." I get to the point. "May we use it?"

He smiles up at us. "Of course. You never have to ask." Sitting up, he places his forearms on the desk. "Just point them out, and I'll have them delivered for you."

EIGHTEEN

BLAKELY

WE'VE BEEN AT the club for three hours now. We've had drinks, shots, and danced our asses off.

"Do you want to talk about it?" she asks as we come up to the bar for a refill. I'm not sure if it's the alcohol or the flashing lights, but it's getting hard to see.

"Nope." My problems are not hers. And I'm still unsure of this ritual shit. Does she have to tell Gunner if he asks her? Would she willingly tell him without him having to ask? I love my friend, but I'm going to keep this to myself. It's not something she can fix anyway.

"Okay," she says, not concerned that I'm keeping something from her. "Just know I'm here if you need me."

"Here you go, ladies. Courtesy of the two gentlemen at the end of the bar." The bartender sets two shots down in front of us.

I look over to my right, my hair flipping across my face expecting to see dipshit again. Thankfully, the guys haven't bothered us since Sarah told them to fuck off. But instead, I'm surprised to see a set of emerald eyes staring at me. He stands there, holding a glass of scotch. Gunner stands next to him, drinking a beer. A laugh bubbles up from my chest, making his eyes narrow on mine. It's funny. I'm not even mad or surprised that the fucker found me.

"I swear I didn't tell him," Sarah assures me, patting my shoulder.

"It's fine." I nod, picking up my drink. I stare at it for a second before I throw it back. Some misses my mouth, and the coldness runs down my breasts since they're on full display tonight.

"Fuck them, B. We came here to have fun. Me and you. Let's go dance," she offers when I set the empty drink down.

"Lead the way," I half joke. I'm fucked up and feel great. He can't ruin my night. Hell, not even Matt can piss me off right now.

She grabs my hand and pulls me onto the dance floor. We make our way through the people, bumping into them until we're in the center. I throw my hands up above my head and start moving my hips to "Taste of You" by Rezz and Dove Cameron.

The lights flash, making it hard to focus on anything. So, I close my eyes and drop my hands, running them over my hips, moving my head from side to side, letting my hair slap my face. I can feel the bass thumping through my body. The bright lights are warming up my skin.

Someone comes up behind me, and rough denim pushes against the back of my thighs. Then a set of hands grabs my waist before falling to my hips. Instead of pushing them away, I hold them and pull them around to my front, knowing exactly who it is. Ryat doesn't know how to stay away. I lean back on him, laying my head on his chest, eyes still closed.

His hand sprawls across my exposed stomach, his other trails up my body. He wraps it around my neck, and I whimper. My ass grinds on his hard cock in his jeans.

Bending down, he nibbles on my ear, and I groan. "Fuck, yes."

My pulse is racing, and my head is spinning. I've already had so much to drink before we even got here. I just want to let go, feel the music, the vibrations, and the sweat that covers my body. It's all so much.

His hand squeezes, taking away my air for a quick second, and my underwear grows wet. My lips part, unable to breathe. Maybe he'll knock me out. When he loosens his grip, I feel an overwhelming rush of disappointment.

Lifting his hand just a bit, he moves from my neck to my chin. His free hand dips lower and up under my dress. "Yes." I moan. "Please ..."

"You're in so much trouble," he growls in my ear, making me shiver.

"Punish me," I tell him, my hands coming up and reaching behind me to grip his hair. He hisses in my ear when I pull on it.

I don't even care at this point. Matt can't do shit right now. Ryat has made that very clear—no one will touch me. No one will hear me.

He owns me for now. And I'm going to revel in it.

"Be careful what you ask for, little one." He kisses down to my neck, where he bites it.

I gasp, my hips pushing forward, feeling his fingers very close to my pussy. I'm so wet that my thong is soaked. The song changes to "Sick Like Me" by In This Moment, and he spins me around, his hands on my hips stopping me from turning too far.

Moving his hand to cup my face, he pushes the hair out of my eyes and rubs his thumb over my parted lips while our hips grind. I stick my tongue out and wrap it around his finger, pulling it into my mouth.

His eyes darken under the flashing fluorescent lights, and I feel a growl from his chest vibrate mine. I close my eyes and suck on his finger as his other hand goes to the back of my neck. Gripping my hair, he yanks my head back, his thumb popping loose from my lips. He lowers his lips to my neck and kisses my skin.

"Ryat ..." I whimper, digging my nails into his shirt. Is this my punishment? Dancing? Teasing? "I want you." I moan, my lower stomach grinding on his hard dick. "Fuck." My hands go to his belt, but he pulls back, grabbing my wrists to stop me.

He looks over my shoulder and nods once. I'm guessing to signal to Gunner. Then he grabs my hand and drags me off the dance floor. My drunken legs can't keep up in my six-inch heels. He takes me to the coat check at the entrance and gets my purse, keys, and phone for me. Guess I didn't have to text him a pic from the bathroom after all.

Grabbing my hand once again, he leads me out the back, and we walk toward his car. I'm stumbling, my vision blurry. I blink, but it doesn't do any good. "Did you ... did you drug me?" I ask as he brings me to the passenger door. He and Gunner had bought us drinks. I wouldn't put it past them to slip something into them.

He pushes my back into the door, coming to stand between my legs. He grips my chin and forces me to look up at him. "No," he answers, his green eyes searching my face. When they find mine, he gives me a devious smirk that lights up his gorgeous face even in the dim parking lot. "I want you to be awake and remember every little thing I do to you tonight."

I whimper, my thighs tightening.

"Starting now." He spins me around to face the passenger car door, pressing my exposed stomach to the cold metal, making me shiver. He yanks my hands behind my back, and my ears still ring from the loud music inside, so I don't hear the handcuffs before they wrap around each wrist. And just like before, he secures them extra tight.

Leaning over, he opens the door and helps me into my seat. He slams the door and I cry out as my arms are crushed behind me.

RYAT

I GET IN the driver's side and start my car. We knew that Sarah had brought them here, so I drove Gunner so we could each drive them back. Leaning across her, I fasten her seat belt.

"It's a thirty-minute drive," she whines, trying to adjust her arms behind her back.

"Should have thought about that." I wasn't all that mad until I saw what she was wearing. A fucking bathing suit would cover more. And I know she dressed this way because of our fight earlier. I reach over and yank both sides of the straps open, exposing her tits. I grab her left one and squeeze. She throws her head back, panting. Leaning over the center console, I suck her nipple into my mouth, making it hard. She lifts her hips the best she can with the seat belt on.

Pulling away, I slap it, making her cry out again. If the car was big enough, I could totally fuck her in it because the windows are blacked out. But I need more room to work with. She'll probably be passed out by the time we get back to the apartment.

I lift her skirt and shove her underwear to the side. "Just how wet are you, Blake?" I ask, running my fingers over her pussy.

"So wet," she moans.

I push a finger into her, and she's not lying. "For who?" I ask.

"You." She wiggles her shoulders, trying to relieve her hands restrained behind her back.

"Whose girl are you?" I ask, shoving another one into her.

She gasps, her tits bouncing at the motion while she spreads her legs farther apart for me. "Yours."

"Mine," I remind her as I start finger-fucking her while she sits in the passenger seat of my car.

She cries out, her legs shifting on the seat, her hips bucking and head banging on the headrest. I don't gag her. I like the way she sounds when she's screaming my name.

My fingers go in and out of her while my free hand pinches her nipples. She arches her back as her cunt clamps down on my fingers while she comes.

I pull them out, and she slumps against the seat. Lips parted while she tries to catch her breath. I push the strands of hair covering her face away and shove my fingers into her mouth. "Clean them," I command.

Her cheeks hollow as she sucks her cum off them, and I pull them out with a pop. Gripping her face, I force her to look over at me. "Don't ever do that again. Do you understand me?"

Her eyes are glassy, her chest heaving and body shaking. I want to drag her across this car and force my cock down her throat. I want to be rough with her. Remind her who the fuck I am and that she belongs to me, but I don't. She licks her numb lips and nods. "Yeah."

After I release her, I sit back in the driver's seat and defog the windows while putting the car in gear and take off.

***

SHE'S OUT LIKE I expected her to be by the time I park at her apartment. Undoing her seat belt, I help her out of the car and carry her inside with her hands still cuffed behind her back.

Getting her into the door, I head toward her room but pause before passing the kitchen. Something on the floor catches my attention—it's glass. Its broken pieces are scattered on the floor, and I frown. *What the fuck happened?* I knew she was home because I had watched her on the cameras, but then I got called to the house of Lords for a meeting. Once it was over, Gunner notified me the girls were going out. By the time I checked on her, she was already on her way to the club.

Moving on to her room, I lay her on the bed facedown. She doesn't even make a sound. I remove her heels and then place her on her side to remove the halter from over her neck. I then slide it down her stomach and legs before tossing it to the floor as well.

That too will be getting burned. I run my hands up and down her bubble ass, giving it a small slap.

She buries her face into the pillow, letting out a moan as she stirs. Moving my hand up to her face, I push the hair off the side. "Good night, little one," I tell her and turn toward the bathroom.

"Ryat?" She moans my name.

I turn to look at her over my shoulder. "Yeah?"

"My wrists?" she asks, licking her dry lips with her eyes still closed.

"They stay on," I tell her.

She whimpers, her face digging into the pillow once again. I walk back over to her. "Did you think your punishment was an orgasm?"

"They hurt." She ignores my question.

"Good," I say and then pause, getting an idea. "They can come off. If ... you tell me what happened today."

She turns her head to face away from me and mumbles, "Good night."

My brows rise. What the fuck happened that she doesn't want me to know? "What happened in the kitchen?" I try another way.

Nothing.

"Okay." I reach down and undo my belt. She's given me no other option. Snapping the leather between my hands, I then slap it down across her upper thighs.

She screams, her body tensing.

Doing it again, I order, "Ass up in the air."

She buries her face into the pillow, whimpering, but she wiggles up onto her knees, arching her back.

Dropping the belt next to her on the bed, I reach out and rub my hands over the red marks that it gave. She wiggles her ass, and I grip her underwear and tear them down the middle. My hand runs down over her ass to her pussy. "Last chance. Tell me what happened today," I say, pushing two fingers into her already wet cunt.

She moans, her hips rocking against my hand. "Nothing ..."

I remove my fingers and slap her pussy.

She cries out, her body jerking, and she goes to pull her knees together. "Don't you dare," I warn, and she pauses, slowly pushing them back to where they were. "You're lying to me, Blake." I sigh, tapping her pussy in warning, and she flinches. My left hand reaches for the chain that connects the handcuffs, and I grip it in my hand, pulling it toward her ass.

Her head comes up off the bed. "Ryat." She gasps. "Please ..."

I tap her pussy again before pushing the two fingers back into her. "You're in control here," I say. Manipulation is important. "All you have to do is tell me, and I'll take them off."

She stays silent, and it pisses me off.

I force a third finger into her pussy and work them in and out while circling her clit. She rocks her body back and forth, whimpering at what my hand is doing. I get more forceful, pulling harder on the cuffs.

She's panting, her body rocking back and forth, trying to fuck my fingers as if it's my cock. Her pussy clamps down on me, and I pull them out. Her body sags, and she groans.

I slap her pussy once again and then shove my fingers back in. "I can do this all night, little one," I say with a smile.

She's close to orgasm again, so I stop. She screams, burying her head into the pillow, getting irritated. I slap her pussy, then start again.

Just as she's about to cum, I let up. "Okay, okay," she rushes out. "Please ... just let me ..." She trails off and I keep going, and this time, I allow her to come. Pulling my fingers out, I bring them to my lips when she breathes, "Matt."

I pause. "Excuse me?" *Did she just call me her ex?*

She stretches her legs out, flattening her body to the bed, and whispers, "He threatened me."

"Matt threatened you?" I growl. "When? What the fuck did he say?"

"It doesn't matter." She sighs. "Never does."

I dig the key to the handcuffs out of my back pocket and undo them. Before she can even move, I'm pushing her onto her back and sitting down next to her. Reaching out, I push her hair from her face. "Tell me what he said." She's pretty fucking drunk, and I'm not even sure how much of tonight she'll remember when she wakes up. So, I need to use this as an opportunity to find out everything before she sobers up and becomes a brick wall again like she was earlier today.

Her eyes are closed, and she's breathing heavily. She's about to pass out again anytime soon.

"Blake?" I bark, and she opens her heavy eyes.

"Today. Earlier." She licks her lips, reaching up and running her hands through her hair. "I saw you talking to your wife."

I frown.

"Well, he caught me watching you talk to your future wife." She chuckles. "I think he thought I was jealous. Like he thinks I already love you." More laughter follows, like that'll never happen. "And he told me that you may have me now, but once you're done with me, I'm stuck with him until I die. And he'll make my life a living hell." She yawns and mumbles on. "Something about not seeing daylight. Your slut, his whore ..." She trails off.

"Blake ..."

"He pushed me up against the wall and licked my face." She shudders. "Thought I was going to puke."

"He what?" I snap, my body tensing while my blood pressure rises at that thought. But she ignores my outburst. "Why the fuck didn't you tell me this when I asked you earlier?"

She looks up at me. Her pretty blue eyes look unfocused and tired. "I don't know what happened between you two, but I know Matt is the reason you chose me."

I sigh. She's not far from the truth. "Blake ..."

"I will not be punished for something he has done, Ryat," she says softly. "You can fuck me, but I told myself that Matt will not dictate my life anymore."

I run a hand through my hair at her confession. She's not wrong. Matt is why I had to pick her. But it wouldn't have happened without her. "Why did you let me choose you?" I ask.

She gives me a weak smile. "Because you made me feel wanted."

Matt is a fool and a dead man.

"I hate everyone," she goes on, eyes closed once again. "My mom for making me marry him. Matt for blaming me for you hating him. And you ..." She trails off and whispers, "I'll just run away once you're done with me."

I stand staring down at her, my hands fisting. Why the fuck was he even talking to her in the first place? He told her I'm marrying Cindy? That may be true, but we don't discuss that shit. How would he know that?

When she starts snoring softly, I place the handcuffs in her nightstand, then I cover her up with her comforter, kissing her forehead good night.

NINETEEN

BLAKELY

IT'S A BEAUTIFUL *fall day here in Texas. "Bad Intentions" by Niykee Heaton is blasting in my ears while I run the old trail behind my parents' house. I've grown up here. Lived in the same house all my life. My father's office is in downtown Dallas, but we live quite a ways from there on twenty acres. He commutes, but for the most part, he's not even in the state. He has to travel a lot for work.*

The hairs on the back of my neck stand, and I come to a stop. Breathing heavily, I yank the earbuds from my ears. "Hello?" I ask, looking around. To my left is a small pond. Other than that, it's just trees back here. "You're being paranoid, Blakely." Matt gets on me all the time for running this trail. He says it's unsafe.

I put the earbuds back in and start jogging again. I've been at it for almost thirty minutes. I'm almost to my turning around point. The song changes to "Mirrors" by Natalia Kills as the trail turns to the right, and I see something out of the corner of my eye. "What the …?" I stop and rip the earbuds out, turning around to go back. "Hello?" I shout this time. "Anyone there?" There are bobcat sightings around here, so maybe it's an animal of some sort.

When I'm again convinced I'm losing it because there's nothing here, I put my earbuds back in and turn back to continue. I jump when I see someone standing in front of me in the middle of the trail. My heart hammers in my chest. It's a man dressed in black jeans and a black short-sleeved T-shirt, stance wide and arms down by his side. He's got to be over six feet, and he's wearing combat boots.

My thighs tighten, wondering how long he's been following me. My earbuds are still blaring in my ears, and I reach up to take them out in case he's talking to me. He's wearing a mask—a white one—so I'm unable to see his face, but something about him seems familiar.

He takes a step toward me, and I take one back. He stops, and I swallow the knot that forms in my throat while my nipples harden.

No. No. No.

Not again.

I can feel his eyes on my legs. I decided to run in shorts this morning. My pulse is racing, and my breathing picks up, making my tits bounce in my sports bra.

"I've been watching you." *My pussy throbs at his confession, and tears sting my eyes. Even his voice sounds familiar. Where have I heard it before? "You run here every day." He tilts his masked head to the side.*

"Please ..." *I whimper, placing my hands up at him. "I just want to finish my run," I say, slowly taking a step back as my body heat rises at the thought of us being out here all alone.*

"Well"—he chuckles behind his mask—"I don't know if you'll finish, but I will." The man charges for me.

I spin around to run, but he barrels into my back, knocking me to the ground. I try fighting him, but he's on my back. He grabs my hands and wraps something rough around my wrists, securing them behind me, and I feel wetness pool between my legs.

God, no.

He grabs my hair and yanks me to my feet, pulling me off the trail. Then he's shoving me deeper into the woods. I trip and fall down onto the ground. Twigs and branches dig into my bare legs. I go to get up, but his fist hits my back, knocking me down again. "Stay down, bitch," he orders, pushing my face to the rough ground.

Tears run down my face as he rips my shorts down my legs along with my underwear. Then he's shoving my legs apart. I cry out when his hand touches my pussy.

"Ahh, you're wet," he says in surprise.

I sob, my body shaking.

"You like being taken, don't you, you little slut." He grips my hair and leans down. "Don't worry, looks like you'll get to finish after all."

I sit straight up, gasping for air in the darkness. Reaching over, I knock a few things to the floor to find a light. When I press a button, the room lights up, and I see I'm at home in my apartment, naked in my bed. Alone.

"Not again." I breathe. Leaning forward, I drop my face in my hands and try to calm my breathing. I look at my cell, and it says it's a little after three in the morning. How did I get home? The club ... drinking with Sarah ... Ryat. He showed up. Must have brought me home and dropped me off.

Lying down on my back, I stare up at the ceiling. My mouth is dry and tastes like lingering alcohol. Throwing off my covers, I get out of bed on shaky legs and open my bedroom door. Stepping out, I come to a stop when I see Ryat sitting on my couch, his cell in his hands and staring straight at me.

"Ryat?" I squeal, taking a step back. "You, uh... what are you doing here?" I stumble over my words, still trying to catch my breath.

His eyes drop to my hard nipples, and I cross my arms over my chest. They lower to my legs, and I cross them as well, leaning up against the doorframe to my bedroom for support. "What were you doing?" he counters, arching a brow.

"Nothing." I shrug carelessly, but his eyes run up and over my body, and I can tell by the look in them, he knows I'm full of shit. I bite my lip to keep from whimpering. *Not again.* This can't be happening again.

"You were doing something." He stands, pocketing his phone, and walks over to me.

I swallow the lump in my throat. "Sleeping." Not a total lie. I literally just woke up like this.

Coming to a stop in front of me, he orders, "Open my legs."

If I know anything about Ryat, it's that he'll get what he wants. No matter what. I push off the wall and uncross my shaking legs for him as humiliation washes over me.

RYAT

SHE PRACTICALLY RAN out of her room, breathing heavily, nipples hard, legs shaking. She looked like she just got herself off. And she was surprised to see I was still here. She knows she's not allowed to do that.

Dropping her head, she closes her eyes and takes in a deep breath. She looks almost ashamed. I place my hand on the inside of her thigh. She flinches but doesn't pull away. I run my hand up between her legs and cup her pussy, sliding my middle finger between her lips.

She's fucking soaked. "Did you touch yourself?" I ask. I'd actually love to watch her get herself off.

She shakes her head, eyes still on the floor.

"You're awfully wet for someone who was just sleeping."

She remains silent.

"Tell me," I say, spreading her pussy wide and pushing a finger into her, seeing just how turned on she is.

"I had a dream," she whispers.

"And?"

"And nothing. It was just a dream," she answers vaguely.

"It was something." I slide a second finger into her, and she whimpers. "Tell me about it."

I gently play with her clit, just trying to relax her. The woman is already worked up. No foreplay is needed at this point. "I was running through the woods." She swallows. "Well, jogging on a trail. And someone was following me."

"Yeah?" I remove my fingers and slide my hand up over my stomach and chest, smearing herself on her skin. I undo her arms crossed over her chest and start playing with her nipple.

"He ..." Moaning, she stops herself.

"What about him?" I ask, telling myself not to get jealous. It was just a dream. "What did he do?"

She's silent for a long second before whispering, "He knocked me down, tied my hands behind my back, and dragged me off the trail." Pausing again, she takes in a shaky breath. "And ..."

"And what?" I lean in and kiss her neck, tasting the salt from her sweat. Pulling back, I lick my lips for another taste.

"And he fucks me," she whispers.

"You mean he rapes you," I correct her.

She whimpers and places her hands over her face.

"Hey." I grab her arms and pull her hands away. Shaking her head, she drops her face to stare at the floor. I grip her chin and force her to look at me. "Don't be ashamed, Blake." I've never been one to kink shame. We all like something different. It takes some of us a little more to get off. Some of us have better imaginations than others when it comes to fantasies.

She sniffs. "This isn't the first time I've had the dream."

"When was the last time you had it?"

"Over the summer. Matt and I were back home, and he was staying over." She swallows. "I woke up wet and horny. I woke him up to tell him about it. I wanted to mess around. He left and didn't talk to me for two weeks." The first tear runs down her face. "He said that there was something wrong with me. That I was fucked up." She covers her face with her hands and starts to cry.

There is nothing wrong with a girl who has forced-sex fantasies. Matt is just a punk-ass bitch. The more I see how he was and is with her, I think he was training her. I thought he had true feelings for her, but I think there were other reasons as to why he was with her. And I'm going to find out what they are.

I pull her into me, wrapping my arms around her. "Good girl." I praise her for telling me, and her body shakes against mine. Bending down, I put my arm behind her legs and pick her up, carrying her back to her room. That text I was in the middle of can wait.

TWENTY

BLAKELY

"MATT?" I SHOVE his shoulder.

"What?" he mumbles, eyes still closed.

"Get up, babe." I kiss his chest. "I want to play around."

"Blakely ..." He opens his eyes and checks his cell on my dresser next to my bed. "It's after midnight."

"I know." I get up and straddle his hips. Lifting his hands, I place them on my boobs. "I just had this dream."

"Oh, yeah?" He chuckles, his hands squeezing my breasts on his own. "Must have been good? What did we do?"

"Well, I was jogging—"

"On that trail I tell you to stay the fuck away from?" He interrupts me.

I roll my eyes. "Yeah, yeah. I was running, and a man was following me. He said he had been watching me." I grind my pussy on his dick. I can feel how hard it is through his boxers. He won't fuck me, but we do other things. My body is craving sex. So bad. I don't know how much longer I can wait. "Anyway, when I went to run away, he chased me down and tied my hands behind my back, and dragged me into the trees ..."

His hands drop from my chest. "What?"

I wave off his concerned tone. "I wanted it. There was just something about it. I was ..."

"You dreamed you were raped?" he snaps.

I bite my bottom lip nervously. My heart accelerates and shoulders sag.

"Jesus, Blakely. Do you have any idea how that makes me feel?" He *glares up at me.*

"You?" I ask, looking at him through my lashes.

"Yeah. Me." He shoves me off him and gets out of bed. "If some guy decides he wants to rape you, you're going to let him. And get off on that shit."

I've had this dream ever since I was fifteen. And at first, I was disgusted with myself. Why would anyone dream and get turned on by something like that when people have experienced something so traumatic in real life? "Lots of women have forced-sex fantasies," I argue. After the fifth time I had this dream, I started doing research, and I found I wasn't alone.

They call it forced-sex fantasy because rape implies violence. And for women who fantasize about this—it's the fact that someone wants them so much, they can't help themselves. Can't take no for an answer. It's more of the domination aspect of it.

He snorts, yanking up his jeans. "Please. No one asks to be raped, Blakely."

I flinch. "Just because I have a fantasy doesn't mean I want it to happen in real life. To me. To anyone for that matter." The studies I found said that those who fantasize about it are the most erotically open and adventurous. I'm neither one of those things because I'm still a virgin. I think I have this dream because I want him to take me. I want him to dominate me, but he turns me down every time.

I think I dream about it happening on that trail because he has warned me about it not being safe. And somehow, I've connected the two.

He pulls his shirt down over his head and looks down at me. His lip is pulled back, and he shakes his head with disgust. "That's fucking sick, Blakely. You're fucked up." And with that, he leaves my room, slamming the door behind him.

Ryat lays me on the bed, and I roll away, unable to face him right now. I hear him removing his jeans and T-shirt before he crawls in behind me.

The bed dips as he gets in. "Blake." He places his hand on my shoulder and rolls me back to face him. "There is nothing wrong with you," he says, running his fingertips along my cheek to push my hair off my tear-streaked face.

I swallow and try to calm my breathing. "It's wrong," I whisper. After that, I told myself that I'd never have that dream again, and if I did, I'd fight, scream, bite, and run faster. But I did none of those things this time. I let him catch me, and I was going to enjoy it if I hadn't woken up too soon.

"No, it's not," he argues. "It's just a fantasy. Everyone has those.

And that's normal."

"It's not the violence I crave," I tell him honestly. "Although I like it rough, I think it's more of the idea of a man being so overcome with desire for me that he can't be stopped. And the fact I have no say over what he does. The feeling of having no control makes me feel in control. I let him catch me even though I run. I let him do it even though I fight him," I ramble, trying to get it all out. Matt didn't want to hear how I felt, and he never mentioned it again.

Ryat's eyes search mine, and I look away, again feeling shame.

"I know, it sounds stupid," I whisper.

"No, it doesn't."

"It's just hard to explain." I lick my wet lips.

"I think it makes perfect sense."

Biting my bottom lip, I add, "I think the man was you."

He adjusts himself on his side and props his head up in his hand. "Why is that?"

"Because up until now, he's never had a face." It's just always been a blur. Or I just never remembered it when I woke up.

"And you saw me this time?" he asks, his green eyes searching my face. He doesn't look disgusted in the least with what I just told him.

"No. He was wearing a mask. The same one you have," I answer softly. I've only ever seen Ryat wearing the mask that one night at the house of Lords party, and at that time, I didn't even know it was him.

He sighs, his free hand lazily running up and down on my arm, "Well, after what we did at the house of Lords party, when I had a mask on ... then you were unconscious when I touched you here in your apartment ... I can see that. It makes sense you'd put me in this guy's place. I've dominated you. And that's what you like."

My cheeks flush, and he cups my face. "It's okay, Blake. You're okay. And I'd be more than willing to give you what you want."

My heart picks up at his words, my eyes widening. "What do you mean?"

"Tell me what you want, along with your limits, and I'll do it. Whatever you're comfortable with."

"You mean my fantasy?" I ask slowly.

He nods.

My thighs clench at the thought. So many possibilities. Scenarios. I've only ever had that same one over and over. "I'll think about it," I tell him, still a little uncomfortable talking about it. I'm not sure I will feel okay telling him what I want. Or what I think I want. I'm not even sure what it is exactly.

139

RYAT

I KISS HER forehead and pull her body into mine. I'm not going to lie to her, but her fantasy turns me on. I had a feeling she'd like being dominated, but this is a fantasy on a whole new level. One that I'm more than happy to fulfill for her.

Matt is pathetic and knows nothing when it comes to sex. Three years without it and the bastard didn't do any research? He never once thought that maybe his girlfriend was craving something that he should look into?

No woman asks to be raped—it's a fantasy about submission. She wants to be dominated in way that she knows she'll enjoy it. It's the act of the coercion.

I'm not sure when the dreams started and I'm no sex psychologist, but maybe it was the fact that Matt turned her down so many times that she had to force herself to enjoy what her body craved. I mean, I loved when she drank the GHB and gave herself over to me, not knowing what I was going to do to her. Hell, she even thought I actually took her virginity at the time.

To her, that was a way of giving herself over to something that she knew she wouldn't be able to control. But it was still her choice.

Matt tried to rape our assignments wife, but he put Blake down for fantasizing about it? That doesn't make any sense. Although one is nothing like the other. He told her she was fucked up? I know Lords who prefer to watch other men fuck their chosens. I'd never allow that but that doesn't mean it's wrong. Fuck, maybe it means I'm insecure, and that's completely fine. That's my issue, not anyone else's. Who the fuck cares? As long as all parties are consenting, then do whatever the fuck you want.

Pulling my chest away from her face, I look down to see her eyes closed and lips parted, she's back asleep. Running my hand through her soft hair, I wonder what she's dreaming about right now. Me and her? Back on that trail in the woods?

I want her to see me with the mask off and know that it's fucking me giving her exactly what she wants. If she wants to role play, then I'll play along. She can give me as much or as little. Doesn't matter, I have an imagination, and I'll make sure she likes whatever I come up with.

I snuggle her back into me, and I close my eyes, thinking a little forced-sex fantasy dream sounds pretty fucking good right now.

TWENTY-ONE

BLAKELY

I STAND IN my bathroom getting ready when Ryat walks in already dressed in his clothes from last night. "You don't have class today," I say to him. He doesn't have any on Fridays. Come to think of it, I never really see him going to any classes or talking about schoolwork. He may be on campus but never actually doing anything there. Makes me wonder if the Lords actually have to attend.

"I've got somewhere to be before my plane leaves this morning," he says cryptically, walking over to me. He slaps my ass while staring down at it. I'm still naked, and my hair is wet. I just got out of the shower. "Fuck, that ass—"

"You pick." I interrupt him.

He steps behind me, reaching up. He gently pulls the hair off my chest and shoulder to lay across my back and leans down to kiss my neck, while his eyes find mine in the mirror. "Pick what?" He kisses my neck again.

"The fantasy," I whisper nervously.

His free hand comes up and wraps around my neck while his other comes around and massages my breast. "What about it?"

"You told me last night to tell you what I wanted in order to act out my fantasy." Something about our conversation last night took a weight off my shoulders. I woke up feeling lighter—more confident in myself and what I want.

"I did," he agrees, his teeth sinking into my skin.

I swallow the moan and focus on what I'm trying to say before I lose my nerve. "I'm telling you now, I want you to pick."

"How I act it out?" he confirms.

I nod. "Yeah."

Smirking, he meets my eyes in the mirror. "Last chance."

I frown. "For what?"

"To rethink that." I go to ask what he means when he continues, "Because you might not want to give me that kind of power."

I swallow nervously but nod. "I'm sure." I'm not backing down. My mind knows right from wrong, but my body craves the wrong. And as little as I know about Ryat, I do know that I can trust him. My body reacts to his touch, his lips, his dominating demeanor. All I ever wanted Matt to do was take control. I would be stupid not to use Ryat when he's offering me that very chance.

"Limits?" he asks. "Anything off the table?"

Biting my lip, I think of one thing. "No anal." He obviously has a thing for asses. I'd like to ease into that one.

"Okay, then." He kisses my neck once again and pulls away from me. "I'll see you Sunday." He slaps my ass and turns, leaving the bathroom.

"Wait. When will we do it?" I ask.

He stops and turns to face me, tilting his head to the side thinking about it. "Do you want to know? Or would you rather be caught off guard?"

The thought of not knowing has my heart racing and my skin tingling. It just takes away another choice that I didn't realize I wanted him to have. "Surprise me."

He nods and then turns to leave.

RYAT

I BRING MY car to a stop in the parking lot at the house of Lords. Entering the double doors, I check the time on my watch. I have two hours before my father's jet is set to leave for New York. I hate to be late, but I'm not going to put this off.

"Hey, where have you been?" Prickett asks as he sees me enter. An apple in one hand, his cell in the other. It's clear that Gunner hasn't filled him in on what we did at Blackout last night. But I didn't expect him to. It wasn't Lord related. Just two overly jealous men who will do anything to prove a point.

"Matt here?" I ask Prickett, avoiding his question. I actually prefer staying at Blake's apartment. It's not as secluded as I'd like, but it's better than this place full of horny fucking men.

"Yeah, he's in the gym." He and Gunner exchange a look.

I run up the staircase, taking a right on the second floor. Then I storm down the hallway to the double doors at the end. I shove them open, noticing Gunner and Prickett are behind me.

The gym is large with everything you could possibly think of, plenty of each station for us all to work out at the same time comfortably. When you tell almost a hundred men they can't fuck, you find a lot of them work out to take their minds off what they really want. Thankfully at this time, most of them are already in classes or still asleep.

Matt's the only one in here at the moment. I spot him over in the corner, working out with the free weights. He smirks when his eyes meet mine in the floor-to-ceiling mirrors. "Pretty sure these weights are too heavy for you," he jokes.

Walking over to him, I pick up a thirty-pound dumbbell off a bench next to him and swing, hitting him on the side of the head.

He stumbles over, dropping the weights he was holding. "Fuck ..." he groans, his hand going to a gash that is now bleeding from the side of his head. I hope he's seeing fucking stars right now.

Gunner's eyes widen while Prickett drops his apple to the floor. Ignoring them both, I grab Matt's hair and yank him over to the bench press. I throw him onto it facedown.

"Load it," I order to Prickett and Gunner. Might as well put them to work if I'm going to give them a show.

Matt is still pretty dazed from the hit to his head, so he's not fully understanding what's going on just yet. Making his body sluggish and slow to get up. His head hangs off the end, and his arms dangle off the sides, touching the floor.

Prickett and Gunner put fifty pounds on each end and then lift it off the bar. Pressing it to his back, they pin him down but hold it steady on both sides, making Matt groan from the weight.

I crouch down in front of his face that hangs off the end of the bench. "I saw you talking to *my* girl yesterday." It's clear that Blake doesn't remember our conversation before she passed out last night because she didn't mention it this morning. And I'm not going to remind her of it, but I'm also not going to rat her out. Matt needs to think I saw it, not that she told me what he said and did. Because I know if I hadn't forced her, she would have never told me. And I don't like that.

Gunner and Prickett push their weight onto either end of the bar, shoving it further into his back, making him bare his teeth at his silence. He coughs, face turning red, but he's fully aware of what's happening right now. "She's not yours." Matt manages to get out through gritted teeth. "Doesn't matter what you fucking do. She will be mine!"

I can't argue that because it's the truth. That doesn't mean I fucking like it. "Here's the thing, Matt. I don't give a fuck about that. She's mine right now. And I don't fucking share. So as a reminder ..." I stand and grip his sweaty hair. Yanking his head up, I bring my knee to his face, hearing a crack, and he cries out. His body jerks, and the guys have to grip the bar tighter to keep it in place.

Keeping my hand fisted in his hair, I crouch back down beside him this time and whisper into his ear. "That was for putting your fucking tongue on her face. Do it again, and I'll cut the goddamn thing out." I let go of him, and his bloody face falls to hang over the bench.

"Stay the fuck away from her, Matt. This will be your only warning. I already took her from you once, and I can do it again." With that, the guys let go of their ends, and it slides off to the right of his back. The weight catches his body and shoves him to the floor with it.

I turn and walk toward the double doors to exit the gym when I hear him shout, "She does not belong to you. She will be my wife." He's screaming as the doors shut behind my exit. Taking the stairs down to the first floor, I head to my room to pack my bag for my trip home.

"What the fuck was that about?" Prickett charges into my room with Gunner behind him.

"Nothing," I lie. I'm not in the mood to go through this with them. My entire body is vibrating right now because I'm so pissed at Matt. At Blakely. I know it's not her fault, but the fact that I may have never found out doesn't sit right with me. And I can't even fucking tell her that because then she'll know she told me last night. *Fuck!*

"What the fuck, Ryat? That was not nothing." Gunner is the one who snaps.

I throw the bag on my bed and turn to face them. "I didn't need your help. So next time don't follow me and get involved."

Gunner snorts, and Prickett runs his hands through his hair.

"Listen ..." Prickett steps into me. "Things haven't been the same since you and Matt returned from Chicago last year. We all know it. We've all seen it. I don't know what the fuck went down there, but you need to get your shit together. Fighting in the Lords over a chosen ...?" He shakes his head. "That's the last thing you want to be seen doing."

I step into him, not about to back down. I love Prickett as a brother, but I'm not past breaking his fucking jaw. "Then he needs to keep his fucking hands off what's mine."

"Jesus, Ryat. Are you falling for her?" Gunner asks, wide-eyed.

"Fuck, no." I hiss at his dumb-ass question. "This is about Matt and him putting his hands on something that doesn't belong to him," I shout. "I didn't give him permission—"

"I'm going to stop you right there." Prickett interrupts me, placing his hands up and stepping back, giving me some space. "Did he fuck her?"

"No." I would have killed that sorry son of a bitch right there in the weight room and hung his body for all to see just to make a point.

"Then you can't go after him, Ryat. Unless he did something with your chosen without your permission, the Lords won't see your tantrum justified."

"Tantrum?" I give a rough laugh.

"What else would you call it?" Gunner shrugs.

My teeth fucking grind because I could explain it to them a million different ways, and they wouldn't understand.

Someone knocks on my bedroom door, and I snap, "What?"

It cracks open, and Sarah pokes her head in. Her eyes go from me to Prickett and then Gunner. "I'm headed to class," she tells him.

He looks at her, then back at me. After a long second, he sighs. "I'll walk you out." Then he leaves me alone with Prickett.

"I ..."

"Leave, Prickett." I'm over this conversation.

He hangs his head, rubbing the back of his neck. "I just hope you know what you're doing, Ryat. I'd hate for you to come this far and lose it over a piece of ass." Then he too turns and walks out, leaving me pissed off.

An hour later, I'm boarding my father's private jet when my cell rings in my pocket. Taking a seat in the white leather chair, I see it's a number that isn't saved and shows no name. Not uncommon.

"Hello?" I answer.

"Hello, Ryat."

I recognize his voice immediately and sit up straighter in my chair. I haven't spoken to him since I met him in the middle of the night in his office when he told me to choose Blakely. "Sir ..."

"I heard there was an issue this morning at the house of Lords."

My teeth grind. How the fuck does he know? Prickett and Gunner may not understand what I did, but they're not rats. There wasn't anyone else in the gym. And I know Sarah doesn't know what happened. That only leaves one possibility. Matt. He's already run his mouth to his daddy. Maybe he thinks if he can get me stripped of the Lords, he'll get Blakely sooner. Maybe that was his plan all along. Go to Blake, threaten her, thinking she'll run to me, and I'll attack him. Fuck, if that was his plan, I fed right into it and gave him exactly what he wanted.

"Yes, sir. It won't happen again," I lie. Matt needs to learn his lesson. If I need to do that again, then so be it. I'll face those consequences, when the time comes.

"No need," he says dismissively.

I frown and repeat. "No need?"

"Yes. I'm not aware of the details, and neither do I care. But just so we have an understanding." He pauses and clears his throat. "You do whatever the fuck is necessary to keep him away from her. And I'll make sure that these pesky rumors are never heard of."

A smile grows across my face. What the fuck has Matt done to piss off this man?

"Am I clear?" he asks at my silence.

"Yes, sir."

Click.

I sit back as the engines come to life on the jet, and that smile grows even bigger, making my cheeks hurt. This game just got a lot more fun.

THE TOWN CAR pulls up to the front of the Victorian mansion in Upstate New York where I grew up.

Getting out, I grab my bag and head up the steps. Before I can even reach the last one, the door swings wide open. My mom shrieks, placing her hands over her mouth before running to me.

"Ryat," she screams a little too loud in my ear as she hugs me tightly.

I drop my bag to hug her back. "Hey, Mom."

"Oh my God, I'm so glad you're home." She pulls away and cups my face with both of her hands. "You're such a grown man." I see the tears start to build in her soft blue eyes.

I never come home. It's not because of her or because of my dad. I just choose to be somewhere else. "I'm only here for the weekend," I remind her.

She smiles at me. "I know. But soon, you'll be living here again."

I don't respond to that.

"Son," my father calls out from inside the house.

"He's been waiting on you," she says softly.

Kissing her on the cheek, I reach down and grab my bag before walking inside.

"I'll take that." She jerks it from my hands. When I go to reach out for it, she adds, "I'll put it in your room." Then she turns and practically skips up the stairs.

Taking in a deep breath, I walk down the hallway and into his study to the right. He sits behind his desk, typing away on his computer.

"I'm glad you could make it home, son," he says, glancing up at me, then going back to his screen.

I fall into the brown leather couch. "You said it was important."

His cell phone rings, and he stands. "Give me a second." Dismissing himself from the room, he answers it.

I pull mine out and enter my passcode before pulling up my app that shows me the inside of Blake's apartment. She's lying in bed. She must have gone back to take a nap after her first class. I know she's tired. After her drunken state last night plus waking up after her dream, she didn't get much sleep.

She's on her right side, facing one of the cameras. The covers are shoved down to the footboard. All she wears is her thong. Her clothes are on the floor by her bed.

"Sorry about that," my father announces, entering, and I lock my cell before he can see what I'm looking at.

"It's fine." I shove it into my pocket and think of anything but her to ignore my hard cock.

He sits back behind his desk, undoing the button on his Armani suit jacket, his green eyes meeting mine. "Mr. Williams called me."

I roll my eyes. "Can't say I'm surprised. I'm sure I know what he wanted too."

He nods. "Cindy told him who you chose, and he wanted to know why."

"Did you tell him it's none of his goddamn business," I growl. God, that family is annoying. The fact that I have to marry into it gives me a migraine. And they keep overlooking the fact that no one chose her. That should be the first hint. I've seen Lords go to war over wanting the same chosen, while refusing to share her with one another.

"Well, she will be your wife—"

"Not by choice," I interrupt him, standing.

He sighs heavily. "Arranged marriages aren't uncommon in our social circle, Ryat."

I walk over to the window and look over the grounds. You can see the horse stables from here. My mom loves her horses. She's been riding since she was a kid. The only kind of horse my father likes are the ones that win him money at the track. "Yeah, well, as long as the prenup doesn't mention anything about remaining faithful." I give him a pointed look. "For either of us." She can fuck who she wants, and I'll fuck whoever I want. I don't want to get caught with my pants down around my ankles and her try to take me for everything I have.

He runs a hand down his face. "The Williamses aren't the issue right now."

"Then what is?" I ask, looking back out the window.

"Matt."

I tense. Does my father know what I did this morning? That Blakely is causing problems? He knows I had to choose her, but does he know why? I decide the best way to find out what he knows is to play stupid about what I did to Matt in the gym this morning.

I snort. "He's always a problem."

"I'm serious, Ryat. He's getting worried. He's offered to pay."

I look back at him and growl. "How much?" So, my knee to his face has made him desperate? He thinks I have the chance to take Blakely away from him.

"Fifty grand."

I roll my eyes. "The Winstons always have been fucking cheap."

"You saying you want to offer more?"

Walking back over to the couch, I sit down and arch a brow. "Since when is that an option?" He's got to be joking, but I'll see where it gets me.

He shrugs. "This isn't about you. It's about Matt." Leaning forward, he places his forearms on his desk. "So, I'm asking you ... How much more are we going to offer?"

"I'm going to marry Cindy," I argue. "Why would I make an offer for a woman who I have to toss to the side afterward?" His logic doesn't make any sense.

"I can't tell you that," he answers simply.

I roll my eyes. "Of course not. How do you even know he wants to *buy* her now?" He's trying to guarantee his future that I threatened to take away from him. He never wanted her. Matt is to marry Blakely because his father told him that's what he'll do. There's no other reason behind it. Now I have the fucker scared. I took his toy, and he knows it won't be clean and innocent when I'm done with it. No, it'll be dirty and tarnished. Used every way imaginable.

When she sucks and fucks his cock in a way that makes his head spin, his first thought will be—did Ryat teach her that? I damn sure did, you son of a bitch.

"I received a call," he answers vaguely.

And I don't ask any further questions because I know I won't get any answers.

"So, I'm going to ask you one more time." He speaks, and I come to a stop and look at him. "How much is she worth to you?"

TWENTY-TWO

BLAKELY

I LIE IN my bed dressed in a T-shirt and a pair of gray boy shorts, watching a Halloween movie and snacking on popcorn while having a glass of wine. Well, technically, I'm drinking it out of the bottle. It just sounded good.

Sarah is at the house of Lords, and I'm home alone because Ryat is out of town for the weekend. It's only Friday night, and I'm already going crazy bored with nothing to do. I've always been a homebody, but it's lonely without Sarah here with me. We've always been homebodies together. And I've spent every day with Ryat since the vow ceremony. It's just weird being here alone. The place seems so quiet.

My cell rings, and I pick it up to see it's Ryat. "Hello?" I answer before taking a swig from the bottle. I'm not nearly drunk. I still have over half left.

"Hey, little one," he says in greeting. "What are you doing?"

"Lying in bed." *I'm a real party animal.*

"Oh, yeah?"

"Yep. Bored as shit. You won't let me go out." I secretly like how controlling and possessive he is. It's like he's feeding a craving. But it's cruel that he tells me this and leaves me here alone. If I have house arrest, I'd much rather it be with him.

He chuckles. "Well, you wouldn't be bored if I was there."

My breathing picks up, and I take another drink. "What would you be doing to keep me busy?" I ask.

"Well, for starters, I'd rip that shirt off you along with that underwear. And I'd take that bottle of wine away from you."

I look up, forgetting he has cameras in this place. I still have no clue where they are in the apartment. But I have a feeling that they're in more places than just my bedroom. Something about knowing he watches me turns me on. I sink further into the bed, getting comfortable. "And?"

"I'd cuff your hands behind your back and then flip you over, pinning them underneath you." I groan at the image he gives me. "I'd then drag you across the bed where your head hangs off the side. I would order you to open your mouth so I could fuck it."

"Ryat," I moan his name as I lick my lips, imagining him in my mouth. I've only given him head that night during the vow ceremony.

"You'd have your legs spread wide open for me while I used a vibrator on your wet cunt. You'd come with my cock down your throat."

He's so vulgar with what he wants and how he wants it. I like that about him. I wish I was as open as him. It takes a lot for me to tell him what I want. I think that's due to so much rejection Matt gave me. He always made me feel dirty. Not just about my fantasies but anytime I showed him any kind of sexual desire. I think that's why I like the way Ryat takes control without me even having to ask.

Reaching up, I grab my breast over my shirt, knowing my nipples are hard.

"Blake," he warns. "Do not touch yourself."

I bang my head on the headboard. "No fair. You're getting me worked up on purpose. What time Sunday will you be back?" I change the subject.

"Not until Monday night," he answers.

"What? You said Sunday." It's only Friday. He left first thing this morning but never gave me a return time for Sunday. I was hoping for early morning.

"Something came up," he says vaguely.

That seems to happen a lot in his life. "Well, then I guess I'll see you Monday." I try not to sound sad or desperate. I went twenty years without sex. I can last three days.

We say our goodbyes, and I lie down, getting comfortable and turning the movie up.

RYAT

I UNLOCK THE door and enter. A quick look at my watch tells me it's almost one in the morning. I walk into the bedroom to find her lying on her left side, sound asleep. The popcorn still on the bed next to her with the TV on the Netflix home screen and empty wine bottle on the nightstand.

I drop the bag next to her and open it up. Reaching in, I pull out everything that I'm going to need. Then I go over to her dresser drawer and pull out a see-through thong. Walking back over to her, I grip the covers and rip them off her. She stirs, moving onto her stomach.

Perfect.

I get on the bed and grab her arms, gently pulling them behind her back and crossing her wrists. She moans, her head moving. I grab the zip tie and wrap it around them, securing it tightly.

"What ...?" she mumbles sleepily.

Then I reach up, grab a handful of her hair, and yank her face off the pillow. She screams, fully awake now. Sitting on her back, I reach around and shove the thong into her mouth and immediately grab the duct tape. Snapping a piece off with my teeth, I place it over her mouth, securing them inside, all the while she's kicking and mumbling into the gag.

I shove her face into the pillow while my free hand grabs the black drawstring bag. Letting go of her hair just for a second, she lifts her head to suck in a breath through her nose, and I shove the bag over her head and pull the drawstring, tying it off at the back of her neck to keep it in place, but loose enough where she can still breathe in fresh air through the bottom.

Getting off her, she's flopping around trying to free herself when I grab her legs and place another zip tie around her ankles. Then I throw her over my shoulder and carry her out of the apartment.

I take her out the side exit where I've already got my SUV parked. Opening the back, I place her on her stomach. I pick up the rope that I already had sitting in the back and quickly slide it between her tied wrists and then also slide it between her tied ankles, pulling it tight—hog-tying her.

Stepping back, I watch her fight the restraints, wearing herself down. She's mumbling nonsense through her gag, and her body is shaking. She can't see me through the bag over her head. I've taken all but her hearing away from her. And even that has to be limited by the rush of adrenaline—the blood rushing in her ears.

Placing my hand on her shoulder, I push her onto her side and rip her shirt up to expose her breasts to me. I reach out, wrapping one hand around her throat while the other squeezes her breast. I lean down and whisper, "Scream all you want, little one. You're mine now."

Then I slam the hatch shut.

———————

THIRTY MINUTES LATER, I pull off the highway to a gravel road and come up to the house. I get out and walk around the back of the SUV. She's still struggling on her side. Reaching into my pocket, I cut the rope but leave the zip ties. Her feet fall to the floor, and I pull her out of the back by her arm before once again throwing her over my shoulder and carrying her into the house.

Making my way down the hallway, I reach up and slap her ass, and she moans.

I kick the bedroom door open and toss her onto the bed. I was here earlier and prepared it by removing the comforter and top sheet, and dropping off what items I would need. Rolling her onto her stomach, I cut the zip tie that binds her arms, then shove her to her back as I straddle her chest.

She screams behind her gag, and her arms slap at me. But I easily grab her left hand and shove it through the slip knot I've already made in the rope that is secured to the bed frame. I then do the same with the right.

Getting off the bed, she kicks her zip-tied feet, twisting her body to the left and right. I walk down to the end of the bed and cut that tie as well. Then I secure each ankle to a bedpost with rope, wide apart, making her spread eagle. Then I stand at the end and look over her. Her shirt has ridden up in her struggle to expose her pierced belly button. My eyes travel down to her gray boy shorts. There's a wet spot.

I knew there would be. This was a fantasy of hers. Fuck Matt for making her feel ashamed for what she wants.

Walking around to the left side of the bed, I take the knife and place it on the inside of her leg. She stills, no longer screaming. Her heavy panting fills the room. I run the blade upward, being careful not to cut the skin, getting to her underwear. I slip it between the material and her skin, cutting them free.

She whimpers, body trembling. Placing my hand between her legs,

I cup her wet pussy. She arches her back, letting out a muffled cry.

I push my palm into her pelvic bone and grip her cunt. Thrusting my three fingers inside her and removing them quickly, I slap her pussy.

Her body jerks off the bed as a muffled cry follows. I slap it again, and she twists and turns, trying to close her legs.

Not happening, little one.

Crawling onto the bed, I sit next to her. I shove the bag up a little to expose her neck to me and wrap my left hand around it, holding her down to the mattress but not cutting off her air. Dropping the knife beside me, I cup her pussy again with my right hand, and this time, I finger-fuck her. Her body rocks back and forth on its own while she mumbles incoherent words behind her gag.

It doesn't take long before her pussy clamps down on me, and she comes.

Removing my fingers, I lick them clean one at a time as they pop out of my mouth. Tasting that sweet fucking honey.

Then I cut the rope that binds her legs. She yanks them closed and brings her knees up. I smile, forcing them apart with my hands and sitting between them. I unzip my pants and pull out my dick. It's been so hard since I called her earlier from the jet on my way back. I didn't stay in New York for very long. After my conversation with my father, I wanted the hell out of there and back here with her. Knowing this was an opportunity I didn't want to miss. She gave me the green light this morning in her bathroom to act out her fantasy however I wanted. Her thinking I was out of town all weekend was the best chance.

As I look at her tied and gagged with a hood over her head, knowing I'm taking advantage of her, I'm turned on just as much as she is.

I grip my cock and slide into her. She sucks me in, and I bite my tongue not to groan in pleasure.

Fuck!

I take the knife to her neck, and she stiffens once again. I cut the tie and rip the hood off her head. She blinks rapidly from the harsh light of the bedroom.

"Hello, little one," I say, smiling as my cock jerks inside her.

She blinks again, her pretty face covered in tears. I reach up and gently push the hair from her face, but I don't remove the tape. I have plenty of time to hear her scream my name over the weekend while we're here.

"So beautiful," I tell her

She whimpers.

I place the tip of the knife back to her neck, and she arches it, panting through her nose. I run it through her shirt, ripping it in half. Then I toss it to the floor.

She wraps her legs around my hips, and I lean forward. Gripping her chin, I turn her head to the side. I lick the tears off her cheek, and my hips start to move.

"Such a good girl for coming for me," I tell her. "I knew you would."

I pull back and slam forward. She pulls on the rope that binds her arms. Her hands are turning blue from how hard she's managed to tighten them. I had just made slip knots to slide them into for easy access because I didn't want to drug her. I needed her awake and aware of what was happening. So, I had to make things as easy as possible to restrain her while she fought me. She's made them tighter by pulling on them during her pointless fight.

I lean down, taking a nipple into my mouth. I suck on it as I fuck her. The bed bangs against the wall so hard, we may break it.

Her soaking wet cunt clamps down on me again, and she's coming.

"That's my girl," I say, licking my way up her chest to her neck. I kiss her racing pulse and slide my free hand under her head. I grip her hair, holding her in place while I sink my teeth into her neck, drawing her salty skin into my mouth, knowing I'll leave a big hickey there.

Letting go, I trail kisses up her chin and the duct tape, so I'm over her lips. I kiss them before pulling back. Her watery blue eyes meet mine before she closes them.

"Look at me," I order softly.

She opens them back up, and I grip the back of her knees, shoving her legs wide open for me, but my eyes fall to watch my cock slide in and out, covered in her cum. Biting my lip, I pound into her, making her tits bounce and her eyes fall closed. She's coming again once more as I am.

TWENTY-THREE

BLAKELY

HE REMOVES THE tape from my face, the sting making me flinch, and pulls the underwear from my mouth. I immediately start sobbing. He undoes my arms and pulls my trembling body into his.

I knew it was Ryat before he even spoke to me. I have the feel of his hands down. I know the touch of his lips. And I know how he fucks. My body has never been so alive. I've never come so hard in my life. I guess that's not saying much since he's the only guy I've ever slept with. But even when I fantasized about it in the past, I've never come like that.

"Shh," he soothes me while I lie on my side, my face buried into his shirt in this unfamiliar bedroom. "You're okay," he says, rubbing my bare back.

I squint my eyes shut and try to catch my breath, letting him hold me like he cares. "I feel guilty," I admit softly.

He pulls me away from him and runs his hand down my face, wiping away the tears. "Don't. Don't do that to yourself, Blake."

"I got off." I swallow the lump in my throat. "I liked it." Shame washes over me like a heavy wave.

"That's okay," he tells me. "It was a fantasy, Blake. I wanted you to enjoy it."

A small part of me is relieved that I enjoyed it, but the bigger part is ashamed of that. The fact that he took my sight, voice, and restrained me had my body screaming with joy. I laid in the back of the car crying and breathing into that hood, so turned on. I kept hearing Matt's voice, saying how fucked up I am. How wrong my body was to be enjoying it.

He pulls away, reaching out for the nightstand. Then he's handing me a bottle of water. "Here, drink this."

I sit up and take a drink, my hands shaking so bad, I miss my mouth, and some runs down my exposed chest. Taking another, I hand it back to him and rub my tear-streaked face. Lying back down, I sniff, and he settles back down next to me, pulling me close once again, hugging me.

"I'm sorry," I whisper, not really sure what I'm sorry for exactly. It just feels like the right thing to say to him at the moment.

"Don't be." He sighs. "There's no reason to be sorry. Fantasies don't hurt anyone, Blake." Feeling his lips on my hair, he kisses it softly. I close my eyes and let him hold me while I try to calm my breathing and stop crying. It feels like hours, but my body starts to relax. Everything hurts. My body is exhausted. Pulling away from him, I lie on my back and stare up at the ceiling.

"You okay?" he asks, reaching out and rubbing my stomach.

I nod. "Where are we?"

"My house."

I look over at him, and his emerald eyes are staring at me intently. "Yours?"

"Yeah. I bought it a couple of years ago, but I never get to stay here. I'm always at house of Lords. I thought of bringing you here because I didn't want to act it out at your apartment. I wanted to take you away from there and give you a new environment. You said in your dream that he drags you off into the woods. I wanted you to use your imagination to see where it would take you. Give you control of where you thought you were going."

I sit up and place my hand on his shirt and notice he's still dressed in his clothes. "Thank you," I tell him. He did something that Matt refused to do. Ryat just listened to me. He didn't judge me. He asked what I wanted, and then he gave me exactly that.

He lifts my hand to his lips and kisses my knuckles. "How do you feel?"

"Better," I say truthfully.

"Tell me about it," he urges. "Is there anything you didn't like about it?"

I blush, wishing he'd turn the lights off so he couldn't see my face. "No."

"Is it something that you want to do again?"

I nod, biting my bottom lip nervously.

He reaches out, pulling it free from my teeth, running the pad of his thumb across it. His eyes follow before they meet mine again. "What would you want done differently?"

"I don't know."

"Blake." He sighs. "I'm more than willing to do what you want, but you have to tell me what that is."

Looking away from him, I feel tears start to sting my eyes again with shame. "I ..." That lump returns, and I can't seem to swallow it down.

He grips my chin gently and forces me to look over at him. "What?"

"I just don't want the choice," I whisper. My body likes to be dominated. However he wants to do that is okay. It's terrifying but also exciting. To me, giving him the power over me gives me power. It's freeing. It doesn't make any fucking sense to me, but that's what feels the best. I thought I would like the surprise factor, but it ended up being the biggest turn-on.

He nods. "Okay." Leaning in, he kisses my forehead tenderly before pulling my body back into his. "Did you like the fact that I spoke to you? I wanted to make sure you knew it was me without ruining it for you."

"I knew it was you before you even spoke," I tell him.

"Yeah?" He arches a brow. "Well, I'll take that as a compliment."

I chuckle and try changing the subject. "Why are you back?"

"I came back early for you," he answers through a yawn.

My brows rise. "You weren't even gone for twenty-four hours."

"I hate New York," he states.

I don't mention Matt told me that Ryat will one day be a judge there. I doubt he knows everything. He was probably just lying anyway to put thoughts in my head.

"Are you hungry?" he asks.

"No." I yawn and stretch out my heavy limbs.

"Get some rest. You must be tired," he says, pulling away from me. A hint that he's not coming to bed with me.

"What time is it?" I ask, all of a sudden feeling drained.

He looks at his cell. "Almost two thirty." Then he bends down and picks up the top sheet. He lays it across the bed and then does the same with the comforter that's folded over in the corner.

I close my eyes and yawn once again. I'm about to pass the fuck out when I open my eyes to see him walking toward the door. "Hey,

Ryat?"

He turns to face me. "Yeah?"

"Thank you," I say again.

"You don't have to thank me, little one," he says, turning off the light and then exiting the room.

I roll over and pull the covers up to my neck and close my eyes, hearing him shut the door as he exits, not giving two fucks about taking a shower right now.

RYAT

SUNDAY NIGHT, I'M standing in the bathroom at the sink brushing my teeth. Spitting out the toothpaste, I turn around and watch Blakely in the bathtub. She's relaxing back with her head on a white pillow and her eyes closed. Her hair is up in a messy bun. Some pieces have fallen down around her face and are wet. Her left knee is bent, popping out of the bubbles that fill the Jacuzzi tub.

I walk over to the side and sit down on the edge. Placing my hand on her knee, I slide it down to her inner thigh, my hand dipping into the scorching hot water. She jumps, her eyes springing open at the touch. "Were you sleeping?" I ask her.

"No," she answers through a yawn.

I laugh at that lie. "Come on." I tap her thigh. "I don't want you falling asleep in here and drowning."

"Aw, you do care about me." She smiles.

"Can't fuck a dead chick," I joke. Well, you can, but then again, that's not a kink I'm into.

She throws some bubbles at me, landing on my shirt. I stand, and she reaches out, grabbing my hand to stop me. "Can we stay here tonight? We can get up extra early in the morning to head back."

"Sure." I wasn't planning on leaving this late anyway. I know she's tired, and frankly, so am I. Leaving the bathroom, I enter the master suite. I just lie down in bed when my cell goes off on the nightstand. Picking it up, I see it's a text from Prickett.

Turn on the TV.

Frowning, I pick up the remote next to my phone and point it at the flat screen that hangs on the wall. It comes on, and I don't even have to change the channel. A news crew stands outside of a home here in Pennsylvania. Police cars, ambulances, and a coroner van are gathered in the large driveway of the three-story, white brick mansion.

"What's going on?" Blake asks, walking out of the bathroom.

I look over at her dressed in nothing but a short towel, and my first thought is to throw her on the bed and fuck her. But I dismiss it and put my eyes back on the TV. "Not sure," I answer honestly.

A brunette steps into the camera, holding a mic to her face. "A manhunt has been issued," she announces. "Behind me, you'll see the police and FBI are at the Mallory family's home ..."

"Oh, shit," I whisper, sitting up straighter.

"Who is that?" Blake asks. "You know them?"

I nod in answer.

"All we know right now is that there was forced entry with one fatality ..."

"Fuck," I hiss, my hands going to my head.

"What?" Blake demands. "What's wrong?"

If it's who I think it is, heads are about to roll. Gregory Mallory is a very important Lord here in Pennsylvania. With a list a mile long of people who would want him dead. His position has enemies lined up wanting his head.

"Ryat ...?" Blake snaps, trying to get my attention to answer her question, but I ignore her.

Three FBI agents exit the front doors of the home and walk over to the reporter. "Shut this down." You hear one demand to the woman.

"I'm Jane, with News One. We're allowed to be ..."

He cuts her off by taking her mic while the other one slams the camera down onto the ground. The picture goes blurry, and they cut back to the station.

I turn it off.

"Ryat, what's going on?" Blake demands.

My phone ringing keeps me from having to acknowledge her. I answer when I see it's my father. "Hello?" I ask, getting out of bed and walking into the living room.

"You see that shit?" he growls.

"Yeah. What the fuck happened?" I demand, catching Blake now standing in the living room at the end of the hallway, arms crossed over her chest, watching me.

"There was a hit out on Gregory. But he wasn't home—"

"Wait," I interrupt him. "They said one fatality. Who the hell did they kill?"

"Remy," he answers.

I fall onto the couch and place my face in my hand. "Fuck." I sigh.

It's worse than I thought.

"Yeah," my father agrees.

I pull it away from my ear to look at the screen when it vibrates. It's a text.

House of Lords. Now!

"I gotta go," I tell him, not even bothering to wait for a response. Standing, I look at her. "Get dressed. We're leaving."

She places her arms out wide, and the towel drops to her feet. "In what? I don't have anything to wear. You cut my shirt and my underwear." Arching a brow, she places her hands on her narrow hips.

My eyes take a second to run over the bruises that cover her body in various places along with my teeth marks. She's got two hickeys— one on her neck, the other on her inner thigh. We've spent all weekend here at my cabin doing nothing but fucking, and I'm still hard. "I have clothes you can wear." I point at the bedroom, ignoring my cock. Now is not the time. We've got to go. "Grab a T-shirt and a pair of sweatpants out of my closet. We're leaving in five minutes."

Thankfully, she doesn't argue with me anymore and goes to get dressed.

"Are you going to tell me what's going on?" she asks the moment we're in my SUV speeding down the highway to get back to the house of Lords.

"I can't," I say honestly.

"Can't or won't?" she snaps, getting irritated.

I shift in my seat. "Can't. I took an oath ..."

She snorts. "Matt used to always say that shit. It was a lie then too."

I give her a quick glance to see she's glaring out the passenger window. The fact that she even mentioned him pisses me off. "Look, even if I could tell you, I wouldn't because it's none of your damn business," I snap.

"Right." She looks over at me. "Sometimes I need a reminder that the only reason you're fucking me is to piss off Matt."

My hands tighten on the steering wheel. "Blake ..."

"So, thanks for that, Ryat," she adds with bite.

"Blake," I snap in warning.

She huffs, crossing her arms over her chest and sitting back in her seat.

I turn up "If You Want Love" by NF to drown out my thoughts and anything else she has to say.

WE'RE WALKING INTO the house of Lords when we run into Sarah and Gunner. She eyes me warily, and I wonder if any rumors are being spread in the house while I'm away regarding Matt and me.

"Where have you two been?" Sarah asks, looking over at Blakely. "You guys have been MIA all weekend."

"We've been staying at the apartment," she answers her.

"We were just there yesterday." Sarah looks at Gunner. "I was actually worried. Your room was destroyed. Stuff kicked over. Looked like there was a struggle of some sort."

Blake's cheeks flush at the same time Matt walks around the corner. I don't miss the black eye he has from my knee connecting with his face the last time I saw him. "We went out to my cabin for the weekend," I answer Sarah's previous question, not taking my eyes off his until he disappears down another hallway before Blake can even see him.

"We left in a hurry," Blake jokes.

"Well, I'm glad you guys are back." Sarah smiles at her.

"Actually, we're just grabbing a few things, then going back to the apartment," I inform them.

"Oh." Her face falls. "I have been texting and calling you all weekend, and you never answered," she tells her.

Blake frowns, and I look at Gunner. He pretends like he's not listening and looks away to the grand staircase.

"Hmm," Blake adds. "I didn't have anything on my phone from you. Maybe I didn't have any reception. We were out pretty far."

I grab Blake's hand, ending this conversation and pulling her away and down the hall to my room.

After I close the door, I turn to her. "I have to attend a meeting," I tell her.

She just stares at me, her pretty blue eyes still heated from earlier. She hasn't spoken directly to me since I snapped at her on the way here.

"Stay in here. I'll come back when I'm done." With that, I turn and exit the room to see Gunner and Sarah in the hallway.

"Sarah is going to hang out with Blakely while we're occupied," he tells me.

I nod and open my bedroom door for her. Sarah doesn't even look at me as she enters, and I yank it shut harder than I mean to.

Gunner laughs. "Trouble in paradise already?"

"Let's get this over with." I ignore him and shoulder past him.

TWENTY-FOUR

RYAT

Stepping off the elevator, Gunner and I step into the basement. The bunker was added after the hotel was given to the Lords. It's an armory down here. More guns, ammo, and weapons we could ever need. It's also where we hold all our important meetings.

The walls are matte black with racks of guns hanging on the far wall. The right wall has knives of various sizes and colors.

There's a black table in the center of the room. Enough seats to fit fifty people. I notice that only the seniors are present. I plop down next to Prickett, ignoring Matt, who sits across from me. Gunner takes the seat to my right.

Lincoln enters the room and doesn't waste any time. Clapping his hands, he gets started. "I'm guessing everyone has seen the news by now and is aware of what's happened."

"Yes," everyone says in unison.

He takes the chair at the head of the table. "I need two volunteers for an assignment. I can't give you any other details other than the job might take a day, might take three weeks. That all depends on how long it takes you to get it done."

I'm about to volunteer when I hear Matt speak. "Ryat and I will handle it."

Gunner's wide eyes shoot to mine while Prickett runs a hand down his face.

"Ryat?" Lincoln looks at me, relaxing back in his chair, waiting for confirmation.

I can't say no. If I do, it'll prove to everyone in here I have a problem with Matt. "Sounds good, sir," I say and then clench my hand in my lap. *Motherfucker!*

"Perfect. You all are dismissed." Lincoln stands and exits in a hurry. I'm sure to go get updated on whatever I'm about to be doing.

"Are you fucking serious?" Prickett snaps in my face the moment we're out of the room and jumping on the elevator. Thankfully, it's just him, Gunner and me. The others stayed behind.

"What was I supposed to say?" I growl.

"No. That you refuse to work with him."

I snort at that.

"He's obviously setting you up." He goes on.

"Let him." I shrug.

"Ryat ..."

"I don't give a fuck about him right now." I snap at Prickett and put my attention on Gunner. "I need a favor from you."

"I've got it covered." He nods, already knowing what I was going to ask.

"Thanks, man." The elevator dings and stops on the first floor. We exit, and Lincoln stands there.

"May I have a moment?" he asks me.

"Yeah," I tell him as Gunner and Prickett walk off down the hall, leaving us alone. "What's up?"

"Sure you want to do this?" he asks.

"Doubting me?" I arch a brow.

He chuckles. "Never." His face gets serious, and he checks his watch. "All I know is that you've got five hours. So, I'd make sure your girl is home and in bed asleep before you leave."

BLAKELY

"IS EVERYTHING OKAY?" Sarah asks me while we sit on Ryat's bed.

"Yeah."

"Why do I feel like you're lying to me?" She laughs softly.

I sigh, pulling the hair tie loose from my hair. The messy bun was falling anyway. "Does Gunner tell you anything about the Lords?"

"Nope." She shakes her head. "And I'm totally fine with that. I'd rather not know."

"It drives me nuts," I admit. "Like what the fuck could they possibly be doing that's so secretive?"

"Listen, Blakely ..." She takes my hands in hers. "Whatever you're thinking, let it go. Okay? I've heard some shit while staying here, and you're much better off not knowing."

"Like what?" I urge.

Letting go of my hands, she tucks a piece of hair behind her ear. "They ..."

The door opens, and she jumps when I look up to see Ryat and Gunner both enter the room. "Hey, babe. Come on." Gunner stands in the doorway, holding the door open, obviously taking her away from me.

She looks back at me, giving me a soft smile. "I'll see you in class tomorrow."

I nod, pissed that they interrupted whatever she was about to tell me, but I guess waiting until morning isn't too bad.

Ryat enters his bathroom, and I get up, following him. He turns on the sink and bends over, splashing water on his face. "Are we staying here tonight?" I ask him.

"No," comes his clipped answer before yanking a hand towel off a hook and running it down his face. Then he just tosses it onto the counter. "We're headed to your apartment." Then he walks past me, going back to his bedroom.

"How long are we going to do this?" I ask, following him.

"Don't, Blake," he snaps. "I'm not in the mood right now."

"Maybe I'm not in the mood to put up with your shit," I push.

He spins around, his hand goes to my throat and shoves me back into the wall. So hard it knocks the air out of my lungs. His face lowers to mine, our lips almost touching, and his green eyes are slits on mine with a tic in his sharp jaw.

I almost forgot how terrifying he could be. He's been nice, understanding even. But it reminds me that this is just an agreement, and I'm nothing to him. Like I said in the car, I'm just here so he can piss off Matt.

"I said I'm not doing this right now. And I meant that. So, unless you want to really see me pissed, I suggest you back the fuck off." His voice is low, his words controlled, but his hand around my throat is shaking, giving away his true feelings at the moment.

I wonder if it's me or something else. Lifting my chin, my lips thin. "I understand."

Letting go of my neck, he steps away. "Let's go."

We exit his room, and I look up across the hall to see Matt walking out of a room. His eyes meet mine, and he gives me a smile. It makes the hairs on the back of my neck rise. His blue eyes go to Ryat, and I notice the black eye that he has. What the hell happened to him? Did Ryat do that? Are they fighting? Is that why Ryat is on edge? Did Matt say something to him about me? It's not like Matt knows any secrets about me. I never got the chance to do anything crazy.

"See you soon," Matt speaks, nodding his head to Ryat with that smile still on his face.

Ryat grabs my hand and yanks me down the hall. I look back at him over my shoulder just as the bleach blonde exits Matt's room, pulling him back into it and shutting the door behind them.

WE ENTER MY apartment, and I'm on edge. I don't like not knowing what's going on. Especially when it could involve me.

"What did Matt mean?" I ask Ryat as we enter my bedroom. "Why will he see you soon?"

"Not now." He sighs heavily, scratching the back of his neck.

"Ryat ..."

"Blake," he snaps, pinning me with a glare. Releasing a sigh, he slowly walks over to me.

I don't move. Coming up to me, he slides his hand in my hair and licks his lips. "Can we just go to bed? It's been a long weekend and an even longer day. We can discuss it tomorrow."

My eyes search his, and I hate that I can't tell if he's lying or not. I knew Matt well enough to tell if he was trying to avoid a conversation or just me in general. Ryat is harder to read.

Nodding, I say, "Sure."

Leaning in, he gives my forehead a soft kiss. "I'll get you a water." He pulls away and goes into the kitchen while I remove his T-shirt and sweatpants before crawling into my cold sheets.

I am tired. I thought I was going to pass out at his cabin, but then the events that followed woke me up really quick.

"Here you go," Ryat says, entering the room with a glass of water for me.

"Thanks." I take it from him and drink more than half of it, not realizing how thirsty I was.

He takes it and sets it on my nightstand before crawling in bed next to me. "Sweet dreams, Blake." He kisses my forehead again, pulling my back into his front.

My last thought is that we won't be having that conversation in the morning.

TWENTY-FIVE

RYAT

WITHIN MINUTES, I hear her softly snoring. The drug working fast. She hasn't eaten in hours. I slipped a sleeping pill into her water while in the kitchen. I needed her out in order to leave without her asking questions. I was tired of not being able to answer them. Not only because of the oath I took, but also because I have no fucking clue what I'm going to be doing. I didn't trust to leave her at the house of Lords, so I had to get her back here and asleep as soon as possible.

Pulling out from underneath her, she doesn't even move. She'll be pissed at me when she wakes in the morning, but I'll deal with that when I'm done with my assignment.

Getting out of bed, I exit her room just as Gunner and Sarah walk through the front door. "Give us a second," he tells her, and she heads to her room at the other end of the apartment.

"She's out. Will be all night," I tell him.

He nods once.

"I'll let you know what's going on as soon as I can." He understood that I wanted him and Sarah to stay here with her while I'm gone. I may not be able to control what she does or where she goes while I'm working. I still don't want her up at the house of Lords even if Matt is away, so I needed to give her a reason to stay away. Sarah being here is as good as I could come up with in such a short time.

"Of course. Just be careful." His eyes go to her closed bedroom door. "And don't worry about her. I'll make sure nothing happens to her while you're gone."

My cell vibrates in my pocket, and it's a text from a blocked number.

Opening it up, I see it's the address of the cathedral. Without saying another word, I exit and head out.

———————

THIRTY MINUTES LATER, I'm walking inside the double doors of the cathedral tucked back in the woods. I look around to see I'm alone. But that victory is short-lived when the doors creak open behind me, and Matt steps inside.

"It'll be like old times." He gives me a fucking grin when I turn to face him.

"Try not to kill an innocent this time." I make a jab at him. But instead of taking offense, he just laughs.

The doors open, and we both turn to face the three men who enter. All three wear black cloaks and white masks over their faces to hide their true identity.

My pulse quickens, and my heart begins to race at the adrenaline pumping through my veins. I forgot how much I've missed this. The action. This is the part of the Lords that I love. I'm not going to pretend not to like the violence. I love it.

"Gentlemen," the one on the far right speaks.

Matt steps toward them.

All three raise guns at us. "Hands up," one orders.

I raise mine as does Matt.

"Turn around. Lie on your stomachs with your hands behind your backs," the one in the middle demands.

Doing as I'm told, I smile to myself. Let the game begin.

TWENTY-SIX

RYAT

I'M YANKED TO a stop and shoved into a chair where each wrist is pulled down to my sides and cuffed to a back leg. My ankles are then also cuffed to the front legs. The hood that's been covering my face is ripped off, and I suck in a breath of fresh air as I blink and look around.

We're in a warehouse of some kind. A quick glance tells me it's underground. No windows, no doors. Just an elevator at the other end of the large space. Concrete floors and walls.

I try to rock the chair from side to side to see how much it'll take for me to break it, but it's no use. The bitch is cemented down to the damn floor. A steel table sits in front of me that I bet is also cemented down.

"A little overkill," I say, testing the cuffs themselves, but they're the real deal, cinched down tight. I know that Blake secretly likes these damn things, and I don't know why.

"Are these necessary?" Matt growls, secured to the chair next to me. The chains to his restraints clank as he tries to break free as well.

After we were cuffed and the hood was placed over our heads, we were dragged out of the cathedral and thrown into a vehicle of some kind.

The officer who stands to my right with his hands on his belt says nothing. Another quick look around tells me that the three guys who picked us up are nowhere to be seen. They were delivery boys and nothing else.

The elevator dings, getting our attention seconds before it slides open. Gregory Mallory himself steps off it. I've never met him before. A ruthless, powerful motherfucker who has a target on his back. The sorry bastard who tried his shot, missed him. I'm guessing that's why we're here. He's followed by two other men. They look like they work for the FBI—three-piece black suits, sunglasses, and earpieces. But none of them resemble the men I saw on the TV.

He pulls the only other seat out from across the table from us and sits down. I notice his moves. Pulling a picture out of the pocket of his Tom Ford Windsor suit jacket, he slams it down and slides it to the center of the table in front of us. "Erik Bates. Remember the name, brand the fucking face into your goddamn memory," he orders.

I look down at it. The guy has jet-black hair, pale skin, and a face tattoo of a fucking Chinese star on his cheek. Hard to forget. "Got it," I say.

"Don't fucking play, boy." He shoots up from his chair, knocking it over as his hand slaps me across the face so hard that if the chair I'm chained to wasn't cemented down, I'd be on my ass.

Taking in a deep breath, I glare up at him. "I said, I fucking got it."

"I want his head!" He stabs the photo with his finger. "I want his fucking balls. I want him in fucking pieces." He slams his fisted hands on the table, making it rattle.

"Anything else?" Matt asks sarcastically.

Gregory bares his teeth at Matt. "If you two do not get it done, I will make sure you rot in a maximum-security prison for the rest of your goddamn lives," he warns.

Matt chuckles. "I like anal. What about you, Ryat?"

"As long as I'm the pitcher," I say, playing along with whatever game Matt is playing.

"Of course," he adds. Then looks up at him. "I'm sure we can find someone who will willingly be our bitch."

Gregory reaches across the table, grabbing his shirt, and tries to pull him toward him, but Matt doesn't go far. When he realizes Matt's cuffed to the damn chair, he slams the side of his face into the table instead. "I'll have your fucking heads ..."

The officer clears his throat, cutting him off. Gregory lets go and shoves him back. Matt very slowly rolls his neck around. Then leans over and spits some blood onto the concrete floor.

"Get it done." With that, he turns and stomps over to the elevator, his two merry men once again on his ass.

The officer removes the keys to the cuffs from his pocket and undoes my wrists first, followed by my ankles. I stand and stretch as he goes to free Matt.

"Don't get too comfortable." The man finally speaks and adds, informing us, "They're going right back on."

BLAKELY

I WAKE UP and groan, rolling over. My body hurts so much. My pussy feels swollen and tender. I think it was from Ryat slapping it. But fuck, it felt amazing at the time.

Grabbing my phone, I see it's a little after ten in the morning. I had gotten seven and a half more hours of sleep after he woke me up in my room and kidnapped me. I get out of bed and make my way to the bathroom. I never did clean myself up after we had sex last night. At that point, I just didn't fucking care.

After using the restroom and taking a nice hot shower, I exit the bedroom to look for Ryat. "Hello?" I call out, walking down a long hallway. I gasp, throwing my arms around my naked body when I step out into an open room. It's the living room.

Nothing but high ceilings with massive windows. The thought of someone seeing me makes me jump back, using the hallway to shield my body. But getting a better look outside, I see it's nothing but woods.

"Ryat?" I ask, but only silence follows.

Going back into the bedroom, I grab the sheet that's been shoved to the end of the bed and wrap it around me. I walk over to the dark gray curtains that hang from the ceiling and pull them back to showcase more woods on the other side of the floor-to-ceiling windows. It's beautiful out here. It has two glass doors that open to a back porch. My hand wraps around the doorhandle but I stop myself, needing to go find him first.

Walking back down the hallway, I look over the bare walls. The furniture is black leather. No rugs, pictures, or artwork in the house whatsoever. If I didn't know Ryat owned it, I'd say that it's vacant.

The kitchen is what any chef would call a dream—all stainless steel appliances, three ovens, two refrigerators, and one large walk-in freezer. The pantry alone is as big as my bedroom at my apartment.

I start to walk up the stairs but pause, realizing I don't have my cell on me. Going back to the bedroom, I pick it up and call him.

"Hello?" he answers on the first ring.

"Where are you?" I ask, looking around the bedroom as if he's going to appear.

"I had to run to Barrington. I didn't want to wake you."

Oh. "How far is that from here?"

"Thirty minutes. I should be back in a couple of hours."

"Okay. I'll see you then." We hang up, and I go into the kitchen and make myself some coffee. I'm going to need it. I could seriously go back to sleep right now.

Once it's done, I open the sliding glass door and walk outside onto the back patio and sit down in a chair. Looking around, I see that it wraps around the whole back of the house. I bet it goes around the front too.

I look to the left, and you can see a gravel driveway from where I am. My heart picks up when I see Ryat's SUV parked in plain sight.

He's here.

That's what he drove me here in. It wasn't his car or mine because he put me in the back. I could tell by the amount of room I had.

My breathing becomes heavy as my cell dings, and I look down at it to see I've received a picture message.

I open it up, and it's of me a second ago while I was sitting down on the porch with my coffee. It was taken from the tree line, but it's from a private number.

I set the coffee on the table. "Hello?" I call out.

The only sound I hear is the birds. My cell dings again, and I read the message.

Come find me.

I place my phone by the coffee and walk down the stairs. My bare feet feel the softness of the grass. Making my way down the path, I get closer to the tree line. I look where it seems the picture was taken from, but no one is there. "Hello?" I ask, circling back around to look at the house. "Ryat? I know you're here." I smile, realizing why he brought me out here. We're going to live out my fantasy several times this weekend.

Someone stands on the back porch dressed in dark jeans and a black T-shirt, a white mask covering their face.

My heart rate accelerates as they take the first step. My mind tells me that it's Ryat, but my skin starts tingling because I can't be a hundred percent sure.

Second step, third step. Slowly, he makes his way down them. When his boots hit the grass, he stops.

The hairs on the back of my neck stand up, feeling his stare. I grip the sheet tighter around me, knowing I'm naked underneath it out in the open. What if someone sees us? That thought has my pussy clenching.

He takes his first step toward me, and I turn, running away from him farther into the trees. I look back over my shoulder, and he's gone.

I stop, my heart pounding and panting from the short run. Turning my head, I feel my hair slap me in the face. I reach up and push it off my face when someone grips it from behind me.

I scream out, my scalp tingling from the action. He drags me backward, and my hands come up to grip my hair, causing me to lose the sheet completely, exposing my body.

He brings me to a stop and shoves me to the ground. I manage to roll over onto my back as he drops to his knees, straddling me.

His hands wrap around my neck, and he squeezes, taking away my air before I even have the chance to yell for help.

My hands dig into the ground while my hips lift, and I arch my back. My pussy throbs as he spreads my legs wide for him. My bare feet kick the loose dirt and tree limbs as I fight to breathe. My face throbs, and blood rushes in my ears, but my pussy is wet and my nipples hard. Dots start to dance around, blurring my vision.

He lets go, and I begin to cough as I suck in a shaky breath while he unzips his jeans and pulls out his hard dick. He grips my legs, dragging me closer to him, my back scraping against the uneven ground, and enters me without any foreplay. I cry out before his hands are back around my throat, taking my air away.

I lie in the middle of the woods while he fucks me with both hands wrapped around my throat. The feel of branches and rocks under me, scratching my naked body. I come, unable to make a single noise. This time, those dots grow larger, my head pounds harder, and just as my eyes start to roll into the back of my head, he lets out a feral growl, stiffening as he comes inside me.

He pulls out just as my eyes close. Unable to open them, let alone breathe now, I feel him lift me into his arms and carry my limp body back to the house, knowing I now need a new shower.

My eyes spring open, and I sit up in my bed. I blink a few times, waiting for my eyes to adjust to the dark room. I'm back at my apartment. Soft light filters in from underneath my black curtains that Ryat had hung up over my window.

Getting up, I make my way to the bathroom. After using the restroom, I turn the sink on and splash my face. The dream of what we did at his cabin has my body wide awake.

We did nothing but fuck all day Saturday and most of Sunday. Hell, he even woke me up twice. I have never been so sore in my life. I'm pretty sure I have a UTI, considering it burned when I went pee.

Of course, that could be due to the fact he fucked me in the middle of the woods. You know, tree branches, dirt, and all of that probably wasn't the best idea.

Turning the water off, I dry off my face and exit the bathroom. I go to turn off the light but pause. It helps illuminate my bedroom, and I see that I was alone in my bed.

That's odd but not uncommon. He must be in my living room or the kitchen. I swear the man never sleeps. He fucks me to the point I black out, and whenever I wake up, he's already awake.

Going over to my bed, I pick up a T-shirt and pull it on before opening my bedroom door. I let out a shriek when I see Gunner standing in my kitchen. My hands immediately going to my chest, forgetting I'm wearing a shirt.

"What's wrong?" Sarah asks, rushing out from down her hall.

"I scared her," Gunner states, smiling. Enjoying himself.

I huff and agree. "It was unexpected." Then giving a quick look around, I frown when I don't see who I was expecting. "Where's Ryat?" I ask.

"He's on an assignment," Gunner answers.

I frown. "What do you mean an assignment?"

"I mean, he's gone."

"He just left?" I ask, trying to understand what he means. My mind is a little slow this morning.

He nods. "Yep. He'll return when he's done." With that, he goes to walk out of the kitchen.

"Well, when will that be?" I demand.

He shrugs. "Don't know. But don't try to contact him. He won't answer."

What the fuck? He just up and left? No goodbye? No hey, I'll see you later? Nothing.

Storming into the kitchen, I go to get a drink because my tongue feels like sandpaper, and I see a bottle of pills on the counter. Picking them up, I read them over. They're sleeping pills. My mom takes them. "Did he ...?" My voice trails off when I remember him grabbing me water last night. He always gives me a bottle, but it had been in a cup. I didn't even question it. I've put too much trust in him.

"Gunner?" I snap.

"Yeah?" He reappears back into the kitchen.

I hold the bottle up. "Did Ryat know last night that he was leaving for an assignment?"

He looks from me to Sarah, who crosses her arms over her chest

184

and arches a brow at him. Running a hand through his hair, he looks uneasy, silently answering my question.

"Dammit," I growl, throwing them across the room. They hit the wall and shatter open. *Fuck him!*

TWENTY-SEVEN

RYAT

I'M SHOVED INTO a chair with my hands cuffed behind my back and my legs shackled.

The female officer looks down her nose at me and smirks. "Good luck, pretty boy." Laughing, she exits the room.

I was brought in here three hours ago. It took them that long to book me, strip search me, and change me into my new orange jumpsuit. After our meeting with Gregory, Matt and I were cuffed and placed in squad cars. We've officially been arrested on bogus crimes and booked under fake names. Come to find out, our target is in jail. Just our luck.

The door opens, and Gregory enters.

My eyes go to the right upper corner to see the red blinking light turn off on the camera. He sits down across from me.

"Two times in the same night," I say, wondering why I'm seeing him again. Didn't he say all he needed to say earlier in the warehouse? Otherwise, why not just come speak to us here instead of before?

"I hear you're the best, Ryat," he says, leaning back in the seat.

"I wouldn't believe everything you hear," I counter.

He snorts. "Most of the best ones are the cockiest in their field."

"What do you want?" I ask, getting to the point.

"I want to make sure you understand the situation."

I tilt my head to the side, running my tongue along the front of my top teeth. "I understand you want revenge on that sorry piece of shit for killing your son." I don't blame him. The bastard who was going to take him out killed his six-year-old son, Remy, instead. I can't even fathom what this man feels right now. I'm the type of man who would never trust my revenge in someone else's hands. I'd take them out myself. I'd want to see the life drain out of their eyes as they choke on their own blood from my hands.

He looks up, checking to make sure the light is shut off as well before leaning forward. "I gave the order to kill him. But the cops who found the motherfucker arrested him and booked him instead."

I frown. Matt and I weren't given any details, so why is he telling me this now? Especially since Matt isn't present. They placed him in a separate room from me after we were done being booked. "You think they're on his payroll?"

He sighs. "I'm not sure what the fuck to think."

"Why are you telling me this?"

"I've got word that he's in solitary confinement."

"Why would they do that?" Gregory has put most of these men in their cells. So, why would they hide his son's killer? Most of these men would praise him. Hiding him doesn't make much sense. Especially if they went against Gregory's demand and arrested him when they were supposed to shoot to kill. No questions asked. A dead man can't defend himself sort of speak.

"I'm not sure. The best I can think of is they know I'd send in someone to finish the job they weren't able to do."

I nod in understanding. "Got it."

He stands, getting what he wanted from me. "Once it's done, you'll be released. You have my word. No one will know it ever happened." Exiting the room, a male police officer enters and helps me up.

He leads me down a hallway and into an open area. It's two stories tall with a guard station in the middle. Someone whistles, and I look over to see a guy leaning up against the bars of his cell. He blows me a kiss.

I smirk as the officer brings me to a stop. He opens the cage, and I enter, where he removes the cuffs and then locks me inside.

"About time."

Turning around, I see Matt sitting on the top bunk. He jumps down. "Where have you been?"

I ignore that. "Was this your plan? Get locked up with me in a little cell?" He didn't know any more than I did what the assignment would entail, but I like giving him shit.

He shrugs. "If you're here, you're not there."

Stepping forward, I say. "I may not be fucking her right now, but I will the moment we're out of here."

"You son of a ..."

I grip his head and slam it into the white brick wall to my left. Blood instantly runs from his nose, covering the wall. I do it again. And again.

I hear the guards shouting from their station, and inmates start raising their voices while I shove Matt to the floor and kick him in the face, knocking it back and making blood fly.

The cell opens, and I'm tackled to the floor, where they cuff me once again. I'm smiling when they haul me out of there, taking me to solitary confinement. I'm not here to play roommates with Matt. I'm here to get a job done and get back to Blake.

BLAKELY

RYAT'S BEEN MIA for three days now. And every day that goes by without any word from him just pisses me off even more.

Is this what people mean when they say they were ghosted? I mean, no one just disappears. But it's like poof, he's gone. Almost like the motherfucker never existed. I'm not sleeping at night. I can't concentrate in classes. It's not because I miss him. It's because I'm fucking pissed.

I spend every second of the day thinking about what I'll say to him if I ever see him again. And none of them are good.

"Hey?" Sarah enters my bedroom.

I look up at her from my bed. I have a serial killer documentary on. It's giving me ideas on what to do to him in his sleep if he ever returns. "Hey." I haven't spoken to her much. She and Gunner are staying here, but I don't see them often. They're too busy fucking most of the time in her room. I know this because I can hear them.

"We're going out for dinner. Want to come with us?" she asks.

"No thanks." I'm not in the mood to eat anything.

She sighs. "Gunner says this is just part of being a Lord."

"Noted." I dismiss her, looking up at my TV.

"Blakely—"

"I'm not trying to be rude, but I want to be left alone," I interrupt her.

Nodding, she turns and closes my door doing as I ask. Sinking farther into the bed, I pick up my cell next to me. I pull up his contact and hover over the number. The inner battle of wanting to say, "go fuck yourself" and "please talk to me" are equally on my mind right now.

And of course, like the dumb bitch I am, I press call. "You've reached Ryat ..." I hang up and toss it across the room the moment his voicemail picks up, letting out a scream. Obviously, he has no intention of having any contact with the outside world, including me.

Rolling over onto my stomach, I shove my head into my pillow and scream again, this time as loud as I can. I hate being ignored. It's my biggest pet peeve and what Matt would do the moment I asked a question he didn't want to answer.

TWENTY-EIGHT

RYAT

I'VE NEVER REALLY cared for people, so the fact that I've been in solitary confinement, AKA administrative segregation, for a five days now doesn't really bother me. But what does, is that I'm away from Blake.

I can't even lie to myself. I've gotten used to being around her all the time. And the sex, fuck, I'm craving her scent, her touch, and her sweet fucking body.

I'm in a six-by-nine concrete block with no window for twenty-three hours a day. I don't even have bars for a door. It's steel with a slot that they give me my meals through. This is the one time in my life I wished I was the type of guy who required a lot of sleep—so I could at least sleep through the night. But nope, I'm up for most of it.

I was told once that when men find themselves in situations like me, they write novels in their heads. Or work out mathematical problems or sing songs to keep themselves occupied to help pass the time. Those that are held here for long periods of time can start to hallucinate.

Me? I'm spending every second of every day remembering my weekend at the cabin with Blake.

"Smith!"

I sit up and watch the door open. The guard that I know by the

name of Henry enters. Shackles hang from his fists. "Shower time."
He smirks at me.

BLAKELY

I'M LYING IN bed, something I seem to do nonstop. If I'm not in a class,
this is where I am, watching TV by myself. Gunner and Sarah are at a
party tonight at the house of Lords. She invited me, but I told her no
thanks. I'd much rather get drunk alone in my bed, wearing nothing
but a T-shirt. Instead of having to get all made up and pretend I like
people right now.

Ryat has me hating the world. It's now been six days since he left.
And still no fucking contact whatsoever.

But whatever, I tell myself I'm over it. Eventually, I'll start to
believe it.

I hear a sound coming from the other side of my bedroom door
and mute my TV. "Sarah?" I call out.

A quick look at my cell shows me it's not even midnight yet. There's
no way they are back. Shrugging, I turn the sound back on when my
door opens.

I stare at a set of emerald eyes that I haven't seen in almost a week.
Ryat stands there, dressed in the same clothes he was wearing when
I saw him last. He's got a cut above his eye, covered in dried blood. A
busted bottom lip and cracked knuckles.

My eyes narrow on him when my heart starts to race. I hate that I
care how he looks. The fact that he's been in a fight has me wanting
to ask a million questions, but I know he won't answer a single one
of them.

Entering my room, he shuts the door behind him. "I'm taking a
shower," he announces and walks into my bathroom.

"What the ...?" I trail off and jump up from my bed, storming into
my bathroom.

He's leaning inside my shower, turning on the water. "Get the
fuck out of my apartment," I order.

Instead of doing what I say, he reaches up and removes his T-shirt
exposing his chest to me. My eyes fall to the bruise over his ribs.
Looks like a fucking boot. Jesus, what the fuck has he been doing?

Giving me his back, he undoes his jeans and shoves them down
his legs along with his boxer briefs. He's got more bruises on his
legs and back. I swallow nervously and go to step toward him, but he

opens the shower door again and steps in.

Going under the sprayer, he places his hands flat on the wall and lowers his head. I watch his stomach suck in while he breathes deeply, making his ribs more prominent. He looks like he's in pain.

Making up my mind, knowing I'll probably regret this later, I remove my shirt and underwear, stepping inside.

I place my hands on his back, and he stiffens under my touch. "You okay?" I ask softly, knowing it's a stupid question but needing him to reassure me that he is.

Instead, he turns around to face me and stumbles into me. I catch him, but his knees give out, and I'm not strong enough to hold him. I fall to the shower floor with him, and he leans his head against the wall, closing his eyes. "I'm so tired," he mumbles.

The water from the showerhead above beats down on us, making me blink rapidly.

"What happened to you?" I ask, shoving my wet hair off my face and pulling my head away so I'm not directly under the water.

His head falls to the right, and he opens his heavy eyes, meeting mine. "It's nothing. I just need some sleep."

My teeth grind at his lie. He's obviously had the shit beat out of him. He's been gone for almost a week. Did he even get any sleep? "Ryat ...?"

"I'm fine, Blake." He pats my thigh. "I just want to clean up and go to bed."

Letting out a deep breath, I nod. "Okay."

TWENTY-NINE

RYAT

SOMETHING HARD HITS me in the back, knocking the wind out of me. I'm shoved to my knees, and my face is held down to the wet shower floor. My head to the side, I stare into a dead set of brown eyes. The Chinese star tattoo on his face.

Erik Bates.

Gotcha.

I killed the motherfucker! Took me a several days in solitary confinement, but I only needed one shot, and I just took it. I'm not stupid. Someone set this up and made sure that I was in here at the same time as him. I didn't even have a chance to get undressed. The moment I saw him, I took the opportunity.

I'm jerked to my feet and dragged out of the showers, down the hallway, and back to my cell. The shackle around my waist is unlocked, but they leave my hands cuffed in front of me. My door is opened, and I'm pushed into it. The door shuts behind me and locks. Looking up, I see a man sitting on my bed who I don't recognize.

Arching a brow, I ask, "Since when do they assign roommates in solitary confinement?"

He reaches up under my pillow and pulls out a short knife that wasn't there before. "It's amazing what they allow us to do when they need us to take care of something."

I don't miss the fact that the guards threw me in here still cuffed. This is a setup. Just like the one where I killed fuckface. "Who sent you?" I ask. It *wasn't Gregory. I did what I signed up for. If he turned on me, he would be terminated.*

The man smirks, showing off his ugly brown teeth. He's been in jail for a while. Probably a lifer. "Let's just say a friend wants me to send you a message."

"Friend?"

He stands, and I take a step back, but there's nowhere for me to go in this concrete box. "I don't know what you did, but he wants you to suffer."

Fucking Matt! It has to be him. I beat him up and left him in our cell. He's obviously been making friends while I've been in here alone. Good for him. The corner of my lips pulls back into a smirk when I confess. "I fucked his girl."

His chuckles softly. "That'll do it." Lifting the knife, he looks over it. Pretty sure if he cuts me with it, I'll need a tetanus shot afterward due to how discolored it is. I'm definitely not the first person it's going to be used on. "Was the pussy worth it?" His eyes meet mine.

"Absolutely!"

He charges me, knocking my back into the steel door. He lowers the knife to my side, and I manage to dodge it, but his free hand lands a hit to my ribs, taking my breath away. He takes a step back from me, and I double over.

"Sounds like I should try it out." He laughs while I cough. "He did offer me a piece of it once I finish with you." I glare up at him. "Brunette? Blue eyes? I didn't catch her name. That's not important anyway. She'll be my bitch ..."

I run at him, hunched over, and my shoulder hits his abdomen, shoving his back into the opposite wall. The small space didn't allow me that much momentum, but it's all I got. The knife clanks to the ground, and I go to hit him, but the handcuffs make it hard. I'm going to have to get him to the floor.

His fist connects with my chest, and my knees buckle, knocking me to the floor. Trying to regain my strength, I hear him laughing as he stands above me. "He said that she's got some nice tits too."

I catch sight of the knife next to me. Grabbing it, I shove it into the top of his foot. "She does."

He throws his head back, screaming, and I stand, kneeing him in the stomach. He doubles over, and I shove him to the floor. Face down. I straddle his back and wrap my cuffed hands around his neck, pulling back, cutting off his air.

The sounds of him gurgling while struggling with me fill my cell. But I don't let up. Not until this son of a bitch is dead because I sure as shit am not letting anyone near her. She's mine. I'll have to remind Matt of that.

His body grows weak, and it doesn't take long for it to sag against the floor. I'm still hanging on for dear life, the tight cuffs pinching my skin, when I hear the door creak open.

Looking up, I see Gregory enter my cell. "What the fuck?" he asks, his wide eyes on the guy I'm sitting on top of.

"Is he dead?" I grind out.

Kneeling next to him, he presses his fingers on his neck. "Yeah," he answers.

I let go and roll off him to my side, letting out a long breath. "Who's next?" I ask jokingly, but he doesn't laugh. Then my heavy eyes fall shut.

Waking up, it takes my eyes a second to focus on Blakely sleeping next to me. Reaching out, I run my hand through her dark hair fanning her pillow.

Fucking Matt tried to kill me while we were locked away. That can't go unpunished. There are a lot of things I can overlook, but that sure as shit isn't one of them. He'll pay for that. And I know the best revenge. She's lying right in front of me.

I push the covers down and off her back, seeing she's naked. I wanted to fuck her so bad the moment I got back, but my body just wasn't having it. I could barely shower, let alone dominate her, but I feel better now. Recharged. The light that filters into her room tells me it's early morning. It's also a Sunday, meaning I have all day with her.

Running my hand down her back, I slide it over her bubble ass before giving it a little slap. She shifts, letting out a moan.

I scoot closer to her, my hand sliding between her legs to find her cunt. She goes to roll onto her back, but I use my free hand and push her onto her stomach. "Ryat?" she whispers.

Pressing my lips to her back, I gently kiss her soft skin while I spread her pussy lips with my other hand. I push a finger into her, and she's not even close to where I want her to be.

I kiss my way up to her neck, where I bite into her skin, making her shiver.

"Ryat?" she speaks, sounding much more alert.

"Wake up, little one," I whisper, my finger entering her again.

"What?" She goes to roll over, but I shove her onto her stomach completely. "Ryat," she snaps, making me smile. "I'm so pissed at you."

"Good." I remove my hands from her legs and sit between them, spreading them wide with my knees.

She gets up on her hands, and I reach around, grabbing them and pulling them behind her back, gripping them in one hand. I slap her ass with the other while her face falls down into her pillow.

"Fuck you, Ryat," she hisses, her body fighting under mine.

I chuckle. "I'm going to." My hand goes back between her legs, and I smile that she's getting wetter. "You missed me."

"I hate you," she growls.

"I can live with that." I enter a second finger, and she makes a noise between a growl and whimper, her body rocking back and forth. "That's it, Blake. Ride my fingers like a good little slut. Show me how much you want to be fucked."

Her back arches more at my words, and her pussy just gets wetter. Thinking about the guy in my cell makes me angry. The fact that Matt offered her to the man in exchange for getting rid of me, puts me on edge. How many will he send after me in order to get to her?

That someone else would get to fuck what's mine. My cock is the only one that's ever been here. And it's going to stay that way.

Removing my fingers, she sags against the bed. I grab my cock and push it inside her, not wanting to play any longer. I want to fuck. "This is my cunt," I tell her.

"Uh-huh." She moans and agrees. "Yours."

I pull out and slam into her, forcing a cry from her lips. "Remember that, Blake." I do it again. "Don't ever forget who owns you."

"Never." She cries.

Thankfully, I have plenty of time to remind her in case she forgets any of that.

I STAND IN the kitchen eating some yogurt in nothing but a towel wrapped around my hips. "We have a ceremony next weekend," I say loudly so Blakely can hear me from her room.

She pokes her head out of the open door. I can tell she's still mad at me but curious at the same time. "Ceremony? Another one?" She arches a brow. "At the cathedral?"

"No." I shake my head. "This one is at the house of Lords."

Stepping out of her room completely, she adjusts the towel underneath her underarms, giving me a quick peek of her tits. I came all over them about an hour ago before we showered for the third time since I've returned last night. "What is it for?"

"It's to show you off," I say truthfully.

She bites her bottom lip nervously, dropping her eyes to stare at her bare feet. "Do I have to ... do anything?"

She means sexually. "Just be mine," I say simply.

Nodding, she turns and goes back into her room.

I take another bite of the yogurt as I hear a key in the front door of her apartment. Then it opens seconds later. I expect it to be Sarah and Gunner, but a bleach-blond enters instead. Her green eyes find me instantly. They drop to the towel that sits low on my hips, not leaving much to the imagination. They slowly run up over my V, pausing on my abs and then rising to my chest. When they meet mine, hers narrow like I'm the one in the wrong here. "Who the fuck are you?" she demands.

I take another bite of the yogurt. "Who the fuck are you?" I ask, although I already know.

"What should I wear ...?" Blakely trails off, exiting her bedroom. Her wide eyes go to the woman. "Mom?" she shrieks. "What are you doing here?"

"Blakely," she hisses when her eyes go to her daughter. They pause on the bite marks and hickeys that dot her neck and run down over her arms. Then drop to her legs. I've left marks all over my girl. "What in the fuck is going on here?"

Blakely looks at me, mouth hanging open and eyes still the size of quarters. I finish off my yogurt, then throw it in the trash. Walking past her mother, I go over to Blake. Cupping her face, I lean down and gently kiss her forehead. "Don't take long." Then I walk into the bedroom, shutting the door behind me.

BLAKELY

"Mom," I GASP. "What are you doing here?" I ask, blinking. The fact that Ryat kissed me on the forehead brought me out of my trance.

"Looks like I got here just in time," she snaps, placing her hands on her hips. "Who the fuck was that, and what have you been doing with him?"

I roll my eyes. "That's none of your business—"

Her rough laugh interrupts me. "I pay for this apartment and this college, young lady. Everything you do is my business. And I've been calling you. Is this why you haven't been answering? Because you've been with him?"

I frown. "I haven't had any calls from you."

"Like I believe that." She snorts. "Where the fuck is Matt?" Her dark green eyes search the apartment as if I have him hidden somewhere. That I've been shacked up in this apartment having a fuck fest with both him and Ryat.

I fist my hands. "We're not together anymore. I told you I dumped him. He was cheating on me." My voice rises.

"And I told you that you will still marry him," she snaps.

I throw my hands up. "You know what, I'm not doing this." After Ryat disappearing and then showing back up nearly beaten to death and acting like nothing happened. To him waking me up and fucking me all morning, I'm still pissed. At him, at her, and at myself for allowing all of this to go on. "You can't force me to be with him. I won't do it." I just need to make it to his graduation. Then I'll run. I can save enough money by then to get away without them knowing. I'll just pull out a little cash every day, so I won't be forced to use my card and leave a trail.

"What? You think that guy in there is better than Matt?" she demands, pointing at my closed bedroom door. "He doesn't love you."

I flinch at her words. Even though I know they're true, I hate that she acts like no one ever could. She makes it sound like Matt is my best option, and I should just settle for that. "Don't worry, Mom. I won't be bringing him home for the holidays. It's just sex."

She slaps me across the face, making me gasp in shock.

"You little ungrateful bitch ..."

I hear the bedroom door open behind me, and my mother takes a step back when Ryat storms out of it. He wraps his hand around her throat, slamming her back into the wall. "Never touch her again." Yanking her from the wall, he shoves her back into it once again, making a picture of Sarah and me fall off the wall beside her, and the glass shatters on the floor next to them. Stepping into her, he asks, "Do you understand?"

She nods the best she can, her hands gripping his forearm with wide eyes. He's cutting off her air.

"Blake isn't going to answer your calls or return your texts. So quit fucking trying." He lets go of her. "Now get the fuck out," he commands as she rubs her neck.

"I don't take orders ..."

He grabs her hair, and she screams out as he drags her across the room to the front door. Opening it, he shoves her out into the hall. "You son of a ..."

"Don't fucking come back." Then he slams the door in her face and proceeds to lock it. "I'll have the locks changed today."

I stay where I'm at, my hand pressed to my throbbing cheek and tears stinging my eyes. He turns to walk back over to me. "You okay?" he asks, cupping my chin and forcing me to look up at him.

"Yeah," I lie, shamed and embarrassed at what she did. My mother has never hit me before. I wish I knew what her obsession with Matt was.

"You sure?" His emerald eyes search mine before dropping to my reddening face.

I nod, looking away from him, and whisper, "Thank you."

Stepping into me, he gently forces me to look up at him once again. I can't tell through the tears that I refuse to let fall, but he looks concerned. "You don't need her, Blake. Not when you've got me." Then leaning forward, he kisses my forehead before pulling me into the bedroom to start round four.

I hate to think of it, but it's obvious he returned just in time.

I'M WALKING DOWN the hallway with Sarah at Barrington Monday morning when I ask, "Have you messaged me lately?"

She frowns. "Not since the other weekend. Why?"

I haven't received any from her, but she's also been staying at the apartment. Except for Saturday night. She and Gunner never did return after they left for the house of Lords party. Something tells me Gunner knew Ryat was back and wanted to leave us alone. "Well, my mother showed up at our apartment yesterday morning ...."

"She what?" she shrieks. "What did she want?"

"Well, that's the thing. She said she's been calling and texting me, but I haven't received any. And I know you had said that you were texting me when Ryat and I were at the cabin, and I wasn't answering."

She nods. "I blew up your phone and nothing."

I adjust the books in my hand. "That's odd ... right?"

She shrugs. "I call it a blessing. Well, not the fact that my calls didn't go through, but definitely regarding your mother's."

"But shouldn't your text have come through once I got service?"

I ask, thinking out loud.

"Maybe. I guess it depends on how long you went without it. You were gone all weekend."

"But ..." It did work. I spoke to Ryat while I was there. I had called him and then received that text from him. Had it been dead when I plugged it in that night? I can't remember. When I'm with Ryat, he demands all of my attention. "Will you call it now?" I ask her.

"Sure." We come to a stop, and she digs her cell out of her back pocket. She goes to her recent calls and presses call on my number. Mine starts ringing immediately.

"Hmm." I decline the call.

"See, like I said. It's a blessing that you're missing her calls," she jokes.

"Guess so," I add skeptically. It just seems odd.

"So, what else did she have to say?" she goes on.

"A lot. She walked in on Ryat and me both in towels fresh out of the shower."

She throws her head back, laughing. "That's fucking gold. Wish I was there to see it. What all did she have to say about that?"

"She went off on me. Said I was still marrying Matt ..." I trail off, not wanting to tell her that my mother slapped me. It was embarrassing enough that Ryat was there.

"God, she's such a bitch." She sighs. Turning to fully face me, she smiles softly. "I'm glad you have Ryat. No matter the situation you have with him, he's way better for you than dick face. I mean," she goes on. "The guy has barely left you alone since the vow ceremony. Unless the Lords demanded his attention. You know for a fact that guy isn't out there fucking around on you, and that's more than Matt's ever done for you."

She's not wrong about him not ignoring me as Matt has done in the past, but that doesn't mean that Ryat isn't fucking other women, right? Can I even call it cheating if he has been? I mean, this isn't a relationship per se. It's more of an understanding. I'm his and he's ... mine? Then I get a new thought. What if the Lords had him shack up with someone else for his assignment? He has spent every second with me, so it wouldn't be farfetched to think they had him do the same with someone else, right?

Jealousy slithers up my back and makes my blood start to boil. Even though I have no right to call him mine, the thought of him touching someone else still infuriates me. I swallow down the bile that wants to rise at that thought.

"How are you and Gunner?" I ask, changing the subject. Trying to tell myself that it doesn't matter. I don't love him, and he'll never tell me anything regarding the Lords.

"God, girl ..." She licks her lips, and we start to walk again. "So fucking good."

I laugh. "Sex that good, huh?" I had to listen to them fuck like rabbits while they stayed at the apartment last week when Ryat was gone.

"Absolutely. The man knows what he's doing." We come up to the door for our class and stop. "Last night, he literally choked me out."

My eyes widen. "Like during sex?" That's what Ryat practically did to me when we were out in the woods.

She nods. "He's got this obsession with breath play."

Breath play? Is it some kind of kink?

"One hundred percent hot as fuck. I came so hard before I passed the fuck out." With that, she opens the door to enter class.

"Blake?" I hear my name being called. Without having to look, I know who it is.

"I'll be right there," I inform Sarah.

Turning around, I see Ryat coming toward me, pocketing his cell phone. He's dressed in a pair of jeans, a plain white T-shirt, and a backward baseball hat. No man should look that good dressed so casually. I hate that I'm mad at him and want to fuck him at the same time.

"What's up?" I ask, crossing my arms over my chest. What if this is all some big game that I'm playing with them? I know he chose me because of Matt, but what if Matt told him to choose me? What if this is their way to fuck with me? He's been too understanding of what I want. At the time, I thought he really seemed to care, but what if that's not the case? Then he just up and leaves me without any explanation. And returns like it never happened.

"I'll be gone tonight."

Every thought that I just had about him not fucking someone else is shattered with those four words. Did I really think I was the only one? He's a fucking Lord. I was told they can do whatever they want—their oath tells them that. "Of course." I snort, making him frown. "Let me guess, the Lords?"

"No. It's personal."

Okay, I'll bite and be a nosy bitch. "Where are you going?"

"Something has come up," he answers vaguely.

How have I not seen this? How many times has he blown off my questions? Or something mysteriously comes up? I bet it's another woman. Good thing I don't love him. I won't be that dumb bitch who believes everything a guy tells me because I want him to be someone he's not. I hate how much my mother was right.

"Okay." I reach out to open the door, but he steps in front of me, blocking it. "Ryat—"

"What's wrong?" he interrupts me, searching my face.

"Nothing," I lie.

He sighs heavily. "Don't let your mother get to you, Blake."

I refrain from snorting. Of course, he thinks it's related to her. My mother may be a bitch, but she's never made me think she was someone else. He's the joke. The liar. And I'm the dummy who never questioned it. Instead of correcting him, I nod. "I'll get over it."

He steps out of my way and opens the door for me. "I'll see you in the morning."

Without responding to that, I walk into class and up to my seat next to Sarah. She's typing away on her cell. I pull mine out of my pocket and pull up *breath play*. By doing some research, I hope it gets shit off my mind.

THIRTY

RYAT

I WALK INTO the office in downtown Dallas with my lawyer behind me and look around the abandoned space. No one is here this late. It's after midnight. This is an off-the-books meeting, just like when I was here last time.

Making our way down the long hallway, I hear laughter coming from the back office. Pushing the door open, I step inside to find my father and another man I have come to know well.

"Ryat." He stands. "Glad you can join us ..." He trails off as he sees the man enter behind me.

"Garrett," my father states, acknowledging our lawyer also standing.

"Mr. Archer." He nods, holding his briefcase in his hand.

I fall down into a high-back chair next to my father. "I'm the one who called this meeting." It's time to iron some shit out. Make sure people understand what I want and that I'm going to get it.

Phil sits back in his chair and sighs.

My father arches a brow at me. "Why are we here, Ryat?" Then he looks at our family attorney that we've had since before I was born.

I had already made up my mind after Matt fucked me over while we were in jail. But Blake's mother's stunt solidified my thoughts on what needed to be done.

"I'm guessing it's because of my wife. She's had plenty to say about you today." Phil Anderson relaxes in his seat. "Said you put your hands on her—choked her and threw her out of the apartment."

"I did. After she slapped your daughter."

His jaw sharpens, slapping his hand on the desk. "She didn't mention that part."

"Why am I not surprised?" I grunt. That bitch will never touch Blake again. "I'm here to make an offer," I say, getting to business, raising my hand to Garrett.

Silence falls over the room. The last time I was in New York, my father asked me how much I'd pay to beat out Matt. I never gave him a definitive answer because I wasn't quite sure. Now I am.

Garrett places the briefcase on Phil's desk and opens it up, pulling out a set of papers.

Mr. Anderson puts his glasses on and reads over it. "I don't understand—"

"Five hundred thousand." I interrupt him, so he doesn't have to search for it.

He clears his throat, pulling his glasses off, and looking at me. "The Winstons ..."

"Fuck the Winstons," I snap. There is no signed contract that states Blake has to marry Matt. I know, I did my homework to make sure. "I want her." He already handed her to me once, ordering I make her my chosen one. I didn't think this would be difficult, but I came prepared just in case.

He tilts his head to the side. "For how long exactly?"

"Garrett," I order, and he pulls out another set of papers and lays them on the man's desk.

Placing his glasses back on his face, Mr. Anderson picks them up and starts reading them over as well.

"Marriage," I say simply.

My father doesn't interject, which means he's given this some thought and isn't going to fight me on this. But I don't think he understands what this means. It's not a temporary fix. I will marry Blake, and she will be my wife—forever. I will not be marrying Cindy

Phil looks up at me through his dark lashes. "And the agreement with ..."

"Did you sign an agreement with the Winston's?" I ask, already knowing the answer.

"Of course not." He snorts. "That was my wife's doing."

Exactly. "It's just a verbal agreement." I shrug. "Not like he can sue you over it. And if it was that important to you, you wouldn't have forced my hand to pick her as my chosen in the first place."

He looks away from me and stares down at a picture of Blakely that sits on his desk. Picking it up, he takes in a deep breath.

I sit up straighter, placing my elbows on my knees. "The Winstons' empire is crumbling. Kimberly—Matt's mother—went to your wife trying to strike a deal." But none of us know what the deal was exactly. "They came to the Andersons hoping to forge your legacy with theirs. To save it. Not the other way around." Matt's father wants to fly on the back of Blakely's family. Marrying her, he gets to help run this business. One day her father will retire, and Matt will take over a hundred percent, making sure to keep the Winstons a part of the one percent. "I don't want your company," I add. "Whatever you decide to leave her when you're dead is hers. I just want Blakely." I'm not sure what she would do with her father's company. She's an only child, so I'm guessing she'd sell it. As far as I know, she's never worked for him before.

"A prenup?" he asks, wanting to make sure that's all in writing.

I laugh. "There will be no prenup." That implies our marriage is going to fail and that's just not going to happen. "But I do have a contract ..." I snap my fingers at Garrett, and he removes it from his briefcase as well. "These papers state that." I also made sure to leave out the part where she can fuck whoever she wants like I told my father to add to mine with Cindy. Blakely will only ever fuck and suck my cock.

"It took her a long time to accept her marriage to Matt. How would you convince her to marry you?" her father asks.

"She'll accept it. I have no doubt." I stand, ready to get this over with. Blakely has no clue that I had to make a quick trip to Texas. I had to fly to New York today to meet with Garrett to get everything in order and the papers drawn up, then we had to fly here for this meeting. I wanted to come to her father, not the other way around.

I had checked the cameras in her apartment on the way here, and she was passed out in her bed. "I've already had everything drawn up, as you can see." Garrett removes a pen from his suit jacket. "All you have to do is sign. If you agree, of course. If not, we can discuss whatever you have questions about." I'm straightforward in the contracts with what I want and how I want it—just her. "Once you sign them, I'll wire the money to your account."

He nods, accepting the fate of his only daughter. *She will be my wife.* I'll fuck over anyone in my way. "How far out will this wedding be?"

"As soon as possible," I answer honestly.

"But you're both in college ..."

"Why is that a problem?" I ask, tilting my head to the side. Lots of people get married before and during college. She doesn't need to attend Barrington after I graduate this year. She doesn't need the degree, and she sure as shit won't be working. I will be the sole provider for our family. Blakely will depend on me for everything, and I will give the woman whatever the fuck she wants.

"It just seems quick." He shrugs.

"Well, I'm sure if your wife had it her way, Blakely would already be married off to Matt," I growl.

He sighs heavily as if he believes that as well. Mr. Anderson starts to read over the contracts once again as my father speaks up. "If this is what you want ..."

"It is," I say firmly.

Her father stands and adjusts his suit jacket. "Do you love her?" he asks.

I've thought about this a million times since I found myself in a jail cell left with just my thoughts. And every time, I came up with the same answer.

No!

They say love is patient and kind. I'm not either one of those things when it comes to Blakely. I'm controlling, possessive, and madly jealous. Which can only mean one thing—I'm obsessed with her. To the point I want to hide her from the world. I don't want another man looking at her, let alone talking to her. Matt helped me understand that.

So, instead of lying to my future father-in-law, I ask, "Did you love Valerie when you married her?"

He places his hands on his hips and lets out a sigh. I know he had an arranged marriage. Blakely doesn't know that, but I do. "I learned to love her over time," he finally answers.

Stepping up to his desk, I place my palms flat on it and lean over. "I promise you, Mr. Anderson, Blakely will be in good hands. I don't need to love her to promise that I'll protect her. And that's more than Matt would do."

He nods to himself a few times. "You're right. But ..." He pauses. "I don't want the money. I'll sign everything. She'll be yours. But I won't take a cent from you for her. If she chooses to marry you, then she's yours."

I smile. *Oh, she'll choose me all right.* "Mighty noble of you."

"I won't be like Valerie." He shakes his head. Reaching out his right hand to me, he adds, "Welcome to the family, son."

BLAKELY

I'M STANDING IN my bathroom, lining my lips, when I see the door open and Ryat enter. I say nothing to him and look back at myself in the mirror. I'm running late as it is. I slept through my alarms. My body was so exhausted that I actually managed to sleep through my anger for him.

I was going to skip my shower but realized I needed to wash my hair, so that put me an extra twenty minutes behind schedule.

He comes up behind me, his eyes dropping to the towel wrapped around my body. Reaching out, he yanks it off me.

"I don't have time," I inform him, pulling away. "I'm late."

"So?" He arches a brow, smacking my ass and making me jump.

"So I can't miss classes." My mom is already pissed that I'm not screwing Matt. She'll have a cow if she found out I'm skipping classes because of Ryat.

"Fuck Barrington." He grips my hips and pulls them from the counter.

"Ryat ..." He reaches up and grabs a handful of my hair, making me hiss in a breath.

His eyes meet mine in the mirror, and his voice drops to a deep growl. "Bend over and spread your fucking legs, Blake."

My heart starts to race, my body temperature rising. I want to tell him to go to hell. Or back to whoever he spent the night with. But the way his emerald eyes are glowing, I don't. Maybe I'm overthinking things. Maybe he wasn't with someone else last night. If he was, why would he still want me? It's not like he only jumps on me when Matt is around. We actually never see him.

"Blake," he warns, pulling me out of my own thoughts.

He lets up on my hair, and I bend over the counter, spreading my legs wide just like he ordered me to do. The cold surface of the counter makes me shiver as he runs his hand between my legs.

When he thrusts a finger in me, I rise to my tiptoes, whimpering. Then he pulls it out, and I hear him undoing his belt, followed by his zipper. His way of inspection, letting him know I'm wet enough. Then the head of his dick is pushing its way into me.

I'm panting. My palms are on the countertop next to my head while my hips are shoved into the side.

He doesn't waste a second. The sound of my heavy breathing fills the room while he fucks me. I blow my hair out of my face the best I can, knowing I'll have to redo my makeup when he grips my hair and yanks me to stand.

I cry out, staring at him in the mirror as he lowers his lips to my ear, his eyes on mine. "Marry me."

I want to laugh, but his cock is hitting just the right spot, so instead, I just stare at him with heavy eyes while breathing ragged.

He runs his nose along my neck and bites into my collarbone while his free hand runs up my body, scorching my skin. He massages my breast and then slides his hand over my neck. I swallow nervously. Thoughts of what I found while searching breath play enters my mind. I lick my lips, wondering what it'd be like for him to take it away again.

As if he can read my mind, his hand then comes up, and he places it over my mouth. I whimper, my pussy tightening around him. I suck in a deep breath through my nose, wishing he would take that away from me too.

Why? Why do I want to be treated like nothing? I wish I could explain how much my body craves to be dominated. How much my mind dreams about it.

"Marry me, Blake," he says again and then pinches off my nose, taking it away as well.

My eyes find his again in the mirror while my ears pop and my body convulses. His hand suctions to my face as I try to suck in a breath through my mouth.

He picks up his pace, slamming the front of my body into the counter, knowing it'll bruise. My knees bang against the cabinets.

My hands come up to grip his arm, but he doesn't budge. My lungs begin to burn, my eyes water. He continues to fuck me, his eyes on mine in the mirror while I begin to go into panic mode, but my body reacts as that sensation builds.

I try to pry his hand from my face, but he lets go of my hair with his free hand and slides his arm between the crook of my arms and my back, pinning them in place, and whispers, "You can breathe after you come for me."

My heart races, and tears fall from my eyes, but a wave is coming. It's going to pull me down so deep I won't be able to break the surface.

The room is spinning, and my eyes fall shut just as the dam breaks and that wave takes me under. Just like I knew it would.

THIRTY-ONE

RYAT

I REMOVE MY hand from her mouth and nose just as her eyes close. She sucks in a shaky breath when I pull out of her, and I pick her trembling body up and carry her to the bedroom. Laying her down, I sit between her parted legs. Her eyes are open but looking around aimlessly, trying to get her bearings back.

Three years having to abstain from sex while watching others have it fucks with your mind. I've read up on every kink and fetish you can think of. Plus, the longer you have to withhold, the dirtier your imagination has to get in order to get off. Erotic asphyxiation can be very dangerous. Some prefer to pass out completely. Others just like their air supply cut off for a few seconds. And then some like the physical aspect of being choked. The total submission is what turns them on.

"You're so beautiful, Blake." I lean down and kiss her cheek, tasting her tears. Sitting back up, I push my hard cock into her soaked cunt, making her trembling body flinch.

I watch her as my hips set a slow and steady rhythm, giving her a chance to catch her breath. Blue eyes start to focus a little more as they land on mine. She reaches up, wrapping her arms around my neck to pull my body down to hers.

Tilting her head to the side, I dot kisses on her slick neck. "Ready?" I ask her.

"Yeah," she answers breathlessly.

"Take a deep breath," I order. She does as she's told, and I slap my hand over her mouth again. I can't pinch her nose because of the position of my hand, but I make sure my palm covers it as well. My hips pick up their pace. Our bodies slap while her nails dig into my back, making me hiss in a breath when I feel them cut my skin.

She arches her back and neck while my body continues to pin her down. I feel the heat from her breath as she tries to let it out while her tight cunt clenches down on me once again.

Removing my hand from her mouth, I sit up and hold her face in both of my hands. She's gasping for breath. "Look at me," I order.

Her eyes are once again unfocused, and tears freely fall from the corners of them. "What do you say, little one?" I ask, wiping them away.

She blinks, her pretty eyes finding mine.

"Do you want to be his whore for the rest of your life, or do you want to be my good girl?" This is her only chance to choose me. I have no problem tricking or forcing her to be my wife. But her choosing to be with me over him makes it all that better.

"Yours," she breathes.

"Mine," I agree.

I pull out and her arms fall to her sides. She's weak, her body still trying to come down from her high. Flipping her over onto her stomach, I yank her hips up in the air, spreading her legs wide with mine. Sliding back into her soaking wet cunt, I pull her up to where she's straddling me backward. I reach around, grabbing her breasts with one hand, making her moan. Her head falls back onto my chest while my other hand comes up and covers her mouth once again, my fingers pinching off her nose, and I fuck her, making the bed hit the wall.

It doesn't take long for her to go slack this time, her body already exhausted. It only takes me a few more thrusts, and then I'm coming inside her.

I remove my hand from her face, and she sucks in a deep breath, her body still slack against mine. I gently lay her down and push her onto her back, propping her head up on the pillow before getting off the bed. I go over to my backpack and pull out the box. Opening it up, I remove the six carat princess cut engagement ring that I purchased while in New York yesterday, and slide it onto her finger. "Here's to being mine forever, Blake," I say, watching her sleep.

BLAKELY

218

I OPEN MY heavy eyes to see it's dark in my room. Whimpering, I stretch and feel the soreness in my body. I just lie here, looking up at the ceiling, and I hear the sound of rain hitting the window.

It's hard to explain, but I almost feel like a new person. I have never come so hard in my life. It felt like I was floating. Dots peppered my vision, and just when I thought I was going to pass out, he'd let go, and everything would come crashing back. Every inch of my body was tingling. It was like the best high you could reach without actually being on drugs.

Even now, my body still lightly tingles. As if a fire that can't be put out still lingers.

Deciding I need to get up, I push off the covers and walk on shaky legs to the door. Opening it up, I find Ryat sitting on the couch, his cell to his ear. His emerald eyes spot me immediately. "I'll call you back." He hangs up, not even bothering to wait for the person on the other end to say goodbye. He stands and walks over to me while I stay in the doorway, unsure my legs will support me to walk that far to him.

Coming up to me, he kisses my forehead.

"What time is it?" I ask. My phone wasn't on my nightstand.

"A little after two in the afternoon."

I frown. "I missed classes." Was that his plan all along?

He nods. "You needed the rest."

"Ryat," I growl. My hands shove him, but he doesn't move. I'm not sure if it's because my body is weak as fuck or because he is just that strong. "My mom will kill me." Turning around, I make my way through my room and to the bathroom. I get a little dizzy and have to use the countertop for support. It's comparable to when you stand quickly out of a hot bath, and you get light-headed while seeing dots.

"It's fine," he argues, coming in behind me.

"That's easy for you to say," I snap, picking up my underwear off the countertop from earlier. I go to put them on, but he yanks them from my hand.

"Ryat," I shriek, reaching out for them, but he tosses them across the bathroom.

I sigh. "Real mature." He grabs my arm and spins me around when I go to get them, pushing my back into the wall. "Ryat ..."

"Calm down," he says softly, his eyes searching my face. "You're getting all worked up over nothing."

"My mom—"

"Fuck your mother," he interrupts me with a growl.

219

I feel like a child wanting to stomp their foot. "You don't understand."

"I understand everything. Your mom thinks she can control you."

"She does," I say through gritted teeth hating to admit that. "She pays for this apartment."

"Move out."

I continue like he didn't just suggest something so idiotic. "She pays for Barrington."

"Drop out."

"Are you insane?" I demand, and he just chuckles. "I'm not a Lord, Ryat," I snap, and he stiffens against me. "I can't do as I please."

He grips my chin, forcing my head back against the wall to look up at him while stepping in closer. "You're mine, Blake. And that holds a lot of power."

Letting go of my neck, he runs his hands down my arms, making me break out in goose bumps. He grips my left hand and brings it to his lips, kissing my knuckles.

"It's not that simple ..." My voice trails off as I spot the ring on my finger, heart starting to hammer in my chest. "Ryat." I breathe. "What?"

Memories of earlier this morning come back like a hurricane hitting a small town.

"Marry me, Blake."

"Do you want to be his whore for the rest of your life, or do you want to be my good girl?"

"Yours."

"Mine."

"This"—he kisses it again—"is the answer to all your problems, Blake. All you need is me. I'll take care of you."

"But ... you were joking," I manage to get out even though I'm having problems breathing. He might as well have his hand over my mouth and nose again. Those spots are back, and I try to blink them away.

"Why would I joke about that?" he asks, tilting his head to the side.

"Because you ... you're seeing other women." That's the only reason I can come up with.

"Who the fuck told you that?" he barks, making me jump.

Have I been wrong? "You. Your behavior. You keep disappearing

...." I rush out, not really having anything else to go on.

He pulls away from me, and my body sags against the wall without his support. I allow my shaky knees to give out, and I slide down to sit on the cold, tiled floor while he starts pacing my bathroom.

"Every time I ask where you go, you don't answer." I go on at his silence because, honestly, I'm starting to question myself. I mean, did the man really ask me to marry him? The look of the rock on my finger is screaming yes. "You're only with me because of Matt." He doesn't even offer a lie for that. "You're a Lord."

"Matt is a Lord, and you were going to marry him," he argues, still pacing.

"No. I wasn't." I shake my head.

"Oh, I forgot. You were going to run away." He snorts. "I'd like to see you try to run away from me ...." He fists his hands. "You wouldn't get far, Blake."

"Wait." I run a hand down my face. "How did you know ...?" Finding strength in my newfound anger, I get to my feet. "How did you know what I was going to do?" I haven't even told Sarah this. Too afraid she'd say something to Gunner.

He comes to a stop and turns to face me. I don't know why but I hate that he's fully dressed and I'm naked. It makes me feel vulnerable. Which is stupid. The man has tied me up, gagged me, blindfolded me, and taken away my air. Not sure why clothes matter all of a sudden. "You told me."

"No, I didn't."

"Yes, you did. That night you were drunk off your ass, and I brought you home from Blackout." His voice rises.

"What else did I say to you?" I demand.

"Enough," he snaps and then storms over to me, pressing my back into the wall once again. He lifts his hands, cupping my face, and glares down at me. I take in a shaky breath. "Just know this, Blake. If you try to run from me, I will find you. And when I do, you will regret the day you left me." Softening his eyes, he gives me a threatening smile. "You were mine yesterday, today, and tomorrow." He gently kisses my forehead. The tenderness a contradiction to his threatening words. "And you will continue to be mine forever."

I want to be terrified, but I'm not. Ryat Archer is possessive, controlling, and extremely jealous. He's fucking toxic. But I can't lay all the blame on him. Maybe I'm the cause of his toxicity. Maybe it's my bad habits that bring out his worst. Hell, maybe I'm wrong, and they are his best qualities.

I want his hands around my throat. I want his body pinning mine down, and I want him to crave me the same way I need him.

So, who's the real toxic one here?

"I'm not going anywhere," I tell him, but even I know it's a lie. Eventually, he'll be done with me, and I'll belong to Matt. I will do everything in my power to stop that.

He lets go of my face, his knuckles running over my jawline to my neck. "I think you're lying." There's a hint of pleasure in his voice, and it makes me shiver.

I swallow nervously. "No ..."

"I think you want to run, Blake." His eyes search my face, the corner of his lips turning up. "Just for me to catch you."

My heart hammers in my chest, and my thighs tighten. Why does that sound like fun? Why does it turn me on to think of him searching for me? Knowing that once he finds me, he's going to punish me?

"Is that what you want, Blake? Want me to chase you?"

"Yes." I say the word before I can even think about it.

His eyes drop to my chest as his knuckles run over my breasts and my hard nipples. "We can play that game. Just know"—his eyes meet mine again—"that once I catch you, I will do whatever I want to you." My stomach flip flops with excitement at his threat. "And after I drag you back here ..." Lifting my hands, he intertwines our fingers and pushes them above my head, pinning them to the wall. "You will be my wife."

I lick my parted lips and take in a deep breath, trying to calm my breathing. "You'll have to find me first."

Leaning in, he kisses my cheek. "I like my odds." Then he lets go and pulls away from me. My arms drop to my sides like ten-pound weights. "I'll see you soon." With one last look at my naked body, he exits the bathroom.

I raise my hands and run them down my face letting out a breath. The ring catches my attention. I stare down at the large square diamond that's surrounded by more diamonds. It's a little gaudy for my taste but so gorgeous. I run my fingertip over it.

What happened to his future wife? Why all of a sudden does he want me?

My parents will never willingly let me be with anyone other than Matt. Well, my father might. My mother is the one obsessed with him.

But if I give myself to Ryat before I have to marry Matt? That would be my way out. My mother hates the idea of a divorce as much as she hates the idea of Ryat and me together. So, if I choose to marry Ryat first, then she'd have no choice but to accept him. She'd hate for her daughter to be divorced in a matter of weeks of getting married. That would just make her look bad.

Smiling, I make my way over to the counter and look at myself in the mirror. I'll run from Ryat for now, but when he catches me, I'll marry him. Just like he said. If for no other reason than to piss off my mother.

Walking into my bedroom, I start yanking on the sheets looking for my cell. I find it on the floor. Calling my dad, I sit on the side of the bed, waiting for him to answer.

"Hello, honey."

"Hey, Dad," I say, smiling. "How are things going there?"

"Good. How about you?" he asks slowly. I haven't spoken to him much since classes started this year. But it's not unusual to go weeks without talking to him. He's always been a busy man.

"Same," I say, holding it with my shoulder and ear to the side of my head. "I need a favor."

He's silent for a long second. "Okay. What is it?"

"I need the jet," I answer, biting on my bottom lip. This wouldn't be the first time I've used it.

"Uh ... where are you going?" he asks, sounding concerned. "Everything okay?"

"Yeah. Yeah. Sarah and I are just getting away. You know, to have a girls' trip." I lie easily.

"What about classes?" he asks.

Fuck! "It's just a couple of days. We've already arranged it with our professors."

"Okay." He clears his throat. "Are you sure everything is all right?"

"Yep," I reply.

"I can have it to you by tomorrow night."

That won't work. "Can it be tonight?" He stays silent. "It's just that we're already packed, and I'd like to be on the beach first thing in the morning ..."

"Sure, honey. I'll have it fueled and sent your way."

I drop my shoulders and let out a breath. "Thanks, Dad." I hang up and don't even bother looking for the cameras. Instead, I ignore Ryat completely. I know he's watching me, but he can't hear me. He doesn't have audio that I know of. And even if he did, that doesn't tell him where I'm going.

THIRTY-TWO

RYAT

I SIT IN my car, watching her through the windshield. It's like old times again. Back when I followed her around for those two weeks. Before I wanted her to know she was going to be mine.

She gets out of the car, wearing a white halter top sundress with dark purple heels and a black umbrella to shield her from the steady rain while the man grabs her three bags out of the trunk.

Interesting.

Blakely thinks I won't find her. I could have saved her the time and trouble packing those because she won't be wearing a goddamn thing while we're away. Well, other than handcuffs and maybe a blindfold.

She walks up the stairs to board her father's private jet, and I grab the bag out of the passenger seat before getting out of my car. Throwing it over my shoulder, I make my way onto the plane, shaking off the rain that's covered me, looking around. Her father has a jumbo private double-decker jet that can sit up to fifty people. It's got white carpet with white leather seats along with brown wood and gold trim—it looks every bit of the millions of dollars it cost him.

"Oh, hello, sir." A bleach-blonde flight attendant who can't be older than twenty-one greets me with a smile. Her brown eyes look me up and down. "I didn't know we had another guest. Would you like a towel to dry off?"

"Where is she?" I ask, ignoring her and getting to the point.

"The back suite, sir," she answers, her eyes falling to my limp dick inside my jeans.

"Ask her if she would like some champagne," I order.

She nods and walks to the back of the plane, pushing open a door. I hear the blonde ask, "Would you like a pre-flight drink, ma'am? We've got some champagne."

"Yes, please." I hear Blake's sweet voice. Almost song like. She's quite proud of herself. I can't wait to see the look on her face when she sees me.

"Of course." She closes the door and comes back to me.

I pop open a bottle of champagne and pour it into a flute. Then I remove the clear vial out of my pocket and dump all the contents into the drink. Taking a knife, I stir it around and then wipe it off on my already wet jeans. Picking it up, I hold it out for the blonde to take.

She looks at me wide-eyed. They drop to the flute, and she swallows nervously, running her hands down her tight black pencil skirt.

"Problem?" I ask.

"No." She shakes her head. "Uh, no, sir." Reaching out, she takes it from my hand and goes back to the bedroom. Leaving the door open, I hear their exchange. "Here you go, Miss Anderson."

"Thank you."

"My pleasure." She closes the door and walks back over to me, nervously tucking an imaginary piece of hair behind her ear.

"You're fired," I tell her.

"What?" Her wide eyes meet mine. "But ..."

"Get your stuff and get the fuck off this plane." I lean into her and hear her inhale sharply. "Or I'll throw you out at fifty thousand feet."

Pulling away, she grabs a purse and all but runs off the jet before the door closes.

I pull my cell out of my back pocket and send a text to Phil.

Me: I just fired your flight attendant. I'll hire someone else who is more capable of doing their job. And by the way, here are the new coordinates to give to your pilot. Gunner and I are crashing the girls' trip.

Then I turn it off before pocketing it once again. The blonde bimbo has no fucking clue who I am, yet she watched me drug Blake's drink and then served it to her. For all she knows, I'm taking her to another country and selling her into sex slavery for one fucking dollar or a million dollars.

That was a test, and she failed.

One of the things I learned as a Lord is if you give someone enough rope they always hang themselves.

I make it to the back of the room. Turning the knob, I open the door slowly to make sure she doesn't spot me right off the bat.

Blakely stands at the end of the bed that is pushed up against the right wall. To the left is a desk and next to it is another door to the private bathroom. She has her back to me while she digs through a black and white Dior bag. My eyes go to the empty champagne flute on the desk.

"We need to have a discussion about you taking drinks from strangers."

She jumps, spinning around, and the action makes her dress fly up, showing me her bubble ass in the process. Placing her hand on her chest, she gasps. "Jesus, Ryat! What the fuck are you doing here?" Her blue eyes scan the large space as if I didn't come alone. "How did you find me?"

Entering the room, I close the door behind me and lean up against it, blocking her only exit. Even though she'll be unconscious in a matter of minutes. "You know, I'm offended on how little credit you give me."

She snorts. "Please ..." Stepping forward, she stumbles but rights herself before falling, regaining her balance. Her eyes shoot to mine.

"Feeling okay?" I ask, not sounding the least bit concerned.

Her hand goes to her head, and my eyes drop to her bare legs. "I'm assuming you wore that dress for me. Since I'd never let you leave the house wearing it." It dips low in the front, showing me her round perfect fucking tits. I just want to yank it down and suck on them. Mark them with my handprints. She loves when I slap them. Gets her so wet. Another reason it needs to be burned.

"Ryat ..." She blinks, trying to get her eyes to focus. "Did you ... drug me?"

"I did."

She steps into me, tripping again, and I catch her.

"Be careful. Don't hurt yourself." Spinning us around, I push her back into the closed door and pin her against it with my body, holding her up. "That's my job."

She whimpers, her heavy eyes blinking. "What? What are you going to do?" She licks her lips. Her mouth getting dry.

"Whatever I want," I remind her of our agreement.

"You cheated," she whispers. "Somehow ..."

"I'm winning," I correct her. "And you, Blake ..." I reach up and run my hand through her hair. "You are my prize."

Her long, black lashes flutter, and her eyes fall closed. This time, they don't open again. Her body goes slack against mine, and I pick her up before placing her on the bed.

I roll her onto her stomach and shove her dress high up on her waist, exposing a light pink cotton thong. I yank it down her legs and place them in my pocket before removing her heels. Then I grab one of the white pillows off the bed and prop it up under her hips, sticking her ass up in the air. Going over to the only bag I brought, I pull out the black silicone plug before crawling onto the bed and sitting between her parted legs.

I run my hands up and down the back of her smooth thighs, digging my fingers into her skin and massaging them. I can't get enough of her. I want to fuck her every second of every day. And what little sleep I get, I dream about her.

She's become my newest obsession.

I make my way to her pussy and push a finger in to see how wet she is. Not nearly enough.

Getting up onto my knees, I unzip my jeans, pulling out my dick. *It's so fucking hard.* Has been ever since she told me she wanted me to chase her. My girl likes to play games.

I spit into my right hand and wrap it around the base of my dick while sticking my other thumb in my mouth to get it wet. Readjusting myself between her legs, I spread them farther apart, her ass and pussy up in the air for me to play with.

I begin to stroke my hard cock while my free hand goes to her ass. I rub my thumb over her puckered hole before gently pushing it into her. I groan at how tight it is. How fucking good it's going to feel when I take it from her later.

My breathing picks up, and so does the rhythm on my dick. My hand tightens to the point it's almost painful, and I hiss in a breath.

Removing my thumb, I bend over and spit on her ass so I can replace it with a finger. Working it in and out until I decide to add another.

Looking over her body lying before me makes my balls tighten. I love that she lets me play with her however I want.

I pull my fingers out and push them back into her. My eyes are glued to her ass, giving way to allow me entrance. I moan, thinking about how good it's going to feel. My balls tighten, and my body stiffens while I stroke my dick a couple of times and remove my fingers quickly before coming all over her ass and pussy.

Panting, I reach over to the plug and run it up and down between her legs, coating the black silicone in my cum. Then I spread her ass wide and gently push it into her.

"Anything I want," I say out loud as if she can hear me.

Sitting back, I look down at it. Her pretty shaved pussy and the black diamond poking out of her ass.

That's all mine!

"Beautiful." Her body is as relaxed as it'll ever be right now. This is the perfect time to get her ready for what I'm going to take later. I'll make sure she's awake for that. A sick part of me wants it to hurt, and I know a part of her will like it.

That's just who my girl is.

Removing the pillow from underneath her hips, I lay her flat on the bed and lie down beside her. Pushing the hair from her face, I rub my knuckles down the side of her cheek, thinking about the look on Matt's face when he sees her at the ceremony with my ring on her finger, knowing she's going to be mine forever.

He'll realize I'm not one to play fucking games with because I always win.

BLAKELY

I GROAN, PUSHING my face into a soft pillow that smells of lavender. Rolling onto my back, I open my heavy eyes and look up to see an unfamiliar matte black ceiling. "What?" My eyes take a second to focus. On the opposite wall is a see-through fireplace with a TV hanging above it. To the right is a sliding glass door. Squinting, I see nothing but trees and what looks like snow on the other side of it.

"What happened?" I ask myself, my hand coming up to my head. It's all so foggy, and everything is sore. Like maybe I got really drunk and fell down a flight of stairs. It wouldn't be the first time I've done that. I can be a klutz.

"I found you."

Looking over to the open bedroom door, I see Ryat leaning up against the doorway. His arms crossed over his chest, dressed in a pair of jeans and a white hoodie with the sleeves pushed up to show his toned forearms. The color makes his skin look even tanner than it already is. His emerald eyes are bright, and his lips twitch as if he wants to smile but refuses to allow himself that simple gesture to let me know he's having fun.

"You cheated," I say, and his eyes fall to my chest. Looking down, I realize I'm naked. "Where's my dress?" I ask, running my hands over my stomach. I'm not even going to ask about my underwear. I'm sure he ripped those.

"Burned it," he answers with no remorse.

"Ryat," I growl, watching as he pushes off the doorway and stalks over to the bed. His eyes slowly rove over my exposed body, and his tongue comes out to run across his lips. "You can't keep burning my clothes." I try to sound like it matters that he scorched an expensive dress, but by the way his eyes are heating up my body, I don't really give a fuck what he did to it.

When I sit up, the room spins, but I freeze when I feel something. "What—?" I trail off when that smile he was holding back appears on his face.

He arches a brow. "Something wrong?"

"What did you do?" I ask, terror gripping my chest at the feel of my ass. There's something there.

He reaches his hand up, rubbing his freshly shaven jaw. "It's what I'm going to do."

Shoving him out of my way, I fumble to get out of the bed, but my knees wobble, throwing my body into his.

Reaching up, he grips my hair and yanks my head back, holding me in place. I hiss in a breath, his force making me stumble on shaky legs, but his free hand wraps around my waist, pulling me into him to hold me up. Lowering his lips to my neck, he whispers, "You need to take it easy, little one. You're still coming down off your sedative."

Once he lets go of me, I make my way to the bathroom. There's a long counter with his and her sinks at either end. Below the countertop is nothing but matte black-painted drawers. There are three rows running down and four across. The countertop is white marble to match the floor. Lights line the top of the tall mirror, making me blink my sensitive eyes.

Turning on the far sink to the right, I bend over but pause. My eyes shoot to his in the mirror when he enters behind me, my heart picking up. "Ryat?" My voice shakes nervously.

I reach around just as he steps up behind me. He grabs my wrists and slams his body into mine, pushing me down onto the white marble counter. I let out a shaky breath, the motion brushing my hair across the smooth surface. "Ryat?" I ask, my heart now racing.

"Shh," he breathes against the side of my head. Letting go of me, he stands up but places his hand on my back to keep me bent over.

His free hand goes between my legs, and he pushes on my ass, and I feel something ... inside me? I tense.

"Have I done anything to you that you haven't enjoyed?" He muses.

"No." My heart is pounding, and my mind is trying to think of what the fuck happened while I was out.

"Do you trust me?" he asks, and I feel pressure where I've never felt it before.

"Yes," I whimper, now panting. I trust Ryat more than I do anyone else, and even I understand how sad that is.

"While you were out, I put a butt plug in your ass."

"You what?" I shriek and try to get up, but his hand on my back prevents it.

"Calm down." He slaps my thigh, and I yelp. "I'm going to fuck your ass, Blake. It's time I get what's mine."

Gripping my hair, he yanks me to stand, pulling my back to his front. His free hand wraps around my throat from behind, forcing me to lift my chin.

The new position has me feeling the plug. I groan at the way it presses into me. So unfamiliar, yet also good at the same time. I can feel it not only in my ass, but also in my pussy. The thought of it just being there makes me feel even more submissive to him.

"Contrary to what you believe, I don't want to hurt you, Blake," he says, his eyes boring into mine in the mirror. "I had to stretch that tight ass in order to get it ready for my cock."

I swallow against his hand. My ass tightening on its own, squeezing it to see if it's truly there. And why the thought turns me on. I already feel so full, I can't imagine what he will feel like inside me.

"I promise it will feel good." He kisses my cheek as if reading my mind.

Tears start to sting my eyes, but I understand what he's saying. And a part of me wants to give it to him. Wants him to take it. It's the fucked-up part that Matt was ashamed of. "I trust you," I manage to whisper.

"That's my good girl." He runs his lips along my face to my ear, where he nibbles on it, making me groan. Pulling away, he meets my eyes in the mirror once again. "Stay right here." Then he turns and walks out of the bathroom.

I bend over a little, tightening my ass once again and feeling the plug inside. It feels good but also uncomfortable at the same time. I have an urge to push it out, but I don't. Instead, I place my hands on the edge and try to calm my breathing.

He returns seconds later with rope hanging from his hands. Blood rushes in my ears when he places his hand on my back and pushes my chest onto the counter. Then he grips my hips pulling them away from the edge a little, leaving some open space.

"Spread your legs," he orders, slapping my ass.

Sweat begins to bead on my forehead. Swallowing, I spread them the best I can, knowing that he's about to have his way with my ass, and he's going to make me like it.

THIRTY-THREE

RYAT

I TAKE ONE of the ropes and double it up, sliding it through the silver handle on the bottom far right drawer and wrap it around her ankle before tying it into a knot, attaching it to the drawer. Going over to her other ankle, I do the same thing—securing her legs far apart.

Standing behind her, I grab her wrists, pulling her arm off the counter and over to the right. Her forearm hangs off the edge. I do the same to her wrists, securing them to a top drawer. Then do the same to her left one.

I look over her tied open for me with the black plug in her ass, and I start salivating. I've been dreaming of this since I saw her on her ass in the hallway at Barrington. Our flight was over four hours. It gave me the opportunity to change her plug out twice. I needed to get her ready for me. As bad as I wanted to just ram my cock into it, I do want her to enjoy it.

Running my palm up her thigh, I give her left ass cheek a hard slap.

She jumps, whimpering.

I do the same to the other one.

Her breathing picks up, filling the large room. Cupping her pussy, she wiggles her ass for me, and I push a finger into her. "You're already so wet for me," I say and then remove it, slapping her cunt as well.

She cries out. Grabbing a hand full of her hair, I yank her face off the countertop and look at her in the mirror. "Do you know why I tied you up in here instead of the bed?"

"No." She whispers. Her tear-filled eyes are so pretty right now.

I knew she wouldn't. "It's because I want you to watch yourself come with my cock in your ass."

She sucks in a ragged breath.

"You will come, Blake," I promise her. Reaching into the front pocket of my jeans, I pull out pink rubber vibrator—Lovense Lush 2. I bought it for her last week but haven't had the chance to use it yet. Now is the best time.

I remove my cell from the other pocket and pull up the app. I turn the vibrator on and rub it against her clit while setting my cell on the counter next to her head. She squirms, her body pulling on her restraints. I gently rub it in circles, just teasing her. I have it turned all the way down right now, not ready for her to come just yet.

When I push two fingers into her, she rises on her tiptoes, a strangled cry leaving her parted lips as I pump them in and out of her, getting her wetter. They pick up their pace, getting a little more forceful. When I think she's ready, I remove them, her body sagging against the countertop.

I take the vibrator and rub it over her wet cunt, getting it lubed up before pushing it inside her. She's panting, the side of her face on the counter, her eyes closed. "Ryat ..." she cries out, lifting her head up, and wide blue eyes meet mine in the mirror.

I know she's used vibrators before. I've seen them in her nightstand at her apartment. But using one on yourself and someone using one on you are two very different feelings. She's not in control here. I am.

I undo my belt and then unzip my jeans, pulling out my dick. Then I pick up the lube and spread it all over my length, making sure to coat every inch of myself until it's dripping off me.

Reaching out, I take the diamond and slowly turn it in a clockwise circle. She sucks in a breath, her body tensing. "Relax," I warn, slapping her ass cheek. "Focus on the vibrator."

I gently pull on the plug, and she whimpers. Before it can pop out all the way, I gently push it back inside her, and she moans. "That's it," I say and do it again.

Her breathing picks up even more, and she yanks on the ropes that keep her open for me.

This time, I pull it out all the way and toss it into the sink that still runs from when she turned it on, replacing it with two fingers that are still covered in lube from applying it on my cock. "Take in a couple of deep breaths," I tell her.

Her watery eyes meet mine in the mirror, and she puckers her lips, sucking in a deep breath, and then relaxes as she lets it out while I push a third finger into her. She cries, and I remove them. "Again," I tell her.

The first tear runs down her cheek, but she does as I say. I repeat the process with just two fingers this time, knowing she's ready.

Letting go, I yank my hoodie up and over my head before tossing it to the floor. Not wanting it to get in the way. Taking my cock in my hand, I step closer to her and slide the head of my dick along her ass, slowly running it up and down, smearing the lube all over her. "One more," I say, reminding myself to go slow. If I tear her, I'll have to wait to have it again.

When she sucks in a breath, I push the head into her, spreading her tight ass. She cries out, and I bite my bottom lip when it opens up for me.

I pull out and push in again, just my head. Letting her get used to it.

"Ryat," she softly cries, her body already shaking under mine.

I reach around between her body and the countertop—this is why I left some space—and begin to play with her clit. Her head falls back onto the countertop, and I pull out, pushing into her again, going deeper this time.

Yanking on the rope, she whimpers.

"Goddamn," I moan, unable to stop myself. Pulling out, I push in, a little deeper once again.

She's gasping for breath, and I'm trying not to fucking come right now. Clenching my teeth, I slide out and watch her ass open for me as I enter her again with more force this time, burying myself in deeper. "I'm halfway," I say, more to myself than her.

The drawers rattle from the ropes I've tied her to while her knees hit them. "You're doing so good," I tell her, making her whimper. "So good, Blake." I pull out and push into her again, my fingers pulling on the vibrator to remind her it's there just in case she's too focused on her ass. The way she pushes against me tells me the little distraction worked.

I do it again, this time pushing all the way into her. Letting go of the vibrator, I reach over to my cell and turn up the level all the way on the vibrator and then lean against her back. Wrapping my hands in her long, dark hair, I pull her face off the marble to look at me in the mirror. It's wet with tears. "Fuck, you're amazing, Blake," I say, kissing the side of her face and tasting the saltiness. "My good girl."

Her lips are parted, and she's panting. Her body already shaking uncontrollably.

"I'm going to fuck your ass now," I warn her, and before she can say anything, I start to move.

BLAKELY

IT HURTS BUT also feels good. I can't catch my breath. Between his dick in my ass and the vibrator in my pussy, I'm having trouble focusing.

At first, it felt like I needed to go to the bathroom. My body wanted me to push against it—refuse him. But then he started to move and fuck if it didn't feel good. I hate that he's right.

"Do you feel how deep in your ass I am, Blake?" he growls in my ear. His green eyes are locked on my watery ones in the mirror. "How tight it is?"

My hips are slammed into the side of the counter, my back arched at an odd angle, and my limbs secured to the drawers. My tits are smashed underneath me, already making it hard to breathe.

"Fuck," he growls, his hands gripping my hair, making my scalp tingle. "Your ass feels so fucking good wrapped around my cock." I manage to suck in a deep breath. "I knew it would."

My face is just inches from the mirror, and every time I breathe, a fog covers it before disappearing. His hand in my hair is the only thing preventing my face from hitting the glass with each thrust.

Everything feels so intense. He feels ten times bigger than when he's in my pussy. Sweat covers my back and my chest—my body starting to slip around on the marble counter. My hands have gone numb from the rope wrapped around my wrists, but I can't help it. My body is reacting to Ryat's dick in my ass and vibrator in my pussy.

My lips fall open on a moan, and my eyes close. The sound of his body slapping mine fills the room, and so do his grunts. They turn me on even more. The fact that he's enjoying himself makes me even wetter. My pussy clenches the toy inside me, and I'm pretty sure I'm drooling, unable to close my mouth.

It's primal. As if he can't control himself. He needed to take it. Just like I told him I imagined when I dream about my forced-sex fantasy. It feels like total surrender. I'm giving him the last bit of me that I have to offer.

He lets go of my hair with one hand and wraps it around my neck. "Open your eyes," he demands with a growl. "You're going to fucking watch."

I open my heavy eyes, fresh tears roll out of them. I'm not even sure why I'm crying. It doesn't hurt as much as I thought it would. My body tenses involuntarily, an unfamiliar feeling starting to build between my legs. My pussy and my ass start to pulsate with contractions. They crawl throughout my body like a million spiders— an explosion starting to build.

He holds me tighter, and the room seems to fade away, my vision going dark even though my eyes are open. I feel like I'm spinning, body shivering.

"That's it, Blake." I hear his voice roughly in my ear as I do exactly what he said I would do, and come, a sound so unreal erupts from my lips. A wave so heavy and hot rushes over me, taking away what little breath I had.

My body goes slack, and he slams into my ass. His dick pulses inside me as he too comes.

Pulling out of me, I whimper. Then he removes the vibrator, throwing it to the floor. It continues to stay on as he rips a towel draped over a silver rod and wipes between my shaking legs, cleaning me up. Then undoes the ropes. I don't even have the strength to get up off the counter. The side of my face sits in my tears and sweat on the marble.

He grabs my shoulders, pulling me to a standing position just in time to pick me up before I can collapse to the floor and carries me to the bedroom. He sits with his back against the headboard and pulls me into his lap.

My body is shaking so badly, I feel like I'm having a seizure. I have no control of my motor skills whatsoever. I realize I'm still crying when I lick my lips and taste the tears.

"Shh." He rocks me back and forth gently. One arm wrapped around my body, the other running down the side of my head. "You did great, Blake." He kisses my hair. "Such a good girl."

I grip the shirt he still wears and bury my face into it, closing my eyes tightly, unable to control my emotions either.

THIRTY-FOUR

RYAT

SHE'S STOPPED CRYING, her body has gone slack, and I can hear her even breathing. She's passed out again. She hadn't been out long enough the first time. It was clear the drugs were still in her system when she woke up.

I hear my cell ring in the bathroom. I gently lay her on the bed and cover her up before making my way into it. I turn off the sink, pick up the vibrator, shutting it off, and grab my cell off the counter. *Dad* flashes across my screen.

"Hello?" I answer.

"Son," he greets me. "I just spoke to Phil. He said you and Blakely went on a trip."

I didn't have to watch the cameras in her apartment to know she'd call her daddy. She needed a quick escape, and his jet would be her only option. Only we weren't going where she had planned—the Hamptons. I told him to inform the pilot of our new destination and that me and Gunner were hijacking the girls' trip. He didn't even question it.

"We are," I answer.

"Well ..."

"We didn't run off to elope if that's what you're wondering." Not like he'll be invited to the wedding anyway.

He sighs, letting me know he's got something on his mind. "You know I'll back you a hundred percent. I just want to make sure this is what you want."

"The contract has been signed. The deal is done." *She will be my wife.*

"But the Lords ..." He pauses. "She has to be initiated in as your wife. You sure you want to put her through that?"

"She would have done it when she married Matt." I shrug, not seeing the problem. Or the difference in the matter. Other than her last name will be Archer.

"Matt won't have the title that you will be awarded, Ryat," he growls.

A Lords wife is much different than a chosen one. As my wife, she will be untouchable. Invincible. Because I will give her as much power as she fucking wants. Matt was going to make her his whore. Probably let anyone who wants a piece of her, have her. He planned on using her to get him whatever his title wouldn't. Not one person will fucking touch her but me. "She can handle it," I tell him.

"We both know that if Matt doesn't marry Blakely, then he won't get anywhere. His father needs the Anderson name to stay alive."

"Your point?" I snap, getting irritated. He's speaking like I haven't already asked her father and gotten his permission. Like I'm going to just wake up and toss her to the side. That was the original plan, but not now. Not after what Matt did to me while we were in jail working for Gregory.

"My point is that giving her your last name isn't the same as taking Matt's."

"Did you call for any another reason, or just to piss me off?" I growl.

He lets out a huff. "I just ... I just want to make sure you know what you're doing. A Lord getting married isn't like taking on a chosen one. You can't toss Blakely to the side when you're done *playing* with her."

"You didn't mind me offering money for her when I was at the house in New York." I remind him. He asked me twice what I'd pay for her while I was there.

"That had to do with Matt. Not you," he argues.

I bend down, pick up my hoodie, and walk over to the doorway, leaning against it. My eyes fall to her sleeping in the bed. A sense of overwhelming jealousy runs over me at the thought of anyone else's lips kissing her body. Their hands running over her soft skin and wet pussy. Fucking her like I have. Her moaning their name. Or her begging them for their cock.

She's mine. It's just that simple.

I'm addicted to her smile, the way she touches me. The sound of her voice. How she says my name. The way her scent lingers on my clothes when I'm not with her. Everything about her feeds a hunger that can never be satisfied. I know it, and she knows it. It's not a matter of if I love her. The question is, can I hand her over to Matt after graduation? *Fuck no!* Call me selfish, but I'm not handing her over to anyone.

"I understand the difference, Father. Thanks for your concern, but Blakely Anderson will be my wife." I hang up before he can say anything else about my decision to marry her.

Walking back over to the bed, I run my knuckles down her cheek.

"Ryat?" she whispers, moving onto her back.

"Yeah, little one?" I ask, my fingers running down her neck, stopping to feel the strong rhythm of her pulse.

Her heavy lashes lift for the briefest second, soft blue eyes meet mine before falling shut once again. "Take a nap with me."

"Whatever my girl wants," I say, removing my clothes and climbing into bed next to her. She rolls, giving me her back, and I cuddle up to her warm body, pulling her into me. Within seconds, she's back to sleep.

BLAKELY

I EXPECTED BEING married to feel different. I always had this dark cloud hanging over my head that I was expecting to open up and drown me once I married Matt. That's not even close to what it feels like being married to Ryat.

It's a freeing feeling that I can't even begin to explain. The only thing I can compare it to is when you're swimming and come up for air. That burning sensation in your lungs, that tightness in your chest. When you break the surface and get that first breath and feeling the sun on your face. That's what Ryat is to me.

My sun. My air.

We spent two days away together doing nothing but having sex when we played the cat and mouse game. We could have literally done that at my apartment or at his cabin in the woods. Instead, he had my father's pilot take us to one of his parents' vacation houses in the middle of nowhere. It was cold, wet, and started to snow. We spent every second indoors screwing all over the house. Even joined the mile-high club on the way back. It was by far the best vacation I've ever had. And not one tan line to show for it. I've been doing it wrong all these years, sitting on beaches with Sarah.

The moment we touched back down in Pennsylvania we went and applied for our marriage license. Three days later we were at city hall getting married.

I look down at the ring on my finger and run my thumb over it. It's still hard to comprehend. It's like a dream. One that I could have never imagined. I guess you would call that weekend we had away our honeymoon because we didn't have time to get out of town after we said I do.

I stand in Ryat's bathroom at the house of Lords, looking at myself in his mirror. My hair is up in a French twist, my makeup done heavily with silver and black eye shadow with thick black liner on top and bottom, with extra thick mascara and matte red lips.

Running my hands down the white satin gown, I take in a deep breath. Tonight's the ceremony. To say I'm nervous is an understatement. I'm not sure what to expect. But one thing is for sure, I'm no longer Blakely Anderson. Now I'm Blakely Archer— Ryat's wife.

It isn't hard to say or comprehend. I understand what we did. I also understand that I'll never leave him. I owe Ryat that. My commitment. My body. My heart? Do I have to love him too? Or is the rest enough?

The fact that he was even willing to save me from Matt is good enough for me.

"Blake, you ready?" I hear Ryat call out, entering his room.

"Yeah," I say, turning around to stand in the doorway of the bathroom just as he enters.

He comes to a stop; his emerald eyes drop to the train on my dress and slowly run up over the fitted material that hugs me like a glove. There's a slit up my right leg, so high, I wasn't even able to wear any underwear because it comes up past my hip. The satin material covers my chest, coming up high up in the front, to where it wraps around my neck, two silk pieces tie in the back in a big bow leaving the leftover satin to fall over the open back. Every time I move, I feel the soft and cool material glide across my skin, making me shiver. The entire back is cut out, dipping to the top of my ass.

I didn't wear a dress to city hall. Instead, I chose a white suit. But tonight, I wanted to dress up for him. He once told me he was proud to call me his chosen after we performed the vow ceremony. I wanted him to feel that way tonight, knowing that I'm now his wife.

My heart begins to race, breaths coming in quick bursts at the way he looks at me. His emerald eyes slowly run up and down several times.

Reaching up, he pulls on his bow tie and clears his throat. Taking a step toward me, I take one back, and he stops. "Are you going to burn it?" I ask nervously. It's revealing, showing off my bare back, leg, and hip along with a little side boob. But somehow, even the parts of my body it covers, I still feel exposed.

He begins to walk toward me again, and this time, I don't retreat.

Coming up to me, he cups my face, his eyes searching mine. "No," he whispers, his eyes dropping to my covered chest. "Blake ... you look stunning."

I blush, letting out a long breath, and drop my head, unable to help the smile that spreads across my face.

There's a knock on the door right before it swings open. "Ryat?" I look up, and he snaps, "What?"

"You're needed, man," Gunner informs him then looks at me. Winking, he gives me a thumbs-up. "Hot wife."

My cheeks burn. I still can't believe we did that.

"Gunner ..." Ryat starts.

"I'm not leaving." He enters the room and crosses his arms over his chest with a playful smile on his face.

Ryat growls deep in his chest and turns to face me. "I'll meet you out there." He places a kiss on my cheek and turns, walking out.

Taking a second to myself, I close my eyes and inhale deeply, trying to slow my racing heart. I exit the room, making sure to shut and lock his bedroom door behind me before pocketing the key in my clutch that barely fits my cell phone.

Making my way to the ballroom, I look for Ryat or Sarah but don't see them anywhere. The place is packed. Decorated with white twinkling lights and soft piano music. So different from when I was here the first time.

"Would you like a glass of champagne, miss?"

I go to tell her no, afraid of my last experience. Now is not the time to get drunk or drugged. But she pops the cork and grabs a flute. "Yes, please."

Handing it to me, I thank her and take a sip.

The lights dim down a little, the music coming to a stop, and so does all the conversations.

"Good evening, ladies and gentlemen."

I turn to face the stage, seeing Ryat stand in the middle with a microphone in his hand. "I want to thank you all for attending the annual house of Lords ceremony."

I take another sip.

"It's been a long four years," he says, running his hand across his chin as in thought.

I frown, wondering what he means by that.

"As a Lord, we're taught to never accept defeat. To never give up on what we want."

His eyes are looking past me, over my shoulder. I turn to see what he's staring at and regret it the moment I do. *It's Matt.* He stands there, dressed in a suit and tie like the others, and his girlfriend is wearing a black sequined dress with a plunging neckline to show off her assets. Giving them my back, I turn to face the stage once again.

"Some of us will never know defeat. Others will never know victory," Ryat goes on. "But what I can tell you is those who don't try will never know what they are capable of."

I take a sip of the champagne.

"Blakely," he calls out my name.

And I snort into my drink. Then quickly wipe it off my chin, praying it didn't spill on my dress. *Not again!* Last time, I left a party here covered in alcohol.

I look up at him wide-eyed.

He stands there, looking every bit of a powerful man dressed in an expensive tux, hair slicked back and clean shaven. He's so gorgeous.

"For those of you who don't know, Blakely is my chosen."

What is he doing? My hand holding the flute starts to shake.

"Sometimes, you get lucky in life. And I can say that I'm the luckiest man in this room."

Oh, God. No. no. no.

"Just look at her." He gestures to me with his left hand and my eyes go straight to his wedding band. The thought that he's mine fills my stomach with butterflies. "She's amazing, breathtaking, good hearted and a hundred percent mine."

Don't do it ...

"As of yesterday, I can add my wife to that."

Audible gasps fill the large room, and I hold my breath. "The stunning Mrs. Blakely Rae Archer, everyone." He introduces me to hundreds of people.

I give a shaky smile to the applause given to us that follows, wishing the floor would fucking swallow me up.

Ryat walks down the stairs and comes over to me, people moving out of his way.

"What are you doing?" I hiss under my breath.

He takes my drink from my hands and passes it off to a server who walks by. He spins me around, pulling me into his body, not answering me.

THIRTY-FIVE

RYAT

FUCK EVERY SINGLE goddamn one of them.

"Ryat," she whispers. Her eyes darting around the room.

I begin to dance with her. One hand on her bare back, the other coming up to cup her face while "Broken" by Lifehouse starts to play through the speakers in the ballroom.

She nibbles on her bottom lip nervously and her eyes continue to look around the room, looking at everyone as they watch us.

Coming to a stop, I run my knuckles down her cheek and along her jaw before lifting her face to mine. She licks her lips, wetting the matte red lipstick. I run my thumb over it, lowering my face to hers. Her pretty blue eyes stare up at me, and it's like everyone else in the room fades away. She only has eyes for me, but everyone is looking at her. My wife.

I never really gave much thought to my marriage. That was because I never really cared about it. I looked at it more like a contract. And even though this is exactly what it was, it feels like more.

She licks her painted lips and I lean down, pressing mine to hers. I kiss her. The first time I kissed her was yesterday standing at the city hall, vowing my life to hers. The thought had never crossed my mind. Now? Now I can't get enough of them. Doesn't matter what we've done, this feels more intimate than any of it.

Her tongue meets mine and I taste the champagne. It's as sweet as her. She kisses me with so much passion, so needy. It's as if she's breathing for me.

She stood in this very spot just weeks ago, and all I could think of was that I was going to take her from a man I hated. Now, all I can think of is spending the rest of my life with her.

I lift my hands to her neck, making sure everyone watching can see my ring, tilting my head to the side of her face and open my eyes. They land on Matt, who stands behind her, just like I knew they would. I hope they say everything I'm thinking.

I fucking win!

The way his narrow on me and his fists clench, he gets the message. He grabs Ashley and spins around, running off with her.

Slowing the kiss down, I pull away. Her heavy eyes slowly open to look up at me. "I owed you a dance, Mrs. Archer." I finally answer her question, and her body melts into mine. A look of pure admiration written all over her Barbie doll face, and it makes me smile. I want to see that more from her.

It can't hurt to have your wife fall in love with you, right?

I feel like it won't take much.

BLAKELY

I MAKE MY way down the hallway to Ryat's bedroom. Three glasses of champagne later and countless handshakes with the congratulations have got me needing to pee. I unlock the door and then shut it behind me. I'm washing my hands when I hear his bedroom door open and close. "Have you seen Sarah tonight?" I ask, turning it off and grabbing a towel to dry my hands.

Spinning around, I go to step back into the bedroom, but someone steps in front of me, blocking my way. I go to scream when they shove me into the bathroom, but a hand is slapped over my face, and I'm shoved up against the wall.

I look up into a set of baby-blue eyes. I start screaming behind his hand.

"Shh, Blakely. I just want to talk." He removes his hand and raises them both in front of him.

I suck in a deep breath, "What are you doing, Matt?" I snap. If Ryat finds him in here, he'll kick his ass.

"I need to talk to you."

I shove his chest, but he doesn't budge. "There's nothing for us to say." Making a fist, I pound it into his suit.

He sighs and steps back, allowing me space to exit the bathroom. I rush through the bedroom, and my hand reaches the doorknob when he speaks. "He paid your father five hundred thousand to marry you."

I stop and turn to face him. A laugh bubbles up in my chest, but I force it down. "You're lying," Men don't pay for their wives. That's the kind of shit you see in movies.

He goes on. "Your phone. He tracks you with it."

My pulse races at his words. "No ..."

"Your incoming calls and texts. He blocks them." He growls.

My knees start to buckle at the blow to my chest his words have on me, but I manage to stay standing. But I argue, "He couldn't ..."

"Think about it. Your mom has told me that she can't reach you. I've tried calling and texting you." He steps toward me, and I'm frozen in my spot. "That weekend he went to New York but came home early, he blocked Sarah's number so she couldn't call you to come party here without him."

Tears start to sting my eyes at how much sense his words are making, but I don't want to believe it. "No. How would he ...?"

"That first night here at the party ... when you caught me with Ashley? He retrieved your phone, keys, and ID from the check-in before driving you home. He downloaded an app to your cell to give him access to everything. Even the things you google. He can hear every call, read every text. He tracks you."

Tears fall from my eyes even as I shake my head at him, refusing to believe what I know is the truth. It has to be. It makes too much sense.

He sighs, "I know there's no hope for us anymore. But I just thought you should know who you've married." His eyes drop to my ring.

"How ..." I clear my throat. "How do you know all of this?"

"Because I did it to Ashley," he replies simply. "All the Lords do it to their chosens. Why do you think we make everyone turn in their cells for the party? It's to give us access to them when everyone else is too busy partying."

I swallow the lump that gets lodged in my throat. It has to be true, right? It explains so much. Why my mother couldn't reach me. Why Sarah's calls wouldn't go through when he was supposed to be gone, but magically did when we returned from our weekend at the cabin. How he found me on my father's private jet. And the fact that he placed his hand over my mouth and nose the day after I googled breath play. "How do you know he gave my father money?" I ask, my shoulders shaking.

He reaches up, scratching the back of his neck. "I know because ..." He pauses, his arm dropping to his side, sighing. "Because I offered fifty for you."

Reaching up, I cover my mouth to hide my sob. I knew he didn't love me, but this? It was all a game to him. I was nothing more than a high-paid prostitute. My father sold me to the highest bidder.

"Blakely ..." He steps toward me, and I take a step back, hitting the bedroom door. He stops. "I'm so ..."

"Get out," I shout. More embarrassed than anything. Ashamed that I thought I was doing something right when it was really the stupidest goddamn thing.

"Blakely ..."

"GET OUT," I scream, stepping out of the way and opening the door for him.

He walks toward it, pausing once he gets to the door. "Ryat was right about one thing. You really do look stunning." Then he exits the room, and I slam the door shut, locking it.

I fall to my ass and bring my knees to my chest, holding a hand over my mouth to quiet the sobs.

Every single person sold me out. Every goddamn one of them. No one was on my side. They never asked what I wanted.

Pulling my hand from my mouth, I look down at my ring and start yanking on it. It pops off and goes flying across the room. I crawl over in my expensive dress and pick it up. Then I walk over to his bed, placing it in the center of it.

Entering the bathroom, I look at myself in the mirror. My makeup smeared across my face. I expected to look this way later this evening for a different reason. Not even bothering to wipe it off, I grab my clutch that has my phone in it, knowing I've got one chance and one chance only to get away. Because if everything that Matt said is true, Ryat will find me within minutes.

THIRTY-SIX

RYAT

"CONGRATULATIONS ON THE nuptials, Ryat." Gregory comes up to me, shaking my hand.

"Thank you, sir." I take a sip of my champagne.

"Remember what I said." He nods at me. "Need anything. Let me know. I owe you."

I give him a nod and pull my cell phone out of my pocket. I notice that Blake's been gone for a while now. Pocketing it, I look up and scan the crowd. I see Sarah and Gunner in the far corner at the bar.

Making my way over to them, I take another drink. "Hey, have you guys seen Blake?" I ask.

"No." Sarah frowns. "I've texted her twice and no response."

Gunner shakes his head. "But by the way ... smooth, man." He gestures to the stage and the little show I put on.

I smirk, but it drops when I spot Matt across the room. He stands with his back to the wall with a drink in his hand. It's the smile on his face he's giving me that makes my skin crawl. Alarms go off as he just stands there staring at me.

My cell rings, and I pull it out, dismissing him. I see it's a blocked number, so I turn and open the sliding glass door, walking outside. I stand on the back terrace, looking over the Olympic size swimming pool lit up with floating white lights and hit answer. "Hello?"

There's a long stretch of silence that greets me. "Hello?" I ask again, and nothing. "Who is this?" I demand.

"Your wife."

The cold tone used for those two words send a chill up my spine, freezing me in place. "Blake?"

"How could you?" Her words shake, telling me she's angry.

"How could I what?" I look up and over the manicured yard. "Where are you?"

She gives a rough laugh. "Want to make sure you get what you paid for?"

My head snaps up, and so does my pulse. "Blake ...."

"How could you?" she seethes. "You know, I never expected you to love me. But I was dumb enough to think you at least respected me."

"Where are you?" I growl through gritted teeth. Spinning around, I yank open the door and enter the ballroom.

"Long gone, Ryat."

"Where?" I demand, running through the ballroom and down the hallway.

"You wanna play games, Ryat? I can play. I can play them all day long."

I come to my bedroom and slam the door open. Looking around, I don't see her. "You better—"

"What?" she interrupts me. "Come back and bow down to you? Not a chance, Ryat."

I catch sight of something on the bed. Walking over to it, I see it's her wedding ring, purse, and cell phone. *Motherfucker!* She's running. "I'll find you," I grind out. "I already told you that once ... and Blake." I take in a deep breath, my hands shaking. "When I do, I will drag you back by your hair, kicking and screaming." I'll do whatever it fucking takes. "Don't make me hurt you."

She gives a soft laugh, like she doesn't believe a damn word I just said. The sound crawls all over me like hot lava, burning my skin, making me even angrier. "You can't find what you can't track, Ryat."

Oh, but I will. "I'll see you soon, Mrs. Archer."

"No. You won't." *Click.*

"Goddammit," I shout, throwing my cell across the room, and it hits the wall, the screen shattering in a million pieces.

My chest is heaving, and my hands reach up to fist my hair. It doesn't matter how she got that ring; she belongs to me. This changes nothing. I will bring her back, but she won't like how I do it.

THIRTY-SEVEN

RYAT

I SIT ON the black leather couch, leaning forward with my elbows on my knees. My right hand absentmindedly spins my wedding band.

Till death do us part is engraved on the inside of the band—identical to my wife's.

She has been gone for two days now. Not a single word, not a clue as to where she went. And no fucking idea where to even start looking. She disappeared—*poof*—like a ghost.

When I find her—and I will—it's going to take everything in me not to fucking kill her. That's how angry I am.

My new phone vibrates in my pocket, and I pull it out to see it's a text from an unknown number.

Negative.

Locking it back, I grind my teeth. *Well, that's interesting.* But something that I don't have time to devote my life to right now. One problem at a time.

"What do we know?" my father-in-law asks, sitting behind his desk in his office overlooking downtown Dallas. Once again, in the middle of the night.

"Nothing," Prickett answers, sitting to my right.

I haven't said much since I found out she decided to run. It seems pointless because there's not much to say.

"She didn't return to her apartment, her car is still in the same spot it was before, and she left her cell at the house of Lords, along with her wedding ring," Gunner informs, sitting to my left.

My father sighs while he stands by the floor-to-ceiling window. "She's just vanished."

"People don't just disappear." Her father slams his hands down on his desk. I'm pretty sure Phil wants to strangle her too. "She needs money to survive."

"She gets a job," Prickett offers.

"She's never had one a day in her life. What skills does she have?" he barks. "But if she does have one, then there's a record of her somewhere out there."

"Not if she's making cash, getting paid under the table," Gunner states, sitting back on the couch. "Vegas and stripper come to mind."

My hands clench at his words, and I want to punch him for even thinking that.

"Matt played her," my father states, turning around to face the room. "He realized his chance with her was gone, so he chose to sabotage her marriage with Ryat." His eyes meet mine. "He was probably planning on her making a big scene in front of everyone but was granted something better when she ran instead."

We had watched the video of Matt and my wife in my bedroom when we first arrived thirty minutes ago, I've watched it more times than I can count by now. You would think that I'd realize that there is no evidence to tell me where she went.

But the video didn't change my mind about the situation she's left us in. I don't give a shit how upset she is with me; she's still going to pay for this. So will Matt, but he'll come later. Right now, she's my main priority.

Phil runs his hands down his face, letting out a deep breath. "Find her." His eyes meet mine. "Find her and bring her back. By whatever force you deem necessary."

I nod once. I'd planned on it anyway, but thanks for the permission.

"Her biggest threats are those who want to hurt Ryat," he goes on. "A wife of a Lord is one who can be used against us. And it was just announced to the goddamn world."

Marriages inside the Lords are always to create power. Wives have been kidnapped for ransom. Some have been raped, others murdered. Any of our enemies can see what we have and take it. Doesn't matter if the couple loves each other or not. It still impacts our world. The wife is our toy and also our weakness.

"She's vulnerable out there by herself." He stands and shoves his computer off the desk. It crashes to the ground. "FUCK!" Placing his hands on the surface, he breathes heavily. "We can't go to the press with this. We can't do anything to let the public know she's missing. It'll bring a fucking war on us. Someone could see her and then grab her before we even find her." His eyes dare me to argue. I don't. "By the time we find her body, it'll be too late."

He's right. We can't trust anyone outside this room. "I'm going to find her," I say calmly, finally breaking my silence. But what no one knows is that I'm the biggest threat she's got right now.

BLAKELY

"You may kiss your bride."

Out of everything I've done since I ran into Ryat in the hall of Barrington, those are the most terrifying words I've heard.

Kiss? The thought just hit me like a brick to the face. The blow almost knocking me out of my heels. We haven't kissed on the lips once yet. I honestly didn't even think of it. That this had to happen.

He steps into me, his right hand cups my cheek, his eyes drop to my parted lips and I suck in a deep breath when his chest presses up against mine.

I tilt my head up to look at him. My heart hammers and beads of sweat form on the back of my neck. Why am I so nervous? I've kissed a boy before. Hell, I've even kissed Sarah before. But Ryat? Kiss my now husband sounds too intimate—forbidden.

But I can't stop it. It has to be done—it's a tradition to bless the marriage. Pressing his lips to mine, my eyes fall closed just as my lips part. His touch is tender, his lips almost needy. I open up for him, giving the last thing that I have to offer him and my body molds into his when his free arm wraps around my waist, holding me tightly.

His tongue enters my mouth, gently meeting mine and I moan into his mouth, wanting more. Needing that aggression that he always has. My hands slide up his back, gripping a hold of his button-up and I cling to him. Needing him closer.

But he pulls away, and I open my heavy eyes, disappointment coursing through me that I hadn't done that before now.

His eyes are already on mine and he licks his lips as if he needed one more taste of me. His hand cupping my face moves to run his knuckles down over my cheek when he whispers, "Now you're mine forever, Mrs. Archer."

"Miss?"

"What?" I blink, trying to get that memory of our wedding day out of my mind. It's been on replay ever since I left him.

"Can I get a Bud Light?" the man calls out, raising his hand to me from his table.

I nod. "Of course. Anything else?" *Get your shit together, Blakely. There was a reason you left him.*

He gives me a soft smile, his amber-colored eyes dropping to my tight booty shorts. "A shot of you."

Cute! After giving him a fake laugh like his joke was funny, I turn and head to the bar to grab his order.

"You just got a new table," Janett, the bartender and owner, nods behind me.

Looking over my shoulder, I see three men sit down. "I need a Bud Light," I tell her, and she pops one open for me. Placing it on my tray, I give it to the man and then go over to my new table. "What can I get for you guys?" I ask, holding my round tray up against my right hip.

This is my life now. A server at a dive bar in the middle of fucking nowhere. I've been gone for three weeks. No phone, no car, no access to the outside world other than who I see in here, which is exactly how I want it. I don't know just how much the Lords reach goes when it comes to the police or the feds.

But Ryat still lives in my head, and I hate it.

I left everything when I ran out of the house of Lords. I knew I wouldn't be returning. In order to escape, I need a new life. I had some cash saved, but I wasn't able to run back to my apartment and grab it, so until I could get some saved up again, I needed a job that was going to fly under the radar.

I applied, and Janett hired me on the spot. I think she knew by my white satin dress and smeared makeup that I was running from someone. And, of course, the fact I had no contact number or ID. She helped me out. I owe her for that.

"I'll have a Corona," one of the guys calls out over the music. The second one nods. "Yeah, that sounds good. Make it two." The third guy puts the menu down and looks up at me. His dark blue eyes drop to my white crop top. It fits extra tight, pulling across the black bra I wear underneath—classy, I know.

I've dyed my hair black with a cheap box from the dollar store just down the road. I was trying to think of a million things I could do to change my appearance in case my picture or name was plastered all over the news. But to my surprise, that hasn't happened.

Every day I'm gone, I feel more on edge. Like my time is running out. I don't plan on staying here much longer. I know I need to keep moving in order to avoid my past. I already feel like I'm being watched. But I keep telling myself that's crazy. If Ryat was here and knew where I was, he'd make himself known. He doesn't have enough patience to hide in the shadows and watch me.

"What's your name?" he asks, placing his forearms on the table, leaning in.

"Rae," I give him my middle name. Still wanting to be careful. That's what everyone calls me here anyway.

"Rae." He runs his tongue across his white teeth. "Well, what do you suggest, Rae?"

"Depends on what you like." I shrug. We're not that experimental with drinks here. The clientele usually prefers the norm. I'm not going to go over the entire list when it's sitting right in front of him.

"I like you." He sits back in his seat, his eyes dropping to my shorts like the last guy, and I have to refrain from rolling my eyes. This is how I make my tips.

"Stop, man." His friend slaps him in the arm, laughing. "She's probably got a boyfriend."

A husband actually.

If I'm lucky, he's given me an annulment, but I highly doubt it. Ryat is more the type to have fake papers drawn up about an excruciating death on my behalf. That's the least that motherfucker could do for me.

"So?" The guy chuckles at his friend. "What do you say, sexy momma? Go out with me after your shift?"

Momma? Does that really work for men? "I don't get off until three," I inform him. The fact that he thinks I would cheat on my imaginary boyfriend is insult enough. It's clear he just wants to fuck. No one goes on a date at three in the morning.

Not going to say I haven't thought of it. Going from as much sex as Ryat and I were having to fucking nothing sucks ass. This morning, I had to lay flat in the bathtub and spread my legs for the damn faucet to hit it just right while on full blast. I have nothing to get me off, and I can't seem to get it done with my fingers. It's frustrating, to say the least.

"That's fine." He links his hands together and places them behind his head, smirking up at me. "I'll wait until you get off. Then we'll get off."

"What do you want to drink, sir?" I ask, holding in a sigh.

His friend's laughter grows. "Dude, just order your fucking drink and leave her alone."

"Surprise me," he finally says.

Giving them my back, I make my way over to the bar. "Three Coronas, please."

She nods and turns to get the beers for me, and he floods my memories like usual.

"Ryat," I squeal when he bends down and sweeps me off my feet, cradling me in his arms in the middle of the driveway. "What are you ...?"

"It's tradition to carry your wife over the threshold," he informs me, entering the cabin.

I smile up at him. "Never thought you'd be the kind of guy who cares about tradition."

Entering the bedroom, he tosses me onto the bed and before I can even get up, he's straddling my hips with a hand on either side of my head, pinning me down. "I think you'll find that I'm full of surprises, Mrs. Archer."

"Here you go." She places the drinks on my tray, once again bringing me back to the present.

"Thanks," I mumble.

"Are you okay?" she asks, stopping me before I can walk away.

"Yeah," I lie, and her light brown eyes look at me skeptically. "I'll be fine."

"Look." She leans over, placing her forearms on the bar top. "I don't know the story, and I don't need to know, but I promise you're better off."

"I CAN'T LEAVE," Janett says into her cell phone, standing behind the bar. We've been closed for almost an hour now and are almost done cleaning. "No," she grinds out. "I have a few more things to do ..."

"You can go ahead and leave if you need to," I tell her.

She looks up at me, and I hope she's not mad at me for eavesdropping on her conversation. We're the only two left here, and the music is off, so it's quiet at the moment.

"Yeah, okay," she says after a long pause. "I'll be right there." Pocketing her cell phone, she looks at me. "Are you sure?"

"Yeah," I say with a nod. "No worries. I'll lock up."

"Thanks, Rae. You're awesome. I'll see you tomorrow." She grabs her purse out from underneath the bar, throws her keys on top of it for me, and then storms out the front door.

I grab the keys and make my way to lock the front doors behind her from the inside. Then I walk over to the bags of trash lined up in front of the bar. I'm in no hurry to get back to my hotel room. It's a shit place, but it's cheap. Again, under the radar. Takes cash. The lady next to me always has visitors, and I'm pretty sure by the way her bed hits the wall, she gets paid for her time.

Picking up two of the bags, I carry each of them awkwardly out the back door into the alleyway to the dumpster. Setting them down, I push the lid open and then throw them each in one at a time. Slamming it shut, I slap my hands together to get the dirt off them and turn around to see a figure standing in front of me.

Jumping back, I scream.

"Hey, Rae," the guy from earlier tonight says, standing in front of the door, blocking my only way back in.

"You scared me," I breathe, my hand on my racing heart. "What ... what are you doing out here?"

"I've been waiting on you."

I take a step back from him, my back hitting the nasty smelling dumpster. We've been closed for over an hour. He's waited this entire time for me? "You need to go," I tell him and try to step around him, but he steps to the side, blocking me.

"Come on." He smirks. "Do you really think I don't know who you are?"

My stomach drops, but I try to fake it. "I don't know ..."

"You're Blakely Rae Archer."

My breath hitches that he knows my full name. My eyes drop to his right hand, but I don't see the ring that I know Ryat wears with the Lord's crest on it. Is this guy a member? "Did Ryat send you?" I ask, voice shaking.

His smile grows.

If this is a test, I feel like I just failed. "Just tell him you didn't find me. Please ..."

Grabbing my top, he spins me around. He slams my back into the back door to the bar, stepping into me. "Why would I do that?"

"Please," I beg. I can't go back. I've thought about it, but it's been too long now. Ryat would kill me. I have no doubt that I stepped over a line that cannot be undone. And I knew the moment I decided to run that I'd be running for the rest of my life. But it was better than the alternative. Ryat, my mother, father, Matt, everyone made me a fool. A stupid, idiotic woman who thought she might actually be worth something.

"What will you do for me?" he asks.

I swallow the lump in my throat. "I have some cash ..."

He throws his head back, laughing. "I don't want your money, bitch," he snaps in my face, making me whimper. "No, I want what Ryat has." Taking a step back from me, he gives me just enough room to bring my knee up, making contact with his balls.

"Fuuuccckkkk." Doubling over, he grabs himself.

I push off the wall to run down the alleyway. But a hand fisting in my hair yanks me to the ground. "Get off me," I shout, kicking my feet out, but he drops and straddles me, his weight pinning me down on the uneven, cold ground. It rained earlier this evening, so the water soaks into what little clothes I wear and my hair.

"Not until I get what he owes me," he growls, wrapping both of his hands around my neck and squeezing.

I arch my back, my hands gripping his forearms and my lips open, trying to suck in a breath, but he's restricting my air. My shoes kick the concrete, and my face pounds like a drum. Tears fill my eyes, making his figure blurry.

"I'm going to send you back to him in fucking pieces," he growls, shaking me.

Dots take over my vision, my chest heaves for a breath of air as my body starts to give up the fight. My hands falling to the concrete beside me, and my eyes grow heavy. Just when I think I'm about to die, his head is yanked back, and I watch a knife slide across his throat. Blood squirts out of the open wound, spraying me, and his hands loosen enough for me to get free.

Coughing, I crawl backward before his body falls to the ground where I was just lying.

Trying to catch my breath, now wet and covered in blood, I look up at the man who stands behind him, and my stomach drops. He's much more terrifying than the man who was just trying to kill me.

Ryat Alexander Archer has found me.

THIRTY-EIGHT

RYAT

I STARE DOWN at her, watching those pretty blue eyes look up at me from her ass in complete and utter shock. She looks just as gorgeous as I remember. Her hair is darker, but other than that, she looks like the blue-eyed, Barbie doll–face woman I became obsessed with. Blood now covers her white crop top, neck, and parts of her face. I like the way it looks on her—really brings out her eyes and red painted lips.

She's sitting on the ground, and her big tits bounce while she pants, trying to regain her breathing after the motherfucker was choking her to death.

If anyone kills her, it'll be me. I get that privilege. She's my wife. I decide when I'm done with her, and my cock stuffed inside my jeans reminds me I'm not quite there just yet.

I lift the knife in my hand and run the blade across my jeans, wiping his blood off both sides on my thigh.

She scrambles backward a little more, getting to her feet. She turns to run, but Prickett and Gunner both stand at the end of the alleyway, blocking her exit. She looks back at me, and then darts inside the bar through the back door.

"Gunner, take care of the security cameras," I tell him, and he nods. "Prickett, you're with me."

I open the back door and step inside, knowing there's nowhere for her to run in here. We already chained the front doors shut from the outside. The sound of them rattling makes me smile. At least she understands the severity of her actions.

She looks at us over her shoulder, her hair slapping her in the face. And she takes off to run, but Prickett grabs her, tossing her on top of a table where she rolls off the side to the floor, taking a couple of chairs with her.

Lying facedown, she lets out a groan as she sluggishly tries to get up on her hands and knees. But Prickett yanks her up, bending her over the side of the table and pulling her arms behind her back with one hand. He reaches into his back pocket with the other to retrieve his handcuffs. She begins to regain some strength and starts screaming while she fights him, but he gets them secure and cinches them tight to make her cry out.

I make my way over to the table and pick up one of the chairs that fell over. Spinning it to where it's backward, I straddle it, placing myself right in front of where her head hangs off the edge. Prickett continues to stand behind her, his forearm in her back, pushing her down onto the wooden surface.

Lifting the knife, I gently press it to her forehead, and her body goes stiff. I slowly run it down the side of her face, pushing her hair out of the way so I can look her in the eyes. They glare at me.

"Hello, Blake," I say lovingly.

"Just fucking kill me," she snaps through gritted teeth.

I tilt my head to the side, running the knife down underneath the tip of her chin, and press on the skin, forcing her to tilt her head up more in order to keep from getting cut. "Why would I do that? I love you."

She snorts at the lie, the action making the pieces of loose hair swirl around her face.

Removing the knife from under her chin, she drops it a little bit, and I dig into my pocket to retrieve her wedding ring. "I thought you'd want this back." I hold it up in front of her face.

"The only thing I want is a divorce." She bares her pretty, white teeth. The table rattles when she starts fighting Prickett's hold.

I forgot how much I enjoyed this side of Blakely. Things were getting a little too comfortable between us before she left. You know, catching those feelings and all because she looked stunning in a dress. Good thing we're back on track now. "Till death do us part, Blake. And I'm not ready to kill you yet."

She starts fighting him harder, but he keeps her pinned down. He removes his forearm from her back and instead lays across her, his hands gripping her hair and yanking her head up. The action forces a scream out of her, and I take the opportunity to grab the two pills out of my pocket and shove them into her mouth before slapping my hand over it, sealing them inside.

Her body thrashes, and I stand from the chair, kicking it out of my way. Crouching before her, I place my other hand around her slender neck, holding it in place but not restricting her air.

My face is inches from hers, and I watch tears start to fill her eyes when she tries to shake her head. "It doesn't matter if you swallow or if they dissolve, Blake. The result is the same."

She blinks, the action forcing the tears to spill down her cheeks to my hand, smearing the blood of the dead guy I killed in the alleyway. Her nostrils flare before she swallows them with my hand around her neck. "That's my good girl," I praise, and she whimpers.

Removing both of my hands, I nod to Prickett. He lets go of her hair as well and gets up off her, walking away to go help Gunner since we'll be leaving soon.

Standing to my full height, I roll her onto her back, pinning her cuffed arms underneath her. I brush her hair from her tear-streaked and bloody face. She blinks, her eyes growing heavy already. "I hate you," she whispers.

"I know," I tell her, running my fingers down over her neck, then her chest to her exposed belly. She's lost some weight. It makes me wonder just how much she's gone without to keep this very situation from happening. "But I also don't care."

Whimpering, she looks away from me to stare up at the ceiling, slowly blinking as fresh tears run down the side of her face. "How?" she sniffs before licking her lips.

I smile down at her, my knuckles brushing through her tears. "I told you ... you can't run from me." Leaning down, I kiss her cheek, tasting them. Fuck, I've missed her so much. I haven't slept much since she left, thinking about what I'd do to her once I saw her again. Now that I have her, I want to tie her down to my bed and remind her just how much she loves being owned. "I'll always find you."

When she closes her heavy eyes this time, they don't open. Her body relaxes, and her breathing evens out. She's got marks on her neck from the bastard trying to kill her. What little clothes she wears are wet with his blood splatter. I'm going to rip them off and burn them.

I place my arms underneath her, picking her limp body up off the table just as Prickett and Gunner come out from the back. "Let's go," I order.

BLAKELY

I SIT UP, gasping for breath. My hand goes to my chest, realizing I'm no longer in my uniform, but now an oversized T-shirt. My eyes dart around aimlessly, seeing I'm in a bed. One that I know all too well. The scent of his cologne lingering in the room is like a cloud of smoke choking me.

He brought me back. The thought is crippling. I failed. Even though I did everything right, I still managed to get caught.

"Good morning, Mrs. Archer."

My head snaps to the left, and I see Ryat standing in the doorway to his adjoining bathroom inside his room at house of Lords. I shove the covers off and scramble out of the bed. My shaky legs have me falling into his dresser, making it rattle. "Stay away from me," I warn, my voice scratchy from the mystery man choking me and whatever Ryat forced me to swallow. My mind is still a little hazy, but I understand I'm in danger.

He chuckles, placing his hands in the front pockets of his jeans, looking every bit of cool and collected as he leans against the doorframe. "That'll be hard since we're married, Blake."

"I told you I want a divorce," I growl.

He pushes off the doorframe, and I run for the bedroom door, but he's faster, my body still weak, giving him the advantage to step in front of me. His hand comes up, and I bow my head, whimpering, hands shaking.

"Shh," he says, gently touching my face, forcing me to look up at him. "I'm not going to hurt you, Blake."

"Yes, you will." I suck in a ragged breath. He promised me in the beginning that he would. Turns out, he was right, and I liked it.

"Is that what you want?" he asks, his eyes searching mine and I swallow nervously. I forgot how intense they can be. "You want me to punish you?"

"No," I whisper, but my heart races at the thought. My body knows what he's capable of, and it's missed him so fucking much.

"Are you sure?" His hand leaves my cheek, traveling down the center of my chest over the shirt. "My cock has missed you, little one." He leans in, tenderly kissing my forehead, and I hold in a breath. "Has my cunt missed me?"

"No," I lie, my thighs clenching at the thought of him between my legs. Even when I was terrified he'd find me, I still dreamed about him. I'd see his face, hear his voice, and feel his body on top of mine. I imagined him finding me, kidnapping me, and fucking me—just like we did with my forced-sex fantasy—but I'll never tell him that.

He frowns. "That's a shame." His fingertips circle my nipple, making it harden at his touch through the shirt, and I realize he's removed my bra. Once satisfied with my body's response, he brings his hand up into my hair and slowly pulls my head back. "But just so you know ..." He leans in with his lips to my ear, and whispers, "You will get on your knees and open your mouth. You will spread those soft and sexy legs for me. And I will take that ass." He pulls away, and his green eyes darken while drilling into mine, making my pulse accelerate. "I will fuck my wife. Whenever and however I want."

I swallow the lump in my throat at his threat while my pussy pulses. *I'm so fucked!*

He pulls away. "And as much as I want to remind you of that right now, we're late. We have a meeting." Grabbing my hand, he yanks me out of the room and down the hall. We enter an elevator, and he presses B for basement. I yank my hand from his once the doors shut. I'm surprised he stays silent. I figured he'd corner me in here, but maybe he's said all he wants to say.

"Where is my uniform I was wearing?" I ask him.

"Burned it," he answers, not even bothering to look at me.

Motherfucker ...

The door slides open, and we enter a hallway and move toward a closed door. Opening it up for me, he steps to the side to allow me to enter. Stepping in, I come to a halt. My legs are unable to take me any farther. My father sits in a chair with a man I don't know next to him.

"Blakely," he growls my name and shoots to his feet.

I spin around to leave, but Ryat shoves me farther into the room, closing the door behind him and caging me in.

"Do you have any idea what you've done?" my father snaps,

rounding the long table.

"Me?" I gasp, pointing a finger at my chest. "You sold me."

He snorts. "I didn't take a penny for you."

I frown. "But Matt ..."

"Matt was pissed because Ryat announced your marriage. He would have said anything to make you leave," the man who remains sitting adds. He seems much calmer than my father, which makes me wonder who he is and why he's here.

No! Matt wasn't just convincing, things he said made sense. Like pieces of a puzzle that clicked together. But just to make sure, I spin around to face Ryat. "So you didn't offer money for me?"

He leans up against the closed door as if to block it in case I try to bolt. Crossing his arms over his chest, he answers, "No. I did."

My mouth falls open. I fucking knew it. "I'm not a whore, Ryat."

He says nothing, but my father isn't done. "I always knew Matt was a sorry piece of shit. That's why I forced Ryat to pick you as his chosen."

I blink. He did not just say what I thought he did. "You what ...?" I look back at Ryat, and once again, he says nothing. Just stares at me like he did when I was on my ass in the hall after I ran into him. Threatening and indifferent at the same time. That playful and carefree Ryat from our wedding night long gone. Back to all business. I'm just a fucking order to him.

"But he chose to marry you," I hear my father add.

"What?" I take a step back, so I can see them both at the same time. The back of my neck is sore, probably from when Prickett was pinning me down on the table. I'm tired of looking back and forth between my father and my husband. "You make it sound like I should be grateful," I snap at my father. What does he expect me to do? Get on my hands and knees and thank Ryat for marrying me so I didn't have to spend a life with Matt? Right now, I'm trying to see how Ryat is any better? Why did it have to be one or the other?

"You should," he demands, stepping into me.

A hand grips my upper arm, and I'm yanked to the side, and I hit a hard body before Ryat places his arm around my shoulders.

My father lets out a long breath. "I'm not going to put my hands on her like my wife did."

I blink, trying to keep up with the change of topics. "How do you know that?" Ryat had to have informed him of what happened. He's the only other person who knows.

My father waves a hand, dismissing me. "Now that you're back, we have shit to take care of," he states.

"Like what?" I ask, my pulse racing. What could possibly need to be done?

"You must be initiated."

That word has my stomach knotting. "What do you mean?" I ask slowly, pulling away from Ryat. Thankfully, he lets go of me.

"I mean, Ryat is going to be powerful—"

"Yeah, yeah, a renowned judge in New York," I interrupt him. "But what does that have to do with me?"

The other man stands from his seat. "Who told you that?" he demands, his eyes glaring at Ryat's over my shoulder.

"Matt," I answer.

Silence blankets the room, making my breathing pick up. Was I not supposed to know that? If so, what will they do now that they know I do. "I haven't told anyone," I add quickly. "Ryat didn't even know that I knew."

"Is this true?" the man demands of Ryat.

"Yes," he grinds out.

Shit! He's mad at me even more now? Was I supposed to tell him what I knew? "Why ... why is that a secret?" I come out and ask.

The man takes his seat, glaring at me now. "Anyway, the Ladies have different tiers, just as the Lords," he goes on, totally ignoring my question. "You will be as high as you can get. A Lady always matches her Lord."

I reach up and rub my temples, closing my eyes for a brief second. "I'm fucking tired, and a little slow from being drugged." My eyes spring open. "So, can someone explain to me what is going on instead of talking in riddles?" I snap. What the fuck is a Lady? And what does it have to do with Ryat being a Lord?

"You will receive a text giving you a name, a location, and a time," my father starts. "This will be the orders of your initiation."

I snort. "I'm not joining this secret society." They've lost their fucking minds. "I want nothing to do with the Lords."

The other man jumps to his feet once more. "You will do what we say—"

"Give us the room," Ryat interrupts the man.

The guy storms out, but my dad takes his time. Coming up next to us, he places his hand on Ryat's shoulder. "I hope you know what you're doing." Then he walks out.

"What is going on, Ryat?" I demand the moment the door closes behind them. "And don't lie to me."

He pulls out one of the black leather chairs at the table and gestures for me to sit. Rolling my eyes, I plop down into it. Ryat pulls out the one beside me and spins it so we're face-to-face. Leaning forward, he places his elbow on his knees. "We're already married, Blake," he reminds me. "If you don't get initiated in, then you are removed as Lady."

My eyes widen. "We can get a divorce?" Maybe there's hope after all.

"No," he snaps, making me jump. Dropping his head, he runs his hands through his hair. A clear sign he's getting pissy with me.

Taking a second to get a good look at him, I see how tired his green eyes look. I wonder if he's lost sleep like me. I wonder if he thought of me like I did him. "I don't understand." I soften my voice. "You just said—"

"You either kill or get killed," he growls, interrupting me.

I laugh at that but stop when he just glares at me. "This has to be a joke, right?"

"There is no way around it," he snaps, jumping to his feet.

He can't be serious. I must still be knocked out. Maybe I'm having a nightmare. Or possibly hallucinating. "I can't ..."

"Yes, you can." He nods. "I knew what you would have to do going into this."

"How could you?" I whisper, feeling my throat tighten. I was an assignment that he tried to buy. And now I'm a Lady who has to kill someone?

"We all make sacrifices in order to get what we want," he states.

I stand on shaky legs, my hands fisting at my sides. Stepping into him, he looks down at me, his green eyes the coldest I've ever seen them. It makes me realize just how good of an actor he was and how stupid I am. "What you don't seem to understand is that I no longer want to be your wife, Ryat. And I don't want to join your stupid secret society. So, no, I don't want to sacrifice anything for you because I don't want to be with you." My heart is hammering in my chest while the blood rushes in my ears at the lie. I can't let him see how much I missed him. I felt something for him the night of the ceremony, but then Matt fucked it all up with what he told me. I hate him too. Maybe Sarah was right—I was better off being in the dark.

Cupping my face, he sighs heavily. "None of that matters, Blake."

THIRTY-NINE

RYAT

SHE HASN'T SAID one word to me since I told her that what she wants no longer matters. It was cruel, but it was the truth. I'm tired of hiding things from her. She needs to know what goes on inside the world of the Lords. She may not like it, but she will learn to live with it.

Blood, death, and secrets are what my life is made of. Hers will be the same.

I quickly look over at her in the passenger seat of my W Motors Lykan Hypersport. She's got her head tilted to the side and her eyes closed. She fell asleep the moment we left the house of Lords. I didn't give her a very high dosage when I found her last night at the run-down bar. I was angry with her and knew she'd fight me every step of the way, so drugging her was my best option to move her without injuring her. It was just a couple of sleeping pills. On a normal person, they wouldn't have worked that well, but I was banking on her already being exhausted. I know my wife pretty well by now. She wasn't getting much sleep, knowing she was on the run.

Pulling into the driveway, I shut off my car, and she stirs. "We're home," I tell her.

Opening her heavy eyes, she blinks. "Why are we here?" she asks, looking around the wooded area.

"This is where we live."

"No ... my apartment ..."

I get out and round the front of the car, opening her door for her. "You no longer have that," I say, grabbing her hand and pulling her out. "I moved all of your stuff into the cabin." After she left, I destroyed her apartment. Not my greatest moment, but I was looking for the slightest clue on where she might have gone. Once I managed to sit back and look at what I'd done, I said fuck it and hired a moving company to pack up all her shit and move it. I knew she wouldn't be going back there once I found her.

She doesn't say anything as we enter the house. I pull her down the hall to the master suite because we both need a shower.

Entering the bathroom, I turn on the shower and then step in front of her. "Lift your arms," I order. She does as I say and places them above her head. I remove the shirt I dressed her in and then shove my sweatpants and underwear down her legs. "Get in. I'll grab some towels."

Walking over to the linen closet, I grab what we need and set them next to the shower, then I quickly undress and join her. She stands with her back against the wall, her arms crossed over her chest and head down. Her now wet hair sticks to her neck and breasts. She sniffs as the blood runs down over her body and disappears into the drain. I didn't clean her up after we returned to the house of Lords. I ripped her uniform off, burned it, and put her in my bed, where I dressed her in some of my clothes and then waited for her to wake up.

"Blake," I say softly, and she looks up at me, tears running down her face.

"You killed him," she whispers, her lips trembling.

I was wondering when this would hit her. When she'd have a second to stop and think about what I did in the alleyway behind the bar. At the time, she feared me and was too concerned with saving herself. Now that we've slowed down and the drugs no longer linger, what I did is coming back full force. "I did."

She sniffs again. "You slit his throat." Her shoulders shake, and her eyes go wide as her hands start frantically wiping the blood off her bruised neck and chest. "It's his blood ..."

"Shh." I grab her face and make her look up at me, taking her attention off what remains of the man. "I had to." She shakes her head, but I steady it with my hands on either side. "Yes." Pressing my body fully into hers, I add, "He put his hands on you. And that is unacceptable." I'll kill any motherfucker who touches my wife. It's just that simple.

At the time, I was pissed at her but also relieved we had arrived just in time. What if I hadn't found her when I did? She'd be dead right now. A second later and I would have found her body in that alley. It made me even angrier with her. The fact that she ran put her life in danger.

She lets out a sob, and I pull her from the wall, hugging her. With one arm holding her to my body, my free hand runs down over her wet hair while she cries into my chest. "You're safe, Blake," I tell her. "I promise."

"I'm sorry," she cries.

I sigh, feeling every ounce of anger I had toward her fade. It's just as much my fault as it is Matt's. I used her and then threw it in his face, so he attacked me the only way he knew how—by going to her. It's a game that we've been playing ever since she became my assignment. But our marriage upped the ante.

I have too much to lose now, and he knows it. Like my father told her, she's important to the Lords now. Matt can't touch her, but he can have someone else go after her. That's the part that scares me the most. I've made too many enemies over the years. Too many Lord members didn't make it through initiation since I started four years ago. How many of them were denied because I beat them out?

"Ryat?" she whispers, pulling her head from my chest, looking up at me.

"Yeah?" I ask, my hand tangling in her hair.

"Thank you for saving me," she whispers, her eyes giving me that same look of admiration she gave me the night of the house of Lords party. Before everything went to shit.

"Don't thank me, Blake," I tell her, my eyes falling to the marks on her neck. I'd go to war for my wife. One man was nothing. "I'll always show up for you."

Fresh tears spill over her bottom lashes, and I almost lean down and kiss her but stop myself. Instead, I pull back and grab the soap off the ledge to help clean her up.

She stays quiet while we both finish in the shower. I make sure to scrub every inch of her. I even wash her hair before tending to myself. Once done, I turn off the water and help her dry off. It's like she's on autopilot—here but not really.

"I'm tired," she says softly and then yawns.

And for once, I am too. I'm exhausted from lack of sleep, stress, and just the feeling of the unknown. I walk out of the bathroom and pull the covers back on my bed. She crawls in, naked with wet hair. I lie down next to her on my back. Snuggling up next to me, she wraps her arms around me, and I let out a sigh, closing my eyes.

I missed her so goddamn much. I didn't realize that until now. I mean, I spent every second of every day searching for her, but it was the fact that she ran from me. Not because I wanted her. It was more of a you belong to me thing and I will find you. Now, I realize it was always more than that.

My phone dings, and I reach over, picking it up off the nightstand. It's a text. Opening it up, I read over it, and my teeth grind.

Fuck!

Deciding to ignore it, I lock the screen and put it back before pulling her into me and closing my eyes.

BLAKELY

I WAKE UP and stretch my heavy limbs. My body is still exhausted, but my head is clear. The lack of light in the room tells me it's not morning yet. But honestly, I have no sense of time anymore. I could have been out for three days, for all I know.

Getting out of bed, I call out for Ryat but am met with silence. Deciding to go look for him, I walk into the living room and turn on the light. He sits in the middle of the couch, dressed in a T-shirt and jeans. His arms are fanned across the back of the cushions, and in his right hand, he holds a glass of scotch. I frown. I've never seen him drink before other than that one time he and Gunner followed me and Sarah to Blackout. His hair dry and spiked to perfection how he usually wears it. I remember lying down with him after our shower, but he looks like he's been awake for hours. "Ryat?"

My eyes drop to the coffee table that sits in front of him. It's got my cell, my wedding ring and clutch—all three things I left on his bed when I ran. A manila envelope sits on the end.

My heart beats faster at the sight of them. I thanked him in the shower for saving me, and I meant it. If he hadn't found me when he did, I'd be dead.

"What are you doing?" I whisper. "Come back to bed with me."

He brings his right hand around, putting the glass to his lips, and throws back his drink. His eyes meet mine and level me with a glare.

"You okay?" I ask, taking a tentative step toward him, already knowing that something is wrong. Ryat doesn't do well with hiding his emotions.

He gives a rough laugh, the sound making the hairs on the back of my neck rise in warning. "Three weeks, Blake. Three fucking weeks." He leans forward, staring at the now empty glass in his hand.

I swallow, knowing it wouldn't be that easy. He won't forgive me. "Matt—"

"Matt wanted you to leave me. Don't tell me that you didn't know what he was doing." He interrupts me. "We both know that you're not stupid. And instead of coming to me, you ran."

I cross my arms over my exposed chest. "You lied to me. Why would I go to you ...?"

He stands and throws the glass into the lit fireplace, cutting me off. The sound of it shattering makes me jump in surprise.

"Don't get mad at me for a situation you put yourself in," I shout, uncrossing my arms. "You had a hundred chances to come clean. To tell me what the hell was going on. You made a decision, and now you don't like the consequences." Spinning around, I give him my back and go to storm off to the bedroom.

"You're right." He sighs heavily.

His words bring me to a stop. Never in my life would I have thought Ryat Archer would be the kind of man to admit someone is right other than himself. Slowly, I turn around to face him, and he falls back down onto the couch.

"Want to know what happened?" He fans his arms across the back again, his legs falling open. His posture and narrowed eyes tell me he's anything but remorseful. "You started off as an assignment. I tried to decline it. Said you didn't belong to me. But that wasn't an option. You don't say no to the Lords." He tilts his head to the side, his eyes running over my bare chest. "So, I followed you. Learned your routine." He laughs softly. "Or lack thereof. Then I made my move."

My brows pull together. "What do you mean ...?"

"You really thought you ran into me by accident?" He shakes his head. "I put myself in your way, Blake. It was my way into your life, It was time for you to see me. To want me."

My hands fist at his confession. "You ..."

"Gunner made sure that Sarah found that flyer. We made it just for the two of you, by the way."

No wonder I had never seen one before.

"I gave you just enough information to make you curious."

Tears start to sting my eyes at how stupid I was. Not a goddamn thing was by chance. It was all a fucking game. Piece by piece, he played me.

He smirks. "You were starving, Blake." My heart sinks at his words. "Matt turned you down for so long that I didn't have to give you much to keep you begging for more."

The first tear runs down my cheek, and he watches it. Then he looks away, pulling his lip back with disgust. "You're not the only stupid one here, Blake," he adds. "I began to feel something for you." He snorts at that confession. "Because you looked good in a fucking dress. I thought, what is wrong with your wife loving you? That maybe we'd have a chance after all."

I hate that my pulse quickens at that thought. That he could actually love me. That's all I've ever wanted. For someone to love me for me. Accept me. I thought he had, but it was part of his game.

"Then you ran ... and it reminded me what this really was. A job. My anger trumped anything else I had felt for the briefest of seconds."

Swallowing the lump in my throat, I step toward the couch again. "Ryat ...?"

"Earlier in the shower made me realize I've gone fucking soft on you, Blake. Know why?" He doesn't let me answer. "Because you cried. Because another man tried to hurt you. That's what I'm trying to protect you from. I should be your biggest threat. But instead, I'm falling in love with you."

My heart hammers, and the blood rushes in my ears. I don't want his words to faze me, but they do. "Ryat ..."

"I've been taught since I was young that obedience is important." He goes on as if he didn't just admit to loving me. "That power and humiliation go hand and hand. I've watched Lords break their chosen ones or their Ladies to keep them in line. And you? You cry a few tears, and I go fucking soft."

"I'm sorry," I say through the knot in my throat.

"Sorry isn't good enough." He jumps to his feet, shouting.

"Punish me," I offer, taking another step forward.

He stares at me with a careless look in his pretty eyes. He's gone. I've lost what little ground we made last night. And I hate that my chest hurts. That I even fucking care. He just admitted to me that it was a game. "Cute." He snorts.

"I'm serious." I take another step, desperate to hang on to what I've spent the past three weeks running from. Yes, he's made mistakes, but so have I. We're not perfect. But he was right. I felt those same feelings at the party before Matt came and ruined everything. Before

I made the decision to leave instead of trying to understand what Matt was doing.

His eyes drop to my bare legs and run up over my body, pausing on my chest before they reach mine. "I'm no longer interested."

Panic grips my chest at his confession. "What do you want, Ryat? Want me to beg? Want to teach me a lesson?"

"No, Blake. I no longer want anything from you." Leaning forward, he picks up the manila envelope and stands. Walking over to me, he places it in my hands, his cold eyes on mine. "Consider this your wedding gift." With that, he grabs his leather jacket off the recliner and walks out, the slamming of the front door making me jump.

I plop down on the couch and open it with shaky hands. Pulling out the papers, I feel fresh tears sting my eyes. They're divorce papers. My heart aches as I flip through the tabs and see he's already signed them.

When I slam them down on the coffee table, the corner hits my ring. I read the engraving on the inside of the band—till death do us part. I slide it on my finger while my stomach knots.

How did we get here? This is what I wanted, except now it isn't. Yes, we started out with a lie. But I'm not innocent. I only became his chosen because of Matt. Ryat was right. I ran when I should have gone to him after Matt cornered me in Ryat's bedroom. No matter how mad or confused I felt, running from my problems wasn't the answer. Even I knew they'd catch up with me eventually.

Leaning forward, I place my elbows on my thighs, my face in my hands, and swallow the knot lodged in my throat. Why do I care that he wants to walk away? Is it the fact that I failed? I felt what he did that night at the house of Lords party, and that's why what Matt said hurt so much. Because I thought I was finally getting what every girl wants—love and acceptance.

He chased me down. Killed a man for me. Saved me. That's more than anyone else has ever done. Ryat promised me in the shower that I am safe with him. That he'd protect me. And then this? I refuse to let him off the hook that easily.

Fuck him and these papers.

Standing up, I grip them and walk over to the fire. I toss them in and watch my only escape plan burn.

Till death do us part, he once said to me. And I'm about to make him eat those words. Walking back to *our* bedroom, I enter the closet and look over my clothes that he had brought over from my apartment. I grab a T-shirt and a pair of white cotton shorts. After getting dressed, I brush my teeth. I'm rinsing out my mouth when I hear the front door open.

Making my way back into the living room, I place my hands on my hips, preparing for a fight, expecting it to be Ryat. He's come back. He's changed his mind too. I have no problem arguing it out with him.

"Ryat?" I hear a female voice call out his name as the front door shuts. Then the last person I expected to see enters the living room. She comes to a stop, and her wide eyes meet mine. "Blakely?" She gasps, swallowing nervously.

My eyes drop to her heels and run up over the black trench coat she wears, already knowing that she's probably naked underneath. A black leather designer bag hangs from her right hand. "What are you doing here?" I demand, my skin tingling as the jealousy courses through my body. My mind races to conclusions as fast as my heart beats.

"I'm here to see Ryat." She gives me a smile. That surprised look no longer on her perfectly done-up face. "What are you doing here?"

"I live here," I say, lifting my chin.

She gives a laugh. "Well, you haven't been here over the past three weeks when I've been here."

No! I don't believe a damn word out of her mouth. Ryat is a lot of things, but a cheater isn't one of them. He's nothing like Matt. And I refuse to let this bitch get to me. I won't make that mistake again. "You're lying."

"Oh, come on, Blakely." She laughs, taking a step toward me. "You didn't possibly think he'd stay faithful after you left him, did you?"

I stay where I am, letting her come to me.

"A man like Ryat has needs." She runs her tongue along her top bleached teeth. "Needs that you weren't here to fulfill." Coming to a stop, she presses her right hip out. "Someone had to keep him satisfied."

"I guess I should be thanking you then, huh?" I ask, arching a brow.

"I should be thanking you." She touches her pointer finger to the tip of my nose, and it takes everything in me not to bite it off. "If you hadn't run like the scared little girl you are, Ryat may have never called me."

I reach down, my right hand spinning my wedding ring around on my left hand, and then I slap her across the face with everything that I have. I need a release. A bitch fight sounds like just the thing to help that out.

Gasping, her hand shoots to her face as she drops—what I'm guessing is her overnight bag—at her feet. Pulling it away, she looks at the blood from the cut my ring left across her cheek. "Bitch," she hisses.

"I'm sorry, did my wedding ring cut you?" I ask, giving her an apologetic smile.

"You fucking bitch ..." She charges me.

I sit on the couch, dressed in Cindy's trench coat. After I was done with her, I did my makeup and hair, then sat back, waiting for my husband to return home from God knows where. I feel like this will be my life a lot—always waiting on him. Not knowing what he's doing or where he's at.

Hearing the front door open and close makes me bite back a smile. Seconds later, he steps into the living room, dressed in the same clothes he left in, and comes to a stop. "What are you still doing here?" he demands, his eyes looking over me. I watch them turn heated in a way that tells me even though he's mad, he'd still fuck me.

Good enough.

"I made you a drink." I ignore his question and lean forward, picking up the glass of scotch off the coffee table.

He just glares down at me, unmoving. I'm sure he thinks I found his stash of drugs and am trying to knock him out or poison him. "Okay, then." I shrug and throw the burning liquid back. Some of it runs down my chin onto my chest. "Oops," I say, pulling the top of the trench coat farther apart to give him a better look. "Wanna lick it off me?" I ask.

"What are you doing here, Blake?" he snaps. "I gave you what you wanted. Take your shit and go."

I smile up at him, refusing to let his words get to me. Ryat has challenged me every step of the way, and now I'm going to do the same to him. "What if I want something else?"

Reaching behind him, he pulls out his wallet and grabs a hundred-dollar bill. "Need money to run this time?" He tosses it onto my lap.

I flick it off onto the floor like a pesky little gnat and ignore the insult that a hundred dollars would get me far. Standing, I say, "I'm not leaving, Ryat."

He runs a hand through his hair aggressively. "Blake ..."

"What if I told you I fucked a guy while I was gone?"

His teeth clench, shoulders stiffening. Exactly the response I was wanting. "You didn't," he argues.

"What if I told you I fucked two guys?" I hold up my right hand, showing him my pointer and middle finger.

"Blake." He growls my name, making my heart race. He doesn't understand that he's giving me exactly what I want. "You better be lying."

"And if I'm not?" I ask, arching a brow. I'm baiting him.

Reaching out, he yanks me to him. "Then I'll hurt you."

I can't help the smirk that spreads across my face. He doesn't seem like a man who wants a divorce. A man done with his wife doesn't give a fuck what she does, let alone what dick she's been riding around on. "It's only fair, baby. You get pussy, and I get dick."

His brows crease, confusion marking his gorgeous face. "What?"

I pull away from him and walk into the laundry room. I open the door and reach in, grabbing the blonde who I tied up and tossed in there two hours ago. Thank God she was actually wearing something under that trench coat, or I would have had to dress her too. "Here." I shove her forward into him.

She trips and he reaches out, grabbing her before she can fall on her face. *Pity.* "What the fuck, Blake?" he snaps, holding a crying and blabbering Cindy. Thankfully the tape over her mouth keeps her somewhat quiet.

"Consider it your wedding gift." I repeat his words and cross my arms over my chest.

"What the fuck did you do?" he demands, yanking the tape from her mouth.

"Ryat ... Ryat, please," she begs him, big crocodile tears running down her face, ruining her once flawless makeup and dried blood from my ring to her cheek. "Help me. She's crazy—"

"Cindy showed up to get her nightly fuck—you know, the one she's been getting for the past three weeks while I was away—and was surprised to see me here," I interrupt her rambling.

He looks at me, his green eyes wide with disbelief. I can't even begin explaining the feeling of relief I have in my gut that he's confirming what I already knew. *He hasn't touched her.* "Are you serious? You honestly think I'm fucking her?"

I shrug. "It is what it is. Call it leveling the playing field."

"You're fucking crazy," she screams, struggling in his grip. "You fucking bitch ..."

He slams the side of her head into the wall, knocking her out, and I bite back a smile of satisfaction. Letting go of her, she falls to the floor, and he steps over her to me. I stay planted in my place, not afraid of him. Not anymore. My husband is powerful, but if I'm going to be a Lady, then I need to raise myself to his level. I'll start by going head-to-head with him.

"I haven't had an affair," he growls, getting in my face.

"She proves otherwise." I point at the unconscious woman.

"So, you're going to believe her just like you did Matt?"

I say the only words that I know will push him even further. "Well, Matt wasn't wrong." He said that Ryat paid my father five hundred thousand, but that wasn't actually true. However, Ryat did offer that much for me. So, it's true enough if you ask me. The tracker in my cell, controlling who I talk to, all that was true.

He steps into me, nose to nose. Bring it. I'm all in. I didn't throw those divorce papers in the fire for nothing. Ryat wants a Lady? I'll give him a motherfucking lady.

FORTY

RYAT

Trying to wrap my mind around what I came home to, I shake my head. "I haven't fucked her in over three years." Back before I took my oath. Blake is the only woman I've been with since I joined the Lords my freshman year at Barrington.

"Sure. And I didn't fuck anyone while I was away." She winks at me, nibbling on her bottom lip playfully.

The fuck?

Giving me her back, she goes to walk off, but I reach out, grab her upper arm, and spin her around. I grip her neck with my free hand. "You better be fucking lying, Blake." I will chase down and dismember any man who she touched. Then I'll beat that fine ass black and blue until she remembers who owns it.

"Is that what you want, Ryat?" she goes on. "Want us to be open?"

"Absolutely not ..."

"You fuck who you want." She tilts her head to the side, her eyes dropping to my T-shirt and the sexiest smirk I've ever seen crosses her face. "I fuck whoever I want."

My hands are fucking shaking. My blood boiling.

"We can share ... Maybe you want to watch another man fuck me."

I spin us around, slamming her back into the wall. Her eyes close, and her lips part, forcing a whimper. "I think those three weeks away made you forget who I am, Blake. Let me remind you." Picking her up, I throw her over my shoulder and carry her off to the bedroom, where I toss her onto our bed, facedown.

She giggles, and it makes my hard cock twitch with anticipation. I can't even think about the fact that I'm playing into her game right now. Blakely knows what to do to piss me off, and she did it.

Opening my nightstand, I grab the handcuffs. Yanking her hands behind her back, I tighten them around her wrists as tight as I can and hear the little whimper she tries to hide. It makes me smile. I lean over her back and whisper in her ear, "You wanted to be punished. Remember that."

Then I stand and flip her onto her back, pinning them underneath her and forcing a cry from her lips. It makes my hard cock twitch. Those three years I had to abstain from sex was nothing compared to the three weeks without her.

It was fucking torture.

Undoing my jeans, I pull my hard cock out and then undo the sash holding the trench coat closed. I rip it open to expose her body to me, and she arches her back, wiggling her arms underneath her to try to relieve the pain. It's not going to help her.

Crawling onto the bed, I spread her legs with my knees, and my hand goes to her pussy. She's wet. I knew she would be. She was already wound up, just begging to be fucked.

I slide into her, no foreplay. A part of me wants to hurt her. After I finish with her, I want her to still feel me between her legs. I lay my body on top of hers, pinning her down even more, bringing tears to her eyes.

"I missed you, Blake," I say honestly, my lips trailing along her jawline. "And I'm going to show you just how much."

My hips start to move, hard and fast. Our bodies slapping together.

She arches her back, a cry coming from her parted lips. I sit up, wrap my hands around her neck and squeeze, taking her air away while I pound into her soaking wet cunt. I watch her eyes grow heavy, and her lips turn blue. Just as her eyes fall shut, I let go, and she sucks in a ragged breath, coughing.

I slow my pace, feeling every inch of her wrapped around my length. "Look at me," I demand, gripping her chin to hold her face in place.

Her watery eyes meet mine. "If another man ever touches you, I'll kill him, Blake." Lowering my lips to her cheek, I lick up her tears, tasting the saltiness. "Painfully ... slowly." I kiss the corner of her parted lips. "It doesn't matter if you wanted him to or not," I inform her. "And then I'll remind you that you belong to me." I slam into her, forcing a whimper out of her. "Do you understand me?"

Sitting up once again, I watch my cock slide in and out of her shaved pussy. My gaze goes back to hers, waiting for a response, but her eyes are closed. I slap the side of her breast, making her pussy tighten around my dick. "Answer me," I demand, slapping the other one.

"Yes." She moans. "I understand."

"Who do you belong to?" I growl, my hips picking up the pace once again.

"You."

"Fucking mine, Blake." I grab her legs, my fingers digging into her thighs, and spread them wide open for me, allowing me to go deeper. I slam into her over and over again until she clamps down around me and comes all over my dick.

I don't let up. The bed bangs against the wall, the room filled with her cries, her body now slick against mine. As I pick up my pace, my balls tighten.

"Ryat ..." She breathes. "Ryat, I'm not ..."

I lean over and place my hand over her mouth. I silence her, knowing exactly what she's about to say, but I don't give a fuck. Thrusting one more time, I come inside her.

I wait for a second while she lies underneath me, body shaking and trying to catch her breath. I pull out and fall down onto the bed beside her, expecting her to yell at me, but she doesn't.

The doorbell rings, and I sit up, rolling her body onto her stomach to undo the cuffs. "Get dressed," I order, slapping her ass, and then exit the bedroom, knowing we've still got shit to deal with. Our fight can wait until later.

BLAKELY

I DRESS BACK in my T-shirt and cotton shorts from earlier before I exit the bedroom and walk down the hallway to find Ryat sitting on the couch, my father in a recliner and that man from the house of Lords in the opposite one.

Glaring at Ryat, I take the couch but choose to sit at the other end. My anger for him once again at a ten.

"Trouble already?" the man asks, amusement in his voice.

"Who the hell are you?" I demand, crossing my arms over my chest. I'm mad that I lost the battle against Ryat. I challenged him, thinking I could win, and the bastard still beat me.

"Blakely—"

"No, it's quite all right," he interrupts my father. "A Lady needs to have some fire in her if she's going to succeed." His eyes slide over to Ryat.

I swallow nervously at those words. I forget that I have to prove myself to the Lords, not just my husband. I have a feeling they're going to be much harder to sway than a man I fuck.

"My name is Abbot Archer," he announces proudly, and my stomach sinks.

Fuuuccckkkk.

"And I'm your father-in-law." He stands from the recliner and walks over to me. I look up at him through my lashes, and he reaches out, taking my left hand. I hold my breath when he runs his thumb over my wedding ring. "I'm guessing you didn't sign the papers."

"What?" My eyes widen. "How did you—?"

"She threw them in the fireplace," Ryat answers, interrupting me.

My head snaps to look at him, sitting at the other end of the couch, but he's typing something on his cell.

"Good," Abbot praises.

I look back up at him. "I don't understand ..."

"You passed your first test of initiation." My father-in-law nods his head once, letting go of my hand, and it slaps my bare thigh.

First test of initiation? I thought I was going to get a text with a name, time, and address? No one said I'd be tested multiple times. How many tests will there be? Ryat said I threw them in the fire. I did, but he had already left.

"How did you ...?" I trail off, trying to piece together everything that has happened over the past twenty-four hours. I thought my mind was clear, but I was obviously mistaken. I look around the large open living room and out the floor-to-ceiling windows that showcase the dark night. He must have cameras here. Of course, he does. I should have known. Matt said that they are always watching. He made up those papers and got in a fight with me. He needed an exit strategy and then once he left, he sat back somewhere and watched me.

"You set me up," I say to Ryat, turning my body on the couch to fully face him.

He's still typing away on his phone. Reaching over, I snatch it from his hands and toss it across the room. The sound of it hitting the glass fills the room, and I secretly hope I broke the damn device. His eyes narrow on mine. "Blake ..."

"I'm fucking talking to you. The least you can do is pretend to listen," I snap.

"Oh, I like her." I hear Mr. Archer whisper to my father.

I stand, glaring down at Ryat. "So, everything you said to me in the room earlier was a lie." How am I supposed to know what is true anymore?

His jaw sharpens, and nostrils flare.

"You tricked me. Made me think you wanted a divorce. What if I would have signed them?" Then what? That would have been considered a failure. Would he have come home and killed me right then?

"You wouldn't have." He snorts, like it's impossible for me to walk away from him. I guess the fact that I burned them proves his point.

"What if I had, Ryat? Then what?" I shout.

He takes the two steps, closing the distance. Reaching up, he places his fingers under my chin and runs his thumb gently over my parted lips. "If you thought for one second that I'd let you walk away from me, then I need to remind you who I am ... again." A smirk tugs at the corner of his lips.

My breathing picks up, and I pull away. The touch and words feel too intimate for our audience. Especially since they're our fathers. "But you signed them," I argue.

"I had to," he growls, giving me his back. "It was an order from the Lords ..."

"The Lords?" I give a rough laugh. "How long will they control our life, Ryat?" I snap, and he spins back to face me. "Huh? What will you do when they tell you to leave me?"

"They won't." He shakes his head.

"How do you know that?"

"Because they won't," he yells.

"I don't believe that," I shout back. "And your loyalty lies with them. Not me."

"Blake." He sighs, running a hand through his hair. "You don't know what you're talking about."

"Test me," I say, holding my hands out wide. Let's get this over with right now. He can give me a test from the Lords, and when I pass, this'll all be over.

"I can't," he growls through gritted teeth. "Not in that way."

"Are you serious?" I snap. "Everything has been a fucking test since the moment I ran into you in the hallway at Barrington, and all

293

of a sudden, you can't. That doesn't make any fucking sense, Ryat!"

"Things have changed."

"What the hell has changed? Because it all looks to be the same fucking game." The room falls silent after my outburst. I drop back down onto the couch. Placing my elbows on my knees, I bury my face in my hands and take a deep breath. "How am I supposed to prove my loyalty to you if you don't trust me with your secrets?" I look up at him, and he's now standing in front of the floor-to-ceiling windows. Bending down, he picks up his cell and then shoves his hands into the pockets of his jeans.

"There is a—"

"No." He interrupts his father, spinning around.

"What is it?" I shoot to my feet.

"It's nothing," Ryat snaps.

"You're lying. And once again hiding something from me."

"I won't risk your life," he screams, his face turning red.

Taking in a deep breath, I walk over to him. "You do it for the Lords. Why should I accept it, but you not?"

"Because I chose this life, Blake," he growls.

"And then I chose you when I burned those divorce papers. So I'm in the middle—"

"Not anymore," he interrupts me. "You will do your last initiation because I'll be there to make sure it goes smoothly, then you're done. You'll be a Lady and my wife. That's it."

That's not the end. Not even close. He's in it for life, and it scares me to know that they have this much control over it. "But the Lords will still call you to do work for them."

"That's what I signed up for," he agrees.

It just makes me even more nervous for our future. "What about what I want?"

"I've told you before, and I'll tell you again, that doesn't matter." This time, his eyes look soft, almost remorseful as if it hurt him to tell me that.

I spin around and look at my father, hoping he can help me out in some way. "Daddy ..."

He raises his hand, stopping me, and my shoulders sag. "I'm afraid he's right, princess. I won't put you in danger any more than you already have been. This all started because of me, and it will end because of me."

My breathing picks up. "What does that mean?"

He looks over at Ryat. "May I speak to you privately?"

"No," I answer for him. "You can't."

"Sure." Ryat ignores me and opens the sliding glass door. "Let's step outside."

I go to run after him, but Mr. Archer stops me. "I must say, I had my doubts about you."

I turn around to look at him relaxing in the recliner. His right ankle propped up on his left knee.

"I never was that big of a fan of Cindy." He shrugs. "That's why I didn't argue when he said he wanted you."

At the mention of her name, I look around the room to see she's no longer here. Where is she? Did she wake up and manage to get free while Ryat and I were having sex in the bedroom? That brings me to another thought. Why did Ryat look so surprised to see her here when he got back when he had obviously watched me burn the divorce papers? "Where is she?" I ask, spinning in a circle, looking for her.

"Who?" he asks, tilting his head in thought.

"Cindy."

"How would I know?" he asks, shrugging.

"Is this another test?" I swallow nervously.

He pushes himself up from the recliner and straightens his suit jacket. "I think you need some rest, Blakely. A lot has happened recently."

"No." I shake my head. I'm not losing my mind; I lost a person. She was right here. I had tied her wrists together. Put tape over her mouth that Ryat took off and then slammed her head into the wall, knocking her out. "She was—"

The sound of the sliding glass door opening behind me cuts me off. "Abbot, let's get out of here. Leave these two lovebirds alone," my father calls out, entering the house.

Coming up behind me, he places his hands on my shoulders and kisses my hair. "I'll call you tomorrow. Get some rest."

Then, without another word, they both leave the house.

I slowly turn around to see Ryat leaning up against the now closed sliding glass door. With his arms crossed over his chest, he glares at me. "I'm not losing my mind," I state as if he accused me of doing so.

He doesn't acknowledge me in any way. Doesn't even blink.

"She was right here." I go over to the wall where she lay on the floor. "You knocked her out. Then carried me to the bedroom."

Again, no response.

"Where did she go, Ryat?" I ask him.

"Don't worry about her," he finally speaks, pushing off the glass.

"Ryat ... she."

"Blake." He comes up to me and cups my face. "Don't worry about it."

FORTY-ONE

RYAT

I HATED THAT I had to force her hand with the divorce papers. I would never tell her this, but a part of me thought she would sign them. She was mad at me, and the Lords knew that. They wanted to test her, and I couldn't tell them no. She has to prove her loyalty to me just like I had to prove it to them. So, I said the only things that made me think she'd want to fight me. I needed to make her mad. Blakely likes the fight. I needed her to find her backbone and stand up to me.

After storming out of the house, I drove a mile down the road and pulled over, watching her on my cell with the living room cameras. I can't even explain how proud of her I was when I watched her throw those papers in the fire with determination. It was more of a I'll make you love me rather than I love you, but I'll take it.

Honestly, I'm not sure what I would have done if she had signed them. But I was telling her the truth when I said I'd never let her go. I probably would have thrown them in the fire, burning any evidence of her signature.

After I witnessed her set them on fire, I quit watching and headed to Blackout. I had to meet with Ty. That's a new issue I have to deal with.

"Ryat," she whispers nervously. "Tell me." Her hands come up to my shirt, and she grips the material. "You have no problem making me prove myself to the Lords, but you won't allow me to prove it to you."

"You already have," I say, running my hand through her long, dark hair, feeling how soft it is.

Her face falls, and her eyes drop to the floor. Stepping back from her, I turn to go take a shower when her words stop me. "I knew you didn't sleep with her."

Turning, I look at her. "How do you know?"

She takes in a shaky breath. "Because you're nothing like Matt."

"You're right." I growl, "I'm not."

Walking over to me, she reaches up, wrapping her arms around my neck and pulling me into her. "Now's your chance, Ryat. To prove to me just how much you trust me."

I look away from her, my eyes going to the large floor-to-ceiling windows that overlook the backyard and woods, knowing it hides my secrets. "What if you can't handle it?" I ask, my eyes going back to hers. "You can't decide to walk away if you see something that you don't like," I say honestly. I won't allow it.

"Who said I was going to leave?" she asks, tilting her head to the side. "Wouldn't you rather have a wife who knows who you really are and chooses to stay than one who pretends you're someone else?"

Letting out a long breath, I think about her words. She's right. I'd much rather her know who I am. A Lord is powerful, but he is also alone in a world full of men. Chosen ones only know the sex and parties. Ladies know more, but still very little. Most prefer to be in the dark, though. My father has never hid who he is from my mother, but I've seen her leave the room, refusing to listen in on a conversation he was having with someone else. I don't fault her for it. Some just don't care to know what kind of evil walks the earth.

Cindy would have been the same way—wanted to be in the dark. All she would have cared about was the power and the lifestyle that my fortune could have provided for us. That's why I didn't want her.

But Blake? I like that she wants to be a part of my world. Even though I'll never allow her to get too close. I can't risk her life, but I can share mine with her.

Making up my mind, I nod. "Okay."

Her face lights up, and she bites her bottom lip to keep from smiling but fails.

"But ..." I add. "If at any point, I think you can't handle it, I get to pull you back."

"That's—"

"The deal." I interrupt her before she can finish that argument.

Rolling her eyes, she says. "Fine. It's a deal."

"Come on," I say, pulling her out the sliding glass door and walking down the steps.

"Ryat, it's pitch black out there," she whispers like someone will hear us. The closest neighbor is three miles away.

"It's fine. I know where we're going." She stays silent while I take us into the woods, walking the path that I've made over the years. Grabbing my phone out of my pocket, I use the flashlight once the lights on the back porch are too far away to find the door that sits in the side of a hill ahead of us.

Walking up to it, I punch in the code and push it open. "Watch your step," I tell her, allowing her to enter first but keeping hold of her hand. Once the door closes behind me, I bring her to a stop and flip on the light.

It lights up the staircase to the bunker below. This time, I place myself in front of her and walk down the stairs with her behind me.

Once we hit the landing, I release her hand and flip on the other light, to illuminate the room and turn to look at her. She comes to a stop, her small gasp filling the large space. Her wide eyes scan the wall in the back—chains, knives, and guns hang from hooks and sit on shelves. There's a cage to the right that's currently empty. But the chair in the center of the room is what gets her attention. Cindy sits tied to it with a black hood over her head. She struggles in the restraints, her mumbled words behind her gag making little sense.

I lean against the table, crossing my arms over my chest, and watch my wife carefully. Her wide eyes are focused on Cindy. "How ...?"

"Your father helped me get her down here while you changed," I inform her. She needs to understand that I'm not the only one who will protect her. He made himself very clear when he spoke to me on the back porch before he and my father left.

Eliminate any threat to his daughter. I had no problem agreeing to that.

She slowly turns, her eyes finally meeting mine. "All of this because she lied about sleeping with you?"

I refrain from smiling at her innocence. That was one of the reasons I didn't want to show her this. Sometimes, I like how innocent she was when she first ran into me. "That was her excuse for showing up, Blake."

"I knew she was lying ... but I don't understand." She licks her lips.

I push off the table and turn to face it. Picking up the black designer bag, I turn it up upside down, emptying the contents out onto it. "This is what she brought to our house."

Blake walks over to me and looks at everything. She picks up a syringe full of clear liquid. "But ... she said she was there to see you."

"She was there to hurt you."

Looking up at me, she frowns. "What do you mean?"

"I bought that house two years ago, Blake. I've never had Cindy over. She wanted you to believe that she had been there several times with me, but that was a lie. Her sole intent was to hurt you while I was gone."

Her frown deepens, and she puts the syringe down. "Then how did she know where it was?"

I smile. "That's a good question. Let's ask her." Walking over to her sitting in the chair, I remove the hood from her head.

She immediately starts thrashing in it. Her hands are tied to each armrest with rope, and her legs are spread wide, secured to each leg with zip ties. I rip the tape off her mouth.

Throwing her head back, she screams, making my ears ring.

"No one can hear you," I tell her.

She leans forward the best she can to look at Blakely. "Help me. Please," she begs. "He's fucking insane."

Blake ignores her and picks up a roll of duct tape that was in Cindy's bag. "What were you going to do with this?" she asks her.

"Did you hear me?" Cindy yells. "He's going to kill me." Tears run down her cheeks as she desperately pulls on the rope.

Placing the tape down, Blake picks up the syringe. "What's in this?"

"Fucking bitch," Cindy hisses. "Listen to me!"

"Let's see." Blake walks over to us, and Cindy starts sobbing. Coming to a stop, Blake looks up at me. "Does it matter where I stick her with it?"

I shrug. "Doubtful." It's probably a sedative of some kind. I can't see Cindy having the skills of a nurse to stick a vein. Especially if Blake was going to be fighting back at that time.

"Okay." Blake stabs Cindy in the upper arm with it, her thumb hovering over the plunger.

"Wait. Wait. Wait. I'll tell you," she rushes out. "Just don't do it. Please. I'll tell you. Anything you want to know," she says through the tears running down her face.

"I'm listening," Blake says but doesn't remove the needle from Cindy's arm.

"Matt told me where you live," she cries.

"How did he know?" I demand. "No one has been out here." Blake was the first person I brought here, other than my father. Well, and now Mr. Anderson.

She sniffs. "He didn't say. Just that he knew you brought her here when you were supposed to be in New York."

"How the fuck did he know I didn't stay in New York?" I bark, making her flinch.

"I don't know," she whines. "Please pull it out."

Blake removes the needle, and Cindy sags into the chair, softly crying. I start to pace. How in the fuck did he know I didn't leave? Was he ...?

"He was watching me," Blake speaks.

I come to a stop. "What do you mean? What makes you think that?"

She puts the cap on the needle. "That night at the house of Lords party—in your room—he told me that the weekend you came home early when you were supposed to be in New York, you had blocked my incoming calls and texts from Sarah so I wouldn't go to the house of Lords." Her eyes meet mine. "What if he was watching me and saw you come back and bring me here?"

My hands fist at the thought of him watching her. I came home to surprise her with her fantasy but what if I hadn't come back? What would he have done?

"We had sex outside. In the woods," Blake announces nervously. "You had texted me to come find you and—"

"What are you talking about?" I interrupt her.

She looks at Cindy who still quietly cries, and then back to me. "When I called you. You lied and said you had to run into Barrington."

"The part about me texting you," I snap.

Swallowing, she repeats. "You sent me a text after the phone call. Told me to come find you."

"Blake." I storm over to her. "No, I didn't."

"Yes, you did," she argues.

"Show me," I snap.

Sighing, she points at the stairs. "My phone is in the bedroom."

BLAKELY

How could he forget that text?

"We'll go get it," he growls, grabbing my hand and yanking me toward the stairs.

"It was me," cries Cindy's soft voice.

"What?" Ryat shouts, making her flinch.

She looks up at us through her watery lashes. "It was me. Matt was using my cell phone. He texted you. He told me that Ryat had blocked his number from Blakely's. His calls and texts weren't going through, so he asked to use my phone. I didn't know at the time what he was going to say to you."

"No." I shake my head, refusing to believe that. "It was Ryat."

"What was the number?" he demands, turning to face me.

"It was ..." My heart hammers in my chest when I trail off.

"What was it, Blake?" he snaps. Gripping both of my shoulders, he glares down at me.

"It was a blocked number," I whisper.

"Son of a bitch," he shouts, stepping away from me. "Why in the fuck would you think that was me?"

"Who else would it have been?" I ask, licking my lips. "You had sent me that picture of myself in the library before." Shrugging, I add, "You said you were gone, but I saw your SUV in the driveway. Then when I went to look for you out in the woods and saw you were standing on the porch." I know that was Ryat. He was the one who fucked me and carried me inside the house. He had removed his mask, and we took a shower. Why would I have questioned the text? "I thought you were playing around."

"Motherfucker," he shouts and turns to Cindy.

She cowers in her chair, dropping her face. He grips her chin and forces her head back, making her whimper. "You knew he was here ..."

"No," she cries, tears running down her face. "He asked to use my phone at the house of Lords party that night. I asked if I could go with him, and he said no, that he'd be out late but would give me my phone back in the morning."

His grip tightens, and she sniffs.

"When he gave it back to me, I looked and saw who he had messaged. There was also a video..."

"What the fuck was on the video, Cindy?" he demands.

With her head tilted back at an odd angle, she manages to try to look at me, and he shouts in her face. "Answer me."

"A video ... of you two having sex in the woods." She sobs.

He shoves her face away and walks over to the table, where he places both of his hands on it and bows his head. His white T-shirt pulls tight across his broad shoulders and back, showing me his taut muscles.

I stay frozen where I'm at, trying to understand what she's saying. Matt watched us have sex that night in the woods, but what if he saw more? Was he sitting in the parking lot of my apartment complex when Ryat showed up and kidnapped me? He had to have been, right? Otherwise, how would he know where the cabin is? If so, does he have a video of that?

"I don't understand," I whisper over her sobs. "Why would he tell me to come find him, knowing you were here with me?"

No one answers. Instead, Ryat shoves all her stuff off the table, and it bounces off the concrete floor, making her flinch. Silence falls over the room, and I'm pretty sure she's holding her breath right now.

He slowly turns around, leaning against it once again. Crossing his arms over his chest, he narrows his green eyes on hers. "One chance. How did you know she was here tonight?"

She bows her head, her shoulders sagging in defeat. "Matt called me and said that she was back in town. He knew you two were at the house of Lords, and if I was going to have any chance with you, this was it."

"Meaning?" he growls.

She lifts her head, her watery eyes pleading with him to have mercy on her, but even I know she's not going to get it. "Meaning, I was going to have to get rid of her. But I didn't ..."

He pushes off the table, stalking over to her.

"No, Ryat ..." she screams, her body thrashing in the chair. "Please, you have to understand..."

He silences her when he walks behind the chair and wraps the rope from her bag around her neck. He pulls it tightly, making her struggle in the chair, her hands clenching and unclenching. Her hips lift while she tries to fight the rope cutting off her air.

He bends down, his lips near her ear while his green eyes are on mine. My breathing picks up when he whispers to her, "Look at my wife, Cindy. I want her to be the last thing you see."

I hate that I'm turned on right now. That the smallest piece of me understands he's about to bring hell down on anyone who wants to harm me. I should feel for her, but I don't. She knew that I was in her way of getting what she wanted. And she was going to do whatever it took to get him.

A part of me can't blame her. I'd do the same.

Her fight grows weaker, her face drains of color, and her lips turn blue. I watch her eyes roll into the back of her head, and her body sags while he holds the rope in place, taking her life. The second one that I know of, for me.

I want to ask how many have to die in order for me to live, but if Ryat asked me that question, I'd say as many as needed.

He undoes the rope from around her neck, and her lifeless body just slumps in the chair. Walking over to the table, he tosses it onto it. "Go to the house. I'll be there in a minute," he orders, his back toward me.

"I refuse to take orders from you anymore, Ryat." I manage to say, squaring my shoulders. My husband just showed me who he really is. I need to show him who I am.

He lets out a growl and spins around. "Blake ..."

I rush over to him, my hands going to his face, and I lean up on my tiptoes, slamming my lips to his, cutting off whatever bullshit he was about to tell me. It doesn't matter. There are situations where words have more impact on someone, and this is not one of them.

He doesn't hesitate. His hands grip my thighs, and he lifts me. Spinning me around, he sets my ass down on the table.

Pulling away, I throw my head back, and he trails kisses down my neck where his teeth sink into my sensitive skin, making me shiver. "Ryat," I breathe.

"Fuck, Blake," he groans, ripping my shirt open, exposing my breasts to him. "Fuck, you're perfect." His hand grips my left breast, and he squeezes it, making me whimper. "Lie down," he orders, slapping my thigh, and it's one that I don't mind following.

Laying my back on the cold metal table, I shiver when he yanks my shorts and underwear down my legs and tosses them over his shoulder. Spreading my legs with his, he steps into me and unzips his jeans. When he pulls his cock out, he's already hard, and my mind wonders if it's because of Cindy or me. Did what he did to her turn him on? Or is it the fact that I'm turned on by what he did?

"You, Blake," Ryat growls. "It's always fucking you." He adds as if reading my mind before he pushes into me, spreading my already sensitive pussy wide to accommodate his size, and I cry out. His hand comes up and wraps around my throat but doesn't cut off my air.

"You're still wet from my cum when I fucked you earlier," he states, his hips slamming into me.

My hands drop to the table, and I reach out, grabbing the edge on either side of us to hold us in place.

"I'm going to fucking fill you with cum again, Blake. Every fucking time your pussy will leak with it, wetting your underwear. A reminder I was there and that it belongs to me."

I understand his need to dominate me after what Cindy told him about Matt watching me. Hell, that's why I wanted him. To remind him that I'm his wife. That no matter how much she wanted him, he belongs to me. But I'm not on birth control. I didn't take it with me when I ran. And I was gone for three weeks. I tried to remind him of that earlier in the bedroom, but he didn't allow me to speak. "Ryat, I'm not ..." His hand tightens around my throat, his fingers digging into either side of my neck, this time cutting off my words again and my air.

He looks down at me, a smile tugging at his lips. "I know, Blake, and I don't fucking care."

I'd moan if I was able to, but his hand around my throat prevents that. He picks up his pace, and my hands fall from the edge, my eyes growing heavy from lack of oxygen. I let go, letting him have his way with me. I trust him with my life.

He thrusts so hard that my head falls off the edge, and I see an upside-down image of Cindy's body slumped in the chair. Her face wet from her tears, and hair a tangled mess. Her body starts to become spotty as dizziness takes over.

My eyes fall shut, and the blood rushes in my ears, blocking out the sound of his grunts. My body is floating, rising like a balloon. Higher and higher to the sky. The pain making it even more pleasurable and the choice to freely give him control.

It's addicting, like I imagine a drug would be. I feel giddy, almost high. My pussy clenches around him, and he hisses in a breath when my body reacts, and I come all over his dick. That wave of heat rushes over me, and he lets go of my throat.

Sucking in a breath, I start coughing but it doesn't slow him down. I feel a rush of blood and loss of the little focus I had left. He thrusts into me one more time, and I feel him pulsing. He comes inside me, just like he said he was going to do.

FORTY-TWO

RYAT

I LOOK DOWN and watch my semi-hard cock slip out of her as cum drips from her wet cunt. I run my fingers through it and then shove them into her, making her moan. "Gotta make sure she gets every drop," I say, and she rocks her hips back and forth on my fingers. She's such a needy slut for me.

"Ryat," she coughs out my name, still trying to catch her breath while her body shakes uncontrollably.

"Shh," I tell her, pulling them out. Leaning over, I kiss her flat stomach. She tangles her fingers in my hair, and I kiss her soft skin again, trailing down to her pussy. "I can't wait to see you pregnant, Blake," I whisper against her skin, my tongue licking her cunt, tasting her and myself.

She whimpers at my words.

I've never really thought about kids. I mean, sure, I knew I'd have them someday. But ever since she's returned, it's all I think about. Her swollen belly and enlarged tits. I want Blakely Rae Archer pregnant with my child, and I'm going to get it.

Throwing her shaking legs over my shoulders, I kneel on the concrete floor at the edge of the table and stick my tongue inside her. Keeping my eyes open, I watch her squirm before me. Her hands grip her breasts, and she pinches her hard nipples.

My girl likes it to hurt a little. That's what gets her off.

I don't stop. I could watch her come over and over and never get tired of it. I could say it's a control thing, but it's more than that. It's the fact that I'm the only one who has ever seen her like this. So vulnerable and unable to control her cravings.

She's become my obsession, but I know I've also become hers.

Her body thrashes on the table, and I reach around her legs, my thumb playing with her clit while her hips ride my face. She arches her back, her breathing picking up once again, and her thighs clench down around my face, holding it in place, coming for a second time.

I suck on her cunt like it's my own personal honey-flavored sucker, filling my mouth with her sweet taste. Her body sags to the table, her legs falling off my shoulders. Pulling away, I lean over the table, standing over her body, and grip her face. She looks up at me through heavy eyes. They're still unfocused from my hand around her throat, restricting her air. Squeezing her cheeks, she understands what I want and the tip of her pink tongue darts out, slowly running across her lips before she parts them for me, opening wide. Leaning down, I spit into her mouth.

"Taste yourself," I order, watching her cum slide down her tongue to the back of her throat. Closing her lips, she swallows, and I press my lips to hers, wanting another taste.

She moans, her tongue meeting mine for a quick kiss before I pull away and she sucks in a breath.

Reaching up, I grab the back of my shirt and rip it up over my head. "Here, you need to wear something while I carry you to the house."

She lets me help her sit up, and I place my shirt over her head. Now that I know Matt is aware of where we live, I need to make sure she's never outside uncovered, no matter what time of the day or night it is. This also means I need blackout curtains for all the windows in the living room. Too many opportunities for him to watch her.

He could be sitting outside right now because he knew Cindy was here.

"Fuck," I hiss. I had forgotten about her.

"What?" Blake asks, her body tensing.

"I'll take care of it," I tell her, yanking the shirt down to cover her.

"Of what?" she asks, and then her eyes fall on the dead girl in the room. "I want to help you."

"Blake ..."

"Ryat, let me help you."

Letting out a sigh, I nod. I can't leave her here alone anyway. I have to take care of a couple of things tonight. She doesn't know it, but I'm about to test her again. Only difference is this time I won't blame her if she doesn't pass. "Okay. We have to go get my SUV first."

I'M DRIVING DOWN the two-lane road, my headlights illuminating what's ahead when my cell goes off, and I pick it up to check it really quick.

Ready!

Exactly what I wanted to see. I had made a phone call while I had Blake pack a bag for us. We're not going back to the cabin tonight, possibly not for a while. I exit the text from Gunner and drop it back into my lap. Pulling off the main road, I turn into the open gate.

"What are we doing here?" Blake asks, sitting up straighter.

"Taking care of business," I say vaguely. She'll find out soon enough. The cathedral comes into view, and I pull into a parking spot. We're the only ones here right now. "Come on." I turn off the SUV.

Getting out, we both go to the back of the vehicle, and I open the hatch. "Take this." I hand Blake a shovel. Then I grab the body wrapped in plastic and throw it over my shoulder. "You okay?" Looking over at her, I make sure she doesn't want to bolt or stay here instead of following me.

She nods in answer.

Adjusting the weight on my shoulder, I start walking away from the SUV and to the side of the building. Blake follows me silently around to the back. We pass the spot where I first fucked her after the vow ceremony and keep going. It's getting darker the farther we get from the cathedral. "Almost there," I tell her.

Coming up to an old wrought-iron gate, I stop. "Open that, please," I ask her.

She rushes past me and removes the broken lock and pushes it open, the creaking sound making her flinch, and she quickly looks around as if someone will hear it.

We enter the graveyard, and I walk over to the right, where I know there's a spot. Dropping the body to the ground, I reach out for the shovel.

Blake hands it to me, not saying a word, and I start digging.

BLAKELY

RYAT GRUNTS, PUSHING the end of the shovel into the ground and then stomps on it, digging a grave. It only took me a second to figure out why we're here.

Looking out over the graveyard, I see most of the headstones are the same—small with nothing but a first and last name and the dates they were born and died. No beloved father, or loving mother ... nothing further mentioned like you usually see. Some are completely blank.

"What is this place?" I ask him.

"An old burial ground," he answers, shoving the tip in again before tossing the excess dirt to the side.

"Why are we burying her here?" I wonder. "Aren't you afraid someone will find her?" They use the cathedral for the vow ceremony, but it could be for more things for all I know.

"Lords, chosen ones, and Ladies are buried here ... Well, that's not the total truth. It's more complicated than that." He stops digging and looks up at me. His eyes look a darker shade of green with only the moonlight. Or maybe I'm just seeing them that way because of what I just witnessed him do to Cindy.

"Mostly members who betray their oath, but if a member has to kill someone, they too are buried here. If a member dies of natural causes, then they are buried wherever they want." He shrugs carelessly, going back to digging. "Or cremated. They get the privilege of choosing before they die."

I bite my bottom lip. "How many have you buried here?"

Stopping again, he shoves the tip into the ground and places his forearm on it, using it for support. I can see a small shine on his forehead where he's started to sweat from the work. "Seven."

I swallow and nod my head. "How many of them were Lords?"

"About half."

Why would he kill someone who isn't a Lord? Was he ordered to kill them? I know the guy who was trying to kill me wasn't a Lord, and he slit his throat. So, that's at least one that I know of. If that guy was brought back and buried here. "How many of those were women?" I wonder.

"This is the first. Any more questions?" he asks, arching a dark brow, and I shake my head.

I understand he's tired. I'm fucking exhausted. It's been a long night, and after what he did to me in that underground bunker, I want to go to bed. But I didn't want to stay at the cabin alone, not after what Cindy told us. Even now, I feel like someone is watching us. But I won't tell Ryat that. I don't want him to worry or, worse, think I can't handle this life.

Finishing up, he tosses the shovel to the side and rolls the wrapped body into the grave. Then he picks up the shovel again, covering it up.

I stand silently, rocking back and forth, arms crossed over my chest, trying to keep warm. Before we left, I put on a pair of yoga pants, tennis shoes and one of his hoodies.

Once finished, he throws the shovel over his shoulder, and silently, we start to walk back toward the cathedral and to his SUV. But he surprises me when he opens a back door to the building and pulls me inside.

We walk down a hallway to a door that he shoves open. It's an office of some sort. He tosses the dirty shovel to the floor and turns to face me.

"What are we ...?"

The door opening behind me makes me jump, my heart starts pounding in my chest, and I squeal when I see Gunner pop his head in.

"We're ready," he says cheerfully.

Ryat nods. "Thanks."

Gunner steps inside, places a box on the floor, and then just stands there, staring at me. My wide eyes go to Ryat. "What's going on?" I ask him.

Stepping into me, he cups my face with his dirt-covered hands and licks his lips. "Do you trust me?"

"Yes," I say without hesitation even though my body shakes with nervousness. Is this another test? What if I fail?

His eyes search mine. "I need you to go with Gunner."

"What?" I shriek. "No, Ryat ..."

"Trust me, Blake." He nods to me. "I need you to go with Gunner."

My stomach is in knots, and my mind runs a hundred miles with all these different scenarios of what is about to happen. Why does he want to get rid of me? Have I not proven that I can stomach what he does? What a Lady is required to do?

"Okay," I whisper, knowing there's no fighting with him. And I wasn't lying. I do trust him. If he wants me to go with Gunner, then that's what I'll do.

He leans in and tenderly kisses my forehead, then he takes a step back. His hands drop to his sides, and I turn, giving him my back, and follow Gunner out of the room.

I stay silent while I follow him down the hall and to a new door. This cathedral is large, but I've walked this hallway before. Last time, I was dripping wet, and my hands were cuffed behind my back.

Coming to a stop, Gunner pushes open a door. "Ladies first." He gestures for me to go.

As I step into the room, my body goes rigid when I see pews filled with Lords. They're all dressed in cloaks and masks while they sit silently. They must have arrived while we were out in the cemetery because when we got here, the parking lot was empty. It took Ryat a good hour to bury her. Maybe even longer than that. All I know is I'm glad it's warmer in here than it was outside.

Gunner takes my hand and forces my heavy legs to walk to the first pew. There's already an empty seat on the end, closest to the aisle. I fall down into it and look up at him, expecting him to tell me something that will help me out with what's going on, but instead, he gives me his back and walks back out the side door, leaving me alone.

My legs start to bounce, and I nervously fiddle with my wedding ring when I hear commotion on the second-story balcony. I look up and see two men dressed in cloaks and masks dragging a woman into the center, where I see a chair already sitting right at the edge of the baptism pool.

All she wears is a T-shirt and a pair of black underwear with a hood over her head. She fights the two Lords, and it causes her already short shirt to show her stomach. They shove her into the chair, where they proceed to zip-tie her wrists to the wooden armrests, then quickly do the same with her ankles.

I swallow nervously, looking around at the Lords sitting in the pews to see a reaction as to what the hell is going on. But they could all be sleeping for all I know since I can't see their faces.

Is this another ceremony? If so, will I be next? What will we vow to?

The two Lords step away from her, and the one on the left rips the hood off. My hands shoot to my face to cover my mouth before the gasp can escape. It's Ashley—Matt's girlfriend.

My eyes dart around the stage, watching both men take several more steps back and cross their arms across their chests.

The sound of a creaking door fills the room, and I look to my right. My stomach drops when I see it's Ryat. He's not dressed in a cloak or mask. He's in his jeans, T-shirt, and combat boots. He's filthy, covered in dirt, and his shirt is wet from sweat while digging out back.

Slowly, he climbs the stairs to the second floor, taking his time like he has all night. Ashley sees him and thrashes in the chair. Ryat comes to a stop next to her, and I tense.

What is he doing?

Why would he hurt her? She should not be held responsible for Matt's actions.

Turning, he walks over to a table in the corner and picks up a knife. I go to tell him to stop but cover my mouth with both of my hands before I can get the words out. He told me to trust him. Maybe he's just going to scare her.

"Ashley," he calls out her name, and she whimpers, pulling on her restraints. The duct tape over her mouth keeps her from talking. "I assume you know why you're here?"

She shakes her head, tears running down her face.

He comes to stand beside her and rips the tape off.

"You sorry son of a bitch," she screams. "Matt is going to kill you." She shakes her head back and forth, making her bleach-blond hair slap her in the face.

"It's funny that you think he gives a fuck about you," Ryat says, and all the Lords chuckle at that.

She bares her teeth at him. "He loves me more than he'll ever love that bitch."

My hands drop from my mouth. She has to be talking about me.

"That must be why he wants her so much." He nods his head. "To prove to you that he loves you more." Reaching out, he places the tip of the knife to her cheek, and she turns her head away from it the best she can. "We're going to play a game," Ryat tells her. "It's called confessional. Fitting, huh? I'm going to ask you a question, and every time you refuse to answer or lie, I'm going to cut you open."

"I won't tell you shit," she screams.

"That's what they all say." He runs the tip of the blade down her neck below her ear, and blood instantly pours from the wound while the high vaulted ceilings fill with her screeching cry.

"We'll start with something easy," Ryat announces. "Did you know that Matt and Blakely were together when you met her at the house of Lords party?"

"Yes," she spits out.

I sit up straighter. She knew who I was? He had told her about me?

"Yet you still agreed to be his chosen before that night?" Ryat asks, tilting his head to the side.

"He told me all about her. The bitch was obsessed with him."

My teeth grind at her words, but I'm not sure why I'm surprised. Men like Matt always make it sound like all women want them. I did because that's who I was allowed to want. If I would have had options, I sure as fuck would have chosen someone else to date.

"She was desperate. A fucking hungry bitch who couldn't take a hint," she shouts at him. "You should know, she married the first guy she's ever fucked."

I think she was trying to make that an insult to Ryat, but he just smiles down at her—proud of that fact he took my virginity.

My hands fist. I actually felt sorry for her, thought that maybe she didn't know what kind of man he was, but she knew we were together. Knew that I was a virgin. How much else did Matt tell her? Sitting back in the pew, I cross my arms over my chest, ready to listen to what he's going to make her confess.

FORTY-THREE

RYAT

SMILING, I MOVE the knife to her neck, and she leans her head back, her chest rising and falling quickly with each breath. No matter how much of a hard-ass this bitch is trying to play, she's terrified.

"Moving on," I say, "Did you know where Blake was when she ran away?" I'm not going to waste much of our time. Gunner and Prickett got the Lords out here for a show, so I'm going to give them one.

"No," she growls.

I lower the knife, slicing a piece of skin off the top of her shoulder. "That's a lie."

She screams, blood flowing down her arm and the chair as the piece of skin sits on the floor by my shoe.

If Matt knew she was back and sent Cindy to get Blake out of her way, then Matt had to have known where she was the entire time, which makes sense. It's just more pieces of the puzzle that I needed. Since I have Cindy's phone now, I have access to a lot of their secrets. All involving my wife and keeping her from me. "Again. Did you know where Blake was when she ran away?"

"Yes," she manages to get out through a sob, dropping her head forward.

Now we're getting somewhere. "How did you know?"

Sniffing and licking the snot and tears that cover her upper lip, she answers me, "Matt told me he was going to talk to her in your room. And that she would run out afterward ...he told me to follow her and let him know where she went."

I hate how much Matt outsmarted me. I knew he told Blake those things to get her to leave, but he knew exactly what she would do, and he wanted eyes on her. I thought it was just the fact that she was leaving me, but he wanted to know where she was when he knew I couldn't reach her.

"You didn't find that odd?" I wave the bloody knife in the air. "That your Lord wanted you to follow his ex?"

"He ... he told me that he just wanted to make sure she didn't return." She yanks on the restraints, and I watch blood start to run from her wrists due to the tightness of the zip ties. Her hands are turning blue. She keeps clenching and unclenching them.

"But she returned," I add. "Because I found her and brought her back."

"No." She shakes her head quickly, throwing her hair around. "She came back for Matt."

I frown. "What makes you think that?"

A soft sob comes out. "He told me so. Said that she returned for him. That she wanted to divorce you ..." Not a total lie when I dragged her back. "And that I had to help him take care of her."

Matt told Cindy that Blake was at the house of Lords—which was true—and that if she wanted me, she needed to get Blake out of the way. The man is just putting every bitch he knows on my wife, hoping someone takes her out. *Over my dead body.* "That's not what Cindy told me."

Her head snaps up, and her wide, watery eyes meet mine. She doesn't know that I've already played this game with her bestie. "Cindy ... no..."

I drag the tip of the blade down her arm, splitting the skin, and she screams. "Try again."

"Stop," she sobs. "Please ... you don't understand."

That's also what Cindy said. "Explain it to me in the simplest form."

Spit flies from her mouth when she speaks. "Blake had been blowing up Matt's phone while she was gone."

"Another lie ..." I grab a handful of her hair and shove her head forward, running the blade across the back of her neck, making sure to only cut the skin and not to cut too deep and sever her spinal cord. "Tell the truth," I shout, getting tired already.

She sobs. "I don't know ..."

I slice along the top of her bare thigh. I'm not stabbing her because I don't want her to die. Yet. I just want to make her feel the sting enough to bleed.

My black combat boots step in the puddles of blood on the floor while I circle her, leaving bloody shoe prints around the chair. Ignoring her cries, I walk over to the table and pick up the cell phone that Gunner put up there for me. Opening up a chat, I read it out loud.

"You know Ryat will look for her again, Cindy tells Matt," I say, jumping midway into their convo. No need to rehash the entire thing. She was part of it, after all, so she should remember it.

"Yeah. I'm counting on it. This time, he won't get so lucky. The only thing of her he'll see will be the videos I choose to send him. That was your boyfriend, by the way." I clarify to Ashley, who just sits there bleeding and crying. "This is where it gets interesting." I scroll down a little. "You join the conversation, Ashley."

"I can get you a sedative to give her. That way, you don't have to fight with her. Just one poke, and she'll be out. You send with a sleeping emoji."

"Don't give her too much. You could kill her. I want her out, not dead, Matt responds to Cindy about your lovely idea."

"But how will I be able to get her to you? Cindy asked your boyfriend."

"I'll be close by. Just message me when it's done, Matt answered."

Lowering Cindy's cell, I look at her. "Do I need to continue?"

Her eyes are narrowed up at me, and her lips pulled back, baring her teeth. "You fucking ruined him," Ashley growls. I've hit a nerve. Good. Finally, we're getting somewhere. "His chance at being a great Lord. Then you choose his girlfriend? You both deserve what you're going to get."

"And you were more than willing to help him?" I ask, tilting my head to the side.

"Of course," she snaps. "A Lady stands by her Lord."

"Aw." I nod my head. "I get it now. He promised you not only retribution but also Lady status." Which has to be a lie because he was still planning on marrying Blake. Lords are a lot of things, but they are still only allowed one wife. Now they can fuck as many women as they want outside of their marriage, but legally—on paper—they have one wife.

"She wasn't even supposed to return. I stayed behind and watched her for three fucking weeks for him. Day in and day out while she worked in that run-down piece-of-shit bar and stayed in that nasty-ass motel." She snorts. "I told him I was done and was leaving to come back, and he sent Derek to watch her." She gives me a chilling smile. "He wanted to pay you back, and she was the best payment Matt could give him."

Taking in a deep breath, she places her nose up in the air, and I tap the bloody knife to my thigh, her blood staining my jeans.

"So, fuck you, Ryat," she snaps, and then her eyes look out over the bottom level. "He'll make her life miserable and make sure you get to watch." Her bloodshot eyes shoot to look up at me.

"This has been informative. Thank you for playing," I say, knowing all I needed to know. I actually was already aware of all of this, but I needed her confession to kill her in front of the Lords. I grip the back of the chair. "Your prize is death."

"No ... wait. Matt ..."

I shove it forward, knocking it in the baptism pool with her still tied to it. Her voice rings throughout the cathedral before her head goes under. Her blood instantly turns the water red, making it look like red wine, and she struggles in the chair as it hits the bottom.

I'm being a little theatrical right now. More than usual, but I thought it'd be poetic to kill her how Matt almost did when he was in that water with her for the vow ceremony. I should have never stood and stopped him. That was a lesson I learned the hard way.

BLAKELY

I FEEL NUMB.

I'm not even sad that Ryat tortured the woman or the fact that he looked like he enjoyed it.

Sitting here, I realize that everything has been a lie. I mean, a part of me already knew that but thinking it and having it confirmed are two very different things.

Now I just look stupid. The entire time I was with Matt, he had someone else. And she knew about me. She was in on everything, pretending that she didn't know who I was. Helping him when I ran. She kept tabs on me like my biggest fan.

All the Lords stand and exit the cathedral one by one, and I stay planted in my seat, unable to move. Instead, my eyes are trained on the glass that showcases the inside of the baptism pool.

Ashley's dead body is at the bottom, still strapped to the chair in the red water. Every moment of my life over the past couple of months have been tracked or forced in some way.

The only real decision I've made was to stay Ryat's wife. He was forced to pick me as his chosen. I felt forced to marry him to save myself from Matt. Ryat said I wasn't paying attention if I thought he wanted to divorce me, but I chose not to sign those papers. I wanted to fight for him. For us. In a world full of smoke and mirrors, he's something real. We got here by chance, but we're still together by choice.

I can't thank him enough for finding me when I ran. I thought Ryat was watching me while I was away, but it turns out it was Matt. He had eyes on me, and when he realized Ryat was getting close, he paid some piece of shit named Derek to kill me.

"Blake?"

I blink, lowering my eyes and see a set of green ones looking into mine. Ryat is kneeling in front of me. I don't say anything. My lips won't work.

He sighs heavily. Reaching out, he runs his thumb across my cheek, then wipes it on his already bloody jeans. *Am I crying?* Not sure why I'd be crying. I feel nothing for that bitch he just killed.

"Come on." He takes my hand and pulls me to stand, but my legs give out, so he picks me up, cradling me in his arms.

My head hangs off the side of his forearm, and I look up to see Gunner and Prickett pulling Ashley's lifeless body from the water. They're still dressed in their cloaks, but their masks are on the floor. I watch them cut the zip ties, and her body falls onto the floor with a thud, then Ryat is walking us out the door, and I can't see her anymore. A part of me wants to watch them bury her. It was satisfying knowing that Cindy was underground in a graveyard where no one would ever look. I want that same satisfaction with Ashley too.

Ryat places me in the passenger seat of his SUV, puts my seat belt on, and then closes the door. I lean my head against the cold window while he drives us who knows where.

I don't even pay attention to where we're going. His cell rings twice, and he speaks to someone on his Bluetooth, but again, I tune it out.

Does any of it matter anymore—Life?

Matt wants me dead. Especially now. What if he succeeds? I want more time with Ryat. I want us to have kids. Should I get that? Do I deserve that? No. I'm no different than the ones trying to kill me. But everyone else is also doing everything in their power to get what they want. I'm going to do the same.

"You either kill or be killed," Ryat had said to me once. I didn't understand how true that was, but I do now. It's just a game, and who knows who will still be alive once it ends.

FORTY-FOUR

RYAT

I PARK IN the back packed parking lot of Blackout and get out. She hasn't said anything to me, and honestly, it's got me worried. I grab the bag out of the back and throw it over my shoulder before going to her door and picking her up. I shut the passenger door, and the back door slams open to the club as I walk across the parking lot. Ty holds it open for me and looks down at her. "Is she okay?"

"Yeah," I lie, trying to convince myself more than him. I keep telling myself it's just been a long night. Between our fight, a fake divorce, sex in my bunker, and two murders—she just needs some rest.

The club is in full swing, but the sound of "Honesty" by Halsey blaring doesn't even seem to faze her. I carry her up the stairs and then in the elevator to the fourth floor, down a long hallway where Ty unlocks a door for me. "Here you go." He shoves a key in my back pocket since my hands are currently full.

"Thanks, man."

"Anytime. You're welcome to stay as long as you need to." He closes it behind me, leaving us alone, and I take us to the back master suite, and straight into the bathroom. I need a shower. I'm covered in not only blood but also dirt from digging a grave.

Setting her on the black marble countertop, I start undressing her, and she remains silent. Her eyes are glazed over—she's looking at me but not seeing anything.

"We need a shower," I tell her, and she slowly nods in agreement. She's listening, so I haven't lost her completely yet.

Leaving her on the countertop, I walk into the Roman shower and turn on the water. After getting undressed, I then pick her up and carry her into the shower. I stand her on her feet but use my body to hold her up against the white subway tile wall, letting the hot water wash over us, washing away another night of dead bodies.

She blinks, her eyes focusing on mine. "There's my girl." I breathe out in relief, running my hand over her wet hair and giving her a smile.

"Do you believe in heaven and hell?" her soft voice asks as I watch her blue eyes fill with tears. "I've never really thought about it ..." She licks her lips. "But there has to be something better than this, right? So much hate. So much deceit. How does anyone know what's real or fake?"

"No," I answer her question honestly. "I don't believe in life after death." Her eyes search mine, and for once, I hate how vulnerable she looks—almost broken. I want to make her whole. That's my job as her husband. She belongs to me, and Matt is still controlling her emotions—making her question everything. "The Lords have shown me that darkness exists. That you don't have to die in order to burn. And then you came along ..." I place both of my hands on her wet face, and she blinks, allowing the first tear to run down her cheek. "I can see you, touch you, and kiss you." I wipe it away with my thumb. "I can love you." My eyes drop to her plump lips, and her bottom one trembles. "You, Blakely Rae Archer, are my heaven." Letting go of her face, I pick up her left hand and bring her knuckles to my lips, kissing her wedding ring. "I made a vow to protect you, Blake, and I'll show anyone who tries to hurt you my version of hell."

I'd set the world on fire, including myself, if it meant saving her.

BLAKELY

THIS IS REAL!

This is what I wanted. All along. Acceptance, love, understanding. What if he's right, and this is all we get? And when you die, you're just ... gone. Eventually not even a memory to anyone.

I can live with that because I have him.

Wrapping my arms around his neck, I pull his face down to mine. His hands slap the wall, leaving the smallest space between our lips. My eyes take in his sharp jaw, the curve of his lips and green eyes—

they look different now that I know who he really is—sexier in a way that has my blood pumping.

I know who you are, Ryat Alexander Archer. I'm not afraid of what I see, nor am I ashamed.

His dark hair is wet, and some of the longer pieces have fallen down across his face into his eyes as the water hits us. Leaning forward, he goes to press his lips to mine, but I pull back just enough to meet his eyes again and whisper, "I love you, Ryat."

His lips capture mine, and I open up for him, letting him take control. It's passionate yet needy at the same time. The water falling down over us makes our lips slippery, the kiss messy. His teeth hit mine, and I moan, wanting them to bite into my skin, to fucking scar me so I'll forever have a reminder of tonight.

I thought I knew what love would be like marrying Matt. Not what I dreamed of but tolerable. Ryat has shown me that there is more out there. I'm no longer settling for something; I'm taking it.

One of his hands tangles into my wet hair, and I lift my left leg to wrap around his hip.

"Fuck, Blake," he growls, pulling his face from mine. His lips drop to my neck, and I tilt my head to the side. "I love you so goddamn much."

I suck in a shaky breath. "I love ..."

His lips capture mine again, and his hand falls between our bodies. Then he's sliding his hard dick into me. Knocking the back of my head into the wall, I gasp when he stretches me open. I'm still sensitive from earlier, but I'm not going to turn him down. Not now. Not ever.

Ryat Archer is a killer, and all I can think of is I wish I could prove my love for him the way he has for me. He deserves that much. Blood for blood. He's spilled so much for me. I'm not afraid to bleed for him.

I'm gasping, my hands digging into his skin, feeling his muscles tense while his fingers dig into my ass, and he lifts me off my feet.

"Yes," I gasp as he pulls out and shoves his dick into me, my back hitting the wall. "Oh, God." My eyes close, and he picks up his pace, fucking me how I like it.

Water from the sprayers slips between my parted lips, and I swallow it, trying to catch my breath. If this is what it feels like to drown, I don't want to be above water.

The bathroom fills with his grunts and the sound of our bodies slapping. My legs tighten around his hips, and I lock my ankles, clinging to his slippery skin. I can't get him close enough, deep enough. I want this man to consume me. Take what little pieces I had left of myself and make them his.

I'm not the type of woman who needs to know who I am. All I need to know is who I am with him. And I know exactly who that is—his. Nothing else fucking matters.

He slams into me, his dick hitting that spot that always makes my body fucking burn from the inside out. My moans grow louder, my breathing heavier.

He yanks me from the wall, only to slam me into the other one opposite us, forcing a cry from my lips.

"That's what I wanted to hear," he growls. His mouth goes to my neck, and I feel him sucking on my skin.

"Ryat!" I shout his name, my heart already racing, the fire starting. He goes harder, faster, knowing I'm right there. Closing my eyes, I let the wave wash over me, knowing that I'm already drowning. Why not let it wash me away?

I LIE IN bed, listening to the pounding music below us. It's not that bad but definitely noticeable. "I need to go back to the cabin," I tell him.

"You're not going back there," he states, entering the bedroom with a towel wrapped around his hips. Water still runs down over his sculpted chest and abs. His arms are red from my nails digging into them in the shower.

"I have to get my books for classes tomorrow." It's Monday, and I have to get back to Barrington. Fuck, I'm going to be so far behind. By now, I'm failing everything. I've missed so much work, only for it not to have been worth it. At the time, I didn't care to go back, but that's when I was going to live my life on the run. That's not the case anymore.

He was in the middle of knocking the water out of his hair, but he pauses. A smile tugs at his lips, and then he starts laughing.

"What's so funny?" I sit up.

"You're done with school, Blake," he announces.

"Excuse me?" I argue.

"You left. You think people weren't going to realize you weren't there?"

I never really thought about it to be honest. When you're running for your life, your college classes don't really matter anymore. "So, what? I just can't not go back. Ryat, I need a degree." And my parents will kill me. Maybe that's another reason my father was so mad at me for leaving town.

"Don't worry, I covered it." He dismisses it.

Arching a brow, I slowly repeat his words. "You covered it?" He nods. "What the hell does that mean?" I'm going to need him to clarify exactly what he's done.

"Told everyone that we took a week off for our honeymoon." He shrugs. "We were newlyweds. It made sense."

"What?" I gape at him. "What about the other two weeks?"

"I paid someone to step in for you. They will be covering for you the rest of the year," he explains casually. As if it's no big deal for someone else to go to school for me.

"Ryat ..." I growl his name but pause, circling around to what he said earlier. Did he say *we*? "You skipped that first week too?"

"I've skipped every day."

I gasp. "Ryat. Why the fuck would you do that?"

"You expected me to go on with my life? Sit in fucking classes while you were on the run and in danger?" he asks with a rough laugh.

I snort. "I was fine."

His eyes go large at the lie, any sense of playfulness now gone. "Are you fucking serious right now?"

Instead of telling another one, I cross my arms over my exposed chest.

"That man was going to kill you," he growls.

"Because of you," I spit out.

He stiffens, his eyes darkening. "Excuse me?"

How dare he make such an important decision for me? But I'm really not sure why I'm surprised. I mean, look how we got here. "He told me you owed him. That he was going to ship me back in pieces—to you. So, I was only in danger because of you." This isn't news to him. Ryat just made Ashley confess that a man named Derek—I'm guessing that's the guy—was sent to watch me. But I hadn't told him what the guy said to me.

"He said that shit to you, and you're just now telling me?" he shouts, his face turning red.

I shrug carelessly. "You never asked. You were too busy drugging me and dragging me back. Oh, and then I had to be tested. Because you know, the Lords said it was time to put even more strain on our marriage—"

He reaches over and picks up a lamp, throwing it across the room. It shatters, hitting a wall, cutting me off. Silence falls between us; the only sound is the faint bass of the music from the club below us, and my shoulders fall while I sit in the bed naked.

Turning around, he places his hands on the dresser and leans over it. I watch the way his back muscles ripple—covered in scratch marks—while trying to calm his breathing.

"I know it wasn't your fault," I say softly. It was Matt's. Everything started because of him. "You saved me—"

"It was, though," he interrupts me and turns around. "How do you think I found you?"

I frown. "I ... don't know."

Running a hand down his face, he leans back against the dresser. "Remember that night Gunner and I found you and Sarah here at Blackout?"

I nod, scrunching my brow. "Yeah, but what's that have to do with anything?"

"A couple of guys hit on you two at the bar," he adds.

I sit up straighter. "How did you know about that?" I never told him that. Maybe Sarah filled Gunner in about our night.

"We were here upstairs, watching you girls and saw them approach you," he admits.

"How did you ...?" I nod my head to myself. "My phone. You tracked us here. I was wondering how you found us." Fuck, I should have fucking known. If I had just opened my eyes, I probably could have pieced it together.

"Long story short, Gunner and I killed them," he confesses as if no big deal.

"What?" I gasp. "Ryat ..."

"They had drugs on them, Blake. Shit that proved they were going to do more to the two of you than buy you drinks," he snaps, then releases a heavy sigh.

"Did you find that out before or after you killed them?" I demand.

"After."

"Jesus, Ryat." I run a hand through my still wet hair. I understand they might have hurt us, but he killed them before that. "You can't keep killing random people."

"I will kill whoever touches what's mine, Blake," he states matter-of-factly. Lowering his voice, he goes on. "They were here with a friend—a third guy. He saw what happened and knew we took care of them. I didn't know at the time, obviously, that Ashley had followed you when you ran, but Ty overheard talk in Blackout that the guy knew where you were. We followed him. It made me think that Matt had told him, and he led us straight to you."

"No ..." I trail off, trying to get my brain to put all the pieces together. It had to have been the guy with the tattoo on the back of his neck. I never saw his face that night here at the bar with Sarah, but it makes sense.

He nods, arguing with me. "Matt sent him when Ashley was tired of watching you. He knew where you were. Maybe he didn't care to go get you at the time. He wanted to sit back and watch what I did when you left. It was more about me at that point rather than you."

"But ... we just found out ..." I trail off at the look on his blank face. He already fucking knew all of this but wanted Ashley to confess in front of the Lords, giving him the reason he needed to kill her. "I can't believe this."

"Which part exactly?"

"All of it," I snap, glaring up at him through my lashes. "God, Ryat, how many secrets are you keeping from me?"

"I don't keep count," he states, his green eyes on mine.

"Is this a joke to you?" I demand, throwing the covers off me and getting out of bed.

"No. I take anything regarding you pretty fucking seriously," he answers, pushing away from the dresser.

I walk over to him, glaring up at him. "What else do you have to tell me at the moment?"

"Nothing."

"You're fucking lying to me."

He lowers his face to mine, a smile tugging at his lips, and says, "Prove it."

I go to slap him, but he catches my wrist with one hand and wraps the other around my throat, pushing my back into the nearest wall. "Want to give that another try, Blake?"

"Fuck you, Ryat," I growl.

When he lets go of my wrist, my arm drops to my side as he steps into me, his nose touching the tip of mine. "Don't mind if I do ..." His hands slide up my bare hips to my ribs. "I can never get enough of you," he growls, his voice rough.

My heart starts beating faster at his words, but I'm still pissed at him, so I say, "Good. Because you're stuck with me until you die."

Tilting his head up just a bit, he lightly kisses the tip of my nose. "That's all I want."

"Aren't you the romantic?" I say, trying to keep my breath steady. Not wanting to show him that my thighs are tightening as we speak. All that's separating us is his towel. I'm already naked.

"Blake, I'll be anything you need."

FORTY-FIVE

RYAT

ME AND GUNNER step down into the basement at Blackout. Ty gave us the green light to use it and Gunner pointed out the two men who were hitting on our girls. Now they lay on the concrete floor, bloody noses and all.

"Thanks, gentlemen." I nod to the two security guards who wear Blackout shirts. "We've got it from here."

They both nod and exit the room, walking up the stairs, leaving us alone.

"What the fuck, man?" One of the guys asks, getting to his knees. He reaches up, smearing the blood on his face.

"Ffuuccckk," the other groans, rolling onto his back.

"Like touching things that don't belong to you?" I ask, arching a brow.

"What are you talking about?" The one on his knees gets to his feet.

"The two women you were hitting on at the bar." I jog their memory, since I know the bouncers fucked them up a bit before bringing them down here. "The ones who you wouldn't take no for an answer from."

The guy snorts. "Fuck those whores .. "

My fist connects with his face, snapping his head back. He stumbles over the other guy lying down, making him fall back to the floor.

"Those whores belong to us," Gunner states, leaning up against the wall casually. "And no, we're not sharing them with you,"

I'm not in the mood to get bloody tonight. Especially since Blake will notice once I make my presence known. So, I walk over to the back wall and remove the chain from the hook. Making my way to the guy who I punched, I wrap it around his neck a few times and then drag him across the floor.

him to his feet.

"What the fuck?" The other guy on the floor growls, getting to his feet, watching his friend struggle while I wrap the chain around a hook on the wall. I yank on it, pulling his feet up off the floor. "What the fuck are you doing?" The guy goes to charge me, but Gunner pushes off the wall and knocks him back to the floor.

"Where is your friend?" Gunner questions.

"Who?" he snaps. "You're fucking ..."

Gunner kicks him in the face, blood goes flying from his mouth. "There were three of you at the bar."

"Fuck ... you ..."

Gunner stomps on his hand, making him cry out.

Once I have my man secured where I want him, I wrap the chain around the hook on the floor. Watching the guy hang there, I dig into his pocket, removing his car keys, wallet and cell phone. "What's this?" I ask, pulling out a pill bottle. The prescription has been scratched off. But it's not hard to figure out what the white pills are—rohypnol. "You were going to drug them." I state. That's why they were so adamant about getting them drinks.

"Hand me one of those." Gunner gestures to another chain. I toss it to him, and he does the same thing with his guy. Also removing his belongings.

We exit the basement and walk up the stairs to find the two security guards standing there, making sure that no one came down to bother us. "Give them an hour." I say and they nod. "Let the bastards fucking hang there."

"Yes, sir," they say in unison and nod.

Blake and I have been staying in the apartment above Blackout for three days, and I hate it. I'm not one to hide out, but it's been our only option. I've had new cameras placed at the cabin and all around the property. I want to watch them for another week to see if Matt is hanging out there. So far, nothing. But he hasn't been at the house of Lords. Meaning the fucker is also in hiding. He won't do that for long, so my question is, what is he waiting on?

What is the opportunity he needs to make his move? And what the fuck is that going to be? Will he take her away from me? Or will he just kill her and leave her where her body falls for me to find? Either one is an option he's considering.

I hate not knowing, and Blake is starting to go stir-crazy. She wants out of this damn club and back to the cabin. Doesn't she understand, I'd much rather us be alone in the middle of nowhere than here?

I just keep telling myself a little longer. Matt will get restless, and when he does, I'll be there to cut his fucking head clean off his body.

I stand on the balcony of the second story of Blackout and watch the girls dance below. Gunner brought Sarah over tonight. I figured some drinks would loosen Blake up and remind her that she's not a prisoner here.

We didn't bring much with us, so Sarah had brought her a dress and a pair of heels. Of course, I didn't approve, but she had nothing else to wear. The moment I rip it off her later, I'm giving it back to Sarah. I'm surprised Gunner hasn't already burned it.

My cell vibrates in my back pocket, and I pull it out to read the text.

Tomorrow night; Blackout.

Shit! My eyes look back down at my wife, and she's smiling with a drink in one hand and her cell in the other. I made her take it with her. She stops bouncing around and takes a drink before holding up her phone. She reads over the text, her body going rigid. Then she turns and looks up at me.

Placing my forearms on the railing, I lean over it and stare down at her, trying to look unfazed by what I just received. Honestly, she's ready. My girl has proven that she's capable of taking on more than I thought.

The black lights bounce off her pretty blue eyes, and I can tell from here how large they are at the moment.

Sarah taps her shoulder, but she ignores her. A second later, she puts her drink down and heads toward the stairs. I push off the banister and go to meet her.

"I got my text," she says, now panting from running up the stairs in heels.

"I know. I got one too." Hers would be different than mine, but they mean the same thing. It's time for her initiation.

She licks her lips. "Ryat, what if ...?"

"You're going to be fine." I place my hands on her shoulders. "You won't see me, but I'll be here, okay?" She nods quickly. "Then you'll meet me at the cathedral," I remind her, and she nods again. "Hey." I pull her into me. "It's not until tomorrow night, so go back down there and have fun with Sarah." I can't believe I just said that. I'd much rather us be in bed than her shaking her ass on a dance floor for other men to watch. The big rock on her hand doesn't hurt, though. I wanted something that said fuck off—I'm married, and my husband will gut you—from far away. I think I made the right decision.

"Okay." She reaches up on her tiptoes and presses her lips to mine. "I love you."

I run my hands through her tangled, sweaty hair. "I love you too, little one." Then she turns and heads back down the stairs, much slower than when she ran up them.

Placing my forearms back on the railing, I watch her make her way through the crowd and back to Sarah. Blake nods a few times, and then they get new drinks.

"Aren't you two the cutest couple?"

I look over to my right to see Ty has joined me. "She has initiation tomorrow night. Here."

"What do you need me to do?" he asks without hesitation.

"Keep an eye out for her."

He nods. "Of course. Just text me when it's going down, and I'll make sure I have all eyes on her at all times."

Pushing off the railing, I reach out my right hand. "Thanks, man."

"No problem." He pulls me in for a man hug and slaps my back. "Come by my office before you call it a night. I'm expecting a phone call that might have an answer to your Matt problem." Before I can respond to that, he walks back toward his office. And I start to feel sorry for Ty. For what he had and lost. I can't imagine what he went through. I saw his rage. His anger controlled him for a very long time until he realized he could get his revenge. And he will—soon.

We always do. That's what we're trained for.

BLAKELY

GUNNER FOUND US on the dance floor and took my friend away from me, so I took that as my hint that I was done too. I make my way to the top of the stairs to see Ryat still standing in the same spot he has for the past three hours. Just watching me. And I'm hoping he doesn't kill those two men who came to talk to Sarah and me. They really were nice and just striking up a conversation. They'd never been here and needed directions to the nearest hotel after they left Blackout.

"Come on." He takes my hand.

"Where are we going?" I ask when he doesn't head to the apartment that we are currently calling home.

"I have to talk to Ty," he answers vaguely. Coming to an end of the hallway, he punches in a code on the keypad with his free hand and pushes the now unlocked door open.

Ryat enters and pulls me inside. I freeze when I see a woman slumped down onto a couch. A man straddles her legs on his knees, his dick in her mouth while his hands pin hers to the top of the cushion with one of his while the other is gripping the hair at her crown.

Her eyes meet mine, and she starts mumbling nonsense around his pierced dick. I look away, turning my body into Ryat, who stands next to me unfazed like I am.

What in the fuck?

Why didn't Ryat knock?

The man picks up his pace, and I hear her start to gag. Turning my head, I look over my shoulder and watch him face fuck her roughly until he shoves it all the way down her throat and growls when he comes.

Pulling away quickly, he slaps his hand over her mouth and orders, "Swallow." She looks up at him, blinking rapidly while tears run down her face, smearing her makeup. She tries to shake her head, but he prevents it and adds, "If you don't, you'll be licking it up."

I look away again, my face heating with his words. Fuck, I'm drunk and horny. Why are we in here?

"Good girl," I hear him praise her, and she whimpers.

I know, girl. I get it. Why do we crave that? To be praised for something that others would find degrading. I'd do some sick and twisted shit for Ryat if I knew he'd praise me for it. I want to please Ryat all the time. And when he tells me good girl, it's like everything I actually did meant something to him.

"Now, go back to work," the man demands, and I hear him zip up his pants.

The girl runs past me in a blur and out the door.

"Ryat," the guy greets him excitedly. "That's the second time you've caught me with my pants down lately." He chuckles.

Second time? Dear Lord, I thought it was bad he didn't knock this time. When will he learn his lesson?

"Guess I should start knocking," he jokes, and I refrain from rolling my eyes at him.

"Well, you know I love an audience."

That makes sense. I turn around and straighten my shoulders, and the guy now sits behind his desk. His black boots are propped up on the surface, and his arms are behind his head, fingers intertwined with a relaxed and carefree look on his face. He's got facial hair, but it's not overdone—more like a five o'clock shadow following the curve of his sharp jawline. His black hair— thick and unkempt—looks like he hasn't cut it in a while. I wonder if he has it that way on purpose or just doesn't care. His baby-blue eyes are on mine, and he doesn't look the least bit ashamed that I was embarrassed by what we walked in on.

"Blake, we finally meet," he announces, giving me a smirk.

Should I know this man? I mean, I've heard Ryat mention him. I know he owns Blackout and has loaned us the apartment above the club, but that's as far as my knowledge of him goes. I've pretty much stayed locked in the apartment these past few days.

"Blake, this is Tyson Crawford. Ty, this is my wife, Blake."

My heart immediately starts racing at his name. I look up at Ryat with wide eyes, and he frowns down at me.

"Uh..." I clear my throat. "It's nice to finally meet you," I say, remembering my manners. "Thank you for letting us stay here."

Oh my God. Does Sarah know he owns Blackout?

"Of course, anything for Ryat and his wife," he says, standing from his chair and walking around it. Leaning back against the edge, he crosses his ankles over one another and his arms over his chest. His eyes dismiss me and go to my husband. "It's all set. I have everyone who is on shift tomorrow up to speed on the situation."

I frown. What is he talking about?

"Thanks, man. It should go smoothly, but just in case—"

"I understand," he interrupts Ryat. "You can never be too careful with the one you love."

"Yeah," Ryat says through gritted teeth. "Anything on Matt?"

My ears perk up at that. This guy is a Lord, so he has to know Matt.

"No." His response is clipped. "But there's already word on the street—two of my guards heard a few guys talking about you taking out his chosen."

Do you ever feel the air shift? Can you tell the moment that the vibe changes in the room? Because I can at this very second. The air gets thicker, the temperature hotter as the man's mood shifts with the mention of what Ryat did. Or maybe it's just me. Afraid of what will happen to my husband when Matt decides to make himself known.

Ryat smiles and lifts his chin a bit. He's proud of himself. And a sick, twisted part of me is proud of him too. This man will do whatever it fucking takes to not only protect me but also love me. "He can't hide forever," he adds.

"Yeah, well, Matt is a piece of shit and deserves to be strung up in the middle of the cathedral where all the Lords can watch him slowly bleed to death," Tyson states, the darkness in his voice making the hair on the back of my neck stand up.

So much so that I reach up and rub the skin like it's going to help.

"Oh, I'm going to teach him a lesson," Ryat agrees, his voice just as threatening.

"I want to be there when you do it." Tyson nods, the corner of his lips pulling back into a sadistic smile.

"Of course," Ryat agrees.

"Let me know if you need anything else, brother." Tyson reaches his right hand out, and Ryat shakes it. Tyson pulls him in for a manly handshake/hug and slaps his back with his free hand. "You two get some sleep tonight. You have a busy one tomorrow."

FORTY-SIX

RYAT

I UNLOCK THE door to the apartment. Stepping aside, I allow her to enter before me, and I shut the door, locking it behind me.

"You okay?" I ask her. It's been a long night, and she's had quite a bit to drink.

Nodding, she heads toward the master bedroom.

"Hey." I follow her. "Talk to me." I can tell something is on her mind.

"Tyson?" she asks about him, surprising me. Out of all the things that have happened this week and what's going to happen tomorrow night, I doubted the man we walked in on fucking a woman was the last thing she'd question.

"What about him?" I wonder.

"He's a Lord?"

Well, that gets my attention. He doesn't wear his ring. Not anymore. Most don't in public after graduation. Only when we have special occasions at the house of Lords. Otherwise, we prefer to blend in with whatever crowd we're in. "Yes."

"Is that how you know him?" she asks slowly.

I nod.

"Why does he own this club?"

I'm even more curious as to what she's getting at. "Why does it matter that he owns Blackout?"

"I thought being a Lord was all about power. This is just a club."

I nod. "It is. But not all Lords prefer to sit in a high-rise office overlooking a large city. A Lord can be anywhere. Ty chose to go underground and work the dirtier side of things." He always liked getting filthy. He was ruthless. Top of his year. He could have picked any profession, and Blackout was where he wanted to be. "Owning Blackout has its perks for the Lords," I assure her.

She licks her lips nervously. "I heard about him ... at Barrington."

I frown. "What did you hear?" It's not uncommon for others to talk about the Lords. Every man who attends Barrington wants to be a member. Not because of the status you get while in college, but what you get once you graduate and are out in the real world. And those who don't make it like to run their little mouths about things they think they know. That's why the Lords have us kill—it's their insurance policy. If you get kicked out before graduation, you're not going to go run your mouth about it when they've got leverage to bury you. I've seen it done before, and those sorry bastards were literally buried alive behind the cathedral.

"That his chosen cheated on her boyfriend to be Tyson's chosen—"

"Don't believe everything you hear, Blake," I interrupt her, reaching up and removing my shirt. I turn and toss it onto the floor, not giving a fuck about it right now.

Her hand grips my upper arm, and she yanks me back to face her. I run a hand down my face, and she glares up at me. "You know what happened?"

Of course, I do. But I say, "It doesn't matter what happened."

"Ryat." She growls my name. "Tell me. When you left me with Gunner and Sarah, we looked up his chosen, and she doesn't exist. No social media pages. No record of ever going to Barrington. It's like she was made up."

I sigh. "She *did*, Blake." The Lords can make anyone no longer exist. If they want. And they wanted to get rid of her existence so fast. Honestly, they failed Ty and her. They guarantee us protection as long as we are faithful to our oath. That was not the case for Ty. But then again, can you guarantee a life? I don't think so. Not the type we live.

"Did?" she asks, wide eyes.

I nod. "Yeah, she never cheated on her boyfriend with Tyson. Because she never had one. He was a stalker."

She blinks, her lips parting. "A stalker?"

I nod. "Yeah."

"What ... what happened to her?" She stumbles over her words and licks her lips, which I know are probably starting to go numb from drinking.

I can't go into detail about what was done to her. It was hard enough to witness Ty go through it, let alone retell it. Cupping her face, I say, "He'll get his revenge."

Frowning, she asks. "What do you mean? On the stalker?"

I shake my head. "Sometimes, the best revenge is to go after something that they love just as much as you loved."

"I don't understand." She frowns.

Kissing her forehead, I pull her into me. It's exactly what I would do if I was put in the same situation Ty was. Only, I'd never wait this long. Being a Lord teaches you patience, but even I wouldn't have this kind of strength.

"Let's get to bed," I tell her, ending this conversation.

BLAKELY

I WAKE TO the sound of a phone ringing. "Ryat?" I mumble, reaching out to wake him up to answer it. It has to be his. No one ever calls me. Pretty sure it's because he's got most people blocked. "Ryat," I growl when it continues to blare in the silent room.

My hands reach farther across the bed, and I feel nothing. Then up to his pillowcase—still nothing. "What the ...?"

Sitting up, I turn to get my phone to use as a light that sits on the nightstand to see that mine is the one ringing.

Holding it up to my face, I shut my eyes because it's so bright. "Hello?" I ask through a yawn. When no one answers, I pull it away from my face and squint to look at the screen. It says **MINE,** and I roll my eyes at what Ryat saved his number under while I was *away*. "Ryat, what are you doing?" I lie down. "Come to bed with me." It's got to be late or early morning. We didn't go to bed until after one, and I can still taste the lingering alcohol on my tongue.

"Want to be my good girl?" he asks in that sexy, deep voice that makes my pussy throb.

Closing my eyes, I stretch out my legs to his side of the bed, all but moaning. Something about those words make my legs weak. Thank God I'm lying down. "Always."

"You know what a good girl is, right?" he goes on.

"Why don't you remind me?"

"Okay." I hear the smirk in his voice, playing along. "It's where I get to do whatever I want to you, and you take it."

"Take it, huh?" I roll onto my back and stare up into the darkness, my free hand twirling a few strands of my hair around my fingers. "In the mood to hurt me?" I joke.

"Yes."

The single word sends a chill down my spine, my nipples hardening, and my legs spread open on their own. Taking in a deep breath, I say, "Big words for a man who isn't even here."

He chuckles softly. "Oh, I'm here, Blake."

"Where—?"

"But," he interrupts me, "before we get started, tell me."

Tell him what? My head is still a little slow, and my lips still kinda numb. I had quite a bit to drink tonight before I passed out, and I didn't even get to sleep it off. Reaching up with my free hand, I push some hair back from my face. "What exactly?" I just come out and ask.

"To have my way with you," he answers simply.

Yes, please. "Have your way with me," I say without hesitation, knowing he's about to fuck with me. And I'm all of a sudden not that tired anymore. Of course, he's not specific. Ryat wants to keep me in the dark, just like when he kidnapped me, and we had my forced-sex fantasy.

"Get up, Blake. And get your ass down here. Now," he commands, his playful tone long gone, before hanging up.

Dropping my phone to the bed, I jump up on wobbly legs and rush to the bathroom. I quickly brush my teeth and swish some mouthwash around to try to get rid of the lingering taste of the rum and Cokes. Then I throw on one of his T-shirts with a pair of underwear, not wanting to go down there naked. We're obviously alone, but I prefer to have something on instead of walking through the club naked. Plus, I don't even know where *down here* is. I'm going to have to find him.

Opening the apartment door, I softly pull the door shut without allowing it to latch because he has a key, but I don't. I make my way down the single hallway to the elevator at the end and step inside when it immediately opens up for me. I press the bottom floor and silently wait for it to open.

I wring my hands in the shirt. They're getting sweaty. I'm nervous because you never know what Ryat will want. Especially here. Like is he planning on fucking me on the dance floor? Bent over the bar? What about on the stage where the bands perform for special events?

The elevator comes to a stop, and the door slides open. "Oh Lord" by In This Moment starts playing. Listening to the words, knowing I'm about to give *my Lord* whatever he wants, makes the lyrics even sexier. Something tells me he picked this song as a warning. The flashing neon lights are on as if the club is open, but it's different being here when no one else is.

Stepping onto the dance floor, I look around at the empty bar and chairs that round the tables. "Ryat?" I shout over the music. It's louder than normal, at least I think so. Maybe that's the start of a hangover coming on.

Patting down the shirt, I realize I left my cell phone upstairs in the bed. "Well, shit," I hiss. When I look up, I throw my hair over my shoulder, and my pulse quickens at what I see sitting back in a corner booth.

It's darker, the lights not hitting in the spot, but I can still make out the body that sits there. He's dressed in a black cloak, and my thighs tighten when I see the white on his face—he's got his mask on.

He wants to fucking play!

The thought makes the blood rush in my ears in anticipation. The song comes to a stop and changes to "All The Time" by Jeremih and Lil Wayne, and I watch him slowly slide out of the booth, then step down onto the dance floor.

I take a step back, and he stands there, tilting his head to the side. He reaches his right hand out and grabs something off the table. His hand falls to his side, and the lights bounce off the metal—handcuffs.

Fuck! My body starts humming even though I'm having trouble catching my breath now. Noticing something else in his hand, it looks like a black leather belt of some sort. No, that can't be what it is. It's too hard to see with the lights constantly flashing.

I keep trying to blink, to try to focus, but in the next second, I realize he's been walking toward me this entire time, and he's getting closer. Taking a step back, he comes to a stop.

It's a dance. Who's going to move first? My heart is racing, and my palms sweaty. I want him to chase me. That's what I like, and he knows it. And he likes to drag me back to him.

So, I give us what we both want. I turn and run like hell, knowing he's going to catch me.

FORTY-SEVEN

RYAT

RUNNING UP BEHIND her, I reach out and grab a handful of her hair, yanking her to a stop.

Her voice rings out through the empty club over the music. "Not fast enough." I growl in her ear then shove her into the side of the bar. Her hands slap the top, and I grab them, yanking them behind her back and cuff them in place, making sure they're nice and tight just how my girl likes them.

Then I yank her to stand, spin her around, and throw her over my shoulder. She whimpers at the position, and I start carrying her off to the door at the end of the hall.

I knew exactly what to say to my wife to get her to come down here. I've watched her reactions, paid attention to how her body responds to me and the things I do to her. My girl has a praise kink. I noticed it before, but today, I felt the way her body melted into the side of mine when we were in Ty's office, and he praised the woman for swallowing.

I know she's nervous about her initiation later tonight, and I wanted to do something for her to try to take her mind off it. Nothing is more effective than getting fucked. So, I'm going to have my way with her and then praise her for allowing it.

Opening up the door, I feel her body bouncing over my shoulder while I carry her down to the basement. Ty had given me the code to turn all the cameras off here at Blackout, so I made sure to do so before I called her and had her come downstairs. The outside ones are still on, but I wasn't going to allow anyone to log in while we're awake or to go back and look come tomorrow.

I was already down here earlier after she passed out and got everything I wanted ready for her. I'm about to show her the darker side of what we both like.

I set her down on her feet, and she sucks in a deep breath. I'm sure my shoulder in her abdomen made it hard to breathe at that angle. She looks up at me, her eyes full of desire. She's ready for whatever I have planned, or so she thinks. She may feel different afterward.

I pull the knife out of my pocket and flip it open.

"Ryat," she breathes and goes to step back, but I reach out and grab her shirt, pulling her to me.

"Don't move," I order and slice through the material, cutting it down the middle and then both sleeves so I can remove it completely.

My eyes fall to her pretty pink nipples and see that they're hard. *They're not the only thing!*

"Spread your legs," I demand, and she widens her feet. I pull her underwear to the side and run my finger over her cunt. "That's what I like to feel." I push it into her easily, feeling how wet she is already. It'll be dripping with cum when I'm done with her.

She gasps when I add a second one, just feeling around. Toying with her. Pulling them out, I grip the material and slowly run them down over her legs, where she steps out of them.

She stands before me naked, hands cuffed behind her back, and I smile down at her. "So gorgeous." I praise her, and her eyes grow heavy. "But I want you filthy."

When she opens her mouth to ask what I mean by that, I reach out and grab her hair and pull her to the center of the room, making her scream instead.

Forcing her to her knees, she whimpers, and I kneel behind her. I pick up the short chain bolted to the floor and fasten the opposite end to the chain that links the handcuffs—securing her to the concrete floor.

Standing, I walk around in front to look down at her. Her shoulders are pulled back, pushing her already large tits out, and they bounce with each intake of breath. "Ryat," she moans my name, staring up at me, shifting on her knees.

"Shh," I say, kneeling in front of her. Reaching out, I run my fingers over her parted lips. "I'm going to make it feel good," I promise her.

She takes in a shaky breath, and I pull my hand from her face to remove what I need from my pocket.

"Open your mouth," I order.

Her eyes widen when she sees what I'm holding, but she complies without hesitation. I place the gag into her mouth, having to force it open a little farther, making sure the O-ring fits behind her teeth. Then I bend over and fasten the buckle behind her head, tightening it so she can't push it out on her own.

Sitting back on my heels, I look at it. I like gagging her. I usually stuff her underwear in her mouth and tape it, but I wanted this time to be different. I want to be able to use her mouth while limiting her voice at the same time.

This particular gag is an open-mouth gag that forces her mouth wide open for easy use. I'm not going to say it's comfortable, but the metal ring is wrapped in leather and so are the straps so it doesn't hurt. Her tongue moves inside of her mouth, and I look over her perfect white teeth and can already see the spit at the back of her throat. She tries to swallow it the best she can and whimpers when she realizes just how difficult that's going to be for her.

Reaching out, I run my knuckles down her cheek and over the leather strap. She closes her eyes, her body trying to fight the cuffs secured to the floor.

Dropping my hand, I reach into my other pocket and pull out a Sharpie. Opening her eyes, she spots it and starts fighting the restraint harder, trying to talk, but it just sounds like grunting.

I pop the lid off and grab her left breast in my hand. Squeezing it to the point she releases what sounds like a cry, I draw a heart around her hard nipple. Then repeat it with the other one. Then I put my hands on her knees and shove them apart. Again, unintelligible noises come from her open mouth. I write MINE above her pussy, over her pelvic bone. "Better," I say, and her body shakes.

I toss the Sharpie across the room, done with it, and run my hands over her cunt since her legs are wide open for me. "Aw," I say, my eyes going to hers. "She's soaked now, Blake."

Her head falls back, and she looks up at the ceiling with her watery eyes, trying to avoid looking at me like she's too ashamed to make eye contact.

That won't do.

Reaching up with my free hand, I place my thumb under her chin and two fingers inside her mouth, forcing her head down. "Look at me."

She sucks in a breath, her body trembling. Her tongue is secured under my fingers, and she tries to move them, but it's no use. She told me whatever I wanted, and what I want tonight is to make my wife my little slut.

To fucking use her!

My hand between her legs thrusts two fingers all the way into her, and her body jerks. I force a third one inside her, and her heavy panting fills the room. I start finger-fucking her, and her hips rock back and forth with my rhythm, unable to stop herself. Her knees fight to close, but I change up my position and kneel before her, using my knees to shove hers open as far as I can. She's completely immobile with no voice and no choice but to kneel and enjoy it.

Her body stiffens, her cunt clamping down on my fingers, and she comes. Removing my fingers from her pussy and her mouth, she sags on her knees. I hold up my now cum-soaked hand and look at it. I want to lick them clean, but I don't. That orgasm wasn't for me.

I stand and look down at her. She's got some drool on her chin but not nearly enough.

"I want that mouth drooling as much as that pussy," I say, and she whimpers. Her tear-filled blue eyes shine up at me.

My right hand grips the top of her hair to hold her head in place, and I stick two fingers into her mouth with her cum on them. I slowly run them along the inside of her cheek before going to the other one. "Stick your tongue out for me," I order softly.

She sticks it through the ring, and I run my fingers over the top of it, pushing them to the back of her throat, making her gag and her body jerk. I do it again and hold them there.

Her body fights me, the chains clinking while she pulls on them. "Breathe through your nose," I tell her.

She doesn't have much experience in the sucking dick department. I've only had my cock in her mouth that one time during the vow ceremony. Women need training to deep throat a dick. Some—but not most I've been with—can do it right out of the gate. Like they practice on dildos at home alone before they even have boyfriends to master the craft.

Her throat works while she tries to swallow, and I run my fingers up and down her tongue before pressing them to the back—repeating the motion. She gags once again, and I watch fresh tears run down her face when she blinks.

Pulling my hand out completely, she chokes, spit flying from her mouth. Drool now runs down her chin and covers her perfect breasts and flat stomach while she sucks in breath after breath. "That's more like it."

Her head hangs forward the best it can, a line of drool leaking from her open mouth reaching the floor, and I watch her shaking body with satisfaction.

My girl.

My wife.

My filthy little slut.

I remove my mask, throwing it to the floor before I remove the cloak, getting more comfortable.

BLAKELY

I CAN'T FEEL my hands or my legs. They're all numb. My body is covered in sweat and drool, and my jaw hurts.

Opening my heavy eyes, I see him widen his stance in front of my kneeling body and know what's coming. The sound of his zipper only confirms it.

His hand grips the hair on top of my head, and he lifts my head, pushing it back. I look up at him through watery eyes while he stares down at me with what I can only explain as raw dominance.

I love it!

This is what my body wants. What it needs. To be his. You can be someone's wife but still want to be used. Ryat never makes me feel ashamed or embarrassed for that.

I try swallowing the excess drool sitting at the back of my throat, but it doesn't work. Biting his bottom lip, he strokes his hard dick a few times before he steps into me.

He slides into my mouth, and the excess drool pushes out the sides of my open lips and runs down my skin to land on my tits. My entire body is wet—if not from sweat then drool or the cum between my legs

His cock slides along the inside of my mouth, and I try to suck on it the best I can, but it's impossible since my lips can't close around it.

"Fuck, Blake," he growls. Letting go of the top of my head, he bends his knees, getting lower, and spreads his large hand across the back of my head, holding it in place while he slowly fucks my mouth, knowing that it won't stay like this for long.

He pushes to the back of my throat, and I gag, my body fighting not to vomit while trying to breathe at the same time.

I blink, fresh tears running down the side of my face, and he looks down at me, his green eyes hooded and needy. He runs his tongue along his bottom lip before pulling it between his teeth and biting down.

My soaked pussy clenches, wanting him to fuck it.

As he pulls completely out of my mouth, the drool runs down my front once again before he pushes back into me, shoving it to the back of my throat harder this time. Right as I gag, he pulls it out. I get a quick breath in just before he shoves his hips forward. His hand on the back of my head keeps it from moving. There's no way for me to fight it.

No. I'm his to use however he wants. And it's got my nipples hard and pussy begging to be fucked.

His good girl.

My nose is running as much as my eyes are crying. I can only imagine how awful I must look, but he is staring down at me like I'm the most beautiful thing he's ever seen.

Pulling out, he forces his way back in, and when his eyes fall shut, I know he's about to fuck my mouth as if it's my pussy when he moans, "Goddamn."

I kneel, cuffed and gagged wide open for him to use, fighting the urge to vomit and trying to breathe every chance I get.

His fingers grip my hair, and my eyes start to roll back into my head from lack of oxygen when he pulls out of my mouth, and a feral growl rips through the room right before his cum hits my mouth, face, and body.

I sag on the floor, trying to breathe, when I hear him zip up his jeans. I open my heavy eyes, looking up at him through watery lashes.

He kneels before me, breathing heavily. He reaches out, his hand wrapping around my throat but not taking away my air. Thank God, because I'm still trying to catch mine. "Good girl, Blake. Good girl."

My eyes fall closed, and an unintelligible whimper comes from my open mouth at his praise. It was worth it.

FORTY-EIGHT

RYAT

I WALK BEHIND her and undo the chain connected to her cuffs. Her body relaxes as if she thinks I'm about to free her from the handcuffs, but that's not the case.

Pressing my hand to her back, I order, "Face on the floor." I know it's hard to move her sore body, so I grab her shoulder and help her. Her face lays down on the cum and drool and she spreads her legs wide for me, showing me that glistening cunt.

I kneel behind her, my hands on her ass cheeks, and she wiggles it for me. I push two fingers into her pussy, and she shifts on her knees. I know the concrete floor is cold and unforgiving, but that's the point. My wife likes a little pain with her pleasure.

I shove a third finger into her, and mumbled cries come from her still gagged mouth. Leaning over, I spit on her ass and move my fingers from her cunt upward. She shifts once again, and I place my hand on her back. "Don't move, Blake," I warn.

Even though I just came, I'm still hard. I'm always ready for her. No matter what. Unzipping my jeans again, I pull out my still wet dick and spread her legs wider with mine, forcing her to arch her back more.

I slide into her wet cunt and reach up to grab the chain connecting her handcuffs, holding them in place while my other hand spreads across her lower back, my thumb sliding into her ass.

She shifts, unintelligible noises fill the room from her open mouth gag and I smile. I don't give her any warning or chance to recover from what I've already done to her. Instead, I take my wife like I'm paying to use her—hard and fast.

My body slapping hers. My knees ache from the concrete floor so I know her entire body is hurting. But it doesn't stop her from cumming again, this time all over my cock. I'm not far behind her.

Pulling out, I stand and she stretches out her body, lying down flat. I remove the key from my pocket and undo the cuffs, followed by the buckle on the gag. She cries when I remove it from her mouth. "Roll over," I demand softly. Her body is sluggish, but she does as she's told, and her heavy eyes look up at me.

Bending down, I place my arms under her shaking body and pick her up, carrying her out of the basement and up to the apartment.

I HELP HER out of the bath after washing her hair and soaping her body for her. I wrap the towel around her before picking her up into my arms.

She's about to pass out. Our little session down in the basement took what little she had left to give. Setting her on the side of the bed, I dry her off a little more, and then she lies down, snuggling into the sheets.

"Here." I hand her two painkillers, knowing her jaw has to be sore along with everything else. I didn't want to keep her down there for long, considering the position I had her in.

She takes them and then hands me her bottle of water. I set it on the nightstand and then crawl in next to her. "Lie on your stomach," I order.

I straddle her back and rub my hands together quickly, warming them up before placing them on her skin. She moans when I start rubbing on her. Maybe a minute goes by before I hear her start softly snoring, but I continue to rub her back, arms, and legs, hoping it will help her soreness when she wakes up in the morning.

Once I'm done, I lie down and pull her into me. Kissing her wet hair, I whisper, "I love you." Hoping she can hear me before I close my eyes.

They spring open when I hear my cell go off.

Groaning, I reach over to the nightstand and pick it up.

Mandatory meeting at house of Lords.

I close it and sigh. It's later on tonight. Thankfully, it's early enough that I can go to the meeting and be back to Blackout before Blake has to do her initiation.

BLAKELY

I'M A LITTLE tipsy. Probably had more than I should have, but I needed the liquid courage to do what needs to be done tonight. It's not the fact that I have to pretend to flirt with a man. It's the fact that I know what my husband is going to do to him afterward. Why does this guy deserve to die? And why was he chosen for my initiation? Are these people picked at random?

I'm wearing another dress of Sarah's, and Ryat literally growled when he saw me in it but didn't say anything. I take another drink before setting it down. Taking a quick look around, I try to find Ryat in the crowd, but it's too busy, and he's not standing on the second-floor balcony tonight.

I can't feel him like usual either. I wonder if it's because I'm just nervous. The fuck fest we had last night in the basement did knock me on my ass, and I slept in until noon today. I woke up sore as fuck and needed another hot bath to help relax my tight muscles. It worked enough. But even now, these heels are killing my feet. Not to mention I've still got hearts on my tits and MINE written between my legs. Wonder how long Sharpie lasts on skin?

"Boo."

I jump when I hear someone in my ear. Spinning around, I see Sarah standing before me. "What are you doing here?" I ask, wide-eyed, pulling her in for a hug.

"I brought you your car."

"Really?" She nods, and I say, "Thank you." I've missed her so much. I haven't gotten to see her much since classes started this year. Between the Lords, my running away, and someone trying to kill me, we've been pulled apart. More so now than when I was dating Matt.

"Of course. I guess the Lords have a meeting back at the house ..."

I frown. *I didn't know that.*

"Ryat called Gunner this morning and gave him the address to the cabin and asked us to bring your car up here. So Gunner took me out there, and he said he'll just catch a ride here with Ryat after they're done at the house."

He promised he'd be here. "When will they be done?" I ask her.

"Should be anytime now." She looks down at her cell. "But I wanted to come help my girl." She winks at me.

Does she know what I'm doing, though? Does she know what Gunner has done in order to become a Lord? I don't even know what all Ryat has done at this point. And I probably never will.

My cell vibrates in my clutch, and I pull it out. Opening up the text, I take a deep breath, thinking it's going to tell me the guy is here but it's from Ryat.

Had a meeting at HoLs. On my way.

Okay. See you soon.

"While we're waiting, I'm going to go out to my car really quick." I'm going to grab a pair of flats in my trunk so I can put them on as soon as this is done. I've hated living out of the small suitcase we brought with us. If I had known we weren't going to return after burying Cindy, I would have packed several bags.

"I'll go with you."

We're laughing as she tells me something that Gunner did last week while walking out the back of Blackout to my car. It was nice of Sarah to drive it here for me. For some reason, it feels like a little bit of freedom has been returned to me. I haven't had the chance to drive my car in almost a month.

I left it behind while I ran, and then we've been hiding here for four days. It's got a big smile on my face.

Unlocking it, it beeps, and Sarah stops. "Dammit."

"What?" I ask her.

"I think I left my cell on the bar." She pats down her dress, knowing damn well it doesn't have any pockets. She yanks her clutch open and starts looking around in it.

I fall into the driver's seat. "Get in. I'll swing you by the back door. That way you don't have to walk." Plus, the sooner she gets there, the better. I don't want someone to take it.

Getting in, I drive through the parking lot since I was in the very back row—the club is packed tonight—and pull parallel to the door.

"I'll be right here," I tell her as she's jumping out. She shuts my door, and I pick up my cell from the cupholder and start to call Ryat but stop. I don't want to be that woman who can't go a second without calling her man. I'm going to be seeing him soon anyway.

My car door opens, and I see her fall into my passenger seat. "That was fast …"

A hand grips my hair, and my face is slammed into the steering wheel. Pain explodes behind my eyes, and I instantly taste blood. Then my head is jerked back, and I don't even get to scream before a hand slaps over my mouth, silencing me.

"You've been very busy, Blakely." I hear a male voice growl in my ear.

My eyes are watery from the impact my face just took, so when I try to look at him, all I see is a blurry figure, but I know who it is. Shaking my head, I try to scream, but he just tightens his grip in my hair, needles pricking my scalp.

"Don't worry, I'm not going to kill you. Yet. This is just a warning." He lets go of my mouth and slams my face into the steering wheel again. This time, my vision goes black, and more blood fills my mouth. I start choking on it, making it fly out of my mouth onto the dash and windshield.

His hand remains holding my hair and his other hand wraps around my throat and squeezes, taking away what little air I had. "You know ..." He leans in, and the wetness from his tongue runs across my pounding cheek, licking up my tears. "I should have taken you up on that rape fantasy of yours." My already racing heart skips a beat, and I try to reach for the door handle, my lungs burning from lack of oxygen while dots cover my already blurry vision.

He removes his hand just before my eyes fall closed, and I suck in a ragged breath before spitting blood out of my mouth once again. "Ryat's going ... to kill you." I wheeze out.

He laughs, the sound filling the small car. "Tell your *husband* that I'll be waiting for him." Then he shoves my face into the steering wheel one last time.

When he lets go of me, my body slumps in the driver's seat, and all I can hear is the blood rushing in my ears. It feels like my heart is pumping in my face, and I can't swallow. Drool and blood run out of the corners of my mouth. I can't see anything, but I'm not even sure my eyes are open.

"Blakely!" I hear my name being shouted. "Oh my God!"

I flinch at the sound. I just ... I just want to go to sleep.

"Help me." The voice screams again. "You're going to be okay," the girl cries.

What's wrong? I'm not sure what she's talking about.

"What the fuck?" someone else barks.

Hands grab my shoulders and roughly drag me out of the car. I can't even fight if Matt changed his mind and decided to come back for me. I'm his at this point as long as he'll let me sleep.

"Get in the car. Drive us," the voice orders, picking me up. I feel that darkness closing in on me, finally allowing me some peace and quiet.

FORTY-NINE

RYAT

I'M DRIVING DOWN the highway, my eyes constantly going to the clock on my dash. The meeting at the house took longer than necessary. Now I'm having to haul ass to Blackout, making sure I get there before Blake receives her text about her initiation.

The sound of my phone ringing blares through the speakers. I see that it's Ty. "Hello?" I answer.

"Ryat," he shouts my name, and it instantly has my heart racing. "I don't know what happened. Man, it was just a second—"

"Let me speak to Blake," I interrupt him.

"I can't." He sighs heavily. "Ryat, she ..."

"What the fuck happened, Tyson?" I snap, and Gunner is already pulling his cell out of his pocket, probably to call Sarah.

"We're at the hospital. Meet us here. I gotta go." He hangs up.

"She's not answering," Gunner growls, yanking the phone from his ear.

"Hang on." I slam on the brake to take the exit that I was almost already past in order to turn around and go the opposite way.

Less than twenty minutes later, I bring my SUV to a screeching halt in front of the emergency room doors. Gunner and I both jump out. Entering, I find the nurse's desk. "Blakely Rae Archer." I shout her name, my hand banging on the surface. "She's my wife."

"Ryat?" I hear my name being shouted from down the hall.

"Never mind," I tell the useless nurse and take off.

"Sir, you can't …"

I ignore her and run toward Tyson. He stands in the center of the hall. "What in the fuck is going on?" I snap, but my eyes drop to the blood on his shirt, and I blink, trying to comprehend what I'm seeing. That can't belong to my wife. I've been around it all my life, but right now, I feel like I'm going to get sick. The thought of something happening to her when I should have been there with her.

He raises his hands. "I don't know what happened. I walked outside, and Sarah … she was screaming for help. Blake … she was bleeding …"

"Where is she?" I demand, about to punch him in the fucking face since he's having problems getting out a single sentence.

"There." He points at the door we stand outside of. "Gavin's on call and already seen her."

I shove it open and rush inside the room to find my wife lying in a hospital bed with Sarah sitting in a chair next to her, holding Blake's hand. Her face is swollen and bruised, and she's got stitches in various places.

"Sarah," I say her name softly. Her makeup is smeared, her face red and splotchy.

"Oh, Ryat." Letting go of Blake's hand, she rushes over to me and throws her arms around my neck, almost knocking me a step backward.

I numbly pat her back while I look over my wife's unconscious body. So small and vulnerable lying there in the bed. They haven't cleaned her, so dried blood is caked all over her face and down her neck. Some even splattered on her arms and hands.

The door behind me opens, and Sarah pulls away from me. "Gunner." She runs to him, and I walk over to her now empty chair and fall down into it. I take Blake's warm hand and clasp it in mine. "What happened?" I ask again, hoping someone will tell me something.

"She wanted to get something from her car … we walked outside. But I forgot my phone." She starts, pulling away from Gunner. "She drove me to the back of the building." She hugs herself. "I was only gone a few minutes. When I came back, she was sitting in the driver seat … like this. I was … screaming." Sarah shakes her head. "For anyone to help. She was just sitting there, covered in blood." Looking over at Blake, fresh tears run down her face. "That's when that guy came up to us …"

"Who?" Gunner interrupts her.

She points at the door. "The guy in the hallway. I don't even know who he is. He pulled her out of the car and ran over to another one. He told me to get in and had me drive while he sat with her in the back." She goes back to sobbing, and Gunner pulls her into him, hugging her tightly.

The door opens again, and I expect it to be Ty, and I open my mouth to tell him to get the fuck out, but it's a different Lord. "Ryat. Gunner." He nods to both of us.

"Dr. Gavin," I say, releasing her hand and setting it on the bed.

"I have some X-rays I'd like to go over with you, if you have a second." He holds the film in his hands.

"Of course." I nod numbly.

"We'll be back," Gunner tells us and then pulls a sobbing Sarah out of the room, excusing themselves.

BLAKELY

I CAN HEAR voices, but they sound far off. Like I'm standing at one end of the tunnel, and they're at the other—echoing inside my head. Which is pounding as if someone is using it as a drum set.

"I told you this would happen ..."

The voices start to come in clearer.

"I told you guys we should have tested her differently." Another voice gets through the drumming behind my eyes.

"The initiation didn't do this to her," a familiar voice snaps.

"No! It was that piece of shit who you were going to allow her to marry," another voice argues, and I recognize it. It's Ryat's.

"I was never going to allow that," the second one shouts back. "Why do you think I made you choose her?" *It's my dad.* "Huh? It sure as shit wasn't for shits and giggles."

"Well, it's not like you ever gave me an answer when I asked."

I open my heavy eyes, blinking a few times before the room comes into focus. I'm lying in a hospital bed. Ryat stands over to the right, leaning back against a windowsill dressed in a white T-shirt and jeans with a black baseball hat on backward and tennis shoes.

My father sits on a couch next to him, dressed in a charcoal suit with his cell in his hand. Looking to my left, I see my father-in-law pacing the large room, also dressed like he just came from a board meeting. "We're not going to accomplish anything if we're arguing," he states, taking in a deep breath.

"Yeah," I manage to croak and flinch. "You're making ... my headache worse."

"Blake," Ryat shoves off the windowsill and comes over to me. "How do you feel?" Before I can even try to answer him, he looks at his dad. "Get the nurse." Who turns and rushes out of the room.

"Hey, princess," my father says gently, coming to the other side of my bed.

"I ..." my eyes close, the light hurting them.

"Turn off the light," Ryat orders, and then I hear the click of the switch, and I open my eyes slowly to a softer lit room with the main light now off. "Better?" he asks, his hand picking up mine and gently squeezing it.

I nod. "Yeah."

The door opens, and Abbot enters with a nurse behind him. "Good evening, Blakely. How do you feel?"

I groan. She's way too chipper with her big smile, bleach-blond hair pulled up into a cute twist, and brown eyes that I notice quickly scan my husband before coming back to mine.

"She said she's got a headache." Ryat answers when he realizes I'm going to ignore her.

"I can give you some pain meds." She nods enthusiastically. And then looks at him again. "I'll be right back with those."

Leaving us, I close my heavy eyes. "What happened?"

"You were attacked," Abbot answers.

Ryat squeezes my hand again. "Do you not remember?"

"No," I answer, opening my eyes and looking at him.

He looks exhausted. His pretty green eyes aren't as bright as I remember. There's stubble on his jaw, and I know he hasn't washed his hair since he has a hat on.

"How long have I been here?" I ask, licking my chapped lips.

"Three days," my father answers.

"Here, I got you some of these when I chased down the nurse." Abbot shoves a cup of ice into Ryat's free hand.

He lets go of mine with his other hand and spoon-feeds me a few ice chips. I just let them melt in my mouth, wanting the water more than chewing ice. I'm so thirsty. After I swallow, I slide my tongue along my upper and lower teeth, making sure they're all there. I feel a little better when they are.

"Want some more?" Ryat asks, and I nod.

The nurse returns with a syringe and that stupid fucking smile on her face. "This will make you drowsy. Probably be in and out—"

360

"No," I say, interrupting her. I've already been out for three days? That's too long. "I don't want ..."

"It's okay, Blake," Ryat tells me and then looks up at her, nodding. His eyes return to mine. "We'll be right here when you wake up." Leaning down, he gives me a soft kiss on my knuckles as my eyes grow heavy.

FIFTY

RYAT

I EXIT HER room and walk down the hallway. I need a fucking energy drink. Hell, I need them to hook me up to an IV of straight caffeine. It's like when she ran all over again, but this time, I know she's right in front of me, not missing.

She could have been, though. Matt could have easily taken her. And I'm more confused as to why he didn't. I mean, thank God that's not the case, but why? What the fuck is he doing?

Is this his way of playing with his food before he eats it?

A way to draw out his torture. I murdered his only two allies, and he just left her when he had the opportunity to take her and make her pay for my sins.

Coming up to a vending machine, I stick in a five-dollar bill and press on the energy drink that I know isn't going to do shit for me.

I'm not sure what the fuck he's up to, but it's not sitting right with me. Nothing about her being in a hospital bed is.

"Come on." I slap the side of the machine when I see it hasn't given me my drink. "Son of a bitch!" I kick it.

"I gave it a twenty earlier and got nothing for it."

I look over at Ty standing beside me and sigh heavily. "What are you doing here?" He promised me he would watch her. I was the one who failed her by expecting anyone else to keep her safe.

He tucks his hands into the front pockets of his jeans and rocks back on his heels, dropping his head. "I can't leave, knowing you're still here."

I roll my eyes and go to walk away. Fuck the five dollars, but his words stop me.

"You were here with me ..." Pulling his hand from his pocket, he runs it through his unruly hair, and my eyes drop to his shirt, realizing he's still dressed in the same one he was wearing when he brought my wife in. I know this because it still has her blood on it. I haven't left this place, but thankfully, Gunner brought me some new clothes. "I just didn't think you should be alone in case ..." He stops himself.

My hands fist. "In case she dies?" I finish it for him. I'm being dramatic. I've spoken to Gavin, and he said that everything looked good as far as no serious injuries. No hemorrhaging. She does have a broken nose and some cuts and bruises, but it's still the fact that it could have been so much worse.

His shoulders drop. "I didn't know ..."

"What, Ty?" I raise my voice. "That Matt was there? Because he knew she was there." We'd been staying there all week. Not like it would have been hard for him to find out. I let her dance with Sarah the night before, wanting her to have some fun. I should have just run with her.

"It's not your fault," he says softly, and I give a rough laugh.

"Thanks for the opinion that I didn't ask for." I turn, giving him my back.

"The Lords are only out for themselves, Ryat," he calls out.

Stopping again, I grind my teeth and turn to face him, but say nothing.

"You want to save her?" He walks over to me. "The only way to do that is to let her go because even if you were to die tomorrow, they would own her." My spine stiffens at his words. "Her father won't be able to save her. Your father won't be able to save her. They take prisoners, Ryat."

I glare at him, "Then why are you still a member, Ty?" Arching a brow, I continue, "Just betray your oath, and they'll make that decision for you."

He smirks, his left hand coming up to rest on my shoulder. "Why do you think I chose the hell I did?" With that, he slaps my shoulder twice and then walks off.

I stare at the energy drink I never got but paid for, and my teeth clench. He was talking about Blackout. The Lords set him up with that club. Purchased the land, built the building, and then handed it all over to him—free and clear. Now it makes me wonder what he has to do to keep it.

Shaking my head, I tell myself not to fucking care about his problems. I did once. I even sat here in the waiting room with him, but I know how that ended. Much worse than my experience here.

I know Blakely will come home, and I know that I won't let her go. I've seen the worst of the Lords, but I've also seen how they take care of their members—like fucking royalty.

I'll do what needs to be done and make sure that Blakely and our future kids are very well taken care of and able to hide if something were to happen to me. That's the best I can do for them.

Walking back over to the machine, I lean over, placing my forehead on the cold glass and sigh heavily. "Fuck it." Then I stand, reach up and grip the back of my shirt. I yank it up and over my head, knocking my hat to the floor in the process.

"Oh my God." Blake's nurse from earlier walks by. "What...what are you doing, Mr. Archer?" she asks, flustered. Her eyes drop to the way my abs flex from my heavy breathing.

Ignoring her, I wrap my shirt around my right hand, make a fist, and slam it into the glass.

She squeals, jumping back. "Ryat."

Pulling my arm out through the glass, she watches me wide-eyed as I unwrap the shirt from my fist, shake the remaining glass out and then pull it back on, along with my hat.

Reaching back in, I grab two energy drinks.

"Your hand." She steps toward me. "You're bleeding."

I have blood running down my arm from where the glass cut me once I broke through. No biggie.

"You need stitches ..."

"I'm fine," I tell her. I've fucked myself up more in a fight.

"But ..." She reaches out, grabbing me. "You may have glass in it."

"Then I'll get it out." I yank my hand back from her. "Go do what you're being fucking paid to do and help the ones who want it."

She gasps like what I said offended her, which I did no such thing. It's literally her job. Leaving her standing there with her mouth wide open, I make my way down the hallway to the waiting room to see Ty still here.

I sigh and plop down next to him, and without saying a word, I pass him one of the drinks I took from the crooked machine.

He chuckles but reaches out and takes it. It's as close to an apology as he's going to get. My wife is the only person who will ever hear sorry from me. But I do understand it wasn't his fault. It was mine. And when she finally gets to go home, I'll allow myself the chance to come up with an idea on how I'm going to kill Matt for laying his hands on her.

"I had Sarah drive us here in my car," he speaks. "That way you can look at Blakely's where it sits. See if he left anything behind."

I swallow, knowing that I'm not going to like what I see on the inside after what he did to her. But he's right, I need to look and see if he left any clues to find him before he has the chance to touch her again. "Thanks."

BLAKELY

"RYAT," I GROWL. "I can do it."

"I know you can, Blake," he lies. If he thought I could, then he'd actually let me.

Shoving his arm away from me, I give up when he doesn't budge and allow him to help me walk back to the bed. I have a broken nose, not a broken leg.

Getting up and into it, I sigh. "When can I leave?" I ask him. I feel like five days—I was out the first three—is a long time for a busted-up face. They keep sending me for all these tests that come back fine every time.

"They said sometime tomorrow."

"Why not today? I'm fine," I say, pushing my split bottom lip out, hoping that will get me some sympathy.

It doesn't.

"If the doctor thought you could leave today, then he'd let you," he says matter-of-factly.

"This is like prison," I say, throwing my head into my pillow and making Ryat laugh. "What's so funny?"

"Coming from someone who's been in jail, this is nothing like it."

I open my mouth to ask when the hell he was arrested, but my door opens, and our fathers step in. They're like best fucking friends now, I guess. Always together. Always here. Maybe they always have been, and I just didn't know it.

I haven't spoken to my mother. I'm pretty sure my father told her to stay the hell away from me after Ryat informed him that she slapped me. It's been nice, actually, and kind of sad that I haven't even missed her.

"Okay, everything looks good at the cabin," my father tells Ryat.

"What do you mean?" I wonder.

"I had all new cameras installed. Inside and out," Ryat answers. "I sent them over there so I could watch them to make sure they were working properly."

"Why would you doubt that they are?" I ask, stuffing a french fry in my mouth that Abbot brought me.

"I've been watching them for over a week now and haven't seen any activity," he states, sitting down on the couch.

"Isn't that a good thing?"

"You can never be too cautious," he answers vaguely.

I stuff another fry into my mouth, close my eyes, and moan. So fucking good. Opening my eyes, I notice everyone is staring at me. "What?" I ask nervously.

My father runs his hand through his hair. "I think it's time ..."

"Phil..." Abbot clears his throat. "We agreed—"

"I changed my mind," he interrupts him.

My eyes go to Ryat, and he shrugs like he has no clue what they're talking about either. "Okay." I sit up straighter in bed. "What's going on?"

"Well ..." My father swallows. "I need to tell you something."

"Then tell me." I'm so over all the secrets. Just get it all out right here in the open.

He sucks in a deep breath and reaches up, removing his tie. *Oh, he's serious.* Unbuttoning his top button on his dress shirt, he says, "I dated a woman at Barrington—LeAnne Mayes. She was my chosen."

It didn't take much to realize my father is a Lord. The fact that he was at the house of Lords after Ryat dragged me back was my biggest clue. I do, however, find it odd that I never paid much attention to his life. Or that he never told me. All the trips he and my mom needed to take for his business. Every time he had to miss a birthday or holiday—was it because the Lords called him to work?

I frown at the name, not recognizing it and wondering why, all of a sudden, it matters. I glance at Ryat, and he's staring down at the floor, face scrunched as if he's trying to decide if he knows who that is or not.

"Should I know her?" I ask.

"No." My father shakes his head, but his eyes shoot to Ryat before returning to mine.

"Why is she so important?" I ask, scanning the room, and my husband is still stuck on the name in deep concentration.

"Because I loved her," he announces, and his broad shoulders sag as if that was a heavy weight he had been carrying.

Okay. I never expected my father not to have anyone before he met my mother. I've never heard either one of them talk about past relationships, but that doesn't mean they didn't exist. So, I'm not sure why this is news. "Did mom know that?" I ask.

His face whitens a little bit, and he undoes another button. "She was already promised to someone else ... LeAnne," he states, ignoring my question. Again, as if this should mean something to me. Or any of us. "But your mom ... you know how we got married shortly after dating?"

"Yeah," I answer slowly.

"Well ..." He scratches the back of his neck. "We had an arranged marriage."

"No, you didn't," I argue as if I was there and laugh it off.

He sighs. "We did. We lied to you."

"Why ... wait?" I sit up even more. "Why would you lie about your marriage?" He drops his eyes to the floor, and I look over at Ryat on the couch. He's already staring at me this time, and he has this look of pity in his eyes. "You knew they lied to me?"

"Yes," he answers without hesitation.

My face scrunches in confusion. "Why would you make that up?"

My father shrugs. "Well, your mother told everyone that story, and as you grew older, it just became the norm."

I look back over at Ryat, and he's watching me intently. It makes me think about when we have kids. Will I tell them how we met? About the ritual? The vow ceremony? The house of Lords? Absolutely not. "I understand why you would hide that as a child, but you could have told me at some point over the past few years. Especially when you were trying to make me do the same thing."

My father sighs. "I never wanted you to marry Matt. That was your mother's doing."

"You could have told her no," I argue. "You know how I felt about an arranged marriage. And how much I didn't want that."

He undoes another button on his shirt. "I couldn't. She threatened ..." Trailing off, I look from him to my father-in-law, who turns his back to everyone and looks out my window with his hands in the pockets of his slacks.

"Threatened what?" I demand as the silence lingers. "What did the Lords have you do that was so bad that you couldn't stand up for me?" My mother pretty much blackmailed him. I'm not surprised.

She's a vindictive bitch like that.

"Well ..." He swallows nervously, and I see sweat bead along his forehead. "My chosen ... it was so long ago. And ..." I've never heard my father stumble over his words so much.

"Motherfucker," Ryat hisses and gets to his feet.

"What?" I ask, watching him start to pace.

He ignores me and runs both of his hands through his hair aggressively.

What did I miss?

"I can't fucking believe it," Ryat mumbles to himself. "Mayes ..."

"Now you understand why we wanted you to tell the Lords what happened," my father snaps at him. Taking the opportunity to avoid my previous question, he obviously understands what Ryat gets and I'm missing. "But here's your chance. Tell your father and me what happened right now."

Ryat stops and turns to face him. He doesn't actually speak, but his tense body says enough. He's pissed.

"We know you didn't do it," Mr. Archer tells him, turning back to face his son. "We just need to know."

"I'm not a fucking rat," Ryat shouts.

Whoa! What the fuck am I missing? I feel like it's several things now. "Dad," I say, trying to calm them both down, but he ignores me.

"A rat?" My father scoffs at Ryat. "Are you serious? He's no longer a Lord. He's on the run, been stripped of his title. This is passed that. Matt has put your wife—my daughter—in the hospital. Why do you think I forced you to choose her in the first place? Huh?" he demands. "I didn't want her near him."

"And he will pay for that," Ryat growls through gritted teeth.

"Or why I didn't take the money when you offered to buy her hand in marriage."

I narrow my eyes at Ryat for that one, still a little sour.

"I was honored to give Blakely over to you," he adds, softening his tone.

Fuck, they act like I'm not even here.

"You knew this whole time." Ryat shakes his head with disgust at his father, who doesn't deny his words.

"Matt needs to be taken down. And you still have the opportunity to do that." My father sighs. "All you have to do is tell us—"

"I didn't work this damn hard, devote my life to the fucking Lords to lose my credibility because of Matt," Ryat shouts, interrupting him.

"So, you will risk your wife?" My father shouts in his face.

Ryat's chest rises as he sucks in a deep breath. "No." He shakes his head, lowering his voice, and my father smiles, satisfied with his answer. "I won't be like you." His words make the smile fall from Dad's face. "You were the one who chose to keep secrets from Blake. You were the one who chose to risk her life by allowing Valerie to continue with the arranged marriage." He looks him up and down with his lips pulled back. "That woman treated her like shit. And you couldn't be a damn man and stand up for *your daughter*." Ryat snorts. "And you call yourself a Lord?"

"Listen here." He gets in Ryat's face, but my husband doesn't back down. "You don't know what I did for my family."

"I don't have to." Ryat takes a step back and points at me, sitting up in bed. "I know what you didn't do." His green eyes find mine. "I'm sorry, Blake." My pulse races at the sincerity of his voice. Ryat never apologizes. "But your father has been lying to you all your life. Valerie isn't your mother."

"What?" I ask, my eyes going back and forth between my husband and my father. "Ryat?" I whisper. "Why ... why would you say that?" The room falls silent, and Mr. Archer runs a hand down his face. "Daddy?" My eyes shoot to his. "Tell him he's wrong." My chest tightens as the silence lingers. As much as I hate my mother on most days, they wouldn't lie about that. Would they?

FIFTY-ONE

RYAT

I SHOULD HAVE fucking known. I should have demanded to know more. The fucking Lords kept me from getting all the information. You can't question them.

I know you killed an important bitch! Is what Lincoln had yelled at Matt afterward before putting him on probation and throwing him out of his office. LeAnne was important because Phil Anderson *made* her important. Mr. Mayes wasn't that high up on the Lords ladder. That's why I never questioned why he needed to die. He betrayed his oath. It was simple.

"Why would you say that?" Blake asks me, her bottom lip quivering. "I ... I don't understand."

I run a hand down my unshaven face. "When I threw Valerie out of your apartment, I ripped a piece of her hair out and had it tested with yours." I received the results when I was sitting in her father's office downtown Dallas after she ran from me. I haven't had the time or concern to dig into who her biological mother is.

Her wide eyes stare up at me, unblinking. "No ..." she whispers.

"I knew about the arranged marriage. It's just par for the course of being a Lord," I add quickly. "I had a hunch." Surprise, surprise, they weren't a match, but I had no idea her biological mother was LeAnne until now. After Phil said her name, it took me a couple of minutes for my mind to put it all together.

"Blake," I walk over to her bed, and she pulls her knees up to her chest, her eyes now on her father, pleading with him to explain everything to her. *I'll fucking do it!* "Blake?" I sit on the side of her bed and pull on her arms, unwrapping them from around her knees to take her hands in mine. Slowly, her watery eyes find mine. "Junior year, Matt and I were partners for an assignment. It was our initiation. We were handed a name and a location. To take out a Lord who had betrayed his oath."

"I don't ..." she whispers, swallowing. "What does this have to do with ... my mom—LeAnne?"

"Something ..." I'm not going to give them the benefit to hear me tell them what exactly happened. "Went wrong and his wife was also killed."

Her eyes go to her father, but he's too big of a coward to face her. Instead, he's staring at the floor, rubbing his neck. "When we got back from the assignment, Matt was put on probation. Then come the following year, two weeks before classes started, I had just taken my oath, your father called me to meet him and told me I had to choose you."

"I was trying to save you from Matt." Her father's voice breaks as he speaks up. "We knew he killed LeAnne." He pauses. "And needed time to prove it."

I can feel his eyes drilling holes in the back of my head as I sit facing my wife. They thought they could talk me down, break me into giving him up, but it wasn't going to happen. Not then and not now. That is what confession is for. When I string Matt up like Tyson suggested at the cathedral, Matt will not only spill blood, but all of his secrets to a room full of Lords. He will be the one who tells everyone what he did that night.

"So"—her brows scrunch together—"Matt killed the Lord's wife?"

"Yes," her father growls. "She was my chosen ... and your mother. I loved her." His voice drops to a whisper. "Still do."

I almost feel sorry for the bastard. Silence falls over the room again, and the first tear rolls down her bruised cheek.

I hear her father sigh. "Blakely, you have to understand—"

"Please leave," she whispers, interrupting him.

He comes around to the opposite side of her. "I know you're upset ..."

"Please." She ignores him, her pretty blue eyes meeting mine. "Please make them leave."

I release her hand and stand, facing her father. "Do I need to show you the way out?" I arch a brow at him.

He straightens his shoulders and grabs his suit jacket and tie off the back of the chair and storms out. My father goes along with him.

Leaning down, I kiss her forehead. "I'll be right back."

Rushing down the hallway, I come to the nurses' station to see them spot me.

Her father sighs. "Ryat, when you're a father, you'll understand."

I step into him, my chest hitting his. "You need to understand the next time I have a meeting with you in downtown Dallas at two o'clock in the morning, I'm going to knock you the fuck out."

"Ryat," my father hisses.

Like I give a fuck what he has to say. I don't. He knew all this time why Mr. Anderson wanted me to choose his daughter. My father never questioned that. He even called me after the ceremony to make sure it was Blake. When in New York, he asked me how much I would offer for her ... and I'd bet my life that's why he didn't force me to marry Cindy. This was their plan.

My hands fist, and I think about just doing it right now. Why the fuck wait until God knows when? But I catch sight of Miss Bleach Blond behind the nurses' station with the phone up to her ear and her wide eyes on me. She's probably already got security on speed dial. The bitch has been staring me down since I broke the vending machine a couple of days ago. So, instead I step away. "I want these men removed from the list of visitors for my wife's room. They're no longer allowed."

"Ryat," her father growls. "You can't keep me from her."

"Watch me." Then I turn around and go back to her room. Entering, I find her on her side in the fetal position with her back to me, crying. I turn off the main light and go over to her bed. When I crawl into it with her, she turns over and snuggles into me, crying harder.

"Shh." I try to calm her by rubbing her back. Knowing if she cries too hard, she's going to give herself another headache

BLAKELY

WALKING INTO THE cabin feels ... different. There are black curtains up that hang from the ceiling, covering all the floor-to-ceiling windows that overlook the woods. It makes the place look darker. Reminds me of Blackout.

"When did you put these up?" I ask.

He places my bag that Sarah had brought to the hospital for me down on the coffee table. "I had Gunner and Prickett do it while we were staying at the club."

"Why?"

"Because I thought maybe Matt was hanging out around here, and I didn't want him seeing inside the house."

I nod in understanding.

Sighing, he comes over to me and kisses my hair. "They won't be here forever," he promises as if he can tell that I hate them.

He walks into the kitchen, and I make my way to the bathroom, wanting to take a hot bath. I'm mentally and physically drained. Getting undressed, I remove my shirt, then shove my shorts down my legs along with my underwear. I turn and stand in front of the mirror. I haven't looked at myself since Matt slammed my face into the steering wheel. I didn't want to have to see what I already knew— he made me ugly.

This was his goal. To make Ryat see me as repulsive. Matt wants Ryat to throw me away. It's no longer that Matt wants me. No. He couldn't beat Ryat, so now he's going to turn him against me. It's the only angle he has left to play.

Ryat enters the bathroom, and I drop my head, unable to meet his eyes in the mirror.

"Hey." Feeling the tips of his fingers on my neck, he pulls my hair off my face with one hand while the other pulls me from the counter to face him. "Blake, look at me."

Feeling defeated, I lift my head.

"Are you hurting?" he asks, concerned the moment he sees me fighting back the tears.

"No," I whisper.

He gives me an apologetic smile. "I'm sorry about your dad."

I look away from him, staring at the white ceiling and refusing to let those tears fall. They're so close to the edge.

"Blake," he demands my attention. "Talk to me."

Swallowing the lump in my throat, I give up fighting him. "He wants you to throw me away," I whisper.

"What do you mean throw you away?" His face scrunches at the question. "Who are you talking about?"

"Matt. He wants to make me ugly, so you'll leave me."

"Blake ..." He sighs heavily. "Is that what you think?"

"It's what I know."

Stepping into me, he slides both hands into my hair and holds my head steady. "I love you," he says, making me sniff. "You are the only woman I've ever told that to. And it'll stay that way until the day I die. Your face will heal, your scars will fade, but my love for you isn't going to change. So, whatever he said to you, or made you feel, don't let it get to you. That's what he wants. Understand?"

His words do what I tried to avoid, and the tears spill over my bottom lashes, just for a different reason. That night is still pretty foggy. I know it was Matt, but I don't really remember any conversation we had if we even did. I just know that this has to be his plan. He wants me away from Ryat, and he knows I'd never leave him.

Leaning down, he presses a soft kiss to my lips, knowing he can taste my tears. When he pulls away, I grip his shirt, not letting him get too far. "Will you take a bath with me?"

"Of course."

―――――――

"Do you have any questions for me?" he asks, sitting across from me in the massive Jacuzzi tub. I overfilled it with a ton of bubbles. He picks up my foot and starts rubbing it as he places it on his thigh under the water.

"About what?"

"About the night Matt and I had our assignment."

"You said you wouldn't rat him out." I'm not sure I want to know. I didn't even know LeAnne existed, and now I'm supposed to just listen to how my ex killed her? Even that's a little too fucked up for me.

"I'll tell you anything," Ryat answers.

"Anything?" I arch a brow at that, and he chuckles, a playful smile on his lips.

"That was probably the wrong answer." His laughter grows.

"You said it."

He nods. "Okay. Anything."

"Tell me about when you went to jail." Ever since he made that remark, I can't get the image of him in handcuffs out of my head. I'm sure he'll look as hot as I imagine it.

"You caught that, huh?" He lets go of my foot for a second and reaches up, running his hand through his hair, getting it wet and making it stand straight up. "Remember when I drugged your water and put you to bed at your apartment before I disappeared?" His hand sinks into the water and goes back to rubbing my foot.

"Yeah ..." What's that have to do with anything? "Wait ... you were arrested? That's where you were?" Prickett told me he was on an assignment and not to call or text him because he wouldn't answer.

"Well, not technically arrested. It was an assignment that Matt volunteered me for."

I frown. "Why would he do that?" Another one of his crazy plans?

"Exactly," he says, confusing me even more. "Remember when we were here before we went back to your place, and I had the TV on? There was a shooting?" I nod. "That was a judge's house. He's a Lord. There was a hit out on him. Someone broke in, but he wasn't home at the time. Instead, they killed his six-year-old son."

I gasp, placing my hand over my mouth. "That's why you were so mean to me?" I ask remembering what he said to me at the house of Lords after his meeting.

"I said I'm not doing this right now. And I meant that. So, unless you want to really see me pissed, I suggest you back the fuck off." His voice is low, his words controlled, but his hand around my throat is shaking, giving away his true feelings at the moment.

He nods. "We had an emergency meeting at the house of Lords. They needed two volunteers. I was going to offer when Matt beat me to it, offering both of us."

The guys weren't on good terms then, so why would he do that? "What did you do?"

"Said yes." He shrugs.

"Then what happened?"

"I had five hours to get my shit together, and one of those things was you. I drugged your water, needing you to be asleep while I took off. Matt and I met at the cathedral and got kidnapped where the judge met up with us and ...."

I sit back and let him tell me all about his experience in jail with Matt while he rubs my feet under the warm water. Every word has my heart hammering. How does he do this every day? Just go blindly into an assignment that he has no idea what it is? Or why he has to do it?

"Wait." I stop him. "You came back to my apartment barely able to stand. You had just gotten out?"

"I had." He nods. "Matt tried to have me killed while in there. He volunteered me for the assignment to get me away from you, but when he realized I'd be back to you in no time, he had to come up with a new plan."

I let out a long breath as the dots start to connect. "Unbelievable." I shake my head.

"What?"

"That's why you married me," I say knowingly. "Because he tried to kill you. So, you needed new ammo to throw in his face." He just watches me while I go on. "And what better place to announce it than the house of Lords annual party in front of everyone?" It was all planned. I can't even be mad at this point. It was pretty well thought out.

"I did." He nods. Reaching forward, he grabs my hands and pulls me toward him, our faces almost touching, our bodies smashing the bubbles. "I've always been a selfish person, Blake. Willing to do whatever it takes to get where I want to be. And out of all the things I've done, you are by far the greatest reward for my selfishness."

FIFTY-TWO

RYAT

I LIE ON my back in our bedroom. It's got to be past midnight, and it's pitch black in here. The sound of the ceiling fan going can be heard along with the thunder outside.

Blake is cuddled up to my left side, and I have one arm under my head, propping it up while the other holds my cell. I watch the cameras on my app that surround the house inside and out. It shows the rain running off the gutters and parts of the ground that are already flooding. And every now and then, lighting strikes.

"Ryat," she whispers. "Aren't you tired?"

"No," I say, my eyes zeroing in on a part in the front yard that looks suspicious. Like something or someone is standing at the end of the driveway. Looking over at the other camera that gives me a better view, I sigh when I see it's the trash can that Gunner put out there for me.

Then it's jerked out of my hand. "Blake ..." I hear it hit the floor.

She pulls back the covers and straddles my hips. "If you're awake, then pay attention to me." Running her hands up and down my chest slowly, she drags the tips of her fingernails softly over my skin, making me shiver.

I place my hands on her naked hips and squeeze. We always sleep naked. I prefer her to dress like it's twenty below outside this house, but inside—nothing.

She bends forward and presses her lips to my neck. Lightning strikes outside the window, lighting up the room through the curtains. "Blake," I warn, my hands moving up to her sides, feeling her ribs.

"What?" she asks innocently.

"We can't," I tell her, hating that she can already feel how hard I am.

"Why?" she whispers, kissing up to the shell of my ear, and my hands move up her back and tangle in her hair.

"Because you just got out of the hospital." As the words leave my lips, she starts grinding her hips on top of me.

Fuck!

"Are you going soft on me?" Her warm breath falls across my skin when she whispers, and I know I'm about to crack.

"No," I say and roll over, taking her with me.

She squeals in surprise, and I pin her underneath. "Good."

Lightning strikes once again, brightening the room and I see the smile on her face. "I don't want to hurt you," I say, bending down to press my lips to her neck. As long as I'm the one on top, I can control what we do and how we do it.

"Since when?"

I give a rough laugh. My wife is trying to push me. "It's not going to work, Blake."

"I want to be your good girl."

I groan at the sound of her voice—so eager to please me. "You are," I tell her.

"Then tell me to fuck your cock," she says softly.

"Blakely," I growl her full name, hoping she understands I mean business.

"Ryat," she counters, her fingers running through my hair and pulling lightly on it. "Fuck me." She orders desperately, her hips lifting to meet mine.

And I feel what little restraint I had left break. Reaching between our bodies I grab my cock and slide into her wet pussy. She was already ready for me, like I was her.

Arching her back, she let's out a sound that can only be described as victory while I promise myself to go slow and be careful with her. I can make love to my wife.

BLAKELY

IT'S BEEN THREE weeks since my stay at the hospital. Life finally seems to be getting back to normal. Well, as normal as it can be. Nothing has really been the same since I ran away. It's weird not going to Barrington now.

Ryat refuses to let that happen. He swears the person he's hired to take over as me has straight A's. When I asked him how he expects to graduate when he's skipping all of his classes, his answer was, "I'm a Lord. We don't have to show up. No matter what, we graduate."

I guess it made sense. They have to do assignments—remain loyal to their oath—and some keep them away for days, even weeks at a time. Barrington is on the Lords' payroll. I always knew the University was crooked. It just took becoming a Lady to find out how much.

Ryat was right—my face has finally healed, and you can't even tell. I'm still getting headaches often, and Ryat took me to see Gavin earlier this week for more tests to look into it, but he gave me the all clear. Said hopefully over time, they will be less and less.

"I'm almost done," Sarah announces while I stare up at Ryat's bathroom ceiling at the house of Lords while she works on my neck.

It's Halloween, and they're throwing a big party. The hotel sits on several hundred acres, and they've set up a haunted house, hayride for the woods, and a walkthrough mirror maze. It's actually pretty cool. I had to beg Ryat to come. I swear, I see himself going crazy while he sits at the cabin watching the cameras. Matt hasn't been seen or heard from since I saw him last in my car at Blackout. It's as if he's dropped off the face of the earth.

"Done." Sarah steps back from me.

Lowering my head to look at her, I turn to face the mirror. "Nice." I smile at myself.

I'm a sacrifice. It's as fucked up as I could think. Halloween is meant to be scary. I didn't want to do the whole look at me, I'm a cute bumblebee. I went the opposite way.

Now, don't get me wrong, I'm still dressed like a slut. I want to get my husband so wound up that when we're finally alone later, he rips this thing off me because he's tired of others seeing me in it. I love being his good girl, but I also enjoy being punished. I've gotten to the point where we need some excitement. He needs me to take his mind off Matt and I know how to do it.

I know how Ryat feels about the Lords—he's devoted his life to them. I wanted to show him that I can do that too. He's sacrificed so much to get where he is, and he'll have to continue to do so. Even after Barrington. So, I'm sacrificing myself to him.

Matt fucked up my initiation, and Ryat told me last week that the Lords aren't going to have me make it up. A part of me was disappointed. I wanted to show him that I could be what a Lord needs. Another part of me wondered if that was what Matt's plan really was—to keep me from doing my initiation, hoping the Lords would exile me. Either way, he lost.

"They're done," Sarah says, reading a text on her cell.

The Lords had a meeting down in the basement once we got here. It gave us time to get ready. "Okay. Let's go and meet them out there." If Ryat finds me dressed and looking like this in his room, we won't be leaving it tonight.

Grabbing my cell off the counter, I flip off the light and hop from foot to foot while shoving my feet into my heels while walking across his room to the door.

"I texted Gunner that we will meet them in the ballroom," she informs me as I lock the door behind us.

"Okay." We make our way through the hotel. They went all out with the decorations. The walls of the hallway are covered in what looks like spiderwebs. Some dip low from the ceiling, and you have to duck. They've got smoke machines sitting on the floor to reduce visibility.

"Let's get a drink first," she calls out over the music, and I nod in agreement.

Yes, please. Ryat and I haven't used a condom, and I'm no longer on birth control, but there have been no signs of being pregnant. I was informed in the hospital that it was standard procedure to test me, and it was negative. Plus, I just got off my cycle last week. I'm honestly surprised by that. But I'm not worried. I would at least like to graduate college first, and that's a year away.

Stepping into the kitchen, she pours us each a mixed drink that looks like fruit punch of some kind out of a witch's cauldron. Once done, we head back through the hotel and to the ballroom. They have the DJ here like that first night in the corner at the head of the room.

I see some of the Lords—non-seniors—walking around holding trays, serving drinks and snacks. They're not dressed in their cloaks and masks tonight. Instead, they are dressed in all black with half of their faces painted like a skeleton.

I did Ryat's face before we left the cabin earlier. I had to lie and say that I needed Sarah to do mine once we got here. I could have done it myself, but he didn't know what I was going to be.

Bringing the straw to my lips, I take a drink, hoping that it doesn't remove my lipstick. When I feel him enter the room, I smile around it to myself.

A hand slaps my ass, making it sting. "Wanting me to fuck that ass to remind you who owns it?" he growls in my ear.

That thought has me sucking harder on my straw. Turning around, I face him.

FIFTY-THREE

RYAT

FUCK ME!

She's got her makeup done heavier than usual. Black eye shadow with thick and long fake lashes. They look like spiderwebs on the top with black liner. It makes her blue eyes stand out even more. Her lips are painted a deep red.

My eyes drop to her neck. She's got makeup on it as well. She's made it look like her neck has been slit from one side to the other. Fake blood runs from the wound and spills over her breasts, displayed by her low-cut dress. In the middle of her chest is an upside-down cross—just like above the main entrance of the cathedral.

Reaching out, I run my knuckles down it and slide my hand into her dress, feeling what I already knew—she's not wearing a bra.

Arching a brow at her, I say, "You're really asking for it, aren't you?"

"Maybe." She places the straw back to her lips and sucks on it.

"It's missing some accessories."

She quits sucking on her straw and frowns at me. "Like what?"

Leaning into her, I lower my lips to her ear. "That open-mouth gag with your body covered in your own drool and my cum." Pulling back, I look down at her, and she swallows.

Fuck, she looks amazing. That dress ripped to shreds on the floor, her body tied, naked, and gagged in the bunker ready for me to use sounds perfect. I'd much rather spend my night with her like that than here.

Her eyes drop to my black jeans, and the outline of my hard cock is on full display. "Yeah," I tell her, and she looks up at me. "My cock is as hard as your pussy is wet." I'm sure.

"Ryat." Shoving my chest, she laughs, thinking I'm joking.

I grab her hand and yank her to me, her body crashing into mine. Lifting my hand, I cup her cheek, my thumb softly running over her painted lips. "I know what you're doing."

"And?" she whispers, opening her lips. Her tongue slides between her lips, sucking my thumb into her mouth.

"It's working." I growl.

Pulling back, I pop my thumb out, and she smiles up at me. "You can prove that later." Then she turns, giving me her back to talk to Sarah.

BLAKELY

I WALK ACROSS the backyard, my heels sinking into the soft ground. It's cold out here, but I needed a second to catch my breath. It was getting hot and crowded inside the house. We've been here for over an hour and the music is too loud. Ryat was talking to Gunner and Prickett, so I took a second to get away.

Looking over to my left, I see the truck and trailer hauling people into the woods for the scary hayride. Ahead of me, at the back of the property, is where they've set up a haunted house with mirrors. I plan on making Ryat take me on all of them at some point tonight.

Lifting my newest drink that Ryat made me, I take a sip and come to a stop when I hear laughter to my right.

"Tyson." A girl squeals.

Squinting, I see him picking up a woman and throwing her over his shoulder. He walks her toward the tree line, and I find myself following them. I stop when they do, making sure to stay far enough away where they can't see me through the heavily wooded area.

He drops her to her feet, and she throws her blond hair over her shoulder, looking up at him. He tosses back his drink before dropping the now empty cup to the ground. "On your knees," Tyson orders her. "Legs tucked underneath you."

My lips pucker, sucking on my straw, making myself more comfortable and leaning against a tree.

She does as she's told, kicking off her heels first and then dropping to her knees in her mini dress, her ass sitting on the heels of her feet. She's got cat ears on top of her head—her nose is painted pink on the end and black whiskers are on her cheeks with her black eye shadow and thick liner, completing the cat look.

Tyson reaches down and unfastens his belt, he rips it from the beltloops, and I take another drink, staring like a peeping tom. Kneeling in front of her, he slides the leather belt underneath her shins and the ground, bringing it around her legs on top of her thighs, pulling it tightly, making her whimper.

I can see her skin pulling from here. Pressing on her shoulders he pushes her back into the skinny tree he's got her kneeling in front of. He stands and grabs a pair of handcuffs from his back pocket.

I suck on my straw some more, the burn no longer even bothering me. I've lost count on how many I've had since we arrived.

"Left arm." He demands and she lifts it to him without question. He wraps the cuff around her wrists tightening it to the point it makes her cry out. Her chest rising and falling quickly. Holding it up, he walks behind her, pulling it behind the skinny tree. "Other one." He snaps his fingers, and she lifts it as well behind herself. Tyson fastens that one, cuffing them above her head and behind the tree. The position has her body pulled tight, chest pushing out, her heavy breathing can be heard from where I stand.

He walks back around in front of her and kneels, running his knuckles down her face. She leans into it, her lips parting and her tongue darts out before he pushes two fingers into her mouth. She gags, her chest heaving before he pulls them out and slaps her across the face, making her whimper.

My pussy pulses and I take another drink. *I should go ...*

"Open," he commands and she parts her lips again for him. "Good girl." He praises her and I swallow, my thighs clenching. Shoving two fingers into her mouth again, he slowly runs them over her tongue that she sticks out for him.

Taking another drink, it slurps, and I freeze, hoping that they didn't hear that. The way he's finger-fucking her mouth and she's gagging, I'd say that they didn't hear a thing. "Keep your mouth open," he orders, pulling them out and standing. He unzips his jeans.

Nope! I turn around to run inside, but hit a wall, making me yelp.

"Shh." A hand goes to my hair and gently pulls my head up to look in a set of green eyes.

It's Ryat. *Fuck!* "I ..."

"Shh," he whispers, his eyes looking up and over my head and I

389

know he can see what I was watching. "You want to watch them?" he asks, his eyes lowering back down to mine.

I shake my head but can't make myself say the words. My numb lips refusing to lie right now.

He pulls away from me and spins me around with his hands on my shoulders. I see the girl still kneeling and cuffed with Tyson standing in front of her, a black combat boot on either side of her restrained legs. He has one hand in her hair, forcing the ears to hang off the side, while the other grips the base of his cock that is in her open mouth.

"Ryat ..." I whisper.

"It's okay." His deep voice assures me before I feel him lowering his lips to my ear. "I don't care if you watch them. I care if someone watches me fuck you."

Swallowing, I feel his hand reach around and slowly pull up my dress. His fingers going between my legs, pulling my underwear to the side.

"Watch him fuck her mouth, Blake, while I play with your cunt."

FIFTY-FOUR

RYAT

I WAS WONDERING where the fuck my wife went. It didn't take me long to find her outside. I watched her follow Tyson and Nicki out here into the woods.

Blake has always been curious when it comes to sex. She has a very open mind and is willing to try anything. And although I'd never share her, or even let someone watch me fuck her, she likes to watch others. I noticed it the first time when we walked in on Tyson and his server at Blackout. She was almost ashamed that it turned her on.

It's dark enough out here and we're in the tree line enough that no one can see us. Well, Tyson could if he looked up, but he's too busy to care. Plus, he likes an audience.

"You're wet," I say, and she whimpers, her body trembling.

I spread her pussy the best I can in this position and slide a finger into her sweet cunt, making her suck in a breath. "Ryat ... I—"

My free hand comes up and wraps around her throat from behind as well, cutting off her words. She doesn't need to explain herself to me. "Just watch them," I order, feeling her swallow against my hand. I'm not cutting off her air just yet.

Tyson pulls out of Nicki's mouth, his pierced dick wet, and drool runs down her chest while she keeps her mouth wide open, staring up at him the best she can. Her back and head are pressed into the tree due to how he's got her wrists cuffed behind it.

I work my finger in and out of Blake before inserting another one, making her breathing pick up. The lights behind us on the outside of the house give us just enough to see them through the trees.

Tyson kneels down and shoves his fingers into her mouth again, pushing her head back at an odd angle, and Blake's pussy tightens around mine.

Nicki gags, her chest heaving. He pulls them out and slaps her across the face. "Please?" She begs, her body fighting the restraints.

"Please what?" he asks her before forcing his drool covered hand between her tied legs. "You want to come?"

"Yes." She nods her head quickly. "God, yes." A cry rips from her when he finds what he was looking for.

Blake moans, her hips rocking back and forth on my hand.

His free hand comes up and wraps around Nicki's neck, holding the back of her head to the tree. "What would you do for that?" Tyson questions. The muscles of his forearm flex while he finger-fucks her cunt.

"Any—thing." She licks her wet lips.

I enter a third finger into Blake and before she can make any sound, I move my hand from her neck to her mouth, silencing her. "Shh," I whisper in her ear. "We don't want to interrupt them," I tell her.

Blake shakes her head and sucks in a breath through her nose.

Tyson removes his hand from between her legs and Nicki sags in disappointment. "When I cum, you cum." He informs her.

She opens her mouth up for him, understanding what he wants. He grips her cheeks, leaning into her and spits into her mouth. "Don't swallow until I tell you to, do you understand?" he commands.

She can't answer because that would require her shutting her mouth, so Nicki nods the best she can with his hand holding her tear-streaked face.

"I want my cock drowning in your drool," he adds.

Blinking, fresh tears roll down her cheeks and he lets go of her face to stand. Gripping the hair at the top of her head, he pushes his cock into her open mouth and doesn't go easy on her.

Blake's breathing picks up, her body rocking back and forth against mine again while I finger-fuck her just as hard as Tyson fucks Nicki's mouth.

My fingers are soaked shoved into Blake's underwear and her cunt tightens down on me while her body stiffens. Her pussy pulses when I feel her cum on my hand seconds later. Removing my hand from her mouth, I pull my fingers out of her and lift them to her mouth.

"Clean them," I order roughly.

My cock is so fucking hard, and I wish it was covered in her cum so she could clean it off instead.

Tyson let's out growl, also cumming in Nicki's mouth. "Swallow," He demands her when I feel Blake's legs give out.

I slide a hand behind her knees and pick her up, carrying her back to the house. I think we've had enough of this Halloween party. It's time to take my wife home so I can cum.

BLAKELY

RYAT AND I lie on the floor in the living room of the cabin. The fireplace is going, the flames heating up the room. I'm covered up with a blanket even though I'm sweaty. We didn't even make it to the bedroom. The moment we entered the house, I jumped on him. I hated to even wait that long. If I had my way, we would have had sex in his car in the parking lot of the house of Lords.

He's on his back, one hand behind his head, the other absentmindedly runs through my hair while my head is on his bare chest. My fingers run over the Lord's crest. "When did you get this?" I ask.

"A couple of weeks before classes started," he answers.

"This year?"

"Yeah."

I sit up and his hand falls from my hair to my bare back. Looking down at him, I ask, "Did it hurt?"

He laughs softly. "Well, it didn't feel good."

"Will I have to get one?"

He sits up, cupping my face. His green eyes search mine. "Why would you think that?"

I shrug. "If the Lords have to have a brand of some kind, I just figured the Lady does too."

"No—"

"What if I want one?" I ask softly.

Silence falls over us and I look away from his stare. My eyes dropping to his brand.

"Blake." His hand comes up and slides into my hair, forcing me to meet his eyes again. "Why would you want one?"

Licking my lips, I answer honestly. The alcohol I had earlier helping me out. "I want something to show my devotion. To prove that I'm all in."

"You do." He frowns, his free hand going to my left hand and lifting it to kiss my wedding ring.

"That's to you." I sigh.

"That's good enough for me." He states.

Pulling away from him, I stand, wrapping the blanket tighter around myself and go to walk out of the living room to our bedroom but he jumps up and grabs my arm, stopping me.

"Hey," he says softly. "I don't need you to prove yourself to me. Do you understand?"

"You did before," I remind him.

"That was then." Letting go of me, he runs a hand through his hair. "This is now."

"And?" My eyes fall to it again. The round circle with three lines through it. I know it represents power. Which a Lady doesn't have much of.

"And I know how you feel about me."

My eyes look up at his. I feel stupid for thinking of it. Of course, a Lady doesn't get the same mark of a Lord. We're beneath them, right? Most Lords have arranged marriages. We're disposable. "It was stupid," I say, feeling dumb. "I just thought ... I wanted to prove to you that I love all of you. Even the part that takes you away from me." At his silence, I lick my lips nervously and add, "You once said that you chose this life. I wanted to show you that I choose it too."

I go to walk away but he wraps an arm around me from behind, my back now to his front. Pulling my hair off my shoulder and to my back, his lips gently kiss my neck, right behind my ear. "Lie on the floor." Comes his command.

My heart picks up, my breathing coming quicker at the sound of his voice. Without hesitation, I pull away and do as I'm told.

He walks over to the fireplace and grabs the tongs off the hook and then removes his Lords ring from his right hand. My heart starts to pound in my chest when I watch him place it on the end and over the fire, heating it up.

FIFTY-FIVE

RYAT

I TRIED TO talk myself out of it. The fact that she wants the Lord's crest on her body, makes me proud. It's just another way for me to claim her. Another way to show she's mine. One that won't fade over time or wash off in the shower with water and soap like that Sharpie that I had used in the basement of Blackout.

She lays by the fire, the blanket wrapped around her chest, hands gripping the material. As much as she wants this, she's still nervous. Which is understandable.

"Remove the blanket."

She opens it up, showing me her naked body and I refrain from growling at the sight of my naked wife. She still has her Halloween makeup on, showing me the fake blood on her neck and upside down cross between her breasts.

Pulling my ring from the fire, I walk over to her and kneel beside her. Then I reach over and pick up her thong from earlier. "Put these in your mouth. Bite on the material," I order.

Grabbing them from my hand, she does as I say. Placing my left hand on her chest, I hold it down. "Interlock your fingers behind your head and take in a deep breath."

She props her head up with her hands and my eyes drop to her body, watching her chest expand and I don't give her any warning, pressing my ring into her skin, right below her left breast on her ribcage. She arches her back, crying into her gag. Her body starts shaking while I hold it there for a few seconds before pulling it away.

Tossing the tongs and my ring to the side, I remove my hand that was pinning her down. Pulling on her body, I yank her up and into my arms, removing her underwear. Her eyes are tightly shut, and tears run down her face. "You did good, Blake," I tell her.

Her long dark lashes flutter open and her watery eyes meet mine.

Pressing my lips to hers, I taste her tears. She opens up for me and I deepen the kiss. Readjusting both of us on the floor, I place myself between her legs, spreading them wide, now that she lies underneath me. "So, fucking good." I praise her and she whimpers, her hands going to my hair, her nails scraping my scalp making me moan.

My free hand goes between our bodies, and I slide my cock into her, making her hiss in a breath. My lips find hers and I don't let them go. I keep them captive while my hips move in and out of her—owning her.

I want her to know that she didn't give herself over to me for nothing. I will take from her, but I will also give her everything that I have. As much as I own her, I fucking need her. "I love you." I pull my lips from hers long enough to speak, then they're back on hers, taking her breath away.

BLAKELY

IT'S BEEN SIX weeks since Halloween night. It was eventful to say the least. Watched Tyson face-fuck a woman in the woods. Had my husband brand me like I was a piece of cattle he owns. But I don't regret it. I wanted him to understand just how far my love for him went.

Things have been going great. We've fallen into a routine that almost makes me feel like we're normal. Going to the movies, out to dinner. It's like we're a real couple that doesn't live in a secret society. Which is crazy since we're actually husband and wife. Sometimes I have to remind myself that he's my husband because it just feels too good to be true.

Ryat unlocks the front door to the cabin. I step into the foyer but come to a stop when I see Matt sitting in the middle of the brown leather couch in the living room. Leaning back, he looks relaxed, his arms fanned across the top of the cushions.

"We've got dinner tomorrow night with Ty," Ryat reminds me as he enters behind me. "Don't let me forget to get that bottle of scotch that he likes."

If I wasn't so terrified, I'd blush at the fact we have plans with a man I openly watched have sex. Instead, I swallow. "Ryat?" I manage to say his name through the knot in my throat, looking over my shoulder at him locking the front door.

"It's a party." I hear Matt say cheerfully.

Ryat looks up, also coming to a stop beside me. His eyes trained on Matt. "What the fuck are you doing here?" Ryat demands.

How did he get past the cameras?

Matt leans forward, placing his elbows on his knees. "Came to get what's mine." His eyes go to me.

I shake my head, my hand unable to hold my purse, and it drops to my feet. "No." The single word cracks, slipping through my lips.

Ryat places his arm on my chest to push me behind him, but Matt jumps to his feet, pulling a gun from the waistband of his jeans, and points it at me. "Don't move, or I'll shoot her," he warns.

"Matt," Ryat growls his name, lifting his hands out in front of him. "Let her go. This is between us. I'm the one you're mad at. It's me you want."

"No ... please ..."

"He's right, Blakely. I wanted you. But you fucking married him," he shouts, the gun shaking in his hand. "And as much as that disgusts me ..." My body trembles, but I can't move. No matter how loud my mind screams to. I can't leave Ryat. "If I can't have you, then no one can."

I'm hit with what feels like a Mack truck. The force knocks me back into the front door. My body shakes like an earthquake as loud bangs go off in the distance. I can't breathe. My body's being crushed. Lifting my arms, I feel soft material. I open my eyes and see a white blur in front of me. Looking up, I meet a set of green eyes. "Ryat ... what?"

Realization returns that Ryat is the one crushing me to the door. His body pinning me to it. I feel wetness against my chest. "What?" I look down, and my T-shirt is soaking up blood.

"You're okay," he assures me, sucking in a ragged breath. "You're okay," he repeats like he's trying to convince both of us.

I look at his white shirt, and I see the blood covering it. "Oh, God." I gasp. "Ryat." He's been shot.

"Blake." He reaches up and grabs my face, his hands feeling cold and clammy. "I'm sorry ..."

Tears sting my eyes while I try and catch my breath. "Don't ...

Don't do this."

"I love you, Blake," he whispers.

"No. No. No. Don't," I shout, gripping his bloodstained shirt. "Why?" Why would he do this to us? To me?

"You think I'd kill for you, but not die for you?" He shakes his head gently. "Silly girl." His words are getting softer. I can barely hear them over the blood rushing in my ears.

"Ryat ..." I sob.

"You deserved better," he whispers.

Tears fall down my cheeks and I lick my wet lips.

"I'm sorry I wasn't better."

"Ryat?" I cry. "Please. Don't leave me." Blood starts to run from his nose. "Please ..." I beg it to stop, my voice breaking.

He smiles, and I watch the color start to drain from his handsome face. It falters, and he places his forehead against mine.

I wrap my arms around him, trying to hold him up, but his knees give out, and I fall to the floor with him. Leaning over his body, I see the blood start to pool around us onto the tile. He lifts his hand to my face. "Why did you do that?" I ask, my hands fisting his shirt.

"Because ... I love you," he says through a cough, and then his hand falls to the floor to his side.

"Ryat?" I shout. My hands pound on his chest. "Ry—at?" My voice cracks when a sob racks my body.

"Get up!" Matt grips my hair and starts pulling me from my husband.

"No! I won't leave him," I scream, twisting in his grip.

"Get your ass off the floor," he demands, bending down and wrapping an arm around my neck. He yanks me backward, and my hands lose their grip on Ryat's shirt.

He picks me up off my feet, choking me, and I kick. Silently screaming while I look at Ryat's dead body lying on the floor. His eyes are now closed, and his head is tilted to the side, facing me.

Matt leans into my ear. "He willingly gave you to me, Blakely. Giving his life for you was fucking pointless. For him anyway. For me, it was everything." Then he drags me out of the house.

My fingers dig into his forearm that chokes me. My feet kick up dirt and rocks, forming a dust storm around us. He gets into a car, dragging me with him. Someone else closes the door while he lets go of my neck. I gasp for a breath while he throws my back onto the bench seat. Then he's pressing his knee into my chest, crushing me.

I try to scream, but nothing comes out. He pulls a syringe out of his pocket and removes the cap with his teeth. I silently cry when he grips my face shoving it to the side. Then I feel the sting on my neck. My body instantly goes numb, my arms and legs dropping like dead weight. He removes his knee from my chest, and I take in a ragged breath. His hand on my face moves it to where I have to look up at him hovering over me. He's smiling down at me.

"I always win, Blakely. And you were always supposed to be mine." Letting go, he runs his knuckles down the side of my face.

"Is she out?" I hear a voice off in the distance.

I blink, taking every ounce of strength I have to open them back up again.

"Almost," he answers.

"Took you long enough," the voice snaps.

And I try to rack my foggy brain to place it. It sounds so familiar.

"I got the job done," he snaps.

This time when my eyes close, they don't open again.

I WAKE UP, rolling onto my side. Grabbing my head and stomach, I feel sick. Nauseous.

Opening my heavy eyes, I see I'm on a bed in an unfamiliar room. It's large with white and purple décor. I roll off it and make my way to the adjoining room. Thank God, it's a bathroom. I fall down at the toilet and hug it while I vomit, hearing the bedroom door open. I sit on my ass, my hand wiping the vomit from my mouth.

"Well, well, well, the whore is awake."

I get sick once again. When I think I'm done, I fall back onto my ass, my back hitting the side of the Jacuzzi tub, and look up to see Matt standing in the bathroom. And the person standing beside him is my mother. "You ..." I grind out. "You helped him do this?" I knew the voice sounded familiar. It was my fucking mother?

"You gave her too much," she snaps at him, ignoring me.

"I gave her less than suggested," he argues. "She needs to eat something." Walking out of the bathroom, he returns seconds later with a tray that must have already been in the bedroom. A piece of toast sits on a plate with scrambled eggs. It all looks old.

How long have I been here?

And Ryat? Oh God, Ryat. The memory hits me like a fist to the face. They killed him. My mother may not have pulled the trigger, but she was there to help Matt. Tears sting my eyes, and my throat tightens.

Matt places the plate on the countertop and tosses the piece of toast at me. It falls onto the floor in front of me. "Eat that," he orders.

Slowly, I look up at him through my watery lashes, wishing I could set his ass on fire. "Fuck you," I growl through gritted teeth.

He smiles. "Oh, we'll get to that. But first, eat."

"No," I tell him. Ryat is dead. My mother helped Matt kill him and kidnap me. Why would I do a damn thing he tells me?

He lets out a huff.

My mother sighs. "You need to eat—"

"Fuck you," I scream, interrupting her. My throat burns, and my ears ring.

"That's it." Matt charges toward me and picks up the toast off the floor. Gripping my hair with one hand, he yanks my head back and shoves the toast into my mouth, down my throat.

I choke on it, pieces flying from my lips.

"Don't do that," my mother hisses, pulling him away from me.

I scramble back to the toilet just in time to puke again.

"She needs a doctor," I hear Matt growl.

"I know what's wrong with her," my mother states.

"Yeah, she's been knocked out for two days. She needs to eat."

"No," my mother disagrees.

I sit back on my ass and wipe the spit from my chin.

"She's pregnant."

I haven't officially confirmed it. I wanted to wait a few more days before I took a test because I've been late before. Even when I was on birth control, and I didn't want to get my hopes up. I drop my eyes to the floor.

"Son of a bitch," Matt hisses. "You let him knock you up, you stupid bitch," he yells at me. "Goddammit, that fucking bastard." He kicks the cabinets.

I look up at him through watery lashes, vomiting so hard, it's made me cry. "He's my husband," I shout back at him. Then a smile pulls at my lips, adding, "He can do whatever he wants with me."

His face goes red with rage. "He's fucking dead, Blakely. Just like that baby is about to be." He begins to roll up his sleeves. Then he fists his hands, walking over to me.

My mother places her hand on his chest, stopping him. "What in the hell do you think you're doing?"

"Getting rid of it," he answers with a huff.

I shove away from the toilet, pressing my back into the side of the tub once again, bringing my knees to my chest. Wide-eyed, I watch them face one another. Ryat may be dead, but I won't let them touch our baby. I'll find a way out of here. I'll buy myself some time.

"You're not touching her." She lifts her chin.

"You can't be serious." He points at me. "She's fucking pregnant. I don't want his kid. Don't tell me you fucking want an Archer baby?"

"Of course, I do." She crosses her arms over her chest. "It'll give me a second chance. To do things right this time." She looks over at me and pulls her lips back with disgust.

"No." He shakes his head.

"Yes," she hisses. "She's not showing yet, so she can't be that far along. You went twenty-one years without her. You can go seven more months."

He huffs. "This brings on more complications."

"I'll handle it. I'll bring in a chef for a special diet. A doctor, she needs prenatal vitamins, an ultrasound. It'll be fine ..."

"You've lost your fucking mind if you think I'll hand my baby over to you," I say through gritted teeth. Is that why Ryat stepped in front of me? Because he knew we were expecting? Maybe I gave off signs that I didn't see, but he did. "Especially since you're not even my biological mother."

I expected that to piss her off, but she just smiles down at me while Matt snorts. "Bless your heart, honey," she says condescendingly. "I will cut that baby out of you myself and then leave what's left of you for Matt."

My stomach drops at her words. My watery eyes dart around the bathroom to see if there's anything for me to use against them. I'll have to check the bedroom. They had to have missed something that I can use to escape.

"Fine." Matt rolls his eyes. "She can keep it, but after it's born, Blakely and I are gone."

She nods. "Deal."

They both turn and exit the bathroom. I hear the bedroom door shut followed by the sound of several locks, letting me know that wherever we are, I'm locked inside these two rooms.

I begin to cry, thinking about Ryat. How could he do this to me? Willingly die to leave me behind. Is that why he did it? Because he knew I was pregnant? How does he expect me to live without him? The bile begins to rise again, and I find myself scrambling back to the toilet.

FIFTY-SIX

RYAT

BEEP ... BEEP ... BEEP ...

I groan, my hands coming up to my head and pressing on it, trying to stop the headache that pounds behind my eyes.

Beep ... beep .... beep ...

"Will someone turn that fucking sound off?" I ask, my voice scratchy, and my throat feels like I've swallowed sandpaper.

"Ryat?" A voice gasps.

"Yeah." I open my eyes to see a blurry shape in front of me. "Blake?" I reach out for it, but my hand misses, touching nothing but air.

Beep ... beep ... beep ...

"Turn it off," I snap, the sound of my own voice making me flinch as it echoes in my head.

"We can't. It's the only thing telling us you're alive," I recognize Gunner say.

"I'm talking, aren't I?" I growl.

"You haven't spoken in a week," he states.

Pressing my palms into my eyes, I rub them once again. They're a little more focused now. I see Gunner on a couch, Prickett standing by a window, and then Sarah sitting on the side of my bed.

"Where's Blake?" I ask, looking around.

The room falls silent.

Beep ... beep ... beep ...

The sound of the machine picks up its rhythm when I don't see her. "Where the fuck is she?"

Sarah looks away from me, and I hear her sniff. She goes to stand, but I grip her forearm, yanking her back down to my hospital bed. "Where the fuck is she?" I shout.

"She's ... gone."

"Sarah," Gunner snaps at her.

She covers her face with her hands and begins to sob.

"What the hell do you mean, she's gone? Where did she go?"

"Matt ..." Sarah cries. "He took her."

Beep. Beep. Beep.

I release her, and she runs out of the room bawling. Sitting up, I ignore the head rush and blurry vision. I start yanking wires off my body and arms.

"Ryat," Gunner begins. "You can't leave. You were shot four times ..."

"I'm fine."

"No, you're not," Prickett argues. "You need rest. Your body needs to recover."

"I need Blake," I shout. "Where is she?"

Gunner sighs while Prickett runs his hands through his hair.

"Where is she?" Panic grips my chest like a vise. This can't be happening. Did he say I've been here for a week?

"We don't know." Prickett speaks softly. "We pulled up to the cabin just as another vehicle was leaving ... we walked inside and found you lying dead in the foyer. Gunner performed CPR while Sarah called 911, and I went after the car. By then, it was too late. It was gone. After we searched the house, we realized she had to have been in the car. We figured by the smear of your blood on the floor that she was dragged away."

Throwing my two legs off the side of the bed, I try to stand, but my knees give out. I fall but catch myself on the side of the bed.

"Ryat ..." Gunner runs over to me and grips my arms to help me stand.

I shove him away. Well, I try but he doesn't budge. "I need my phone. I have to go get it..."

"No."

"Yes. I can't be here." Not while she's out there. Somewhere alone. Lost. Terrified. I should be with her. I should be protecting her. "My phone ..."

"Ryat," Gunner snaps as Prickett runs out of the room.

I yank the IV out of my arm, and blood squirts onto the bed.

"Ryat, get back in bed," Gunner demands.

"No. I need my goddamn phone." *Why aren't they listening to me?* "It was in my jeans ..."

The door bangs open, hitting the interior wall, and Prickett enters with a couple of nurses. They don't even give me the chance to explain.

Prickett shoves his elbow into my back, forcing me to bend over the side of the bed when I feel a pop in my hip. Then my eyes close with her name on my lips.

———————

"WHAT ...?" MY HEAD is foggy once again. The light blinding. I blink, tilting my head to the side. I go to rub my eyes but realize my wrists are restrained to the hospital bed.

Sighing, I mumble, "You've got to be fucking kidding me."

"I'm afraid it's the only option you left them."

Opening my eyes, I see my dad standing next to the bed.

"I need to leave," I say, feeling my tongue stick to the roof of my mouth.

"You need to recover," he argues.

"Why does everyone keep saying that. Blakely ..."

"We'll find her."

I open my eyes to see my father-in-law entering my room with two cups of coffee. He's the last person I want to see, but he might be the only one who will want to find her as bad as me. "I know where she is," I growl. "If anyone would let me get my goddamn phone."

"I have it." My dad pulls it from his back pocket. "After they sedated you, Gunner ran back to the cabin and pulled it from your jeans. I guess when the paramedics arrived, they had to cut them off you. It was still in your pocket."

I go to reach for it, but the damn restraints stop my actions. I throw my head into the flat pillow and grind my teeth to keep from screaming. I don't want them to sedate me again.

"Open it," I growl. "I have an app on there that tracks her."

My father looks across the bed to my father-in-law, who stands on my left. "Uh," my father starts. "Ryat, her cell was left behind. You can't track it."

I close my eyes, hating having to explain what I did, but also glad

409

that I did it.

Gavin sighs. "I have to ask Ryat. Are these injuries from you?"

"No," I snap. I'm rough with Blake during sex, but I've never physically beaten her. Matt slammed her face into the steering wheel, not me.

He arches a brow.

"Why would I lie about that?" It's not like I'd be in trouble if I did do this. The Lords specifically place members into the legal system. Unfortunately, beating your wife isn't a criminal offense. They don't want a Lord in prison for assault or domestic violence cases when he's needed for an assignment.

"During my initial exam," he goes on. "I noticed the writings on her body—in Sharpie. I figured maybe things got out of hand."

I'm not even mad about the fact that he thinks I did this, but the thought of him seeing her naked makes my fists clench. "No," I repeat. "I didn't beat my wife."

"You know how it is with the Lords and their chosens," he adds. "I've seen my fair share in here over the past twenty years since I graduated from Barrington." He then places her X-rays up on the wall and flips the switch to the light behind it, illuminating the film. I can see all of her bones from her chest up. And Gavin takes the end of a pen and points at the spot between her right shoulder and neck. "Is this what I think it is?"

"Yes." I growl and add, "Leave it there."

He nods once. "I just wanted to also let you know that we ran a pregnancy test. It was negative."

I didn't expect it to happen that fast, but I'm definitely going to keep trying.

"It's standard procedure," he adds.

"When I got her back after she ran, I implanted a tracker between her neck and shoulder." I look up at her father. "So, unless Matt found out about it and cut it out, it's still there." No one knew.

Phil runs his hand through his hair and nods to himself. Probably fighting the fact that I did something so morally wrong, but also, it's the only thing that might save her life now. I was never going to let her get away again.

"Okay. Yeah, okay," he finally agrees. "Let's track it, and I'll go get her."

"Hell no," I sit up, pulling on the restraints. "I'm going with you."

"You're not leaving this hospital until they release you," my father snaps.

"He's not going without me," I argue. I want to hold her, pick her up in my arms, and know that at that moment, she's safe. I don't want a fucking phone call that she was found and have to talk to her over the phone. Or worse, what if they find her body? No. I won't believe that. She's not dead. She's alive, and I'm going to make sure of it with my own two eyes.

"You're wasting time! Take these off, and let's go." Who knows what Matt is doing to her? But I have a hundred ideas of what I'm going to do to him. He won't like any of them.

My father places his hand on my shoulder. "Not until your body is healed."

"She's pregnant," I state.

Silence falls over the room.

"She told you?" my father asks.

"No."

"Then you're not sure ..."

"I fucking know, okay," I snap. I first realized it a couple of weeks ago. I think it happened Halloween night. We had sex three times that night by the time we finally went to sleep. There have been signs. I'm not even sure she's seen them, but they've been there. I know my wife's body better than herself.

My father sighs, running a hand down his face. "Did you tamper with her birth control?"

My wife straddles me while I lay on my back in our master suite at the cabin, my hands propping up my head. She runs her finger over the Lords crest that was burned into my chest, lightly tracing it. "We should get divorced in six months. My mother would flip."

I snort at that thought. "That won't be happening."

Her finger pauses, and her eyes trail up over my chest and face to meet mine. "I understand why we did this, Ryat."

"Oh, yeah? Enlighten me." I want to hear her thoughts on why I made her mine forever.

"You don't love me." She shrugs. "I don't love you. You wanted to marry me to rub it in Matt's face. I said yes because I didn't want him and, as an added bonus, it will piss off my mom. I understand neither one of us meant forever in city hall earlier today." Yawning, she lays her head on my bare chest.

I'm still hard. I could fuck her all night, but I'll let her rest. After all, I have the rest of my life to fuck my wife. Because no matter what she thinks, when I took my vow today, it was forever. After several minutes of silence, her hands fall off the side of my body, and her breathing evens out.

She's passed out.

Unlinking my fingers from behind my head, I run them through her curled hair a few times. Then gently, I roll over, placing her down next to me. I get up from the bed and make my way into the bathroom. I remove her birth control pills and then the pack that I've kept stashed in my bag at the back of the closet. I punch the dates she's already used and place the placebos back in the drawer. Blakely isn't going anywhere. If I have to keep her knocked up every day of our lives, I will.

"Yes—no," I spit out. Sighing, I add, "She ran and didn't take it with her." That very next night was the ceremony at the house of Lords where she left me. When I brought her back, I didn't even bother with giving her the fake shit. My wife wasn't going to be taking it anymore.

Mr. Anderson places his cup of coffee on a tray next to my bed and undoes my left wrist.

"What are you doing?" my father barks when he undoes the other.

"Didn't you hear him? My daughter is pregnant. We need to find her now. The tracking device will lead us right to her."

"He needs medical attention," my father argues.

"I'll hire a doctor. Gavin. I'll pay for him to travel with us."

Finally! Someone gets it!

"Hand me my cell," I order my dad while my father-in-law exits the room, leaving us alone.

He pulls it back. "Ryat …"

"Don't give me some bullshit," I snap and flinch. My free hand now pushing into my side to try relieving the burning pressure I feel. It doesn't work.

"How in the fuck are you going to save her?" he demands. "Ryat, you're injured. I know you love her but risking your life to save hers just puts you both in danger. Again."

Baring my teeth, I glare up at him. "Hand me my goddamn phone."

The door swings open, and my father-in-law returns along with Gavin. "I must advise against—"

"I'm fucking going," I interrupt the doctor. My heavy breathing fills the room, and I bite my inner cheek to keep from whimpering at the pain in my side. *Fuck me, I can't breathe.*

"I'll send you with pain pills, but Ryat … I can't go with you," Gavin informs me.

"That's ... fine," I manage to get out, I'll eat them like candy. Enough drugs can make you feel invincible.

My father runs his hand through his hair aggressively and hisses in a curse. "Goddammit, Ryat. You don't even know she's alive."

There it is. The reason he doesn't want me to risk my life for hers—because he thinks it's not going to be worth it. "I've risked my life for the Lords over and over," I say, taking a deep breath. "I will do no less for my wife. She deserves that." This is all because of me. I put her in this life, this situation. I will be the one to save her from it.

After a long second, he holds out my cell, and I take it. Letting out a long breath, I pray Matt hasn't found the tracker. It's not common for the Lords to use them. It should be mandatory if you ask me. But then again, I actually love my wife.

Then, without another word, he turns away from the bed and picks up his jacket off the couch and exits the room.

"Ryat—"

"Give me a hundred," I interrupt Gavin. After a long second, he concedes.

"I'll need an hour."

"You've got twenty minutes," I snap. I lie back on the bed, and he too turns and storms out of the room, and my father-in-law follows him.

I unlock my phone and go to the app. "Please, please, please," I chant. When I see the red dot, my eyes start to sting, and I let out a breath I didn't know I was holding. Laying my head on my pillow, I sniff. "I've got you, Blake. I'm coming." Then I pull up a contact and press call.

BLAKELY

SITTING IN THE middle of the bed, I rock back and forth. I'm pretty sure I'm starting to go insane. I've cried until I made myself sick to my stomach. Multiple times. Over Ryat jumping in front of me and slamming me into a door to be a human shield. Now—I'm pissed at him. So fucking angry that he allowed Matt to win and left me behind.

Getting up from the bed, I walk to the adjoining bathroom to use the restroom. This is my life. Loneliness and boredom.

It makes me wonder if this is what Ryat felt like those days he was in jail. But only he knew he'd be released when his job was done.

Me? I'm in for life. And my mother plans on ripping my baby not only from my arms but my actual body. I can't allow that. I won't. I have a plan, but I'm not sure how I'm going to execute it. And if I try and fail? What will they do to me then?

Finishing going to the bathroom, I go to the sink and wash my hands. Drying them off, I go back to the bedroom for another long afternoon of staring at the wall. I don't even have a TV. I'm guessing that's so I have no idea what is going on with the outside world.

Exiting the bathroom, I yelp when I see Matt standing by the side of the bed, inspecting my breakfast. I had to pretty much shove it down my throat. I'm not hungry, but I won't starve my child.

He turns to face me, and I take a step back into the bathroom. Chuckling, he walks over to stand in the doorway, his large frame now blocking my only exit.

Great, Blake! Real smart. "What do you want?" I demand.

His blue eyes drop to my bare legs and run up over my thighs until they reach the bottom of my shorts. Then over my shirt. "I think you know exactly what I want."

I shake my head. "My mother ..."

He reaches out, wraps a hand around my neck, and shoves my back into the wall to the right. His body presses into mine, and the fact that I can feel his hard dick inside his jeans makes me want to vomit again. "Your mother isn't fucking here." He smiles down at me. "Plus, I can come inside you and not have to worry about knocking you up."

I whimper, my hands trying to pry his away that's wrapped around my neck, but it's not working.

Leaning down, he runs his wet tongue along my face, and I gag as tears sting my eyes.

"You know. I pretended to be repulsed by your fixation of being raped."

"It's called forced-sex fantasy ..." I grind out through clenched teeth. "Asshole."

"No." He shakes his head once. "I'm talking about rape, Blakely. Because I'm going to make you cry." His eyes narrow on mine. "You're not going to enjoy it or get off on it. Not like you did when I watched Ryat kidnap you from your apartment and then again in the woods." He snorts. "I'm going to fucking hurt you, beat you, and humiliate you."

My stomach sinks at the thought of what he'll do to me if he gets the chance. And how whatever he has planned could hurt my baby.

"But I will give you a head start." He lets go of my throat and takes a step back.

I sag against the wall, sucking in a breath while rubbing it.

"Just because I know how much you like the chase." His eyes drop to my chest.

"I won't ..."

"Ten minutes," he states, lifting his arm and looking down at his watch.

"Matt," I snap. "I'm not going to ..."

He backhands me across the face, knocking my head to the side. I gasp, my hands coming up to the wall so I don't run into it.

He grips my hair and yanks me over to the counter, shoving my hips into it, and I scream for help. Even though I know no one will be here.

Holding me in place, his free hand comes up and grips my neck again. "Why, Blakely?" He sighs as if disappointed. "You let Ryat play with you." I tremble, trying to get away from him. "But I guess ..." He yanks my head to the side and starts kissing my cheek. "If you don't want to play, then I'll just fuck you here and now."

"No. No. No." I rush out through a gasp. "I'll play." I try to nod my head, my watery eyes pleading for him to give me another chance in the mirror. "I'll play."

"Good." He steps back and shoves me by my hair into the bedroom. "Go. The clock is ticking."

I run out of the bedroom and slam the door shut behind me. Having to open it may give me an extra second. I'm going to need it. I have no clue where we are, but I decide to take the stairs to the lower level, hoping I can get out. When I hit the landing, I trip over the edge of a rug, falling onto my face. I quickly jump up and run to the front doors and try to open them.

Fuck! They're locked. I twist the deadbolt and try again. Nothing. What the fuck? Looking up, I see another lock that's too tall for me to reach.

"Oh, by the way. All the doors have added padlocks. And only I have the key."

I spin around, my hair slapping me in the face. Looking up, I see him bent over the balcony, a knife in his hand, and he slowly runs the blade down the side of his face pretending to shave. "And all windows are bulletproof." He gives me a chilling smile. "I've had time to prepare your homecoming, baby."

I shove off the door and run farther into the house. The sound of his wicked laughter bounces off the walls, carrying throughout the house. I see another set of stairs and decide maybe I should go up since he thinks I'm down here. I grip the wooden banister, to stop my momentum and fling myself around to run up when I run right into him.

The blow knocks me down. I cry out when my side hits the unforgiving floor and roll onto my stomach to crawl away from him.

"Isn't this fun?" He laughs. His hands wrap around my ankles, and he starts dragging me backward across the tile.

I scream, trying to grab onto anything I can find, but all I do is drag a rug with me, and pull a table down that was up against the wall.

He drops my legs, and I scramble to get up, but his hands grip my hair, and he yanks me to my feet before slamming me face-first into a wall. His large body pins me to it from behind.

"Matt," I sob, "Please ..."

"Shh, Blakely," he says soothingly in my ear. "It's okay, babe. It's just a game. We're both going to win here."

I try to shake my head, but he yanks it back even farther, forcing me to look up at the high ceiling. My fists hit the wall, trying to push away from it and give me some space.

"Your mother plans on doing whatever it takes to get that baby out of you." He presses the tip of the knife to the side of my stomach, and I stiffen, my breathing stopping. "So, while she's away, we're going to play. That way, I still get what I want. And she gets what she wants."

"Valerie is not my mom. You killed my mother," I growl, hating how fucking helpless I am. Hating Ryat for doing this to me. To us. He promised to protect me.

Matt laughs in my ear, making that taste of vomit rise once again, and I swallow it down. "I just wanted a taste of her. I was going to be fucking her daughter for the rest of her life. She was lying there, naked and waiting. Begging to be fucked. What man would pass up the opportunity to have both?"

"My husband would." I growl.

His laughter grows. "He had no clue who she was. But if he had, I bet he would have changed his mind."

"You're sick," I scream. "You fucking bastard!" He yanks me from the wall and shoves me forward so hard that I trip and fall to my knees.

Then I feel his hands on me. He tosses me onto my back and straddles me. He shoves my shirt up to expose my bra to him, and I slap at his face. He grips my wrists, pinning them down by my sides. "You do know that your parents had to sign you up to be a chosen, right?"

"No," I choke out.

"Not just any woman can give herself to a Lord. We can only pick from who is on the list." His hands tighten their grip, and I whimper. "Even they recognized the whore that you are."

I arch my back and scream for help, but it turns into a sob.

"Don't cry, baby. This is your fantasy. This is what you want."

"No," I sob, my hair sticking to my wet face.

"Yes. I saw Ryat. I watched him carrying you tied, and gagged, and put you in the back of his SUV where he then hogtied you. He even lifted your shirt and played with your tit. Then the woods—now that was interesting. I wanted you to come find me, but it was him you found instead. So I watched him get what was supposed to be mine. I watched him fuck you in the woods," he whispers. "And you know what I did? I jacked off watching you get off while he fucked and choked you. You loved every second of being treated like the whore you are. I underestimated you, baby. But it's okay. I can admit my mistakes."

I whimper.

"I'm going to line them up for you." He licks across my face, and I try to turn my head but can't with how he has me pinned down. "Put my Lady to work for the Lords. You'll be the talk of the ..."

"You're not a fucking Lord," I shout over him. I heard someone saying that he was stripped of his title. On the run after Ryat killed Cindy and Ashley.

His face morphs, red with rage, and he leans down into mine so close, his forehead rests on mine while he screams, "I AM A LORD ..."

I move my head just enough to sink my teeth into his nose. As high up as I can, feeling the skin tear and bones breaking. His blood fills my mouth when he yanks back, breaking it free of my teeth, and I take the skin off in the process. Then I spit it on him.

Sitting back on his knees, he brings shaking hands to his face, screaming in agony.

"Fuck you." I roll onto my side for better leverage, propping myself up on my left arm and slam my foot into his face, knocking him back even farther. "You motherfucker."

He throws his head back, his arms out to his side while blood pours from his face, screaming so loud my ears ring.

I get to my feet, turn, and run out of the hallway only to come to another one. It's got door after door. I try them all, needing a place to hide. To regroup. To wash up. Now I'm covered in his blood. It's dripping off my chin onto the floor. He'll be able to track me. Plus, it's making me want to puke.

A door finally opens and it's a set of stairs. I close it behind me and run down them, skipping the last three. Landing on my feet, I trip but manage to stay standing this time. I see a door to my right and open it. Shutting it behind me, I lock it and listen to myself sucking in breath after breath.

It's pitch black. My hand slides along the wall by the door, looking for a light switch, but when I find it, I pause. I can see the light from the hallway underneath the door. So I keep it off, not wanting to give myself away.

"BLAKELY!" I hear him shouting my name.

I throw my hands over my mouth, trying to silence my sob while walking backward from the door in the dark.

"You fucking bitch," he goes on. "You will beg on your knees. Your fucking knees, BITCH."

Taking another step back, I hit something hard and thankfully my hand muffles the scream I make. It's a wall.

Panic grips my chest, and I turn around to face it. My hands frantically reach out, hoping to find a door handle of some sort or any way of an exit. But the thought of any escape vanishes when the door to the room bursts open.

Spinning around, I watch a blood-covered Matt step inside the dark room. The light from the hallway behind him makes only his outline visible.

"I found you, you little bitch."

I try catching my breath, but I can't. My chest is heavy, and my side hurts from running. "I knew you liked the fight." He steps closer into the room, reaching behind him, he pulls two pairs of handcuffs from his back pocket, and a lump gets lodged in my throat. He smiles. "We'll see how hard you fight once these are on you."

FIFTY-SEVEN

RYAT

"Do you hear that?" Phil asks me, holding up his hand to listen. It's faint, but I hear it. "BLAKELY!"

"It's Matt," I confirm what we already expected.

"Yeah." And he sounds pissed. "Let's keep moving."

We tracked her to a place around Niagara, on the lake of Ontario. It's about four hours away by car. Phil's private jet got us here in one. We have no clue as to why he picked this place, but my guess is that he plans on relocating her to Canada at some point.

Thanks to another Lord, we were able to get a hold of the prints and saw tunnels that ran underneath the structure. Thankfully, we were able to enter from the outside. The plans didn't show the buildout complete.

I hold the gun in my right hand down by my thigh as we come up to a right turn. Pressing my back into the wall, I lift my finger to signal him to be quiet. Right before I go to look around the corner, he grabs my arm and whispers, "Someone's coming."

I pause and listen, and sure enough, I hear footsteps. And ... are they humming? The sound grows louder, the steps closer. Sounds like high heels. Looking over at my father-in-law, he shrugs. Who the fuck would be here with them? Especially a woman?

They get closer and closer. I close my left eye, lifting the gun. I'm not going to shoot whoever it is, but I want them to think I am.

I hear the last step before I see the person step into view. "I will blow your head ..."

The person spins around, and my arms immediately drop to my side, lowering the gun. Wide green eyes meet mine. "Valerie," Phil whispers, looking at his wife in complete shock.

Fuck!

She takes a step back, and he steps forward. I watch her open her mouth to scream just as he reaches out and yanks her to him, spinning her around so her back is to his front.

"Get the syringe," he orders, turning her to face me.

I dig into the bag and pull out the drugs, removing the cover of the needle with my teeth. Mr. Anderson moves her neck to the side with his hand on her face while she screams into it. I stab her neck and administer the drugs. Her body instantly drops in his arms, and he lets her fall to the floor.

"Fuck," he hisses, running his hands through his hair. "MOTHERFUCKER!"

"Keep it down," I hiss. "If we can hear Matt, then he can hear us."

He paces, his hands gripping his hair.

"We need to keep moving," I growl. "Not like we have a lot of time. Take her back—"

"No," he interrupts me, his eyes snapping up to mine.

"Take her back to the car," I demand, not in the mood to fight with my father-in-law, but I will if need be. "I'll go get Matt."

"I need ..."

A shrill scream cuts off whatever he was about to say, and I fist my hands. "We're wasting fucking time," I snap at him. "Take the bitch to the goddamn car and wait for us." With that, I give him my back, not even bothering to see if he complies.

BLAKELY

MATT'S GOT HIS hand fisted in my hair while he drags me up the stairs back into the main part of the house. Once he gets me through the door, he shoves me forward, and I sprawl out on the floor.

"Fuck! I never knew you could be this much fun, Blakely." He laughs from behind me.

I get up on my hands and knees and start to crawl away, but he grabs my ankle, yanking me back. I sob, my hands gripping at anything but get nothing while my body slides against the cold tile.

We finally come to a stop, and he grips my hair again, yanking me to my feet, and leads me into the living room. I catch sight of something sitting in the high-back chair, but my hair covers most of my face, restricting my vision.

I'm shoved over the back of the couch, and he yanks my hands behind my back before cuffing them, and every little bit of hope I thought I had is gone.

I sob, and he yanks me to stand, his hand coming up around my neck from behind. "Shh, Blakely. It's okay. It's just a cock. You've taken one before."

Closing my eyes, I bite my inner cheek to keep from giving him any satisfaction of crying.

He leans over and whispers in my ear, "I've watched Ryat fuck you, baby. He wasn't gentle by any means."

"That's what she prefers."

I look up to now see a familiar face sitting in the chair, and I almost cry in joy. "Tyson—"

Matt cuts off my words, slapping his hand over my mouth from behind.

"You should have seen what he did to her in the basement at Blackout." His eyes drop to my legs.

My chest tightens. Ryat let him watch us. He promised me ...

"What the fuck are you doing here?" Matt snaps at Tyson.

He holds out his hands to show they're free of weapons before crossing his arms over his chest. "Just came to collect Blakely."

Matt yanks me back from the couch. "How did you ...?" He snorts. "He fucking put a tracker in her."

My eyes widen.

"No, I did." Tyson gives a cruel smile, making his handsome face look evil.

Matt snorts. "Why the fuck would you track Ryat's wife?"

"Because she's a gift."

I shake my head, not believing that one bit. Ryat would never ...

"A gift? You expect me to believe that Ryat would hand her over to you?"

"Oh, God. No." he throws his head back, laughing. "She's a gift from the Lords."

Matt stiffens against me, and I try to calm my breathing so I can hear over the blood rushing in my ears.

"You know ..." He looks around the room. "Since they owe me a wife and all." He shrugs, his eyes looking me up and down while he pulls his lips back. "She's not my first choice but ..." Tyson shrugs carelessly. "You know how it works. Once a Lady is a widow, they re-gift her to another Lord."

This can't be true. I refuse to believe it.

Matt lets out a curse under his breath, and fresh tears sting my eyes.

"I knew you'd take care of Ryat eventually. I just had to sit back and wait. You know I'm a patient man." He reaches up and runs a hand down over his unshaven face. "Plus, you owe me." Tyson glares at Matt, rising to his feet. "For that stunt you pulled outside of Blackout."

Matt chuckles. "I knew you'd like that."

Wait? Tyson has been in on it the whole time?

"Once again, I knew you'd show up that night." Tyson goes on. "Ryat was too blinded by Blakely to think clearly. You weren't going to allow her to go through initiation to become a Lady. No man likes a woman having more power than him."

Matt laughs that off but doesn't deny it.

"Why didn't you take her, though? That was the only flaw in your plan. You had a perfect opportunity and passed on it." Tyson tilts his head to the side.

"I wanted him to know that I was right there in front of him the whole fucking time. And if I wanted to, I could have her," he answers.

"Well, he's dead now. So, you have nothing else to prove. Not to him anyway. Hand her over." Tyson orders, stepping closer to us.

"This could be fun." Matt's words seal my fate and it's like a fist to my chest knocking the air out of me. "The two of us and her."

I try to free my head from Matt's hand, but he just tightens his grip. "Tell him, Blakely," he urges. "Tell him about your fantasy of being raped."

I sob at his words, embarrassed and terrified.

"It'll be even better with two of us." He goes on while Tyson just stares at me. "Oh, and she loves breath play." He pinches my nose, taking away my air. "We can choke her out."

I blink, causing fresh tears to run down my cheeks, and I see Tyson roll his eyes. "Fucking an unconscious chick isn't any fun. But I don't expect you to understand that. You always have been lazy."

Matt just laughs off the insult. "This will be fun. I'll take her cunt. And you, well—you've always been a sucker for a mouth."

Tyson leans over and reaches into a bag that I hadn't seen until now and pulls out a roll of duct tape. I whimper, my knees buckling, but Matt keeps me held in place while dots start to cloud my vision, my chest burning trying to get a breath into my lungs.

"I guess I have some time." Tyson nods.

I can't fight one of them, let alone two of them.

"I like to play with my toys," Tyson announces, ripping a piece of duct tape free off the roll with his teeth. "What about you, Matt?" He places the tip of that piece on his arm, then rips off another. Then another. Until he's got four pieces total.

I start thrashing in his hands, my scream muffled, and I can feel how hard Matt is. They're going to kill me, but not before they rape me.

"That's the best part," Matt agrees. "What do you have in mind?" Matt shoves me forward, and I manage to get a quick scream out before I hit Tyson, and his hand wraps around my throat, cutting off my air.

His once pretty blue eyes are burning into mine. His hand squeezes my neck painfully so that he picks me up off my feet and throws me down onto the large coffee table, pinning my arms under me once again.

I kick and wiggle, but as usual, it does no good. Tyson holds out his right arm with the four pieces of tape on it. "Shut her up," he orders Matt.

He rips off the tape and places them over my mouth, each one like a punch to my gut. Knowing I won't be able to get it off. When the last one is on, Tyson lets go of my neck, and I suck in a deep breath through my runny nose.

Tyson steps back, and I roll over onto my side, my body convulsing on the coffee table before I hit the floor.

"Fuck, I'm glad you could join us." Matt chuckles and slaps him on the back.

Tyson ignores him and wraps a hand in my hair, yanking me to my feet. "You've got five minutes." Then he shoves me away from them.

Matt's laughter grows, and I know I've lost. It's over. My worst nightmare just doubled. Tyson was playing Ryat all along. Just another lie. Another part I never saw coming.

I turn, my hair whipping me in my tear-streaked face, and I run out of the living room, knowing I have nowhere to go but I have to try.

I'm running down a hallway when I feel a hand grab the back of my shirt and pull me into a blacked-out room.

I scream into the tape when my back is shoved into a wall, a hard body pressing into mine.

"Shh, Blake. It's me."

FIFTY-EIGHT

RYAT

SHE STIFFENS, HER screaming stops, but she's breathing heavily.

"It's me, Blake," I say again. Then I reach over and flip on the light. She blinks several times before her pretty blue eyes meet mine.

I run my hand down the side of her bloody and duct-taped face. "I'm going to take this off, okay? But you have to stay quiet."

She nods, blinking, and tears run down her face.

I rip off all four layers as quick as I can.

"Oh my God! Ryat, what ... how ...?"

I slap my hand over my mouth. "We have to be quiet," I tell her.

She nods once again, and I remove my hand. She sucks in a deep breath but does as I say. "That's my good girl."

She whimpers, and I pull her from the wall. Digging my hand into her front shorts pocket, I pull out a handcuff key and spin her around, undoing them.

"Ryat ..." She sobs softly, her shaking hands coming up to her mouth to try to quiet it. "I don't ..."

"I'll explain it later, okay?" I kiss her forehead. Her hands come up and dig into the material of my shirt. "Fuck, I've missed you, Blake," I whisper and pull her into me, hugging her tightly.

"I love you," she sobs, digging her face into my chest.

"I love you too." I pull away, grabbing her tear-streaked face. "I need you to stay here."

"What? No." Her eyes widen as panic takes over her features.

"Ryat ... no."

"I need you to stay here. In the dark. I'll be back, okay?"

"Please." She chokes out, her knees give out. Before she can fall, I grab her, gritting my teeth at the pain it causes in my side to help her to the floor. I popped several pain pills on the plane ride here, but they're not really doing any good.

"I promise, Blake. Look at me," I order, roughly gripping her face. I wait for her eyes to focus on mine. "I promise we'll be going home soon. But I have to get Matt."

"But Tyson—"

"He came with me, Blake. He's here to help us."

I lie in my hospital bed waiting for Phil to return with my pain pills so we can get the fuck out of here, and I hold my cell to my ear. "Hello?"

"Hey, Ty, I ...."

"Fuck, Ryat! It's good to hear your voice."

"I need a favor," I say, getting to the point of this call. I don't have the luxury of time right now.

"Name it," he comments without hesitation.

I've been unfair to him. None of what happened to Blake that night at Blackout was his fault. Plus, he was the one I got the tracker idea from after she ran from me. Let's just hope I don't find what he found when I get to her.

She sniffs and nods quickly. I turn off the light and lock the door before shutting it behind me so Matt can't enter without kicking the damn thing down.

"Here we come. Ready or not." I hear Matt call out with excitement.

I pull the Glock out from behind my waistband and grip it tightly in both of my hands. It's going to take everything in me not to shoot him between the fucking eyes, considering what he's done with Blake. I almost want to say fuck the confessional and just get rid of him right here and now. But that would be the easy way out for him.

"Hey, Ty?" Matt's voice carries down the hall.

"Yeah?" He asks.

"How'd you get in?" Matt questions and my teeth grind. *Fuck! I thought we'd have more time.* We were planning on Matt being more into the chase than wondering how Tyson got into the house.

"Tunnels." Comes his clipped answer.

I come to the end of the hall and see Matt still standing in the living room, hands on his hips. "When did you get the chance to be alone with Blakely that you were able to put a tracker in her, without her knowing?" He wonders.

"Really, Matt?" he barks, standing behind the couch, pulling a collar and leash out of his bag. "We going to play a hundred questions or are we going to play with the bitch?"

My teeth grind at Ty mentioning touching my wife, but I understood this was going to be needed. Doesn't mean I like it though.

"Oh, we'll play," Matt assures him. "But you won't be touching her."

What the fuck? My eyes widen when I see someone enter the room behind Tyson. Rushing out into the living room, I lift my gun and point it at the man. "Don't fucking move."

Matt spins around to face me, shock covering his features. "Ryat." he growls.

"Get the fuck back," I order the man who holds a gun to the back of Ty's head.

"Jesus," the man hisses but stays where he is. "You can't do one fucking job, Matt."

Matt's jaw tightens. "He was dead when I left him, Dad."

"Dad?" Ty chuckles, his body softening, no longer finding the man behind him a threat. "You were in on this too?"

"Of course, he was." Matt snorts. "She was going to kill him."

My brows pull together. "What does that mean?" I bark. "Why would Blake ..."

"Her initiation," Ty interrupts me, spinning around to face Jake Winston. "You were the one supposed to be at Blackout. You're the reason Matt was even there in the first place."

He presses the gun into Ty's chest and shoves him backward into the couch. "That bitch has become more of a problem than pussy should be," Jake snaps.

Blake had only ever received her first text the night before initiation. I had checked her cell in the hospital and never saw where she got another one with her assignment details the night of the attack. Now I know why. That's why Matt didn't kill her, or take her, it was a diversion. He was just trying to save his father.

"Why would the Lords want you dead, Jake?" I demand. "What have you done?"

He gives me a chilling smile. "It's what I'm going to do." Lifting the gun, he places it between Ty's eyes.

I pull the trigger, the sound of my gun firing, rings out in the room, shooting his hand. Jake cries out, the gun falls from his hands and Ty knocks a fist into his face.

Matt turns and charges me. I pull the trigger again, but he's already on me, the gun firing off into the ceiling as he picks my feet up off the floor. He slams my back into the coffee table, and it takes my breath away. Pain shoots up my side and a burning sensation follows that makes me see dots floating around.

Fuuuccckkkk!

"Don't worry, Ryat." He laughs in my face. "I'm going to make your wife my whore."

No! "Over my dead body," I grind out.

Laughing, he ignores that and adds, "I won't be stingy like you. I'll make sure that everyone else gets a taste as well." Getting up off me, I start coughing, sucking in a ragged breath. I feel wetness on my back and know that the impact has done something to my already injured body. I'm bleeding out. Probably ripped open my stitches. I might die right here and now, but I will take Matt with me.

Gritting my teeth, I land a punch in his face, knocking him back, knowing I'm running out of time to do what I came to get done.

BLAKELY

I EXIT THE bathroom at the sound of gunshots. Ryat told me to stay here but I can't. *He's alive.* He came for me. I have to help him. In any way that I can.

Running down the hall, I hear people struggling—men grunting. Coming to a stop, I see Tyson kicking a man huddled on the living room floor by the couch. He stops and the man rolls onto his back, moaning in pain, face covered in blood and cradling a bloody hand to his chest.

Tyson leans down, retrieving a gun from the floor and straightens, pointing it down at who I now recognize is Mr. Winston—Matt's dad. "If the Lords want you dead, then you already are." Tyson fires the gun at him, shooting Jake in the face.

I yelp, jumping back and my ears now ringing.

"DAD," Matt yells, running over to him.

Tyson takes a step back, the gun hanging at his side.

Matt drops to his knees and pounds his fists into his father's chest. His heavy breathing fills the room when he wipes his own bloody face with the back of his hand.

I smile, the scene all too familiar. I was doing the same thing to Ryat when Matt shot him. But only I know Ryat really didn't die. Jake is dead. The fact that half his face is gone, says it all. "Karma is a bitch," I say, but I don't think anyone hears me.

Matt jumps to his feet. He goes to charge Tyson, but he lifts the gun again, pointing it at Matt's chest. He comes to a stop, his nostrils flaring and chest heaving. "You son of a bitch. I will fucking own you," Matt shouts.

"You always were a worthless Lord." Tyson tilts his head to the side. "They should have killed you years ago."

Matt's face turns red and his blue eyes narrow to slits at his words. "Do it!" He slaps his own chest like a gorilla. "Fucking kill me, you sorry son of a bitch," Matt screams.

"In time," Tyson tells him calmly.

"You don't have the fucking balls." He eggs him on, stepping into the barrel.

Tyson takes the gun and slaps Matt across the face with it. So hard it knocks him to his knees "You of all people should know the Lords don't allow us the easy way out." Tyson squats down next to him. "They make us suffer more than anyone." Then he looks up and I see Ryat stepping behind Matt.

He grips a handful of Matt's hair and yanks his head back, before sinking a needle into his neck. Matt's body falls to the floor next to his dead father.

"Ryat." I gasp, running to him.

"Blake," he mumbles my name when my body connects with his.

I wrap my arms around him, and he stumbles back. His hands go to my hair, but he doesn't hug me as tight as I do him.

"Whoa." Tyson grabs my arms and yanks me free of Ryat.

"What's wrong?" I ask, wiping the tears that run down my face. I didn't even realize I was crying until now.

"We gotta get them to the plane," he snaps, helping a pale-face Ryat over to the couch. He sits him down and I see he's bleeding.

"Oh my God Is he going to be okay?" I ask panic gripping my chest. What happened? Did Matt shoot him again?

"I'm fine," Ryat coughs out.

And the look that Tyson gives me says the opposite. "Ty—"

He places his hands on my shoulders, giving me a little shake. "I need your help, okay?"

"I'M GOING TO get Matt on the plane and secured, and then I'll come back and get Ryat," Tyson informs me.

"Okay." I nod, running my hand through Ryat's dark hair while his head rests in my lap in the back seat. "I can't believe you," I say angrily. He shouldn't have even come. He wasn't ready to leave the hospital.

"You were in trouble," he manages to wheeze out.

"You're right. *You* are in trouble," I snap at him. "Putting your life in jeopardy. Again."

He coughs. "You did it ... too." Pushing off my legs, he rises.

"Ryat. You're supposed to wait ..."

"I can walk, Blake." He shoves the car door open and gets out.

"Shit." I jump out on my side and run around the back just in time to see his knees buckle. "I got you." I grab his arm and wrap it around my shoulders, holding him up.

"I told you to wait," Tyson snaps at me, running down the stairs from my father's private jet.

"It was his idea," I growl, tattling on my husband like a child.

Coming up to us, Tyson grabs his arm and takes my position. I help the best I can to get him up the stairs and into the plane, but I feel like it's more of jobs better suited for one person sort of thing.

"Open the bedroom door." Tyson gestures with his chin to the back of the plane.

I run ahead of them and shove it open, holding it while he helps Ryat inside. He sets him on the edge of the bed. "Stay right here." Then he looks at me. "Don't let him lie down. Keep him sitting up." Before digging into his pocket, handing me a pocketknife. "Cut his shirt off him."

I nod, taking it. "Okay."

"Blake," Ryat whispers when I just stand here.

"I know," I sniff and fumble with trying to open the damn thing. I drop it on the floor. "Shit." And pick it up.

He reaches up, placing his bloody hands on my shaky ones. My eyes meet his—he looks exhausted. "I'm sorry."

He frowns.

My throat closes. "For this ... for you. I did this ..." Sniffing, my bottom lip begins to tremble.

"No. You didn't, Blake." He shakes his head once.

A tear runs down my cheek. "Thank you for saving me." I'm still having trouble believing he's alive in front of me. I've seen the vision of him laying dead on the cabin floor too many times to now accept this is real. That I get another chance to be with him.

"I told you." He gives me that Ryat smirk. "I'll always find you."

The door to the room opens, and Tyson enters once again with a bottle of scotch in his hand and pills in the other. "Take these." He shoves them into Ryat's hand and then opens the bottle before also handing that over. Then his hard blue eyes look at me. "I need that shirt off."

Carefully, I cut down the front of it, making sure I don't cut Ryat on accident. Once I'm done, Tyson rips it off the rest of the way and tosses it to the floor. "Stand in front of him. I'm going to need you to hold him in place."

"What do you mean in place?" I rush out.

But he ignores me and climbs onto the bed and sits behind him. "Ryat, man, I gotta close this up."

"I know," he acknowledges before taking another gulp of the liquor.

Tyson opens up a briefcase of some sort, and my eyes widen when I see what's in it. But I'm not sure why. I should have expected this kind of shit on my father's private jet since he's a Lord. I'm sure this situation happens often when they go on assignments. "I have a needle and thread, but that'll take too long. My other option is staples—"

"Burn it," Ryat growls, interrupting him. "Cauterizing will be the fastest way."

"What?" I ask, that panic gripping my chest. "No. There has to be something ..."

"Do you want him to bleed out?" Tyson snaps at me, and I swallow, shaking my head.

"Hey." Ryat takes my shaking hands in his and pulls me into him, looking up at me. And all I can think about is those pain pills aren't going to kick in fast enough. *He's going to feel this.*

"Do we have any drugs?" I ask, licking my wet lips. We need what Ryat gave me when I ran. It knocked me out almost instantly. Tyson shakes his head without even looking up at me.

"It'll be okay. I promise," Ryat assures me when he sees the way my shoulders tense.

"Hand me the scotch," Tyson demands, pointing at it on the small ledge next to the bed. I do as he says. "Put this in his mouth." He hands me a washcloth.

Before I can do anything, Ryat snatches it from my hand and shoves it into his mouth, and then wraps his arms around my waist, while I stand between his parted legs. Letting out a shaky sigh, I wrap my arms around him, holding the side of his head to my chest.

Tyson takes a lighter and runs it along the blade of the knife, heating up the metal that he's going to use to stop the bleeding. I blink, allowing the fresh tears to fall so I can see better.

Placing the handle of the knife between his teeth, he picks up the scotch and pours it over my husband's back. Ryat tenses, and a muffled sound comes from his gagged mouth.

I whimper, and Tyson's blue eyes glare up at me as if I'm making it worse.

I gently scratch Ryat's head, holding him to me, and I know he can feel me shaking. Then Tyson heats the knife up once again before pressing it—blade flat—along the cut on my husband's back, who tightens his hold on me.

The smell of burning flesh is enough to make me want to vomit. Then to know it's my husband literally has me gagging. But I manage to keep it down.

Once done, Tyson drops the knife beside him before grabbing something from the briefcase and taping it up.

I look up at the ceiling, trying to stop the tears from falling before I have to look at Ryat in the eyes again. I don't want him to see me upset.

"That'll be good enough until we can get him to the hospital. I'll let the pilot know we're ready. Make sure he lies on his stomach." And with that, he leaves us alone.

I EXIT THE bedroom, leaving the door open so I can hear if he needs me. I walk down the aisle and come up to the front where Tyson sits. Typing away on his cell, I sit across from him, thinking it would be awkward if I chose anywhere else since we're the only two awake. "He's asleep," I inform him, and he nods but doesn't look up at me.

"I didn't watch you and Ryat in the basement," he says out of the blue.

Frowning, I argue, "But you told Matt ..."

"I gave Ryat the codes to shut off the security cameras. I knew you two spent some time in the basement that night when he turned them off along with the others inside the club."

I let out a lone breath at his words. Ryat was right—he was a hundred percent on our side.

Another awkward silence falls over us, not really having anything to say to that. I feel stupid now that I believed him. But in my defense, it was very convincing. "I ... thank you." I hold out his pocketknife for him.

He finally looks up but makes no move to take it from me. "It's bad luck to close a knife that someone else opened."

Sighing, I close it and hand it out again. He takes it this time.

He finishes typing on his cell and then puts it away, sitting back in his seat, and grabs a glass of scotch that sits on the table between us. I notice there's another one. "I made you a drink."

I just stare at it, making him chuckle and add, "I didn't drug it."

"I wish. I could use a good nap right now." Then my eyes slide over the empty plane. "Where is Matt?"

"Where he belongs—with the luggage."

Looking back down at the drink, I almost take a sip but then remember the possibility of being pregnant. I doubt he knows that, though. I wonder if he knows I know what happened to him. Or the rumors about his chosen?

"Can I give you some advice?" he asks.

I look up at him through my lashes. "Yeah." Honestly, I'm fucking drowning. Out in the middle of the ocean with my hands tied behind my back. My husband is passed out in a room behind me after his friend took a heated knife to his skin to stop the bleeding from a gunshot wound my ex gave him trying to kill me. *Fuck, yeah. Give me all the advice you got.*

"Don't ever make him choose."

I frown. "I don't under ..."

"Between you and the Lords."

Why would he think I'd make Ryat choose? I understand that he took an oath for them. And if they betray that, the penalty is death. "I would never ..."

"You will. You may not mean to, but you'll fight. Every couple does." He takes a sip of his drink. "And when you get mad, he'll yell and say some hurtful shit and then he'll get called away for an assignment. And when he should be working, he'll be checking his phone to see if you ever responded to his five apology texts." He looks over at the window, the glass of scotch resting on his knee. "I'm not saying he'll choose the Lords over you if you put him in that position." His eyes come back to mine. "I'm telling you that he will pick you. And that's what will get him killed. I know it's selfish. To tell you to forget about your feelings and always put his first."

"Isn't that what you do when you love someone?" I ask softly.

He lifts his drink to his lips and snorts before throwing some back. "No two people love the same way. And everyone has a different opinion on what love actually is."

I sigh. Ryat and I do fight. A lot. Will it always be like this? Once everything is out in the open and there are no more secrets, will we still go at each other's throats? I can't answer those questions, but I do understand that Tyson isn't wrong. Ryat would go crazy if he had to leave, and I was mad and ignoring his texts. "How often will they take him from me?"

"There are no set dates. But Ryat is one of the best, and the Lords know that. It could be three times in one year or it could be twenty." He shrugs carelessly. "He could get called out after breakfast and return before dinner. Or he could miss Christmas, anniversaries, and the birth of every child you guys decide to have." Lifting the drink, he finishes it off. Setting it down on the table, he runs a hand down over his lips and unshaven face. "A Lord serves whenever he is called. We're machines bred for war. And someone, somewhere is always trying to wage one."

His answer doesn't make me feel any better. But it makes me wonder how he knows this. Is it from experience? I know something happened to his chosen, but he also doesn't wear a wedding ring. Which makes me curious why he never moved on. "Can I ask you something?"

"Sure." He surprises me with no hesitation.

"You're older."

A sly smile spreads across his face, making his blue eyes shine brighter. "That's not a question."

I swallow nervously. "Three years older than Ryat. Why aren't you married to a Lady?" He just stares at me, that smile now gone, and I feel I need to explain. Shifting in my seat, I tuck a piece of hair behind my ear. "I thought, you know, pretty much all Lords are arranged to marry someone before they graduate from Barrington."

He nods. "They are. The Lords feel a man is better respected with a wife. It makes them look dependable and trustworthy to the outside world."

"So you never had an arranged marriage in place?" I'm not sure if his chosen was just for fun or if she was the one he planned on marrying, but I'm not going to ask him that.

"There was." He relaxes back into the leather of his seat. "But circumstances change. And I saw an opportunity. The Lords needed someone to do their dirty work."

"Blackout?" I make sure I'm following.

He nods. "I was supposed to wear a suit and tie, run a multibillion dollar business—have the gorgeous wife with a dog, two kids." He waves his hand in the air. "All that shit. Which, at one point, I thought I wanted. But just like anyone else, I changed my mind and presented the Lords with an offer. I choose to take Blackout for one reason."

"Which is?" I ask slowly, wondering if I'm digging in too much, but he's willingly giving me information. Ryat would never tell me about Tyson, and I respect that about him. But that doesn't mean I don't want to know.

"They agreed to let me pick who I marry. When the time comes." A slow devious smile spread across his face, showing off his perfectly white teeth.

My frown deepens. "You wanted freedom to pick who you marry so much that you gave up your higher title of a Lord?"

That smiles widens into something sinister. "I'm the kind of man who will crawl across the floor and lick the dirt off your shoes like a peasant begging a king for some scraps. Just to make you think I'm weak. So, when they look away from me, I can slit their throats."

FIFTY-NINE

RYAT

I OPEN MY heavy eyes and smell the sterilized room before I even see the white walls and realize I'm in a hospital bed. I go to lift my right arm, and it doesn't budge. "Not again ..." My eyes fall to look at it, half expecting it to be handcuffed to the railing, but instead, there's a brunette cuddled up to my side, sleeping on it.

Blake! Thank God. Leaning down, I kiss her forehead, letting my lips linger to feel the touch of her skin on my lips.

Her eyes flutter open, and it takes her a second to focus on me. "Ryat?" She gasps. "You're awake." She goes to get up, but I hold her in place.

"No, Blake ..."

"But Dr. Gavin—"

"No, please." I pull her into me. "Stay here." I take in the smell of her hair, that familiar strawberry smell making me smile. "Stay here with me. For just a bit longer."

"Okay, Ryat." She looks up at me and gently kisses my cheek.

"God, I missed you," I say, and her eyes fill with tears.

"Don't ever do that again," she growls. "Just so you know, I'm going to kick your ass when you get to go home."

I laugh and kiss her forehead. "Are you okay?"

"Yeah."

The moment she answers, I see the bruise on her eye. "He hit you?"

"I'm fine ..." She pulls away.

"Blake." I growl. "Tell me what he did to you." I'm going to make him confess his sins of LeAnne to the Lords at confessional but not what he did to her. I don't want everyone knowing what my wife went through.

Sighing, she runs her hand through her hair. "He told me to run."

I frown, remembering something about a game. "Why would he ...?"

"He wanted to act out my fantasy," she whispers nervously. "Told me to run from him. He wanted to catch me and rape me."

My teeth clench, my muscles stiffening, making my already sore body worse.

"I was able to keep him off at first. Then he caught me, and Tyson was there ..."

"We needed Matt to believe that Tyson was there for you," I inform her. Matt was going to be suspicious no matter how it went down, but we knew he wouldn't pass up on having the extra help to use her. "He had to play a part."

She snorts. "He played it well. Tyson had me thinking he was in on the attack at Blackout. He even threw me onto the coffee table ..."

"He had to get close to you," I say even though I hate the fact that he touched her. Not pissed that he was rough with her, but that he put his hands on her in any way. Or the fact that Matt honestly thought he and Tyson were going to rape my wife. "We knew he'd have you restrained somehow. It was either rope, zip ties, or handcuffs."

She frowns, her brows pulling together. "That's why the key was in my pocket?" I nod. "Tyson put it there while I was lying on the coffee table."

The moment that Tyson saw she was cuffed, he had to get close to her. "I'm sorry, Blake."

"I'm fine." She grabs my hand. Giving me a soft smile, she adds, "Matt never touched me."

She's lying. The mark on her face proves that he did get his hands on her before I could get there. "You saved me. Again."

Cupping her soft cheek, I run my thumb over her warm skin. I don't know what I'd do if I never got to see her again. "I love you, Blake."

"I love you too." She leans forward, gently pressing her lips to mine.

When she pulls away, I look around the room, but it's still just the two of us. "Where is Matt? Please tell me he didn't get away again."

"No. Tyson has him in the basement at Blackout. He told me to tell you that when you're ready, he'll hand deliver him to the cathedral."

I start to push myself up. "We can do it tonight."

She places her hands on my chest and pushes me back down. "No."

"Blake ..."

"I need you back to yourself. And Ryat, that's not going to happen until you heal."

"Blake," I growl. *Not her too.*

"We need you."

"We don't have time ..." I pause. "We?"

A smile covers her face, and she nods. "We, Ryat." Reaching over, she picks up a black and white picture and holds it out to show me. "We're having twins. And we're going to need you ..."

"Twins?" I ask to make sure I heard her right.

She nods, a gorgeous smile on her perfect face. I've never seen her eyes so bright. "Two babies."

I reach over, grabbing her face, and pull her into me. This time, I kiss her deeply, passionately. I ended up going after her, but she was the one who brought me back. This woman is incredible. And I'm the luckiest man to call her mine.

BLAKELY

RYAT HAS BEEN in the hospital for three weeks. He ended up needing surgery again due to internal bleeding. He overdid it and required a lot of rest. I've made sure that he's gotten it. I'm actually surprised he's been so compliant. He must have really needed it, considering how stubborn he is. But I can match it. As a Lady, I understand what my Lord must do. I also understand that even he has limits. And before too long, there'll be two more people for us to care for. I needed him to recover a hundred percent.

I've spent every moment here in this room with him. But I know once he gets discharged today, it'll be out of my control. He's been antsy. He wants revenge, and I do too.

I spit out my toothpaste and wipe my mouth off, exiting his private bathroom and walking into his room.

He stands by his hospital bed, pulling his jeans up over his legs still shirtless.

I lean up against the doorway and watch him. Ryat Alexander

Archer is ripped. From his chiseled abs to his broad chest and muscular arms—the man is delicious. And I've been craving him.

He looks up and smirks, catching me staring. Then he reaches into the bag that sits on his bed, pulling out a dress. "Wear this," he orders.

I laugh like he's joking. Then look out the window to see the snow covering the ground and building. "Ryat, it snowed yesterday. I'll freeze to death."

He walks over to me. "I'll keep you warm."

"I'm serious."

"Me too." He arches a brow, daring me to argue.

I snort. "How did that get in there anyway?" I'm surprised he hasn't burned it.

"I told Sarah to pack you something sexy."

"It's a little revealing, don't you think?"

"Maybe I want to see what's mine," he counters.

I sigh, knowing that Ryat is a hundred percent back to himself and that my track record sucks when it comes to winning these battles with him.

Rolling my eyes, I reach down and remove my sweater, letting it fall to the floor, and then undo my jeans and shove them down my legs, kicking them away.

"Lift your arms," he commands, and I raise them above my head, allowing him to slide it on over my body. The cool material is soft against my warm skin. "Perfect," he praises, running the tips of his fingers over my breasts that the V cut design shows off, and I blush.

He places his hand between my thighs and runs it up to cup my pussy. I moan, wanting to feel him there. To feel him all over me. I don't know if it's the pregnancy or what, but I'm always horny. More than usual. Maybe it's just the fact that I couldn't have him while he was recovering.

"Come here." He grabs my hand and pulls me over to the bed. Reaching out, he shoves the bag off it and onto the other side of the floor. "Bend over and spread your legs," he growls in my ear.

I don't argue. Instead, I'm thanking God. When I bend at the waist, he yanks up my dress and slaps my ass.

I bury my face into the bed so someone walking by his room won't hear us in here. He slides his fingers into my thong and runs his knuckles up and down over my soaking wet pussy. I push my hips back.

"Someone is eager," he muses.

"Please," I beg, knowing that no matter how much he's trying to go slow, he wants to fuck just as bad.

He doesn't respond, but the sound of his zipper being lowered is all I need to know. Seconds later, the head of his cock pushes its way inside me, and I moan at the feel of him spreading me to accommodate his size. My eyes almost roll back into my head at the sensation. It's been too long.

He pushes all the way in, and my breath catches. Then he leans over my back and wraps his hand around my throat, squeezing, but not enough to take my air away. "Fuck, Blake," he growls before his lips are on my neck, sucking on my skin while his hips pick up their pace, fucking me up against the side of the bed.

I place a hand over my mouth to quiet my unintelligible noises that he forces from me. His teeth sink into my skin, and then he stiffens, coming inside me.

He pulls out, and I sag against the bed. "That's no fair," I whine.

Laughing, he slaps my thigh, making it sting. "You're not done." He kneels behind me.

"What are you ...?"

"Stay like that." He slaps my pussy, and I yelp, before burying my face into the bed again.

His fingers spread me wide open, and I suck in a deep breath when I feel something cold and rubber being pushed into me. "Ryat—what ...?"

"Just a little fun." He stands and grabs my hand, helping me to stand as well.

SIXTY

RYAT

"ARE YOU HUNGRY?" she asks, looking out the passenger window of my car that I had Gunner drop off at the hospital for me this morning.

"For you," I answer, my eyes running over her smooth and defined legs. My cock is hard knowing that my cum is running out of her cunt right now.

She rolls her eyes. "For actual food. I need to stop at the store on the way home. What would you like for dinner?"

"I could live off your pussy, Blake." I reach out and slide my hand between her thighs.

"Ryat," she protests, swatting my hand away. "You're driving." Looking around once again, she asks, "Where are we going?" Her head whips around to see I just passed our exit.

"I have to see someone before we go home," I answer vaguely. Knowing she's about to argue with me, I pick up my cell in my lap and turn on the app.

"Ryat," she squeals seconds later when the vibrator inside her pussy comes on.

"We've got a thirty-minute drive, Blake," I inform her, smirking over at her discomfort. "How many times can you come in that amount of time?"

"You can't be serious." She whimpers, throwing her head against the headrest while I speed down the highway.

"Of course, I am." I drop the phone to my lap, leaving it on.

"Fuck," she whines, her hands fisting the hem of her pretty sundress. I'm ripping that off her and burning it the moment I get my wife home. She was right. It's way too revealing, but it serves a purpose.

Unable to help myself, I reach over again, sliding my hand into the top of her dress and squeezing her breasts.

"Ryat, please. I can't ..."

"You can and you will," I say, giving her hard nipple a pinch before removing my hand. "I want your underwear soaked with my cum and yours. Fucking drenched, Blake."

Her hands grip her thighs while she rocks her hips back and forth. I didn't let her cum when I fucked her in my hospital room. I made her wait on purpose, knowing that she's been dying for a release.

She throws her head back, arching her back, and a sound of pure torture and relief fills the car before she sags against the seat. "That's one." I count, and she immediately starts adjusting herself once again.

———

I PULL INTO the back parking lot of Blackout and turn off the car. She sinks into the seat when I turn off the app, utterly spent.

Leaning over, I slide my hand between her legs. "Perfect." I praise her, my fingers running up and down her thong. It's soaked just like I wanted. Slapping her thigh, I order, "Spread your legs. Wide."

She closes her eyes, swallowing, and does as I say. I pull her underwear to the side and grab the vibrator, slowly pulling it out. She whimpers at the loss of it.

Unable to stop myself, I bring it to my mouth and lick up the side of it, tasting that sweet honey I love. Then I drop it and get out. Going over to her door, I open it up for her and pull her out.

I then toss her over my shoulder, and she squeals. I slap her exposed ass and carry her across the parking lot so she doesn't have to get her heels wet. The ground is covered in snow and dirty puddles.

Entering the side door, I drop her to her feet and press my body into hers up against the painted black wall. "Who are you?" I demand, my eyes roaming her pretty face. She's still trying to catch her breath.

"Your good girl," she answers softly.

"You're goddamn right, you are." I grip her face and kiss her, allowing her to taste what I just did in the car. She opens up for me, and I deepen the kiss before quickly pulling away. Then I'm pulling her down the stairs, entering the basement.

Tyson stands in the center of the room with his legs spread wide and a water hose in his hand while spraying down a chained Matt. "You gotta look your best for your company," Ty tells him.

"Fuck you," Matt shouts, spitting water out of his mouth.

He's tied to a chair in the center of the room. Drains are placed throughout the concrete floor for these exact reasons.

"I see nothing has changed," I announce our presence. "I wanted to stop by and see how you're doing. You know, before I gut you."

Matt thrashes in the chair.

I had spoken to Tyson this morning before Blake ever woke up. I wanted to stop by and give Matt a little gift before I kill him. "But first ... I wanted to come by and give you a little something." Tyson and I both turn to look at my wife who leans against the far wall, her arms crossed over her chest and looking a little unsure as to why we're here. "Remove your underwear." I order.

Her wide eyes meet mine, and she swallows. But she only hesitates for a second before she uses the wall as support and pushes her thong down her still shaking legs. I walk over to her, and she hands them over, her cheeks red.

I turn back to Matt. "You wanted a taste." It took some time, but that was all Blakely and I had in the hospital room. I got her to tell me every little detail that happened while he had her. "I thought I'd oblige. Consider it your last meal." I shove her cum-covered underwear into his mouth. And then slap my hand over it while Tyson rips off some duct tape from the roll and places multiple pieces over his face when I remove my hand.

Matt's body starts convulsing as if he's fighting not to throw up and choke on his own vomit.

I grip his face and force him to look up at me. "I fucked that sweet cunt thirty minutes ago and came inside it." I give him a chilling smile at the horror in his wide eyes. "In case you were wondering why they're so wet."

His face goes red with rage while he glares up at me.

I told my wife that no one would ever hear or watch me fuck her, and I meant every word. But I never promised that another man wouldn't taste my cum out of her cunt, smeared on her underwear. It's why I bit her neck and slapped her inner thigh in the car. I wanted to show her off to him. Show what I have that he'll never get. No matter what he does. I needed to remind him that I fucking own him as much as he wishes he owned her. I could have come in a cup and forced him to swallow it, but this was sweeter. Thinking he was getting her but not without me—my wife and I are a team. A Lord and a Lady.

I slap the side of his face, making him flinch. "I'll see you soon."

With that, I turn and grab Blake's hand and exit the room with Tyson behind us. "When do you want him delivered?" he asks, after locking the door.

I look at my wife and see her cheeks flushed and eyes on the floor, knowing that I have some time to make up with her. "I'll make it for Sunday night." It's Thursday, so that gives me the rest of the week and all weekend to spend at home alone with my wife, reminding her that she belongs to me. Till death do us part.

BLAKELY

Sunday night, I sit on the couch inside of the office at the cathedral. Ryat silently sits at the desk when a soft knock comes on the door.

"Come in," Ryat calls out.

I look up from the couch to see Tyson enter. I don't know why I expected him to be dressed in his cloak and mask, but he's not. Instead, he wears a pair of black jeans and a black V-neck T-shirt. His dark hair just as unkempt as usual. "He's ready."

Ryat nods. "Thanks. I'll be right there."

Tyson looks at me, and I have a feeling he's challenging me. This is one of the times when I'm going to have to put my feelings to the side for my husband. Exiting, he shuts the door behind him.

Silence lingers among us, and I look down at my wedding ring when Ryat talks. "Blake, you don't have to—"

"I'm staying," I interrupt him, meeting his stare.

His lips thin, but he nods once. "I just need a minute." He goes back to typing away on his phone.

There's another knock, and Ryat slams his cell down with a sigh. "What?" he snaps.

The door opens, and my father steps inside, closing it behind him. I stand. "I should go ..."

"Wait." He holds out his hands in surrender.

I stop, dropping my eyes to the floor. I haven't spoken to him since I was in the hospital. He hasn't even tried to call or text me.

I'm not sure if that's on his part or if Ryat blocked him from my cell. At this point, I don't even care to ask. "I'd rather not," I state and walk past him. But just as I grab the door handle, I pause and turn back around. My husband sits at the desk, his fingers interlocked behind his head, relaxing back in his chair, eyes on mine. My father, however, looks like a wounded puppy, staring at the floor. "I need to know something."

"Anything." His eyes meet mine, and he takes a step toward me.

"Matt told me that a Lord can't choose any woman. That they have to come from a list."

He swallows nervously but nods his head once and whispers, "That's true."

I let out a rough laugh that makes him flinch. "You were whoring me out?" I snap, thinking that Matt had lied to me. But nope. It was the fucking truth. "That's what a chosen is, Father—a whore." I didn't understand it then. Hell, I still don't a hundred percent, but it's obvious these parents loan these women out to the Lords to serve them for their devotion. We're a prize. An offer of servitude. What if I'm having daughters? I will never allow this to happen to them. Or sons? I sure as fuck wouldn't want our sons to have to take a chosen. Fuck, I don't even know what all happened to Tyson's chosen, but I know she wasn't the first one to die.

"No." My father shakes his head quickly, taking another step toward me. "It wasn't like that."

"Then what was it like?" I demand.

Ryat drops his hands from behind his head and stands. "Blake ..."

"No. I got this." My father lifts his hand to my husband. I cross my arms over my chest and push my hip out, impatiently waiting. "Your mother—Valerie." He corrects himself. "Signed you up because she wanted you to be with Matt. That was her and Kimberly's plan. When I found out, we got into an argument. I didn't want you to be a chosen, but it was too late. I couldn't stop it. My only other option was to intervene. So, I gave Ryat the assignment that I did, knowing that his loyalty was with the Lords, and he wouldn't turn it down." He takes another step toward me, and I match it, my back hitting the door, and his face falls. "I never thought it would go this far. Please, Blakely. You have to believe me. I was just trying to save you from Matt."

I look at Ryat, who stands behind his desk, hands shoved into the pocket of his jeans. His emerald eyes on mine give nothing away. Does he regret it? That's my biggest fear. I know we didn't get here by chance. It was forced. But I still fell in love with him, nonetheless. What if this is just his commitment to the Lords? What if I'm just some game he refuses to lose? A game that he will do whatever it costs.

"Give us a moment," Ryat tells my father.

He lets out a sigh and drops his shoulders, making his way to the door, and I step out in front of it so he can exit.

Silently, I look down at my wedding ring when Ryat walks up to me and places his hands on my face, gently forcing me to look up at him. "Stop," he orders.

I go to look away, but his hands prevent it. "I see that look on your face, Blake. I want you to know this ... whatever is said out there, or whatever I do—just know that I love you."

I nod, and tears sting my eyes.

"I mean it." Pulling me to him, he gives me a tender kiss on my forehead. "You might have started out as an assignment, but you are my life now." He drops his hands to my baby bump and rubs it gently. "You three are my life. And you guys will always come first. Do you understand me?"

His words make my heart race, and I swallow nervously. "I love you," I whisper.

Giving me a tender kiss on the lips this time, he pushes open the door, and we enter the cathedral. All the Lords are present in the pews dressed in cloaks and masks. Ryat leads me to the front row, and I sit down in the same spot I had last time I witnessed him torture someone who tried to destroy my life with him.

Ryat makes his way up the stairs, and he walks over to a black sheet that hangs from the ceiling. He reaches up and yanks it down, exposing what's behind it—Matt.

He's got his arms tied above his head by a rope secured to the ceiling. His feet are spread wide, chained to the floor, and all he wears are his boxers.

He's covered in blood, and I wonder just what Tyson's been doing to torture him for the past month while Ryat recovered. It wasn't enough to kill him, but definitely enough to fuck him up by the bruises and dried blood on him.

Ryat moves to stand behind the baptism pool and faces the congregation. "Lords, I find this to be a teaching moment for you all." He starts. "This here is a fellow Lord who decided to betray his oath and be disloyal to us."

Matt lifts his head and glares at the back of Ryat's head.

"What is his penalty?" Ryat asks.

"Death!" Everyone answers at the same time, making me jump.

"Go ahead," Matt growls, "I won't say shit."

A smile spread across Ryat's face. "You don't have to ... but she will."

The sound of a door opening and closing on the second floor fills the large space, and then I see my dad dragging Valerie onto the stage. I sit up straighter, my eyes shooting to Ryat. His eyes are already on mine. He tried to tell me I didn't have to stay here tonight. Is this why? I thought he was trying to save me from what he was going to do to Matt, but maybe it was to protect me from the woman who I grew up thinking was my mother.

My father brings her to a stop and forces her to her knees. She whimpers behind her gag. Stepping up to her, he removes it, and she cries harder. He grips her hair and yanks her head back. "You get one chance to explain yourself," he says calmly.

I've known my father was a Lord since Ryat brought me back, but I never expected to see him in action. Is this what he wanted to talk to me about in the office? Prepare me for what he had planned on doing? Maybe he didn't want me to be here either.

She sobs, her body shaking. "He killed her."

"Valerie," Matt snaps. "Shut the fuck up, you stupid bitch."

Ryat walks over to him and yanks something out of his back pocket. It's a black ball gag. He shoves the rubber ball into his mouth and then fastens it behind his head. "You'll have your turn," he assures him.

"It's okay." My father runs his hands over her hair and her body shakes with fear at the single touch. "Keep going."

She sniffs. "I ... I found where you had been talking to LeAnne. You guys wanted to tell Blakely about her ..." Her tear-filled eyes meet mine. "I couldn't let that happen. I couldn't ..."

Dropping my eyes to the floor, I dismiss her. I honestly thought she was my mother my entire life, and even though I loved her, I can't get over that she was going to take my babies. That she thought I had failed her so badly, that she wanted a do-over.

"Go on." My father urges her. His hand still in her hair lovingly, but she's shaking like a leaf in a tree.

"He was just supposed to scare her. But Matt took it too far." She cries. "And killed her ..."

"You're correct." My father takes a step back from her and she sags with relief. Thinking he's going to reward her for telling the truth. "Matt did take it too far." He agrees, nodding his head once. "But LeAnne is still very much alive."

My eyes shoot to Ryat and he's looking at my father, confusion written all over his face, informing me he was in the dark just as much as I am.

"No." She shakes her head quickly. "He killed her ..."

The sounds of the double doors opening behind me squeak. Everyone in the pews turn around to stare at whoever entered but I can't. I'm frozen in place. Staring up into the loft at my husband. His already sharp jaw clenches, body going rigid, and eyes darken.

The sound of a pair of high heels on the concrete floor is all you hear as someone—no—some woman walks down it. I wrap my arms around my growing stomach protectively, not knowing what to expect while tears fill my eyes.

"Don't stop on my account." A woman's voice announces to the congregation, making my chest painfully squeeze.

No. No. No. I don't believe it.

"LeAnne." My father says the name and smiles. "I thought you'd want to join in on the fun."

Blinking, tears roll down my face.

Matt thrashes in his restraints while Valerie sobs on her knees.

I see a figure out of the corner of my eye start climbing the stairs to the left. I can't help but look at it. Long dark hair that flows down her back in big waves. She's dressed like she's going to a funeral. Big black hat with a black lace veil covering half her face. A tight-fitting black dress with a long train. Coming to the loft, she turns to face the congregation and I hear the Lord members sitting in the pews gasp at her beauty. The woman screams power and radiates wealth. She's stunning with sun-kissed skin and big blue eyes. Lips that look to be done—but not overly big—painted fire engine red.

I look just like her.

"I don't understand," Ryat is the first one to speak. "I saw you die."

"No. you saw me lying on the floor. You never checked to see if I was dead." LeAnne corrects him.

He scratches the back of his neck, taking a step back. The fact that he's truly bothered by this, makes me even more nervous.

She goes to stand in front of Valerie, her hands on her slim hips. "You put a hit out on me." The sounds of her slapping her follows. "Because you didn't want Blakely knowing the truth." She laughs, gripping her face and shoving her head back, forcing Valerie to look up at her. "If it wasn't for me, you would have never had the chance to be a mom. It's not my fault you failed." LeAnne shoves her away.

Valerie sobs, her head falling forward.

"And you." She walks over to Matt who continues to thrash around. "You wanted to rape me. Men always think their dick gives them power." She reaches out and grabs him between the legs, making him throw his head back and scream into his gag. "This makes you weak." She snaps her fingers, and my father walks over to her, a knife in hand. He holds it out to her, and she let's go of Matt just in time to stab him between his parted legs. The Lords all groan when she yanks it out and blood pours down Matt's legs to the floor, screaming into his gag. "And let's make it clear—you pushed me."

My eyes fly to Ryat, and he's seemed to have composed himself. His fisted hands and heavy breathing show his anger over the turn of events. "How ...?"

"I knew you were coming." She interrupts my husband and looks over at my father. "He gave me a heads-up." She laughs softly. "I ordered the hit on Nathaniel. I requested you." She presses a black pointed fingernail into my husband's chest and my teeth grind at the contact. "Then Phil informed me that you had a partner. I knew his reasons for tagging along immediately. All because of your wife."

Ryat stiffens but shoves her hand away from his body while I sit up straighter when her eyes land on mine. "Bring her up."

Two men grip my upper arms and I'm yanked up from my seat. "Don't touch me," I shout, trying to get my arms loose but they effortlessly drag me up the stairs.

"What the fuck," Ryat barks, rushing over to me once we hit the landing. He yanks me free of the two men.

"It's quite alright." LeAnne says, gesturing to me, and Ryat shoves me behind him, shielding me and the babies. "I'm not here to harm her."

"Then don't have your fucking dogs touch her," He snaps.

"Quite the opposite actually." She holds up the knife that's still covered in Matt's blood, handing it out to me handle first. "I'm here to give her what she wants. Revenge."

My heart is pounding, my adrenaline soaring. Swallowing, I step out from behind Ryat and look at her. I reach out with a shaky hand and take it from her. "Is this ... is this an initiation?" I ask and my voice shakes. Am I being tested? If so, why isn't Ryat in on it? He looks confused and pissed.

"No." She takes a step back. "This is for fun, darling. Mommy here sold you to the Winston's to keep her secret of sending Matt to kill me."

My eyes widen and look down at Valerie. She's still sobbing, rocking back and forth on her knees. "That's why you were so obsessed with me marrying Matt?" I demand. "You were willingly going to hand me over to him because Dad was still talking to my birth mother?"

She lifts her head, snot and tears running down her face. "I am your mother. You ungrateful little bitch!" Her eyes go to LeAnne who places her bloody hand on her hip, looking bored. "All you had to do was marry him."

"He didn't want me," I scream.

Snorting, she licks her lips "You think I wanted your fucking father? You make sacrifices for the Lords."

My hand shakes, holding the knife, and my grip tightens. "You were going to take my baby." I don't want anyone to know that I'm having two. That's for me and only my husband to know.

"She what?" Ryat demands, stepping into me.

He thinks I told him everything that went on those days that I was in lockdown with Valerie and Matt, but I didn't. I ignore him and step closer to her, "You said that you would cut my baby out of me yourself and leave what's left of me for Matt." Angry tears fill my eyes. "A mother would never say that to her child."

Growling, she lifts her chin. "Good thing I'm not your mother." Her eyes go to Ryat who stands to my left. "He doesn't fucking love you. You're a game, Blakely. To Matt. To him. I was going to do you a fucking favor." Her green eyes move to my stomach. "I deserve that baby. I deserve my chance. And I'm going to get it ..."

Cutting her off, I drop to my knees and shove the knife into her stomach, horizontally. Valerie's mouth falls open, a single breath leaving her parted lips before I yank on the handle, pulling it across her abdomen, splitting her fucking open—gutting her—like she had planned on doing to me.

Kneeling in front of her, I feel the blood on my skin and soaking up into my jeans. I watch, unable to look away—the life draining out of her green eyes—and I hope that Ryat was wrong about there not being a heaven and hell. Because I hope she's burning. When my day comes and I have to face my God, I will gladly go to hell for the life I took, because it saved two others. My children deserve a chance at a life they want. Not one that this bitch was going to dictate.

SIXTY-ONE

RYAT

"WONDERFUL." THE CRAZY bitch claps her hands, turning to face the congregation. "You are dismissed, Lords," LeAnne announces. "This is a family matter. Shoo." She waves her hands in the air.

Ignoring her, I kneel next to my wife. She's still on her knees, shaking and her hand gripping the handle of the knife that is inside of a dead Valerie. "Blake?" I say softly, brushing the hair off her shoulder to her back so I can get a better look at her profile. "Blakely?"

"She's fine, darling." LeAnne laughs as if this is a joke.

I look up at her, narrowing my eyes on hers. "You can leave too."

She opens her mouth but Phil steps in next to her. "Come on. Let's give them some space."

"But ..."

"You've got plenty of time to talk to her." He assures LeAnne and all I can think is *over my dead body*! That bitch isn't going to come near my wife. I don't trust her.

"Alright." She nods and looks over at a bloody, but very much alive Matt hanging from his restraints. "But what about ...?"

"I'll fucking handle it," I snap, getting to my feet. "Get the fuck out."

Her face hardens and she steps into me. "Listen here, boy." She points a finger in my face. "Everything you have is because of me. I can take it away just like that ..." Her fingers snap and I fist my hands to keep from snapping her goddamn neck.

"Now, now, now. It's been a long day." Phil grabs her shoulders and pulls her back from me. "We're leaving." He nods and then takes her hand, pulling her over to the stairs.

"Blake?" I bark with a little more bite than I meant to. It doesn't faze her.

She sits on her knees, her clothes now soaked in blood, and sniffing. "Come on." I lean over, grabbing her under her arms and yanking her to her feet.

"I ... killed her ... I ..."

I spin her around to face me, grabbing her face in both of my hands. "Look at me."

Tears run down her cheeks, smearing her once pretty makeup. "She was going to take our babies ..." She rushes out.

"Hey," I say softly.

"I couldn't ... wouldn't let her do that." She licks her wet lips.

"You don't have to explain yourself, Blake. It's okay."

"And Matt ..." Her watery eyes go to his bloody body. "He was going to let her."

"They can't touch you, Blake. Never again." I reassure her when I see something out of the corner of my eye. Taking a quick look, I expect it to be LeAnne but it's Ty joining us.

"I promise." She begins to cry. "I promise to protect them ..." Dropping the knife at our feet, her arms cover her stomach.

My heart breaks for her. How unsure she must feel right now. All the lies she's been told throughout her life. Hell, even I didn't expect LeAnne to be alive. That for sure threw a curve ball. "I know." I decide to say. Knowing that anything else won't get through to her right now. "You did good, Blake," I say, running my hand over her long dark hair. "You're my good girl."

Her bloody hands grip my shirt, and she buries her face into it. Wrapping my arms around her shaking body, I hold her to me. I look over at Tyson who stands next to Matt, and I nod to him.

Tonight did not go how I had planned, but at this point I just want it to end. I want to take my pregnant wife home, give her a bath, and move on with our life together.

Ty picks up a rope from the table and walks behind Matt. He wraps it around his neck multiple times and then throws it up to hang over the rafters. Pulling a knife out of his pocket, he leans down and cuts both that are wrapped around his ankles. Then Ty yanks on the new rope around his neck, pulling his bare feet up off the floor.

I slide an arm behind Blake's knees and the other around her back, picking her up, and start carrying her down the stairs while I listen to Matt struggle before silence falls over the cathedral.

EPILOGUE

RYAT

TEN WEEKS LATER

I ENTER THE cabin. "Blake?" I call out but am met with silence. "Blake?" I say a little louder but again get nothing in response. When I rush into our bedroom, the door hits the interior wall from my force. "Blakely?" I snap her full name.

Still nothing.

Entering the bathroom, I let out a sigh when I see steam coming from the shower. I start kicking my shoes off and undo my jeans, followed by my T-shirt. Opening the glass door, I find her standing with her back to me and her head under the water.

Reaching out, I wrap my arm around her and pull her off her feet, making her squeal. "Ryat."

I spin her around and pin her back to the wall, cupping her face, and she laughs.

"You scared me."

"Sorry." I smile, and she gives me a face that says she knows I'm not the least bit sorry. "How much do you love me?" My hands drop to her growing belly. We just found out last week that we're having twin boys. I couldn't be more ecstatic, but a part of me feels sorry for my wife. The fact that she's going to live in a house with me and two boys just like me. Good thing she's stubborn and hardheaded.

Her face falls, and she stiffens against me. "What did you do?"

"I lied," I admit.

"About?" she growls.

I had told her that I had an early meeting at the house of Lords, but that's not where I've been for the past two hours. "I had a meeting, but it wasn't with the Lords."

She frowns. "Why would you lie about that? Haven't I proven myself, Ryat? That I can handle this."

"Of course, you have." I didn't want to get her hopes up just in case it didn't work out, but it did. And now I'm dying to tell her. "I had a meeting with Gregory Mallory."

Her frown deepens, tilting her head to the side. "I ... wait, isn't he the judge that you went to jail for?"

I nod. "He owed me a favor."

"What kind of favor?" she asks skeptically.

"Remember how you said if you had the choice, you'd choose to stay living here in the cabin, in Pennsylvania?"

"Yeah," she answers slowly.

"Well, I just cashed in my favor."

"I don't understand." She licks her wet lips.

"He's going to be retiring, and when that happens, I'm going to take over his position." Being a Lord is a fast-track to your career. But it'll still be about ten years out before I'm a judge. In the meantime, I'll be a high-priced attorney to get the courtroom time needed. If I start right out of the gate, it'll raise too many questions.

She gasps, her hands going to her mouth. "Are you serious?"

I nod. "Yep."

"We're staying here?" Her hands hit my chest excitedly. "We don't have to go to New York?"

"Nope." I shake my head.

She jumps up and down before she slams her lips to mine. My hands go to her wet hair.

I never wanted to go to New York. My wife's reluctance just solidified it for me. I can be powerful anywhere I go. The Lords want me to be a judge, so that's what I'll be, but they never said where I had to live. Everyone just expected me to go back home, but things have changed. This woman has become my home. She's having my sons. And even more of my kids after that. I want a house full of them. I'm going to keep her knocked up. She deserves for me to give her the life that she wants. And that is here, in this cabin, with me and our growing family.

I can't guarantee that I'll grow old with her, but I will spend every second of every day that I'm alive proving to her that she comes first no matter what.

BLAKELY

I ENTER THE house I grew up in, in Texas. Shutting the door behind me, I walk down the hallway to my father's study. Turning the doorhandle, I pause and knock on it instead.

"Come in." The voice calls out.

Taking in a deep breath, I enter. LeAnne sits behind his desk, looking like the queen sitting on her throne, dressed in a black off the shoulder dress with her fake tits popping out the top. Her dark hair up in a tight twist.

I hate how much I look like her. It's a reminder of how stupid I was all those years that I believed the lies I was told about my mother.

"Does Ryat know you're here?" Is her first question.

"Of course." *Lie.* "I don't keep secrets from my husband." There's no way in hell he'd let me come and see her without him. He hates her. Doesn't trust her. I feel the same way, but a part of me couldn't turn down her request to see her today. Ryat got called away for an assignment late last night and I feel like that wasn't a coincidence. Something tells me that this woman has a lot of pull with the Lords. I'm just praying that he's too busy to check the tracker he placed in me after I ran. A part of me wants to rip it out. The other part reminds me that it saved my life and being a Lady means I'm never truly safe.

She smirks, gesturing to the chair across from the desk. "You'll learn that even in a marriage, sometimes the only person you can trust is yourself."

"Coming from the woman who left her family." I bite. I feel bad for my father too, I wasn't the only one she left behind. But she's got him fooled. Considering he still seems to love her.

She opens up a drawer in the desk and hands me a piece of paper. "What is it?" I ask, keeping my hands in my lap.

"Have a look."

Reaching out, I take it and read over the writing. It's a marriage license with her and my father's name on it. "I don't understand."

"Me and your father got married his senior year at Barrington."

I frown. "What's this have to do with me?" Tossing it onto the desk, I sit back in the chair. "Just further proves my point that you left not only your daughter but also your husband."

"Bigamy is illegal in every state," she answers.

My eyes drop to her ring finger and see a massive diamond on it. "So, you got a divorce and married someone else?" I nod. "Not sure why that was so important." I remember Tyson and Matt discussing once a Lord dies, his Lady is given to a new Lord. I wonder if she requested my father since Ryat killed her husband last year, now that Valerie is dead also.

"I've only ever been married to one man, Blakely." She opens another drawer and pulls out a picture, placing it on the desk in front of me.

Picking it up, I see it's a younger version of her, but it looks like me. The guy she's standing next to is my father. "I ... no." I shove it away. "You were married to the man Ryat killed." I can't remember his name, not sure anyone ever even told me that information.

She tilts her head to the side. "Your father's marriage to Valerie was the lie. It was never legal because we were already married."

I run a hand through my hair. "Why does this fucking matter?"

"Because I want you to know the truth."

I snort. "Nothing is true. All I'm told are lies."

"You think I left you behind because of your father. I left you because the Lords called me. And you never, ever tell them no."

"Why would they tell you to leave him?" I scoff. I know the Lords have to obey their oath, but I've never been told that a Lady has to do that.

"Because Nathaniel Myers was my assignment."

My spine stiffens at her answer.

"An assignment that ended up lasting much longer than it should have. That's why I had the hit put out on him. I was done and needed it to end."

Swallowing, I shift in my seat. "Still not sure what this has to do with me."

"Men come and go, Blakely. But your child? That's where they get you. These Lords prefer arranged marriages because they refuse to fall in love with their wives because that'll show weakness." She snorts. "Men can get pussy anywhere. Woman can get dick anywhere. It's the kids that makes us savages. You have already proven that with how you handled Valerie at the confessional. You took her threat of taking your child personally."

I admit that I panicked after what I did set in. But if I had a chance to redo it, would I? Absolutely. In a heartbeat. "Is that what you plan on doing? Force me to do what you want or take my child?"

"Of course not." She snorts as if that's absurd. "I just want you to understand that I did what I had to do ... for you."

I slam my hands on the desk. "Quit lying to me." Getting to my feet, I lean over it. "You haven't been around for twenty years. None of what you did was for me."

She leans back in her seat, crossing one leg over the other, not fazed by my outburst. "Ryat."

My husband's name on her painted red lips makes my heart beat faster. "What about him?"

"That was me." She tilts her head to the side.

"No." I refuse to believe that. "Dad ..."

"Valerie signed you up for a chosen in order to pay off her debt to Matt for killing me. But how do you think you ended up with Ryat?"

I fall into my seat. "Dad made him choose ..."

"I made that decision."

No. It can't be. My father told me that he knew Ryat was the better choice. He was saving me from Matt. But my father has lied to me more than once. This woman who says she's my biological mother has no reason to lie to me, right? "Why?" I'll bite.

"I saw how he was that night. He got in, got the job done, and he never told a soul about what Matt did. Or tried to do. That's a great Lord."

I roll my eyes. "I'm so tired of the fucking Lords."

"And Janett?" She laughs. "Did you really think that woman was going to hire you? You had no experience. No ID, money. Nothing. Not to mention you were underage." She holds her hands out wide. "I made sure that she took you in."

"No," I whisper. My father was mad when I got back. "No one knew where I was." If she was aware of where I was, then my father would have known. He would have never let me stay away as long as they did.

"Oh, I did. Of course, I kept that to myself." She gives me a smile. "I wanted to see just how far Ryat would go to find you. He didn't disappoint. That's when I knew I had made the right choice."

I sit frozen, listening to her. How much this bitch orchestrated everything. It played out like a game to her. "And the fact that Dad and Mr. Archer wanted Ryat to confess to what Matt had planned on doing to you?" I question. It doesn't make sense. When I was in the hospital, Dad wanted Ryat to confess. If they knew LeAnne was alive, then they already knew the truth about what Matt did that night.

She throws her head back, laughing like I'm too stupid to catch onto something that should be easy to comprehend. "He was being tested. See, the Lords are always making the other Lords prove themselves. And well, the fact that he wasn't a snitch saved his life."

"So, his father was testing him, knowing that if he failed, they'd kill him?" That's what they do to a Lord who goes against their oath.

She waves a manicured hand in the air as if it's no big deal. Live or die, didn't matter to her what happened to my husband. "He had no choice."

That's the same thing that Ryat told me when I asked him about the divorce papers. The Lords had ordered it and that was that.

LeAnne reaches out and grabs a cigarette, lighting it up. Lifting it to her lips, she goes to take a drag, but I yank it out of her hand, putting it out on the surface of the desk. "I'm fucking pregnant," I remind her

"Oh, yes." She smiles. "With my grandsons."

I slowly sit back and the look on my face makes her laugh.

"I know everything," she says matter-of-factly.

"What do you want?" I ask, tears building in my eyes. "I'm tired of games. Just tell me why you wanted me to meet with you today."

She runs her tongue along the top of her teeth and then gives me a soft smile. "I just wanted to see you."

My brows pull together.

"I wanted to tell you—face-to-face—that I'm proud of you."

I hate the way my heart accelerates with those words. I don't know this woman and I have no want to know her. "I don't need your validation."

"I know, but that doesn't mean I can't tell you." She shrugs.

"Unbelievable." I shove myself up from the chair and make my way to the door.

"A Lord is nothing without his Lady," she calls out, making me pause. I turn back to look at her. "Ryat without you is just another ordinary man." Standing, she walks around the desk and makes her way over to me. "You make him a Lord, Blakely." Reaching out, I suck in a deep breath when her fingers grab a piece of my hair. "Don't ever kneel thinking that you need to serve him. Kneel because you want to serve him." I swallow nervously. "You have the power to make him hear, see, and believe whatever you want to. Keep that in mind when he tells you he loves you."

Knocking her hand away from me, I snort. "I'm nothing like you, *mother.* I won't abandon my family or manipulate my husband."

"Maybe not right now." She agrees, her eyes dropping to my growing stomach. "But by the time they're ready to start initiation, you will be."

I slap her, the sound bouncing off the walls of my father's study. Stepping into her, I press my chest into hers, my blood boiling at her choice of words. "You will stay the fuck away from me, my husband and my kids. Do you understand me?"

She rubs her cheek, laughing softly. "It is inevitable."

"No." I refuse to believe that. "My children will not be a Lord, or a Lady. I refuse ..."

"The only problem with that, darling, is that it's not your decision to make." My chest tightens. "Why do you think your father and I didn't want you to know about our life?" She arches a brow. "Our real story?" Shaking her head, her eyes soften. "You cannot keep them from it, no matter how hard you try. You might as well accept that now."

The first tear spills over my bottom lashes because she's right. I know it. There's no way Ryat can get out of the Lords and there's no way I can keep it out of our future. "I'll do whatever needs to be done," I finally say.

A smile, making her look like the Cheshire cat, appears on her face. "And that right there is what makes you just like me, whether you like it or not."

EPILOGUE TWO

RYAT

EIGHTEEN YEARS LATER

I STAND IN our kitchen, dressed in my suit, a cup of coffee in one hand, papers in the other. I have court this afternoon. Day two of a trial that I already know will take months. It's a Lord who fucked up. But to the world, he's another corporate billionaire who deserves to rot in hell. I already know the outcome, but we have to give the world the show they want. Once he's sentenced and forgotten, he'll be terminated. Like all the Lords before him that betrayed their oath.

Looking up, I see Reign enter, dressed in a pair of basketball shorts and nothing else, looking like he hasn't slept in days. "Want to tell me why I got a notification that the alarm was turned off at three in the morning?" I ask, setting my cup down on the counter.

He smirks. "I think you'd rather me not." Opening the fridge, he grabs a jug of milk and tosses it back without grabbing a glass. He knows his mother hates when he does that.

"Whoever she is, she better be gone," I inform him when he lowers it.

That smirk back on his face. The look in his green eyes tells me that she's definitely still in this house. "You have ten minutes." I warn.

"He only needs two." Royal—his twin brother—enters the kitchen not looking any better. His hair a disheveled mess. It's hard to miss the scratches on his bare back and bite marks on his neck. He's only dressed in a pair of sweatpants.

"Your mother will be home any minute with your sister, and I'm not going to cover for you two." I shake my head.

They both snort, trying to act unfazed. They tower over her five-foot four frame, standing at six-two, but I've seen her level them with a single look. "Hey, I've only got one girl in my room, dipshit here, has two." Reign points over at Royal.

Me and Blake have always been open with the boys about sex. We understood that it was going to happen. They're seniors in high school, about to graduate, but that doesn't mean she openly allows it under our roof. "Roy—"

"They already left," he assures me.

"So, Dad ..." Reign leans against the opposite counter, facing me and I already know what's coming. "We both need to talk to you."

Royal shakes his head, his unruly hair falling into his eyes. "There is no *we*. This is a *you* conversation."

Reign rolls his eyes at his twin before they meet mine again. "Graduation is coming up. Just three more weeks. Then initiation at Barrington starts this summer ..."

"We should have this conversation when your mother gets here," I interrupt him.

"We know how she feels about the Lords." He sighs. "But we want to join."

"No." Royal shoves his shoulder playfully. "You want to be a Lord. Why the fuck would I want to abstain from sex just to prove I'm a man?" Snorting, he adds, "I like pussy too much for that shit."

I run a hand over my shaved face. "Boys ..."

"Maybe if you'd stop fucking for five seconds, you'd be able to see the bigger picture here." Reign snaps at Royal. "Being a Lord ..."

"Is overrated." Royal looks at me. "No offense, Dad."

I shrug. "None taken." A part of me is proud that Reign wants to join, but a bigger part wants him to be himself. It took me a long time to realize just how much the Lords controlled my life. I dedicated everything to them long before initiation even started. But no matter what, I can never regret my decision to join because it led me to Blake.

"I ..."

The sound of the front door opening and closing cuts off Reign and his lips thin at the fact his mother is home. She has made herself very clear how she feels about them joining the Lords—not going to happen. We've spoken to them about it over the years. Of course, there were some personal details that we didn't tell them, but we wanted them to see the kind of evil that lives out there. That the devil does in fact come to you in the most alluring form.

"Good morning." My wife enters the kitchen with our daughter behind her. Her long dark hair down and in big curls, dressed in a charcoal suit and black heels. She's still just as stunning as she was when I ran into her at Barrington.

"Morning." I grab her hand and pull her into me, cupping her face. "I missed you." She was only gone for two days but it felt like forever.

"Missed you." She leans up in her heels and gently kisses my lips before pulling away.

"How was Stanford?" I ask, looking at our daughter. Ryann looks just like her mother, but I don't worry much because Royal and Reign don't even let boys around her. They protect her like I protect their mother. It's been nice having backup. She's a junior this year in high school. And she reminds me of Blake—she can't wait to get the hell away from here.

When I first met Blake, she longed for a different life than the one her parents allowed her to have. And we've done everything in our power to make sure our daughter is going to get a chance at what she wants.

"Amazing." She smiles.

"You guys can't be serious about letting her go to Stanford?" Reign demands. "I thought it was a joke."

"Not everyone wants to stay home with Mommy and Daddy." Ryann places her hands on her hips. "Some of us have dreams."

Reign scoffs. "It's like thirty hours away ..."

"Try forty," Royal corrects him.

"They make these things called planes," Ryann says sarcastically. "We do have one. You can come and visit me anytime." She looks at Royal. "Lots of hot girls there. Think hot weather—beach and swimsuits."

"Really?" He arches a dark brow with interest.

"Speaking of girls. Looks like you lost a fight with a tree." Blake observes Royal, her eyes looking over his scratches with disapproval.

Reign starts laughing, Ryann pulls her lips back, and Royal just shakes his head. "Something like that."

"I hope you use protection," Ryann states.

"What the fuck, Ry? You shouldn't know things like that," Reign tells her.

"Condoms?" She asks, tilting her head to the side.

"Sex," Royal answers.

"I'm seventeen, not ten." She throws her long dark hair over her shoulder and exits the kitchen.

"Dad ...?" Reign's eyes go from mine to his mothers, when he nods his head.

"We'll discuss it later," I tell him as Blake exits the kitchen. I follow her down the hallway to our master suite.

"Does this conversation we're having later have anything to do with the two girls driving down our driveway at seven in the morning, or the one I watched sneak out the sliding glass door?"

I smile, she sees everything. "No. He wants to join the Lords."

Her body stiffens. "No." She shakes her head.

"Blake—"

"The answer is no, Ryat. You know how I feel about that." She removes her suit jacket and throws it down onto the bed.

"We all do, but he wants to join them as bad as you wanted to go to Stanford." My wife never wanted to attend Barrington, but again, she wasn't given that option. For the last two months her and Ryann have been visiting colleges to see which one is her favorite choice after her high school graduation next year. So far, looks like Stanford is winning.

"That's not fair." She places her hands on her hips and glares at me.

"I know."

"No, I mean not fair to me. One is an education, the other could get him killed," she snaps.

"We always told the kids that we would listen to what they want," I remind her.

"Except this." She pulls away from me and turns her back to me.

"You're being unreasonable."

Stopping, she spins around, her mouth falling open. "And you seem to forget everything you went through because of them."

Walking over to her, I grip her hips, keeping her in place. "He doesn't need our permission."

Her bottom lip starts to tremble. "I know," she whispers. "I just didn't want her to be right."

"Who?" I frown.

"Doesn't matter." She avoids answering.

A knock comes on our door before our daughter steps in. "Hey, my car is on E ..."

"Again," Royal yells from down the hall.

"So, I'm going to ride with the boys to school," she informs us.

"Okay," Blake nods. "Are you sure you got enough sleep on the plane?"

"Yeah." She smiles at us. "Love you guys. See you after school."

"Love you," we say in unison.

Turning her back toward me, I hear her sniff. I sigh, "Blake ..."

"We're out." Reign pops his head in.

"Wait," she hollers, reaching up and wiping her face before spinning around to face him. "Your dad said you wanted to talk about the Lords."

He glares at me and then looks back at her. Answering, he squares his shoulders, "Yeah, I do."

She places one hand on her hip, the other in her hair, and she nods more to herself than him. "Okay. We'll talk when you get home."

"Really?" he asks, his face lighting up.

"Really," she tells him.

"Thanks, Mom. Love you guys." He takes off and we both stand silently, listening to doors shut, the kids argue. Then we hear Royal's car start before they drive away. Leaving us in silence once again.

I walk over to her, and she looks up at me with tear-filled eyes. "I don't want him to hate me." She chokes out.

Pulling her into me, I hug her tightly, kissing her hair. "He could never hate you, Blake."

She pulls away. "I hated my dad and Valerie for so long because I didn't understand what was really going on. I thought being truthful with them was the right thing."

"It was."

"How?" She points at the door. "He thinks it's some game."

"No. He doesn't." Reign understands more about the Lords than I did at his age. I jumped headfirst not knowing what to expect. I've tried giving him as much information as he could possibly need, knowing that this day would come. "All we have to do is listen. We've still got a few months before initiation even starts."

Nodding, she runs her hand through her hair. "I guess," she says quietly. "I just feel like my hands are tied."

"They're about to be." My eyes drop to the way her silk button-up blouse pulls against her chest.

"Ryat—" She shoves my shoulder and I grab her wrists, pulling her into me. Her body crashes against mine, cutting her off.

Letting go of one, I slide it into her long, dark hair and pull on the soft strands, forcing her to lift her chin so she has to look up at me. "We have the house to ourselves, and I have a few hours before I have to leave." My wife has been gone for two days and I plan on making up for that lost time.

She swallows, her pretty blue eyes searching mine. "What should we do?"

I smile, lowering my lips to her neck. "I know several things that I can do." The first thing is to rip these fucking clothes off of her.

After she killed Valerie, and Matt was taken care of, everything settled down. Our life turned somewhat normal—as much as it can being a Lord and a Lady. I offered to give her a big wedding—a proper one—with friends and family. I wanted my wife to have the chance for the world to see me profess my undying love to her. After all, being a Lord has taught me if there's not an audience to witness, it didn't exist.

She declined. My wife understands how much I love her and didn't need an audience. Instead, she took pictures. All the time. Of me and her. Of our twin boys and our daughter. I wanted us to have a big family but complications during her pregnancy with Ryann resulted in an emergency c-section and a hysterectomy. And although I imagined us having more, I couldn't be happier with the family that she gave me.

I bought this cabin out in the middle of nowhere to be alone. To get away from everything. My wife made it a home. The once empty house is now filled with photos over the years we have spent together on vacations, date nights, our kids succeeding in school and sports. It tells our life story.

Of course, it hasn't always been pretty. I didn't expect it to be. Blake can be just as stubborn as me. We fought over the Lords, my career, the kids. She once asked me if I believed in life after death. If there was anything better than this. Almost twenty years later and my answer hasn't changed.

I was forced to pick her as my chosen, but she continues to choose me every day. And that is what I call heaven. Because life without her would be hell.

THE END

Thank you for taking the time to read The Ritual. Did you enjoy it?

Check out **The Sinner.** **The Sinner** is a full-length standalone based in the world of the Lords.

Want to discuss **TR** with other readers? Be sure to join the spoiler room on Facebook. **Shantel Tessier's Spoiler Room.** Please note that I have one spoiler room for all books, and you may come across spoilers from book(s) you have not had the chance to read yet. You must answer both questions in order to be approved.

Do you like dark Mafia romance? Keep on reading to get a look into my **Dark Kingdom series.** Starting with **Code of Silence.**

PROLOGUE

LUCA

Ten years old

"WHO DID YOU fucking talk to?" my father demands.

"No one, John," Uncle Marco snaps. "You know that—"

"I know what I've been told and what you are saying doesn't add up." He pokes his brother in the chest. "And you." He points at my aunt who stands in the corner of the living room with her back against the window that overlooks their backyard. "You've been running your fucking mouth too much."

Tears fill her brown eyes as she stares at my father. Her shoulders shake, and she bites her bottom lip, trying to swallow a sob.

John Bianchi puts the fear of God in you. Because he is god. As the Don—the ringleader of the Italian-American Mafia—he decides when your time is up and how you pay for your sins. He was born in New York, but he and my uncle moved to Las Vegas when my father was fourteen. Uncle Marco was twelve. The laws in Sin City were more fluid back then, so my father was able to get his hands dirtier. He likes life messy.

"Don't talk to her like that." Marco shoves my father.

"I'll talk to the bitch however I fucking please." He punches my uncle, knocking him to his knees.

Aunt Ava cries out as blood runs down his chin, but she doesn't dare go to her husband. No, she stays in her corner, knowing damn well there's nothing she can do. At this point, all she can hope is that my father spares her life.

"You son of a bitch," Marco growls, wiping the blood off.

My father pulls the gun from the waistband of his dress slacks and points it down at his brother.

"John." He throws up his hands, eyes so dark they're almost black, pleading with my father to spare his life. "Come on. We'll figure this out. I swear it wasn't me …"

My father pulls the trigger.

I jump, momentarily deafened by the sound except for the ringing in my ears. Ava cries out, falling to the floor. Bringing her knees to her chest, she openly sobs.

I look back at my uncle. He never did live up to the expectations of the Bianchi family. My father was born in the mafia, and he will die in it, but his younger brother always played a role. Marco has wanted out for years, and this was the only way he was going to get it. Putting a bullet in his head was John Bianchi's way of sparing him. He could have made my uncle suffer.

He turns to face my aunt. "No," she screams. "Please …" She shakes violently as tears run down her face, smearing the makeup she put on earlier. It's their anniversary. We caught them on their way out to dinner to celebrate fifteen years of marriage.

"Strip," my father orders.

"Please." She sobs, shaking her head.

"Remove your dress. Now," he shouts.

Using the window for support, she slowly gets to her feet. With shaky hands, she undoes the hook that holds her dress around her neck. It falls down her chest, stomach, and hips before pooling around her black heels. Her frail body shakes as she covers her bare breasts with her arms.

My father smiles at her, obviously happy with what he sees. Or what he doesn't see. A wire. Someone has been feeding information to the feds, and he suspects it's her. But the things that have gotten back to my father were spot-on, so if she wasn't the snitch, then her husband was.

He walks over to her, grips her auburn hair, and jerks her head back. Placing the gun under her chin, he shows no emotion as she closes her eyes and sobs uncontrollably. "You keep your goddamn mouth shut; do you understand me?"

She begins to nod, but he shoves her head back farther with the barrel of the gun.

"Fucking say it, Ava," he growls in her face.

"Keep … my ... mouth … shut," she chokes out.

He releases her, and she cries out when he shoves her to the floor once again. Turning to face me, he places his gun back in his waistband. Coming over to me, he says, "Never let anyone stand in your way, son. Not even fucking blood. They'll be the first to undercut you, and they should be the first to die for it."

Twenty-two years old

THE MORNING AIR is cool on my skin. The harsh wind whistling as it blows through the tall trees on this mountainside. The sun is just starting to rise on this glorious Friday. My heart pounds with adrenaline.

Anticipation.

The sound of screaming is like music to my ears. A beacon of hope calling to me, letting me know I'm close to my destination. But as much as I like the sound, I don't need it. I know where he is because I set the traps.

A week ago, my father called me to his home office in New York and ordered me to go *hunting*. But this isn't the kind of hunt where you hang your kill on the wall as a trophy to impress others. No, this is the kind you let the wild animals feast on and then leave to rot once you've trapped your prey.

I come to the clearing and see a man by the name of Bernard lying on the ground. He looks up as I approach with my two men. His lips pull back in a snarl, and drool runs down his chin like a rabid dog. Seems fitting since he's on a leash.

"You." Spit flies out of his mouth. His eyes go to Nite, who stops beside me. "You will pay for this."

He's not lying. The life of the Cosa Nostra is an endless circle of revenge. It's something we all came to terms with long ago. Every one of us understands that you live one day just to possibly be killed the next. But in this day and age, it's not just limited to the mafioso. There are too many angry people in the world who feel they have the right to take your life.

I take a step toward him. He tries to crawl away, but the teeth from the bear trap bite into his leg, preventing it. Gritting his teeth, he throws his head back in pain. His veins protrude from his neck, and the spit flies as he pants.

"Would you like me to set you free?" I ask, watching the puddle of blood grow underneath him. I was taught to play with my food. Sometimes the mind game fucks them up more than the actual violence.

"Fuck you, Luca," he growls.

"What do you think, Nite?" I look over at the man who stands next to me. His hands are tightly fisted, and his shoulders shake with fury, but he says nothing. He turns to me, his green eyes almost glowing with rage.

"I agree." I nod as if I can read his mind. "I think we should give him a fighting chance."

It's all about the hunt. That's what makes this so exciting and gets my blood pumping. I was raised on violence.

Plus, my father sent me to do a job, and I won't fail him. If I do, I'll be the one in a trap. And I refuse to give him any reason not to need me. Useless men end up dead and buried in the desert. My father doesn't show favoritism, not even to his own sons. You either kill or get killed. It's the Bianchi way.

The man yanks on the chain that secures the bear trap into the dirt. He won't be able to get it out. I set all twenty traps out here myself. We raided their log cabin an hour ago, entering from the front to push the fuckers out through the back, knowing they would try to escape through these woods.

And we were ready. We spent all of last night getting things in order.

Reaching down, I grab the knife out of my black boot and lift it in the air. Bernard raises his hands to shield himself, thinking I'm going to throw it at his face. As if I would give him that kind of mercy. Instead, it lands blade down in the dirt next to his bloody leg. "Start cutting," I order.

"Wh … what?" he cries and yanks it from the ground. "This won't cut through the chain." He seethes, shaking it at me.

"It won't." I agree with him.

His eyes widen once he understands what I'm saying. "I'm not going to cut my leg off," he shouts.

I look back over at Oliver Nite. The man has been a member of the Bianchi family for fifteen years now. My father found him fighting off a group of thugs trying to steal what little he had. He took Nite in because he saw an opportunity. One—he could fight. And two—he was a child who had no one. My father could use the boy to his advantage. "What do you think?" I ask him.

He takes a step toward the man.

"Stay back," Bernard orders, lifting the knife that I gave him to cut through his leg. His only chance to free himself from the trap. His only chance at freedom.

I throw my head back, laughing.

"I mean it," he screams. "I already cut you once. I'll do it again." He swings the knife around aimlessly in the air.

Nite goes to him, gripping Bernard's wrist and squeezing so hard that he releases the knife with a cry.

"Pathetic," I spit.

As a member of the Mafia, you are trained for situations like this. And this guy has apparently forgotten all his beatings. I never will.

"Luca?"

I turn to face my father's right-hand man, Diaz. He made it sound as though I needed the protection, but we all knew Diaz was sent to spy. To report back to my father how I did and whether I passed the test.

He holds his finger to his earpiece. "We have another one. Snake pit, sir."

I smile. The snake pit is another trap I set for these sorry bastards. A ten-foot-deep hole that I had my men dig last night, then place five snakes in. None of them venomous. I wanted them captured and scared, not dead. "Tell them to take him back to the cabin." Then I turn back to the man. "We're going to wrap this up."

Diaz hands me a pair of Lineman's pliers and a razor blade. "Nite, you may do the honors." I pass him the razor blade. He stares down at it, his eyes glazing over with excitement. I watch the vein in his neck throb with anticipation.

Payback is sweet. And bloody.

Walking over to Bernard, I grab his arms and pull him toward me. He screams out as the chain on the bear trap pulls taut, stretching his body. Falling to my knees at his head, I order, "Open your mouth."

He clamps it shut, brown eyes glaring up at me. They promise retribution. He knows his hours are numbered, but he also knows his men will retaliate. It's just a matter of when, so I'm going to make it worth it.

"Nite," I call out.

He stomps on Bernard's trapped leg, and the man screams out in agony. I use the opportunity to reach into his mouth and grab his tongue with the pliers. He mumbles a few choice words and tries to shake his head. His tongue instantly begins to bleed when I squeeze, securing the grip. His arms flail around, trying to push me away, but he is unsuccessful.

I look up at Nite as he bends down next to me. And without a second thought, he takes the razor blade and slices it through Bernard's tongue, cutting it off.

I stand, the pliers still in my hand and his tongue hanging on the end. Bernard thrashes on the ground as blood gushes from his mouth. The sounds of gurgling and vomiting follow.

I hand the pliers to Nite, and he stares at it as if it's his firstborn. The most prized possession he'll ever own.

"We could make him swallow it," I offer.

Nite shakes his head and hands it to Diaz to hold.

"Good idea. Keep it as a souvenir." I pick up the knife from the ground. "You had your chance at freedom. You should have taken it." I place it back in my boot. Bernard lies there. He's twisted around to where he's on his hands, his mouth wide open as the blood continues to run down his chin and cover his shirt along with the ground. His body shakes, his leg yanking on the bear trap and causing the chain to clank. His skin is so torn up, you can see the tendon and muscles.

"Diaz?" I snap my fingers, and he hands me the ice chest.

I bend down, opening the small red cooler. Most of the ice has melted, leaving it full of water and a white washcloth. I make sure to dunk it into the freezing water and turn to Bernard. I kick his shoulder, pushing him onto his back, and straddle his chest. He fights me, but again, he's unsuccessful as I cram the washcloth into his bloody mouth. "We need to apply pressure," I tell him while he tries to breathe. Blood sprays me from around the corners of his mouth as he coughs and chokes on the water. His body convulses while trying to breathe. "To make the bleeding stop."

His hands slap at my body aimlessly. I stand and step away from him. His shaky hands yank the washcloth out and throw it to the ground before he grabs at his blood covered chest and neck.

I snort, watching his sorry ass flop around like a fish out of water. I turn, giving him my back, because I'm done playing with him. I get bored easily. "Boys, shall we?"

We walk off, leaving the man behind us with his leg in the trap and bleeding from his mouth. An animal will smell the blood, and he'll either be eaten alive, or he'll eventually die from blood loss or dehydration. Either way will be painful.

Nite slaps me on the back.

"You okay?" I ask, giving him a quick glance.

This week has been rough for him, and I hate it. I've always looked up to him like an older brother. And he's the reason we're five hundred miles away from home to begin with.

He nods because, well, that's all he does. That sorry bastard we just walked away from cut out Nite's tongue seven days ago because he wouldn't give up intel on my family.

We're the Bianchis, the Italian-American Mafia who runs most of Las Vegas. We've all got bounties on our heads and are always a target. If you don't take out your enemies, they will take you out first.

The Mafia is the world's most exclusive men's club, and once you're in, you're in for life. Nite and I both wear the ring on our right hand. It's gold and big. Heavy. The thing is tacky, but it represents power. Nite is the only Bianchi who wears the ring that wasn't born into the family. My parents adopted him soon after my father found him, making him Oliver Nite Bianchi for life. So, like me, death is his only way out.

I didn't have a choice. Twenty-two years ago, I was born into it, and I've been proving my worth and loyalty to my father and his men ever since. This trip will not be any different. I made this trip to show my loyalty to Nite as he has shown to me and my family. Heads will roll. Literally. And it'll be by my bloodstained hands.

CONTACT ME

Shantel's Facebook Spoiler Room. Please note that I have one spoiler room for all books, and you may come across spoilers from book(s) you have not had the chance to read yet. You must answer both questions in order to be approved.

Join **Shantel Tessier's mailing list** for exclusive material and giveaways: https://bit.ly/37clfEM

Facebook Reader Group: The Sinful side
Goodreads: Shantel Tessier
Instagram: shantel_tessierauthor
Website: Shanteltessier.com
Facebook Page: Shantel Tessier Author
TikTok: shantel_tessier_author

If you would like to join the street team or review team, please send all inquiries to shanteltessierassistant@gmail.com